MURDERERS' ROW

MURDERERS' ROW

BASEBALL MYSTERIES

EDITED BY OTTO PENZLER

NEW MILLENNIUM PRESS
Beverly Hills

Design: Susie Dotan
Typeface: Body - Cheltenham Book, Titles - Machine BT, Subheads - Helvetica Compressed

Library of Congress Cataloging-in-Publication Data

Murderer's Row: baseball mysteries / edited by Otto Penzler.
    p. cm.
    Contents: Keller's designated hitter / Lawrence Block — Pinch-hitter / Max
Allan Collins — Strike Zone / K.C. Constantine —A family game / Brendan
duBois — Chicasaw Charlie Hoke / Elmore Leonard — Sacrifice hit / John
Lescroart — Ropa vieja / Laura Lippman — The Shot / Mike Lupica — The
power / Michael Malone — Harlem nocturn / Robert B. Parker — The closer /
Thomas Perry — Killing Teddy Ballgame / Henry Slesar — Pick-off play / Troy
Soos.
    ISBN 1-893224-25-2
    1. Baseball stories, American. 2. Detective and mystery stories, American.
I. Penzler, Otto.

PS648.B37 M87 2001
813'.087208355–dc21

                                                              2001018688

New Millennium Press
A Division of NMWorldMedia, Inc.
301 N. Canon Drive
Suite 214
Beverly Hills, CA 90210
www.newmillenniumpress.com

Printed in the United States of America

For Lorraine Errante
The best and most loyal friend
that anyone could have

TABLE OF CONTENTS

INTRODUCTION

I t has been said that baseball is a microcosm of life. As you will see in this collection of stories, it may also be viewed as a microcosm of death.

The best things that the fortunate among us are allowed to bring into our lives - passion, surprises, triumph, excitement, grace, and the joy of meeting challenges that are physical, intellectual and emotional - are all captured on a baseball field.

Occasionally, it's all too much to bear. The agony of defeat, the despair of being eight runs down going into the ninth inning, the rage at a real or perceived injustice ("Kill the umpire!"), all momentarily contrive to squeeze every bit of pleasure out of the game.

As you will soon see, it is entirely possible for that agony, that despair, that rage, to bubble over into violence.

The phrase "Murderers' Row" was coined for the devastating line-up of the 1927 New York Yankees of Babe Ruth, Lou Gehrig, Tony Lazzeri, Bob Meusel (who is often overlooked in the midst of that extraordinary team of power hitters but who hit 47 doubles that year while batting .337), not to mention the equally overlooked Earle

Combs, who led the league in hits with 231 and triples with 23 while batting a lofty .356. No wonder Gehrig led the league with 175 runs batted in!

"Murderer's Row" has a different, more literal, meaning between these covers. Guns show up on these pages and, not surprisingly, so do baseball bats as singularly appropriate weapons.

And talk about an All-Star line-up! The authors whose works fill these pages are among the most distinguished mystery writers in America.

Jim Bouton is equally noted for his baseball career and his authorship of *Ball Four,* which The New York Public Library listed as one of the 100 most important books of the 20th century, joining Hemingway, Steinbeck, Faulkner and other literary lions of the past 100 years. As a pitcher for the New York Yankees among others, Bouton had his best year in the majors in 1963 when, at the age of 25 and in only his second big league season, he posted a 21-7 record with an ERA of 2.63.

Lawrence Block is [at one and the same time] one of the most popular and prolific authors in the mystery world. He has created several memorable series characters, most notably the dark and very tough Matt Scudder, the recovering alcoholic who solves crimes for friends and acquaintances who need his help; Keller, the utterly amoral hit man who kills people for money; and Bernie Rhodenbarr, the burglar who owns his own bookshop. He was named a Grand Master by the Mystery Writers of America for lifetime achievement.

Max Allan Collins is the author of more than twenty novels,

many about Nate Heller, all of whose adventures involve real-life people and some element of real history. He has made films with Patty McCormack and Mickey Spillane and wrote the Dick Tracy comic strip for many years.

Michael Connelly, one of the truly outstanding younger writers of mystery and crime fiction, is the creator of Hieronymous (Harry) Bosch, a very tough member of the LAPD who has starred in such books as *The Black Echo,* which won an Edgar Allan Poe Award as the Best First Mystery in 1993, *Black Ice, The Concrete Blonde* and *A Darkness More Than Light.* "Two-Bagger" is his first short story.

K.C. Constantine has long been a favorite of the mystery genre's cognoscenti, the author who other crime writers admire. Set in the decaying coal mining region of central Pennsylvania, the novels about police chief Mario Balzic and Ruggiero "Rugs" Carlucci are often - and correctly - described as the finest regional novels being written in America. *Joey's Case* was nominated for an Edgar for the Best Novel of the year in 1988.

Brendan DuBois is the author of four novels, one of which, *Resurrection Day,* has been acquired as a major motion picture property. He is a frequent contributor to *Ellery Queen's Mystery Magazine* and *Playboy,* among other publications. His story, "The Dark Snow," was selected for *The Best American Mystery Stories of the Century,* edited by Tony Hillerman.

Elmore Leonard, a Grand Master of the Mystery Writers of America and winner of the Edgar for Best Novel in 1984 for *La Brava,* is one of the giants of 20th-century crime fiction. His realistic dialogue and memorable characters have inspired such movies as *Get*

Shorty, Jackie Brown, Hombre, 3:10 To Yuma, The Tall T, Stick, and many others.

John Lescroart, whose courtroom novels are among the most suspenseful of contemporary thrillers, makes *The New York Times* bestseller list with regularity. *The 13th Juror, A Certain Justice, Guilt* and *Nothing But The Truth* (the latter two featuring San Francisco defense attorney Dilmas Hardy) have roared onto the list. As Larry King has said about Lescroart, "(he) never wrote a bad page."

Laura Lippman, a feature writer for the *Baltimore Sun,* wrote four paperback original mystery novels before her first hardcover, *The Sugar House.* The series about Tess Monaghan, the private eye who owns Baltimore the way Spenser owns Boston, has earned numerous awards, including an Edgar, an Anthony, a Shamus and an Agatha.

Mike Lupica may be the best sportswriter in America, and he is certainly the most famous. In addition to his regular column for *The New York Daily News,* he has written features for most major sports publications and appears on the weekly television program, *The Sports Reporters.* He has written several mystery novels, including *Limited Partner,* which has a baseball background. "The Shot" is his first short story.

Michael Malone has written two mystery novels and several mainstream novels, including such highly regarded classics as *Dingley Falls, Handling Sin,* and *Foolscap,* and was the head writer for several daytime serials, including *One Life To Live.* His exquisite evocation of small-town life in the South, "Red Clay," won the Edgar for best short story of the year and was selected for *The Best American*

Mystery Stories of the Century.

Robert B. Parker won the Edgar award for *Promised Land,* the fourth in his ongoing series of instant classics involving Spenser, the tough, wise-cracking Boston private investigator who is equally comfortable handling yeggs in the alley and eggs in the kitchen, where he demonstrates that he is a terrific cook. Parker also played first base in the Lynnfield Twilight League and was a dead pull hitter. Apart from "Surrogate," which was published in an obscure magazine, *Club,* and then privately printed, "Harlem Nocturne" is his first published short story.

Thomas Perry's first novel, *The Butcher's Boy,* won the Edgar award in 1983, and his Jane Whitehead series consistently makes the bestseller lists. Although he has not published short stories before this anthology, he has started chapters and been so unhappy with them that he tossed them, so he claims he is not new to writing shorter works.

Henry Slesar is among that select coterie of authors who has had both a prolific career and a distinguished one. He wrote *Edge of Night,* the daytime serial, for a dozen years, presenting and solving numerous mysteries within that confining format. Many of his stories were filmed by Alfred Hitchcock for his television series, and Slesar won the Edgar for Best First Novel in 1960 for *The Gray Flannel Shroud.*

Troy Soos has made the baseball mystery his particular franchise. His series character, utility infielder Mickey Rawlings, is busy solving murders, playing ball and generally coping with life and its struggles in the not-always golden days of the 1920s and before.

xiii

Rawlings is frequently traded and moves through adventures with the St. Louis Browns, the New York Giants and the Boston Red Sox of Tris Speaker and Smokey Joe Wood.

Now that the line-up has been posted, turn the page and let's play ball!

Otto Penzler

FOREWORD

by Jim Bouton

A s a former baseball player who averaged $19,000 a year, in the days before free-agency, I am quite familiar with crime and mystery. Crime being the theft of our money by the owners before Marvin Miller became our union leader in the '60s. And mystery being why the owners didn't throw us a bone to keep us from hiring Miller in the first place. With the minimum salary at $7,000, the players would have jumped at a raise to $10,000 and told Miller to take a hike. Hell, the owners could have bought all the votes they needed against Miller with a *$3 per day increase in the meal money!* To $18.

So the question is this: What kept the baseball owners from taking the few simple steps that could have prevented the economic revolution that has spread to the entire sports world. Mere stupidity and greed, you say? Arrogance? Think bigger, crime fans. There's more to it than that. Way more.

Look at the evidence. In crucial battles between Miller and Baseball Commissioner Bowie Kuhn, Miller was 48 and 0 in court decisions, NLRB findings and arbitration rulings. Suspicious? If it had been a boxing match there would have been Congressional hearings. Open your eyes, people! It's the grassy knoll all over again. I'm talking C-0-N-S-P-I-R-A-C-Y. Moles, double agents, fake mustaches.

This is bigger than baseball; that's just the breeding ground. Our economy is flying high right now. That's the plan. Then a team goes bankrupt, which everyone expects so nobody gets alarmed. Then another team goes under, and pretty soon the domino effect causes a drop in the overnight rate, leading to a collapse of the dollar. Greenspan knows what I'm talking about, *but he won't say anything.* Not publicly, anyway. That's what the Communists are waiting for, down in Cuba.

And where is Bowie Kuhn today? That's what I'm trying to say. Living in Florida and playing tennis in *the very same community* with the Savings and Loan crooks! The same guys who.... Aw, the hell with it. I can't do it all by myself.

We're swimming in crime and conspiracy.

A guy can't even get a book out anymore. Not even two guys, working together. In 1994 I co-wrote a novel with Eliot Asinof, author of *Eight Men Out,* the story of the Black Sox scandal. Our book was *Strike Zone:* a "dramatic and funny inside look at baseball and the crime that scares the hell out of professional sports: the fix," according to the press release. How would the establishment react to *this* book? I wondered.

The story is told in alternating chapters and alternating voices; Asinof is Ernie Kolacka, the home plate umpire who's fixing the game; I'm Sam Ward, the rookie pitcher against whom the game is being fixed.

We agreed on a time frame: twenty-four hours. And the setting: historic Wrigley Field. We mapped out a game, working backwards from a climactic pitch in the ninth inning, with a full count and the bases loaded. Asinof, as the umpire, would make the call when the narrative reached that point.

It was a pretty decent book. "One ball game seen from two utterly different points of view," said the flap copy which we also co-wrote. "A double blind study of balls and strikes, right and wrong, life and death." One writer could have never come up with something that good.

Viking, the publisher, printed sixty thousand copies and sent me out on the road to promote it. Since the book was Eliot's idea, I had to do the tour. Thirteen cities in twenty-one days. First stop: a Barnes & Noble in San Francisco.

Money, here we come.

The front window of the Barnes & Noble was filled with *Strike Zone.* Inside, next to a table piled high with copies of *Strike Zone,* was my picture and a sign announcing that I'd be autographing *Strike Zone.* There were *Strike Zones* everywhere.

But no people.

No customers. No manager. No store personnel. No one even watching the cash register! I looked at my watch; it was time to be signing books. Maybe it was a joke, I thought. Everybody's going to jump out from behind the bookcases and yell "royalties!"

I wandered around the empty store. It was like a neutron bomb had exploded—the people were vaporized but the books were intact. Hell, I could have hauled off a wheelbarrow full of Stephen King books and nobody would have noticed.

Suddenly I heard voices in the back, and went to investigate.

Sure enough, there were people back there. About a hundred of them. They were all crowded around a television set. Just staring at the TV, not saying anything. I stood on my tip-toes to try and see what they were watching. It didn't look that exciting to me. Just a white Ford Bronco driving down a highway.

Little did I know what that Bronco ride would mean for *Strike Zone,* not to mention Eliot's and my bank accounts.

The rest of the promotional tour consisted of cancellations due to lack of air time. Of course. The few interviews I *did* do went something like this: "Before we talk about your new book, *Strike Out*, do you think he did it?"

There are many questions about the so-called "Crime of the Century," but the ones no one is asking, for reasons I can't get into right now, are these: why did it happen the night before publication of a sports-fix book? Why a professional athlete? Why did he get off? Why was Mark Fuhrman seen at Dodger stadium on more than one occasion? And where was Bowie Kuhn during all this? That book hasn't been written yet.

And it may *never* be written as long as certain individuals... Well, you know what I mean. Diversionary tactics. Bait and switch. I don't have to spell it out. If you people don't get it, nobody will.

Meanwhile, our publisher tells me you can buy *Strike Zone* at stores that sell remainder copies. There are approximately fifty-five thousand of them out there. Books that is.

KELLER'S DESIGNATED HITTER

by Lawrence Block

Keller, a beer in one hand and a hot dog in the other, walked up a flight and a half of concrete steps and found his way to his seat. In front of him, two men were discussing the ramifications of a recent trade the Tarpons had made, sending two minor-league prospects to the Florida Marlins in return for a lefthanded reliever and a player to be named later. Keller figured he hadn't missed anything, as they'd been talking about the same subject when he left. He figured the player in question would have been long since named by the time these two were done speculating about him.

Keller took a bite of his hot dog, drew a sip of his beer. The fellow on his left said, "You didn't bring me one."

Huh? He'd told the guy he'd be back in a minute, might have mentioned he was going to the refreshment stand, but had he missed something the man had said in return?

"What didn't I bring you? A hot dog or a beer?"

"Either one," the man said.

"Was I supposed to?"

"Nope," the man said. "Hey, don't mind me. I'm just jerking

1

your chain a little."

"Oh," Keller said.

The fellow started to say something else, but broke it off after a word or two as he and everybody else in the stadium turned their attention to home plate, where the Tarpons' clean-up hitter had just dropped to the dirt to avoid getting hit by a high inside fastball. The Yankee pitcher, a burly Japanese with a herky-jerky windup, seemed unfazed by the boos, and Keller wondered if he even knew they were for him. He caught the return throw from the catcher, set himself, and went into his pitching motion.

"Taguchi likes to pitch inside," said the man who'd been jerking Keller's chain, "and Vollmer likes to crowd the plate. So every once in a while Vollmer has to hit the dirt or take one for the team."

Keller took another bite of his hot dog, wondering if he ought to offer a bite to his new friend. That he even considered it seemed to indicate that his chain had been jerked successfully. He was glad he didn't have to share the hot dog, because he wanted every bite of it for himself. And, when it was gone, he had a feeling he might go back for another.

Which was strange, because he never ate hot dogs. A few years back he'd read a political essay on the back page of a news magazine that likened legislation to sausage. You were better off not knowing how it was made, the writer observed, and Keller, who had heretofore never cared how laws were passed or sausages produced, found himself more conscious of the whole business. The legislative aspect didn't change his life, but, without making any conscious decision on the matter, he found he'd lost his taste for sausage.

Being at a ball park somehow made it different. He had a hunch the hot dogs they sold here at Tarpon Stadium were if anything more dubious in their composition than your average supermarket frankfurter, but that seemed to be beside the point. A ball park hot dog was just part of the baseball experience, along with listening to some flannel-mouthed fan shouting instructions to a ballplayer dozens of yards away who couldn't possibly hear him, or booing a pitcher who couldn't care less, or having one's chain jerked by a total stranger. All part of the Great American Pastime.

He took a bite, chewed, sipped his beer. Taguchi went to three-and-two on Vollmer, who fouled off four pitches before he got one he liked. He drove it to the 396-foot mark in left center field, where Bernie Williams hauled it in. There had been runners on first and second, and they trotted back to their respective bases when the ball was caught.

"One out," said Keller's new friend, the chain jerker.

Keller ate his hot dog, sipped his beer. The next batter swung furiously and topped a roller that dribbled out toward the mound. Taguchi pounced on it, but his only play was to first, and the runners advanced. Men on second and third, two out.

The Tarpon third baseman was next, and the crowd booed lustily when the Yankees elected to walk him intentionally. "They always do that," Keller said.

"Always," the man said. "It's strategy, and nobody minds when their own team does it. But when your guy's up and the other side won't pitch to him, you tend to see it as a sign of cowardice."

"Seems like. a smart move, though."

3

"Unless Turnbull shows 'em up with a grand slam, and God knows he's hit a few of 'em in the past."

"I saw one of them," Keller recalled. "In Wrigley Field, before they had the lights. He was with the Cubs. I forget who they were playing."

"That would have had to be before the lights came in, if he was with the Cubs. Been all around, hasn't he? But he's been slumping lately, and you got to go with the percentages. Walk him and you put on a .320 hitter to get at a .280 hitter, plus you got a force play at any base."

"It's a game of percentages," Keller said.

"A game of inches, a game of percentages, a game of woulda-coulda-shoulda," the man said, and Keller was suddenly more than ordinarily grateful that he was an American. He'd never been to a soccer match, but somehow he doubted they ever supplied you with a conversation like this one.

"Batting seventh for the Tarpons," the stadium announcer intoned, "number 17, the designated hitter, Floyd Turnbull."

"He's a designated hitter," Dot had said, on the porch of the big old house on Taunton Place. "Whatever that means."

"It means he's in the lineup on offense only," Keller told her. "He bats for the pitcher."

"Why can't the pitcher bat for himself? Is it some kind of union regulation?"

"That's close enough," said Keller, who didn't want to get into it. He had once tried to explain the infield fly rule to a stewardess, and he was never going to make that sort of mistake again. He wasn't a sexist about it, he knew plenty of women who understood this stuff, but the ones who didn't were going to have to learn it from somebody else.

"I saw him play a few times," he told her, stirring his glass of iced tea. "Floyd Turnbull."

"On television?"

"Dozens of times on TV," he said. "I was thinking of seeing him in person. Once at Wrigley Field, when he was with the Cubs and I happened to be in Chicago."

"You just happened to be there?"

"Well," Keller said. "I don't ever just happen to be anyplace. It was business. Anyway, I had a free afternoon and I went to a game."

"Nowadays you'd go to a stamp dealer."

"Games are mostly at night nowadays," he said, "but I still go every once in a while. I saw Turnbull a couple of times in New York, too. Out at Shea, when he was with the Cubs and they were in town for a series with the Mets. Or maybe he was already with the Astros when I saw him. It's hard to remember."

"And not exactly crucial that you get it right."

"I think I saw him at Yankee Stadium, too. But you're right, it's not important."

"In fact," Dot said, "it would be fine with me if you'd never seen him at all, up close or on TV. Does this complicate things, Keller? Because I can always call the guy back and tell him we pass."

"You don't have to do that."

5

"Well, I hate to, since they already paid half. I can turn down jobs every day and twice on Sundays, but there's something about giving back money once I've got it in my hands that makes me sick to my stomach. I wonder why that is?"

"A bird in the hand," Keller suggested.

"When I've got a bird in my hand," she said, "I hate like hell to let go of it. But you saw this guy play. That's not gonna make it tough for you to take him out?"

Keller thought about it, shook his head. "I don't see why it should," he said. "It's what I do."

"Right," Dot said. "Same as Turnbull, when you think about it. You're a designated hitter yourself, aren't you, Keller?"

"Designated hitter," Keller said, as Floyd Turnbull took a called second strike. "Whoever thought that one up?"

"Some marketing genius," his new friend said. "Some dipstick who came up with research to prove that fans wanted to see more hits and home runs. So they lowered the pitching mound and told the umpire to quit calling the high strike, and then they juiced up the baseball and brought in the fences in the new ballparks, and the ballplayers started lifting weights and swinging lighter bats, and now you've got baseball games with scores like football games. Last week the Tigers beat the A's fourteen to thirteen. First thing I thought, Jeez, who missed the extra point?"

"At least the National League still lets pitchers hit."

"And at least nobody in the pros uses those aluminum bats. They show college baseball on ESPN and I can't watch it. I can't

6

stand the sound the ball makes when you hit it. Not to mention it travels too goddamn far."

The next pitch was in the dirt. Posada couldn't find it, but the third base coach, suspicious, held the runner. The fans booed, though it was hard to tell who they were booing, or why. The two in front of Keller joined in the booing, and Keller and the man next to him exchanged knowing glances.

"Fans," the man said, and rolled his eyes.

The next pitch was belt-high, and Turnbull connected solidly with it. The stadium held its collective breath and the ball sailed toward the left field corner, hooking foul at the last moment. The crowd heaved a sigh and the runners trotted back to their bases. Turnbull, looking not at all happy, dug in again at the plate.

He swung at the next pitch, which looked like ball four to Keller, and popped to right. O'Neill floated under it and gathered it in and the inning was over.

"Top of the order for the Yanks," said Keller's friend. "About time they broke this thing wide open, wouldn't you say?"

With two out in the Tarpons' half of the eighth inning, with the Yankees ahead by five runs, Floyd Turnbull got all of a Mike Stanton fastball and hit it into the upper deck. Keller watched as he jogged around the bases, getting a good hand from what remained of the crowd.

"Career home run number 393 for the old warhorse," said the man on Keller's left. "And all those people missed it because they had to beat the traffic."

7

"Number 393?"

"Leaves him seven shy of four hundred. And, in the hits department, you just saw number 2988."

"You've got those stats at your fingertips?"

"My fingers won't quite reach," the fellow said, and pointed to the scoreboard, where the information he'd cited was posted. "Just twelve hits to go before he joins the magic circle, the 3000 Hits club. That's the only thing to be said for the DH rule - it lets a guy like Floyd Turnbull stick around a couple of extra years, long enough to post the kind of numbers that get you into Cooperstown. And he can still do a team some good. He can't run the bases, he can't chase after fly balls, but the sonofabitch hasn't forgotten how to hit a baseball."

The Yankees got the run back in the top of the ninth on a walk to Jeter and a home run by Bernie Williams, and the Tarpons went in order in the bottom of the ninth, with Rivera striking out the first two batters and getting the third to pop to short.

"Too bad there was nobody on when Turnbull got his homer," said Keller's friend, "but that's usually the way it is. He's still good with a stick, but he hits 'em with nobody on, and usually when the team's too far behind or out in front for it to make any difference."

The two men walked down a succession of ramps and out of the stadium. "I'd like to see old Floyd get the numbers he needs," the man said, "but I wish he'd get 'em on some other team. What they need for a shot at the flag's a decent lefthanded starter and some help in the bullpen, not an old man with bad knees who hits it out when you don't need it."

"You think they should trade him?"

8

"They'd love to, but who'd trade for him? He can help a team, but not enough to justify paying him the big bucks. He's got three years left on his contract, three years at six-point-five million a year. There are teams that could use him, but nobody can use him six-point-five worth. And the Tarps can't release him and go out and buy the pitching they need, not while they've got Turnbull's salary to pay."

"Tricky business," Keller said.

"And a business is what it is. Well, I'm parked over on Pentland Avenue, so this is where I get off. Nice talking with you."

And off the fellow went, while Keller turned and walked off in the opposite direction. He didn't know the name of the man he had talked to, and would probably never see him again, and that was fine. In fact it was one of the real pleasures of going to a game, the intense conversations you had with strangers whom you then allowed to remain strangers. The man had been good company, and at the end he'd provided some useful information.

Because now Keller had an idea why he'd been hired.

"The Tarpons are stuck with Turnbull," he told Dot. "He draws this huge salary, and they have to pay it whether they play him or not. And I guess that's where I come in."

"I don't know," she said. "Are you sure about this, Keller? That's a pretty extreme form of corporate downsizing. All that just to keep from paying a man his salary? How much could it amount to?"

He told her.

"That much," she said, impressed. "That's a lot to pay a man

9

to hit a ball with a stick, especially when he doesn't have to go out and stand around in the hot sun. He just sits on the bench until it's his turn to bat, right?"

"Right."

"Well, I think you might be on to something," she said. "I don't know who hired us or why, but your guess makes more sense than anything I could come up with off the top of my head. But I feel myself getting a little nervous, Keller."

"Why?"

"Because this is just the kind of thing that could set your milk to curdling, isn't it?"

"What milk? What are you talking about?"

"I've known you a long time, Keller. And I can just see you deciding that this is a hell of a way to treat a faithful employee after long years of service, and how can you allow this to happen, di dah di dah di dah. Am I coming through loud and clear?"

"The di dah part makes more sense than the rest of it," he said. "Dot, as far as who hired us and why, all I am is curious. Curiosity's a long way from righteous indignation."

"Didn't do much for the cat, as I remember."

"Well," he said, "I'm not that curious."

"So I've got nothing to worry about?"

"Not a thing," he said. "The guy's a dead man hitting."

The Tarpons closed out the series with the Yankees—and a twelve-game home stand—the following afternoon. They got a good outing from their ace righthander, who scattered six hits and held the

New Yorkers to one run, a bases-empty homer by Brosius. The Tarps won, 3-1, with no help from their designated hitter, who struck out twice, flied to center, and hit a hard liner right at the first baseman.

Keller watched from a good seat on the third base side, then checked out of his hotel and drove to the airport. He turned in his rental car and flew to Milwaukee, where the Brewers would host the Tarps for a three-game series. He picked up a fresh rental and checked in at a motel half a mile from the Marriott where the Tarpons always stayed.

The Brewers won the first game, 5 to 2. Floyd Turnbull had a good night at bat, going three for five with two singles and a double, but he didn't do anything to affect the outcome; there was nobody on base when he got his hits, and nobody behind him in the order could drive him in.

The next night the Tarps got to the Brewers' rookie southpaw early and blew the game open, scoring six runs in the first inning and winding up with a 13-4 victory. Turnbull's homer was part of the big first inning, and he collected another hit in the seventh when he doubled into the gap and was thrown out trying to stretch it into a triple.

"Why'd he do that?" the bald guy next to Keller wondered. "Two out and he tries for third? Don't make the third out at third base, isn't that what they say?"

"When you're up by nine runs," Keller said, "I don't suppose it matters much one way or the other."

"Still," the man said, "it's what's wrong with that prick. Always for himself his whole career. He wanted one more triple in the record book, that's what he wanted. And forget about the team."

After the game Keller went to a German restaurant south of the city on the lake. The place dripped atmosphere, with beer steins hanging from the hand-hewn oak beams, an oompah band in lederhosen, and fifteen different beers on tap. Keller couldn't tell the waitresses apart, they all looked like grown-up versions of Heidi, and evidently Floyd Turnbull had the same problem; he called them all Gretchen and ran his hand up under their skirts whenever they came within reach.

Keller was there because he'd learned the Tarpons favored the place, but the sauerbraten was reason enough to make the trip. He made his beer last until he'd cleaned his plate, then turned down the waitress's suggestion of a refill and asked for a cup of coffee instead. By the time she brought it, several more fans had crossed the room to beg autographs from the Tarpons.

"They all want their menus signed," Keller told the waitress. "You people are going to run out of menus."

"It happens all the time," she said. "Not that we run out of menus, because we never do, but players coming here and our other customers asking for autographs. All the athletes like to come here."

"Well, the food's great," he said.

"And it's free. For the players, I mean. It brings in other customers, so it's worth it to the owner, plus he just likes having his restaurant full of jocks. About it being free for them, I'm not supposed to tell you that."

"It'll be our little secret."

"You can tell the whole world, for all I care. Tonight's my last night. I mean, what do I need with jerks like Floyd Turnbull? I want a pelvic exam, I'll go to my gynecologist, if it's all the same to you."

"I noticed he was a little free with his hands."

"And close with everything else. They eat and drink free, but most of them at least leave tips. Not good tips, ballplayers are cheap bastards, but they leave something. Turnbull always leaves exactly twenty percent."

"Twenty percent's not that bad, is it?"

"It is when it's twenty percent of nothing."

"Oh."

"He said he got a home run tonight, too."

"Number 394 of his career," Keller said.

"Well, he's not getting to first base with me," she said. "The big jerk."

"Night before last," Keller said, "I was in a German restaurant in Milwaukee."

"Milwaukee, Keller?"

"Well, not exactly in Milwaukee. It was south of the city a few miles, on Lake Michigan."

"That's close enough," Dot said. "It's still a long way from Memphis, isn't it? Although if it's south of the city, I guess it's closer to Memphis than if it was actually inside of Milwaukee."

"Dot. . . "

"Before we get too deep into the geography of it," she said, "aren't you supposed to be in Memphis? Taking care of business?"

"As a matter of fact. . ."

13

"And don't tell me you already took care of business, because I would have heard. CNN would have had it, and they wouldn't even make me wait until Headline Sports at twenty minutes past the hour. You notice how they never say which hour?"

"That's because of different time zones."

"That's right, Keller, and what time zone are you in? Or don't you know?"

"I'm in Seattle," he said.

"That's Pacific time, isn't it? Three hours behind New York."

"Right."

"But ahead of us," she said, "in coffee. I'll bet you can explain, can't you?"

"They're on a road trip," he said. "They play half their games at home in Memphis, and half the time they're in other cities."

"And you've been tagging along after them."

"That's right. I want to take my time, pick my spot. If I have to spend a few dollars on airline tickets, I figure that's my business. Because nobody said anything about being in a hurry on this one."

"No," she admitted. "If time is of the essence, nobody told me about it. I just thought you were gallivanting around, going to stamp dealers and all. Taking your eye off the ball, so to speak."

"So to speak," Keller said.

"So how can they play ball in Seattle, Keller? Doesn't it rain all the time? Or is it one of those stadiums with a lid on it?"

"A dome," he said.

"I stand corrected. And here's another question. What's Memphis got to do with fish?"

"Huh?"

"Tarpons," she said. "Fish. And there's Memphis, in the middle of the desert."

"Actually, it's on the Mississippi River."

"Spot any tarpons in the Mississippi River, Keller?"

"No."

"And you won't," she said, "unless that's where you stick Turnbull when you finally close the deal. It's a deep-sea fish, the tarpon, so why pick that name for the Memphis team? Why not call them the Gracelanders?"

"They moved," he explained.

"To Milwaukee," she said, "and then to Seattle, and God knows where they'll go next."

"No," he said. "The franchise moved. They started out as an expansion team,—the Sarasota Tarpons, but they couldn't sell enough tickets, so a new owner took over and moved them to Memphis. Look at basketball, the Utah Jazz and the L.A. Lakers. What's Salt Lake city got to do with jazz, and when did Southern California get to be the Land of Ten Thousand Lakes?"

"The reason I don't follow sports," she said, "is it's too damn confusing. Isn't there a team called the Miami Heat? I hope they stay put. Imagine if they move to Buffalo."

Why had he called in the first place? Oh, right. "Dot," he said, "I was in the Tarpons' hotel earlier today, and I saw a guy."

"So?"

"A little guy," he said, "with a big nose, and one of those heads that look as though somebody put it in a vise."

15

"I heard about a guy once who used to do that to people."

"Well, I doubt that's what happened to this fellow, but that's the kind of face he had. He was sitting in the lobby reading a newspaper."

"Suspicious behavior like that, it's no wonder you noticed him."

"No, that's the thing," he said. "He's distinctive looking, and he looked wrong. And I saw him just a couple of nights before in Milwaukee at this German restaurant."

"The famous German restaurant."

"I gather it is pretty famous, but that's not the point. He was in both places, and he was alone both times. I noticed him in Milwaukee because I was eating by myself, and feeling a little conspicuous about it, and I saw I wasn't the only lone diner, because there he was."

"You could have asked him to join you."

"He looked wrong there, too. He looked like a Broadway sharpie, out of an old movie. Looked like a weasel, wore a fedora. He could have been in *Guys and Dolls,* saying he's got the horse right here."

"I think I see where this is going."

"And what I think," he said, "is I'm not the only DH in the line-up. . . . Hello? Dot?"

"I'm here," she said. "Just taking it all in. I don't know who the client is, the contract came through a broker, but what I do know is nobody seems to be getting antsy. So why would they hire somebody else? You're sure this guy's a hitter? Maybe he's a big fan, hates to miss a game, follows 'em all over the country."

"He looks wrong for the part, Dot."

"Could he be a private eye? Ballplayers cheat on their wives, don't they?"

"Everybody does, Dot."

"So some wife hired him, he's gathering divorce evidence."

"He looks too shady to be a private eye."

"I didn't know that was possible."

"He doesn't have that crooked-cop look private eyes have. He looks more like the kind of guy they used to arrest, and he'd bribe them to cut him loose. I think he's a hired gun, and not one from the A-list, either."

"Or he wouldn't look like that."

"Part of the job description," he said, "is you have to be able to pass in a crowd. And he's a real sore thumb."

"Maybe there's more than one person who wants our guy dead."

"Occurred to me."

"And maybe a second client hired a second hit man. You know, maybe taking your time's a good idea."

"Just what I was thinking."

"Because you could do something and find yourself in a mess because of the heat this ferret-faced joker stirs up. And if he's there with a job to do, and you stay in the background and let him do it, where's the harm? We collect no matter who pulls the trigger."

"So I'll bide my time."

"Why not? Drink some of that famous coffee, Keller. Get

17

rained on by some of that famous rain. They have any stamp dealers in Seattle, Keller?"

"There must be. I know there's one in Tacoma."

"So go see him," she said. "Buy some stamps. Enjoy yourself."

"I collect worldwide, 1840 to 1949, and up to 1952 for British Commonwealth."

"In other words, the classics," said the dealer, a square-faced man who was wearing a striped tie with a plaid shirt. "The good stuff."

"But I've been thinking of adding a topic. Baseball."

"Good topic," the man said. "Most topics, you get bogged down in all these phony Olympics issues every little stamp-crazy country prints up to sell to collectors. Soccer's even worse, with the World Cup and all. There's less of that crap with baseball, on account of it's not an Olympic sport. I mean, what do they know about baseball in Guinea-Bissau?"

"I was at the game last night," Keller said.

"Mariners win for a change?"

"Beat the Tarpons."

"About time."

"Turnbull went two for four."

"Turnbull. He on the Mariners?"

"He's the Tarpons' DH."

"They brought in the DH," the man said, "I lost interest in the game. He went two for four, huh? Am I missing something here? Is that significant?"

"Well, I don't know that it's significant," Keller said, "but that puts him just five hits shy of four thousand, and he needs three home runs to reach the four hundred mark."

"You never know," the dealer said. "One of these days, St. Vincent-Grenadines may put his picture on a stamp. Well, what do you say? Do you want to see some baseball topicals?"

Keller shook his head. "I'll have to give it some more thought," he said, "before I start a whole new collection. How about Turkey? There's page after page of early issues where I've got nothing but spaces."

"You sit down," the dealer said, "and we'll see if we can't fill some of them for you."

From Seattle the Tarpons flew to Cleveland for three games at Jacobs Field, then down to Baltimore for four games in three days with the division-leading Orioles. Keller missed the last game against the Mariners and flew to Cleveland ahead of them, getting settled in and buying tickets for all three games. Jacobs Field was one of the new parks and an evident source of pride to the local fans, and the previous year they'd filled the stands more often than not, but this year the Indians weren't doing as well and Keller had no trouble getting good seats.

Floyd Turnbull managed only one hit against the Indians, a scratch single in the first game. He went 0-for-3 with a walk in game two, and rode the bench in the third game, the only one the Tarpons won. His replacement, a skinny kid just up from the minors, had two hits and drove in three runs.

19

"New kid beat us," said Keller's conversational partner du jour. He was a Cleveland fan, and assumed Keller was, too. Keller, who'd bought an Indians cap for the series, had encouraged him in this belief. "Wish they'd stick with old Turnbull," the man went on.

"Close to three thousand hits," Keller said.

"Lots of hits and homers, but he never seems to beat you like this kid just did. Hits for the record book, not for the game—that's Floyd for you."

"Excuse me," Keller said. "I see somebody I better go say hello to."

It was the Broadway sharpie, wearing a Panama fedora with a bright red hatband. That made him easy to spot, but even without it he was hard to miss. Keller had picked him out of the crowd back in the third inning, checked now and then to make sure he was still in the same seat. But now the guy was in conversation with a woman, their heads close together, and she didn't look right for the part. The instant camaraderie of the baseball notwithstanding, a woman who looked like her couldn't figure to be discussing the subtleties of the double steal with a guy who looked like him.

She was tall and slender, and she bore herself regally. She was wearing a suit, and at first glance you thought she'd come from the office, and then you decided she probably owned the company. If she belonged at a ball park at all, it was in the sky boxes, not the general admission seats.

What were they discussing with such urgency? Whatever it was, they were done talking about it before Keller could get close enough to listen in. They separated and headed off in different directions, and Keller tossed a mental coin and set out after the woman. He already knew where the man was staying, and what name he was using.

He tagged the woman to the Ritz-Carlton, which sort of figured. He'd gotten rid of his Indians cap en route, but he still wasn't dressed for the lobby of a five-star hotel, not in the khakis and polo shirt that were just fine for Jacobs Field.

Couldn't be helped. He went in, hoping to spot her in the lobby, but she wasn't there. Well, he could have a drink at the bar. Unless they had a dress code, he could nurse a beer and maybe keep an eye on the lobby without looking out of place. If she was settled in for the night he was out of luck, but maybe she'd just gone to her room to change, maybe she hadn't had dinner yet.

Better than. that, as it turned out. He walked into the bar and there she was, all by herself at a corner table, smoking a cigarette in a holder — you didn't see that much anymore — and drinking what looked like a rust-colored cocktail in a stemmed glass. A Manhattan or a Rob Roy, he figured. Something like that. Classy, like the woman herself, and slightly out-of-date.

Keller stopped at the bar for a bottle of Tuborg, carried it to the woman's table. Her eyes widened briefly at his approach, but otherwise nothing much showed on her face. Keller drew a chair for himself and sat down as if there was no question that he was welcome.

"I'm with the guy," he said.

"I don't know what you're talking about."

"No names, all right? Straw hat with a red band on it. You

21

were talking to him, what, twenty minutes ago? You want to pretend I'm talking Greek, or do you want to come with me?"

"Where?"

"He needs to see you."

"But he just saw me!"

"Look, there's a lot I don't understand here," Keller said, not untruthfully. "I'm just an errand boy. He coulda come himself, but is that what you want? To be seen in public in your own hotel with Slansky?"

"Slansky?"

"I made a mistake there," Keller said, "using that name, which you wouldn't know him by. Forget I said that, will you?"

"But. . ."

"Far as that goes, we shouldn't spend too much time together. I'm going to walk out, and you finish your drink and sign the tab and then follow me. I'll be waiting out front in a blue Honda Accord."

"But. . . "

"Five minutes," he told her, and left.

It took her more than five minutes, but under ten, and she got into the front seat of Honda without any hesitation. He pulled out of the hotel lot and hit the button to lock her door.

While they drove around, ostensibly heading for a meeting with the man in the Panama hat (whose name wasn't Slansky, but so what?) Keller learned that Floyd Turnbull, who'd had an affair with this woman, had sweet-talked her into investing in a real estate venture of his. The way it was set up, she couldn't get her money out without a lengthy and expensive lawsuit—unless Turnbull died, in which case the partnership was automatically dissolved. Keller didn't try to follow the legal part. He got the gist of it, and that was enough. The way she spoke about Turnbull, he got the feeling she'd pay a lot to see him dead, even if there was nothing in it for her.

Funny how people tended not to like the guy.

And now Slansky had all the money in advance, and in return for that she had his sworn promise that Turnbull wouldn't have a pulse by the time the team got back to Memphis. She'd been after him to get it done in Cleveland, but he'd stalled until he'd gotten her to pay him the entire fee up front, and it looked as though he wouldn't do it until they were in Baltimore, but it really better happen in Baltimore, because that was the last stop before the Tarpons returned to Memphis for a long home stand, and—

Jesus, suppose the guy tried to save himself a trip to Baltimore?

"Here we go," he said, and turned into a strip mall. All the stores were closed for the night, and the parking area was empty except for a delivery van and a Chevy that wouldn't go anywhere until somebody changed its right rear tire. Keller parked next to the Chevy and cut the engine.

"Around the back," he said, and opened the door for her and helped her out. He led her so that the Chevy screened them from the street. "It gets tricky here," he said, and took her arm.

The man he'd called Slansky was staying at a budget motel off an interchange of I-71, where he'd registered as John Carpenter. Keller went and knocked on his door, but that would have been too easy.

23

Hell.

The Tarpons were staying at a Marriott again, unless they were already on their way to Baltimore. But they'd just finished a night game, and they had a night game tomorrow, so maybe they'd stay over and fly out in the morning. He drove over to the Marriott and walked through the lobby to the bar, and on his way he spotted the shortstop and a middle reliever. So they were staying over, unless someone in the front office had cut those two players, and that seemed unlikely, as they didn't look depressed.

He found two more Tarpons in the bar, where he stayed long enough to drink a beer. One of the pair, the second-string catcher, gave Keller a nod of recognition, and that gave him a turn. Had he been hanging around enough for the players to think of him as a familiar face?

He finished his beer and left. As he was on his way out of the lobby, Floyd Turnbull was on his way in, and not looking very happy. And what did he have to be happy about? A stringbean named Anliot had taken his job away from him for the evening, and had won the game for the Tarpons in the process. No wonder Turnbull looked like he wanted to kick somebody's ass, and preferably Anliot's. He also looked to be headed for his room, and Keller figured the man was ready to call it a night.

Keller went back to the budget motel. When his knock again went unanswered, he found a pay phone and called the desk. A woman told him that Mr. Carpenter had checked out.

And gone where? He couldn't have caught a flight to Baltimore, not at this hour. Maybe he was driving. Keller had seen his car, and it looked too old and beat-up to be a rental. Maybe he owned it, and he'd drive all night, from Cleveland to Baltimore.

Keller flew to Baltimore and was in his seat at Camden Yards for the first pitch. Floyd Turnbull wasn't in the lineup, they'd benched him and had Graham Anliot slotted as DH. Anliot got two singles and a walk in his first three trips to the plate, and Keller didn't stick around to see how he ended the evening. He left with the Tarpons coming to bat in the top of the seventh, and leading by four runs.

The clerk at Ace Hardware rang Keller's purchases—a roll of picture-hanging wire, a packet of screw eyes, a packet of assorted picture hooks—and came to a logical conclusion. With a smile, he said, "Gonna hang a pitcher?"

"A DH," Keller said.

"Huh?"

"Sorry," he said, recovering. "I was thinking of something else.

"Yeah, right. Hang a picture."

In his motel room, Keller wished he'd bought a pair of wire-cutting pliers. In their absence, he measured out a three-foot length of the picture-hanging wire and bent it back on itself until the several strands frayed and broke. He fashioned a loop at each end, then put the unused portion of the wire back in its box, to be discarded down the next handy storm drain. He'd already rid himself of the screw eyes and the picture hooks.

He didn't know where Slansky was staying, hadn't seen him at the game the previous evening. But he knew the sort of motel the man favored, and figured he'd pick one near the ballpark. Would he use the same name when he signed in? Keller couldn't think of a reason why not, and evidently neither could Slansky; when he called the Sweet Dreams Motel on Key Highway, a pleasant young woman with a Gujarati accent told him that yes, they did have a guest named John Carpenter, and would he like her to ring the room?

"Don't bother," he said. "I want it to be a surprise."

And it was. When Slansky—Keller couldn't help it, he thought of the man as Slansky, even though it was a name he'd made up for the guy himself—when Slansky got in his car, there was Keller, sitting in the back seat.

The man stiffened just long enough for Keller to tell that his presence was known. Then, smoothly, he moved to fit the key in the ignition. Let him drive away? No, because Keller's own car was parked here at the Sweet Dreams, and he'd only have to walk all the way back.

And the longer Slansky was around, the more chances he had to reach for a gun or crash the car.

"Hold it right there, Slansky," he said.

"You got the wrong guy," the man said, his voice a mix of relief and desperation. "Whoever Slansky is, I ain't him."

"No time to explain," Keller said, because there wasn't, and why bother? Simpler to use the picture-hook wire as he'd used it so often in the past, simpler and easier. And if Slansky went out thinking he was being killed by mistake, well, maybe that would be a comfort to him.

Or maybe not. Keller, his hands through the loops in the wire, yanking hard, couldn't see that it made much difference.

"Awww, hell," said the fat guy a row behind Keller, as the Oriole centerfielder came down from his leap with nothing in his glove but his own hand. On the mound, the Baltimore pitcher shook his head the way pitchers do at such a moment, and Floyd Turnbull rounded first base and settled into his home run trot.

"I thought we caught a break when the new kid got hurt," the fat guy said, "on account of he was hotter'n a pistol, not that he won't cool down some when the rest of the league figures out how to pitch to him. He'll be out what, a couple of weeks?"

"That's what I hear," Keller said. "He broke a toe."

"Got his foot stepped on? Is that how it happened?"

"That's what they're saying," Keller said. "He was in a crowded elevator, and nobody knows exactly what happened, whether somebody stepped on his foot or he'd injured it earlier and only noticed it when he put a foot wrong. They figure he'll be good as new inside of a month."

"Well, he's not hurting us now," the man said, "but Turnbull's picking up the slack. He really got ahold of that one."

"Number 398," Keller said."

"That a fact? Two shy of four hundred, and he's getting close to the mark for base hits, isn't he?"

"Four more and he'll have three thousand."

"Well, the best of luck to the guy," the man said, "but does he

27

have to get 'em here?"

"I figure he'll hit the mark at home in Memphis."

"Fine with me. Which one? Hits? Homers?"

"Maybe both," Keller said.

"You didn't bring me one," the man said.

It was the same fellow he'd sat next to the first time he saw the Tarpons play, and that somehow convinced Keller he was going to see history made. At his first at-bat in the second inning, Floyd Turnbull had hit a grounder that had eyes, somehow picking out a path between the first and second basemen. It had taken a while, the Tarpons were four games into their home stand, playing the first of three with the Yankees, and Turnbull, who'd been a disappointment against Tampa Bay, was nevertheless closing in on the elusive numbers. He had 399 home runs, and that scratch single in the second inning was hit #2999.

"I got the last hot dog," Keller said, "and I'd offer to share it with you, but I never share."

"I don't blame you," the fellow said. "It's a selfish world."

Turnbull walked in the bottom of the fourth and struck out on three pitches two innings later, but Keller didn't care. It was a perfect night to watch a ballgame, and he enjoyed the banter with his companion as much as the drama on the field. The game was a close one, seesawing back and forth, and the Tarpons were two runs down when Turnbull came up in the bottom of the ninth with runners on first and third.

On the first pitch, the man on first broke for second. The

throw was high and he slid in under the tag.

"Shit," Keller's friend said. "Puts the tying run in scoring position, so you got to do it, but it takes the bat out of Turnbull's hands, because now they have to put him on, set up the double play."

And, if the Yankees walked Turnbull, the Tarpon manager would lift him for a pinch runner.

"I was hoping we'd see history made," the man said, "but it looks like we'll have to wait a night or two . . . Well, what do you know? Torre's letting Rivera pitch to him."

But the Yankee closer only had to throw one pitch. The instant Turnbull swung, you knew the ball was gone. So did Bernie Williams, who just turned and watched the ball sail past him into the upper deck, and Turnbull, who watched from the batter's box, then jumped into the air, pumping both fists in triumph, before setting out on his circuit of the bases. The whole stadium knew, and the stands erupted with cheers.

Four hundred homers, three thousand hits—and the game was over, and the Tarps had won.

"Storybook finish," Keller's friend said, and Keller couldn't have put it better.

"Try that tea," Dot said. "See if it's all right."

Keller took a sip of iced tea and sat back in the slat-backed rocking chair. "It's fine," he said.

"I was beginning to wonder," she said, "if I was ever going to see you again. The last time I heard from you there was another hitter on the case, or at least that's what you thought. I started thinking maybe you were the one he was after, and maybe he took you out."

"It was the other way around," Keller said.

"Oh?"

"I didn't want him getting in the way," he explained, "and I figured the woman who hired him was a loose cannon. So she slipped and fell and broke her neck in a strip mall parking lot in Cleveland, and the guy she hired—"

"Got his head caught in a vise?"

"That was before I met him. He got all tangled up in some picture wire in Baltimore."

"And Floyd Turnbull died of natural causes," Dot said. "Had the biggest night of his life, and it turned out to be the last night of his life."

"Ironic," Keller said.

"That's the word Peter Jennings used. Celebrated, drank too much, went to bed, and choked to death on his own vomit. They had a medical expert on who explained how that happens more often than you'd think. You pass out, and you get nauseated and vomit without recovering consciousness, and if you're sleeping on your back, you aspirate the stuff and choke on it."

"And never know what hit you."

"Of course not," Dot said, "or you'd do something about it. But I never believe in natural causes, Keller, when you're in the picture. Except to the extent that you're a natural cause of death all by yourself."

"Well," he said.

"How'd you do it?"

"I just helped nature a little," he said. "I didn't have to get him drunk, he did that by himself. I followed him home, and he was all over the road. I was afraid he was going to have an accident."

"So?"

"Well, suppose he just gets banged around a little? And winds up in the hospital? Anyway, he made it home all right. I gave him time to go to sleep, and he didn't make it all the way to bed, just passed out on the couch." He shrugged. "I held a rag over his mouth, and I induced vomiting, and—"

"How? You made him drink warm soapy water?"

"Put a knee in his stomach. It worked, and the vomit didn't have anywhere to go, because his mouth was covered. Are you sure you want to hear all this?"

"Not as sure as I was a minute ago, but don't worry about it. He breathed it in and choked on it, end of story. And then?"

"And then I got out of there. What do you mean, 'and then?'"

"That was a few days ago."

"Oh," he said "Well, I went to see a few stamp dealers. Memphis is a good city for stamps. And I wanted to see the rest of the series with the Yankees. The Tarpons all wore black arm bands for Turnbull, but it didn't do them any good. The Yankees won the last two games."

"Hurray for our side," she said. "You want to tell me about it, Keller?"

"Tell you about it? I just told you about it."

"You were gone a month," she said, "doing what you could have done in two days, and I thought you might want to explain it to me."

"The other hitter," he began, but she was shaking her head.

"Don't give me 'the other hitter'. You could have closed the sale before the other hitter ever turned up."

"You're right," he admitted. "Dot, it was the numbers."

"The numbers?"

"Four hundred home runs," he said. "Three thousand hits. I wanted him to do it."

"Cooperstown," she said.

"I don't even know if the numbers'll get him into the Hall of Fame," he said, "and I don't really care about that part of it. I wanted him to get in the record books, four hundred homers and three thousand hits, and I wanted to be able to say I'd been there to see him do it."

"And to put him away."

"Well," he said, "I don't have to think about that part of it."

She didn't say anything for a while. Then she asked him if he wanted more iced tea, and he said he was fine, and she asked him if he'd bought some nice stamps for his collection.

"I got quite a few from Turkey," he said. "That was a weak spot in my collection, and now it's a good deal stronger."

"I guess that's important."

"I don't know," he said. "It gets harder and harder to say what's important and what isn't. Dot, I spent a month watching baseball. There are worse ways to spend your time."

"I'm sure there are, Keller," she said. "And sooner or later I'm sure you'll find them."

PINCH HITTER

A Nathan Heller story by Max Allan Collins

My buddy Bill Veeck made many a mark in the world of big league baseball, owning his first club at twenty-eight, winning pennants, setting attendance records. Two of Bill's teams beat the Yankees in their heyday—the '48 Cleveland Indians and the '59 White Sox; only one other team managed that feat, the '54 Indians, which was mostly made up of Veeck's former players.

And, of course, Bill Veeck was a character as colorful as his exploding-paint-factory sportshirts—one of his many trademarks was a refusal to wear coat and tie—a hard-drinking, chain-smoking extrovert with a wooden leg and a penchant for ignoring such quaint customs as doctors' orders and a good night's sleep. Veeck thought nothing of commuting from Cleveland to New York, to hang out with show biz pals like Frank Sinatra and Skitch Henderson at the Copa, or to fly at the drop of a cap out to Hollywood for a game of charades with Hope and Crosby.

"Baseball is too grim, too serious," he liked to say. "It should be fun. Most owners are bunch of damn stuffed shirts."

Many of Veecks stunts and promotions and just plain wild

ideas indeed had irritated the stuffed shirts of baseball. During World War Two, when the draft had drained the game of so much talent, Veeck told Commissioner Kenesaw Mountain Landis that he planned to buy the Phillies and fill the team with black ball players (another buyer was quickly found). Still, Veeck did manage to put the first black player in the American League, Larry Doby, and even brought the legendary Negro Leagues pitcher, Satchel Paige, into the majors.

Nonetheless, Bill Veeck was resigned to the fact that— no matter what his other accomplishments, whether noble or absurd— he would go down in baseball history as the guy who brought a midget into the majors.

Back in June of '61, when Veeck called the A-1 Detective Agency, saying he had a job for me, I figured it would have something to do with his recent resignation as president of the White Sox. A partner had bought out both Bill and his longtime associate, Hank Greenberg, and I wondered if it'd been a squeeze play.

Maybe Bill needed some dirt dug up on somebody. Normally, at that stage of my career anyway, I would have left such a shabby task to one of the agencys' many operatives, rather than its president and founder—both of which were me.

I had known Veeck for something like fifteen years, however, and had done many an odd job for him. And besides, my policy was when a celebrity asked for Nate Heller, the celebrity got Nate Heller.

And Bill Veeck was, if nothing else, a celebrity.

The afternoon was sunny with a breeze, but blue skies were banished in the shadow of the El, where Miller's nestled, an undistinguished Greek-run American-style restaurant that Veeck had adopted as his favorite Loop hangout, for reasons known only to him. Any time Veeck moved into a new office, his first act was to remove the door—another of his trademarks—and Miller's honored their famous patron by making one of Veeck's discarded doors their own inner front one, with an explanatory plaque, and the inevitable quote: "My door is always open—Bill Veeck."

At a little after three p.m., Miller's was hardly hopping, its dark front windows adding to the under-the-El gloom. Bill was seated in his usual corner booth, his wooden leg extended into the aisle. I threaded through the empty formica tables and, after a handshake and hello, slid in opposite him.

"Well, you look like hell," I told him.

He exploded with laughter, almost losing his corner-of-the-mouth cigarette. "At last an honest man. Everybody else tells me I look in the pink—I'm getting the same kind of good reviews as a well-embalmed corpse."

Actually, a well-embalmed corpse looked better than Veeck: his oblong face was a pallid repository for pouchy eyes, a long lumpy nose and that wide, full-lipped mouth, which at the moment seemed disturbingly slack. His skin—as leathery and well-grooved as a catcher's mitt—hung loose on him, and was startlingly white. I had never seen him without a tan. Though I was ten years older, Veeck in his mid-forties looked sixty. A hard sixty.

"It's a little late to be looking for dirt on Allyn, isn't it?" I asked him, after a waitress brought Veeck a fresh bottle of Blatz and a first one for me.

35

Arthur Allyn had bought the White Sox and was the new president.

"This isn't about that," Veeck said gruffly, waving it off. "Art's a pal. This sale clears the way for Hank to relocate in L.A. When I get feeling better, Hank'll take me in as a full partner."

"Then what is this about, Bill?"

"Maybe I just want to hoist one with you, in honor of an old friend."

"Oh.... Eddie Gaedel. I guess I should have known."

We clinked beer bottles.

I had seen Eddie's obit in yesterday's paper—and the little story the *Trib* ran in sports. Eddie had died of natural causes, the coroner had said, and bruises on his body were "probably suffered in a fall."

"I want you to look into it," Veeck said.

"Into what?"

"Eddie's death."

"Why? If it was natural causes."

"Eddie's mother says it was murder."

I sipped my beer, shook my head. "Well, those 'bruises' could have come from a beating he got, and deserved—Eddie always was a mouthy little bastard. A week after that game in St. Louis, ten years ago, he got arrested in Cincinnati for assaulting a cop, for Christ's sake."

Veeck swirled his beer and looked down into it with bleary eyes—in all the years I'd known this hard-drinking S.O.B., I'd never once seen him with bloodshot eyes... before.

"His mother says it's murder," Veeck repeated. "Run over to the South Side and talk to her—if what she says gets your nose twitchin', look into it.... If it's just a grieving mother with some crazy idea about how her 'baby' died, then screw it."

"Okay. Why is this your business, Bill?"

"When you spend six months bouncing back and forth between your apartment and the Mayo Clinic, you get to thinking... putting your affairs in order. Grisly expression, but there it is."

"What is it? The leg again?"

"What's left of it. The latest slice took my knee away, finally. That makes seven operations. Lucky seven."

"Semper Fi, mac," I said, and we clinked bottles again. We'd both been Marines in the South Pacific, where I got malaria and combat fatigue, and he had his leg run over by an anti-tank gun on the kickback. Both of us had spent more time in hospitals than combat.

"My tour was short and undistinguished," he said. "At least you got the Bronze Star."

"And a Section Eight."

"So I lost half a leg, and you lost half your marbles. We both got a better deal than a lot of guys."

"And you want me to see what kind of deal Eddie Gaedel got?"

"Yeah. Seems like the least I could do. You know, I saw him, not that long ago. He did a lot of stunts for me, over the years. Last year I dressed him up as a Martian and ran him around the park. Opening day this year, I had midget vendors working the grandstand, giving out cocktail wieners in little buns, and shorty beers."

"And Eddie was one of the vendors."

"Yeah. Paid him a hundred bucks - same as that day back in '51."

That day when Eddie Gaedel—3'-7", sixty-five pounds—stepped up to the plate for the St. Louis Browns, batting for Frank Saucier.

"Funny thing is," Veeck said, lighting up a fresh cigarette, "how many times I threatened to kill that little bastard myself. I told him, I've got a man up in the stands with a high-powered rifle, and if you take a swing at any pitch, he'll fire."

"You got the mother's address?"

"Yeah... yeah, I got it right here." He took a slip of paper out of his sportshirt pocket but didn't hand it to me. "Only she's not there right now."

"Where is she?"

"Visitation at the funeral home. Service is tomorrow morning."

"Why don't I wait, then, and not bother her..."

The gravel voice took on an edge. "'Cause I'd like you to represent me. Pay her and Eddie your respects... plus, your detective's nose might sniff something."

"What, formaldehyde?"

But I took the slip of paper, which had the funeral home address as well as Mrs. Gaedel's.

He was saying, "Do you know the *New York Times* put Eddie's obit on the front page? The front goddamn page.... And that's the thing, Nate, that's it right there: my name is in Eddie's obit, big as baseball. And you know what? You know damn well, time comes,

Eddie'll be in mine."

I just nodded; it was true.

The pouchy eyes tightened—bloodshot maybe, but bright and hard and shiny. "If somebody killed that little bastard, Nate, find out who, and why, and goddamnit, do something about it."

I squinted through the floating cigarette smoke. "Like go to the cops?"

Veeck shrugged; his wrinkled puss wrinkled some more.... "You're the one pitching. Hurl it any damn way you want to."

Of course this had all begun about ten years before in the summer of '51 - when Veeck called me and asked if I knew any midgets who were "kinda athletic and game for anything."

"Why don't you call Marty Craine," I'd said, into the phone, leaning back in my office chair, "or some other booking agent."

"Marty's come up blank," Veeck's voice said through the long-distance crackle. "Can't you check with some of those lowlife pals of yours at the South State bump-and-grind houses? They take shows out to the carnivals, don't they?"

"You want an athletic midget," I said, "I'll find you an athletic midget."

So I had made a few calls, and wound up accompanying Eddie Gaedel on the train to Cleveland, for some as yet unexplained Bill Veeck stunt. Eddie was in his mid-twenties but had that aged, sad-eyed look common to his kind; he was pleasant enough, an outgoing character who wore loud sportshirts and actually reminded me of a pintsize Veeck.

"You don't know what the hell this is about?" he kept asking me in his highpitched squawk, an oversize cigar rolling from one corner to the other of his undersize mouth.

"No," I said. We had a private compartment and Gaedel's incessant cigar smoking provided a constant blue haze. "I just know Bill wants this kept mum—I wasn't to tell anybody but you, Eddie, that we're going to Cleveland to do a job for the Browns."

"You follow baseball, Nate?"

"I'm a boxing fan myself."

"I hope I don't have to know nothing about baseball."

"Veeck didn't say you had to know baseball—just you had to be athletic."

Gaedel was a theatrical midget who had worked in various acrobatic acts.

"Ask the dames," Gaedel said, chortling around the pool-cue Havana, "if Eddie Gaedel ain't athletic."

That was my first clue to Eddie's true personality, or anyway the Eddie that came out after a few drinks. In the lounge car, after he threw back one, then another Scotch on the rocks like a kid on a hot day downing nickel Cokes, I suddenly had a horny Charlie McCarthy on my hands.

I was getting myself a fresh drink, noticing out the corner of an eye as Eddie sidled up to a pair of attractive young women—a blonde and brunette travelling together, probably college students, sweaters and slacks—and set his drink on their little silver deco table. He looked first at the blonde, then at the brunette, as if picking out just the right goodie in a candy-store display case.

Then he put his hand on the blonde's thigh and leered up at her.

"My pal and me got a private compartment," he said, gesturing with his cigar like an obscenely suggestive wand, "if you babes are up for a little four-way action."

The blonde let out a yelp, brushing off Eddie's hand like a big bug. The brunette was frozen in Fay Wray astonishment.

Eddie grabbed his crotch and grinned. "Hey doll, you don't know what you're missin'—I ain't as short as you think."

Both women stood and backed away from the little man, pressing up against the windows, pretty hands up and clawed, their expressions about the same as if a tarantula had been crawling toward them.

I got over there before anybody else could—several men stood petrified, apparently weighing the urge to play Saint George against looking like a bully taking on such a pint-sized dragon.

Grabbing him by the collar of his red shirt, I yanked the midget away from the horrified girls, saying, "Excuse us, ladies... Jesus, Eddie, behave yourself."

And the little guy spun and swung a hard sharp fist up into my crotch. I fell to my knees and looked right into the contorted face of Eddie Gaedel, a demented elf laughing and laughing at the pitiful sight that was me.

A white-jacketed conductor was making his alarmed way toward us when my pain subsided before Eddie's kneeslapping laughter, giving me the window of opportunity to twist the little bastard's arm behind him and drag him out of the lounge, through the dining car, getting lots of dirty looks from passengers along the way for this cruelty, and back to our compartment, tossing him inside like the nasty little ragdoll he was.

He picked himself up, a kind of reassembling action, and came windmilling at me, his highpitched scream at once ridiculous and frightening.

I clipped him with a hard right hand and he collapsed like a string-snipped puppet. Out cold on the compartment floor. Well, if you have to be attacked by an enraged horny drunken midget, better that he have a glass jaw.

He slept through the night, and at breakfast in the dining car apologized, more or less.

"I'm kind of an ugly drunk," he admitted, buttering his toast.

"For Christ's sakes, Eddie, you only had two drinks."

"Hey, you don't have to be friggin' Einstein to figure with my body size, it don't take much. Anyway, I won't tell Mr. Veeck my bodyguard beat the crap out of me."

"Yeah. Probably best we both forget the little incident."

He frowned at me, toast crumbs flecking his lips. "'Little' incident? Is that a remark?"

"Eat your poached eggs, Eddie."

In Veeck's office, the midget sat in a wooden chair with his legs sticking straight out as the Hawaiian-shirted owner of the St. Louis Browns paced excitedly—though due to Bill's wooden leg, it was more an excited shuffle. I watched from the sidelines, leaning against a file cabinet.

Suddenly Veeck stopped right in front of the seated midget and thrust an Uncle Bill Wants You finger in his wrinkled little puss.

"Eddie, how would like to be a big-league ballplayer?"

"Me?" Eddie —wearing a yellow shirt not as bright as the sun —squinted up at him. "I been to maybe two games in my life! Plus, in case you ain't noticed, I'm a goddamn midget!"

"And you'd be the only goddamn midget in the history of the game." Tiny eyes bright and big as they could be, Veeck held up two hands that seemed to caress an invisible beach ball. "Eddie, you'll appear before thousands— your name'll go in the record books for all time!"

Eddie's squint turned interested. "Yeah?"

"Yeah. Eddie, my friend.... you'll be immortal."

"Immortal. Wow. Uh.... what does it pay?"

"A hundred bucks."

Eddie was nodding now—a hundred bucks was even better than immortality.

"So what do you know about baseball?" Veeck asked him.

"I know you're supposed to hit the white ball with the bat. And then you run somewhere."

Veeck snatched a little toy bat from his desk; then he crouched over as far as his gimpy leg would allow, and assumed the stance.

"The pitcher's gotta throw that white ball in your strike zone, Eddie."

"What the hell is that?"

"It's the area between the batter's armpits and the top of his knees.... Let's see your strike zone."

Eddie scrambled off the chair and took the toy bat, assuming the position.

"How's that, Mr. Veeck?"

"Crouch more. See, since you're only gonna go to bat once in your career, whatever stance you assume at the plate, that's your natural stance."

Eddie, clutching the tiny bat, crouched. His strike zone was maybe one and a half inches.

Then he took an awkward, lunging swing.

"No!" Veeck said. "Hell, no!"

Eddie, still in his crouch, looked at Veeck curiously.

Veeck put his arm around the little guy. "Eddie, you just stay in that crouch. You just stand there and take four balls. Then you'll trot down to first base and we'll send somebody in to run for you."

"I don't get it."

Veeck explained the concept of a walk to Eddie, whose face fell, his dreams of glory fading.

"Eddie," Veeck said pleasantly, "if you so much as look like you're gonna swing, I'm gonna shoot you dead."

Eddie shrugged. "That sounds fair."

On a hot Sunday in August, a crowd of twenty thousand—the largest attendance the chronically losing Browns had managed in over four years—came out to see Bill Veeck's latest wild stunt. The crowd, which was in a great, fun-loving mood, had no idea what that stunt would be; but as this doubleheader with the Tigers marked the fiftieth anniversary of the American League, the fans knew it would be something more than just the free birthday cake and ice cream being handed out.

Or the opening game itself, which the Browns, naturally, lost.

The half-time show began to keep the implied Veeck promise of zaniness, with a parade of antique cars, two couples in Gay Nineties attire pedalling a bicycle-built-for-four around the bases, and a swing combo with Satchel Paige himself on drums inspiring jitterbugging in the aisles. A three-ring circus was assembled, with a balancing act at first base, trampoline artists at second and a juggler at third.

Throughout all this, I'd been babysitting Eddie Gaedel in Veeck's office. Gaedel was wearing a Browns uniform that had been made up for Bill DeWitt, Jr., the nine year-old son of the team's former owner/current advisor. The number sewn onto the uniform was actually a fraction: 1/8; and kid's outfit or not, the thing was tent-like on Eddie.

We could hear the muffled roar of the huge crowd, and Eddie was nervous. "I don't feel so good, Nate."

The little guy was attempting to tie the small pair of cleats Veeck had somehow rustled up for him.

"You'll do fine, Eddie."

"I can't tie these friggin' things! Shit!"

So I knelt and tied the midget's cleats. I was getting a hundred bucks for the day, too.

"These bastards hurt my feet! I don't think I can go on."

"There's twenty thousand people in that park, but there's one whose ass I know I can kick, Eddie, and that's you. Get going."

Soon we were under the stands, moving down the ramp, toward the seven-foot birthday cake out of which Veeck planned to have Eddie jump. Big Bill Durney, Veeck's travelling secretary, helped me lift the midget under the arms, so we could ease him onto the board inside the hollowed-section of the cake.

"What the hell am I?" Eddie howled, as he dangled between us. No one had told him about this aspect of his appearance. "A stripper?"

"When you feel the cake set down," I said, "jump out, and run around swingin' and clowning. Then run to the dugout and wait your turn at bat."

"This is gonna cost that bastard Veeck extra! I'm an AGVA member, y'know!"

And we set him down in there, handed him his bat, and covered him over with tissue paper, through which his obscenities wafted.

But when the massive cake was rolled out onto the playing field by two of the fans' favorite Browns, Satch Paige and Frank Saucier, and plopped down on the pitcher's mound, Eddie Gaedel rose to the occasion. As the stadium announcer introduced "a brand-new Brownie," Eddie burst through the tissue paper and did an acrobatic tumble across the wide cake, landing on his cleats nimbly, running to home, swinging the bat all the way, eating up the howls of laughter and the spirited applause from the stands.

Then Eddie headed for the dugout, and the various performers were whisked from the field for the start of the second game. The fans were having a fine time, though perhaps some were disappointed that the midget-from-the-cake might be the big Veeck stunt of the day; they had hoped for more.

They got it.

Frank Saucier was the leadoff batter for the Browns, but the announcer boomed, "For the Browns, number 1/8 - Eddie Gaedel, batting for Saucier!"

And there, big as life, so to speak, was Eddie Gaedel, swimming in the child's uniform, heading from the dugout with that small bat still in hand, swinging it, limbering up, hamming it up.

Amazed laughter rippled through the crowd as the umpire crooked a finger at Veeck's manager, Zack Taylor, who jogged out with the signed contract and a carbon of the telegram Veeck had sent major league headquarters adding Eddie to the roster.

By this time I had joined Veeck in the special box up on the roof, where visiting dignitaries could enjoy the perks of a bar and restaurant. Veeck was entertaining a crew from Falstaff Breweries, the Browns' radio sponsors, who were ecstatic with the shenanigans down on the diamond. Newspaper photographers were swarming onto the field, capturing the manager of the Tigers, Red Rolfe, complaining to the umpire, while pitcher Bob Cain and catcher Bob Swift just stood at their respective positions, occasionally shrugging at each other, obviously waiting for this latest Bill Veeck gag to blow over.

But it didn't blow over: after about fifteen minutes of discussion, argument and just plain bitching, the umpire shooed away the photogs and—with clear reluctance—motioned the midget to home plate.

"Look at the expression on Cain's puss!" Veeck exploded at my shoulder.

Even at this distance, the disbelief on the pitcher's face was evident, as he finally grasped that this joke was no joke: he had to pitch to a midget.

"He can't hurl underhand," Veeck was chortling, "'cause submarine pitches aren't legal. Look at that! Look at Swift!"

The catcher had dropped to his knees, to give his pitcher a better target.

"Shit!" Veeck said. His tone had turned on a dime. All around us, the Falstaff folks were having a gay old time; but Veeck's expression had turned as distressed as Cain's. "Will you look at that little bastard, Nate...."

Eddie Gaedel—who Veeck had spent hours instructing in achieving the perfect, unpitch-to-able crouch—was standing straight and, relatively speaking, tall, feet straddled DiMaggio-style, tiny bat held high.

"Have you got your gun, Nate? That little shit's gonna swing...."

"Naw," I said, a hand on Veeck's shoulder, "he's just playing up to the crowd."

Who were playing up to him, cheering, egging him on.

Then pitcher Cain came to Veeck's rescue by really pitching to the midget, sending two balls speeding past Eddie before he could even think to swing.

"I wouldn't worry now," I said to Veeck.

Cain had started to laugh; he was almost collapsing with laughter, which the crowd aped, and he could barely throw at all as he tossed two more looping balls, three and then four feet over Eddie's head.

The littlest Brown trotted to his base as the crowd cheered and cameras clicked; then he stood with one foot on the bag as if he were thinking of stealing, which got a huge, roaring laugh.

Finally pinch runner Jim Delsing came over and Gaedel surrendered the base to him, giving the big man a comradely pat on the butt.

The crowd was going wild, Veeck grinning like a monkey as I made my exit to go down and meet my midget charge in Veeck's office. Eddie had his clothes changed—he was wearing a bright green and yellow shirt that made Veeck's taste seem mild—and I warned him that the reporters would be lying in wait.

"Veeck says it's your call," I said. "I can sneak you out of here—"

"Hell no!" Eddie was sitting on the floor, tying his shoes—he didn't need any help, this time. "It's great publicity! Man, I felt like Babe Ruth out there."

"Eddie, you're now what most every man in the country wishes he could be."

"Yeah? What's that?"

"A former major-leaguer."

Since Veeck had been talking about using Gaedel again, the little guy really warmed up to the reporters waiting outside the stadium, telling them "Two guys I'd really like to face on the mound are Bob Feller and Dizzy Trout."

But it didn't work out that way. First off, despite the midget ploy, the Browns lost 6-2 to the Tigers, anyway. And before Veeck could put Gaedel into a White Sox game in Eddie's hometown of Chicago a month later, the baseball commissioner banned midgets from baseball.

Veeck had responded to Commissioner Harridge by saying, "Fine, but first you gotta establish what a midget is—is it three foot six, like Eddie? If it's five six, great! We can get rid of Phil Rizzuto!"

The commissioner's ban was not only complete, but retroactive: Eddie didn't even make it into the record books, the Gaedel name nowhere to be seen in the official 1951 American League batting records—though the base-on-balls was in Cain's record, and a pinch-running appearance in Delsing's.

Nonetheless, this stuffed-shirt revisionist history did no good at all: record book or not, Eddie was immortal over Bill Veeck's stunt, and so was Bill Veeck.

Immortal in the figurative sense, of course. Their fame didn't stop Veeck from staring death in the face, nor, apparently, had it spared little Eddie Gaedel from murder.

The Keurtz Funeral Home was one of those storefront numbers, with a fancy faux-stone facade in the midst of pawn shops and bars. This was on the South Side, Ashland and 48th, the business district of a working-class neighborhood of two-flats and modest frame houses, a hard pitch away from Comiskey Park.

I left my car three blocks down, on a side street, mulling over what I'd learned from several phone calls to contacts in the Coroner's Office and the Homicide Bureau. The death had never been considered a possible homicide, so there'd been virtually no investigation.

A midget had died in his sleep, a not uncommon occurrence, considering the limited life expectancy of little people. Yes, there'd been some bruises, but Gaedel was known as a rough customer, a barroom brawler, with several assaults on his record. The unspoken but strongly implied thread was that if Gaedel hadn't died of natural causes, he'd earned whatever he'd gotten.

The alcove of the funeral home was filled with smoke and midgets. This was not surprising, the smoke anyway, being fairly typical for a Chicago storefront funeral parlor—no smoking was allowed in the visitation areas, so everybody crowded out in the entryway and smoked and talked.

Seeing all those small, strange faces turned toward me, as I entered, was unsettling: wrinkled doll faces, frowning at my six-foot presence, the men in suits and ties, the women in Sunday best, like children playing dress up. I took off my hat, nodded at them as a group, and they resumed their conversations, a high-pitched chatter, like half a dozen Alvin and the Chipmunks records were playing simultaneously.

The dark-panelled visitation area was large, and largely empty, and just inside the door was the tiny coffin with Eddie peacefully inside. He wore a conservative suit and tie, hands folded; it was the only time I hadn't seen Eddie in a loud sportshirt, with the exception of that kid-size Browns uniform. Quite a few flowers were on display, many with Catholic trappings, a horseshoe arrangement ribboned MY FAVORITE BATTER - BILL VEECK prominent among them.

The folding chairs would have seated several hundred, but only two were occupied. Over to the right, a petite but normal-sized woman in black dabbed her eyes with a hanky as a trio of midgets—

two men and a woman—stood consoling her. Eddie's mother, no doubt.

The female midget was maybe four feet and definitely quite lovely, a shapely blue-eyed blonde lacking pinched features or ungainly limbs, a miniature beauty in a blue satin prom dress. She was upset, weeping into her own hanky.

In the back sat a human non sequitur, a slim, rangy mourner in his late thirties, with rugged aging-American-boy good looks— anything but a midget. His expression somber, his sandy hair flecked with gray, he looked familiar to me, though I couldn't place him.

Since Eddie's mom was occupied, I wandered back to the full-size mourner and he stood, respectfully, as I approached.

"Nate Heller," I said, extending a hand. "I take it you were a friend of Eddie's, too. Sorry I can't place you..."

"Bob Cain," he said, shaking my hand.

"The pitcher!"

His smile was embarrassed. "That's right. You're a friend of Bill Veeck's, aren't you?"

"Yeah. I've done a number of jobs for Bill... including body-guarding Eddie for that stunt, way back when."

Cain smiled again, a bittersweet expression. Then he moved over one and gestured to the empty chair, saying, "Sit down, won't you?"

We sat and talked. I was aware that Cain, after a contract squabble shortly following the midget incident, had been traded at Veeck's request to the Browns. Cain played the '52 and '53 seasons for him.

"Bill's a great guy," Cain said. "One owner who treated the players like human beings."

"Even if he did embarrass you?"

"That's just part of the Veeck package. Funny thing is, in the time I played for him, Bill never mentioned the midget thing. But I always wondered if he'd traded for me to make it up to me, or something. Anyway, I had a fine career, Mr. Heller."

"Nate."

"Beat the Yankees fifteen oh, in my first major league start. Pitched a one-hitter against Feller. I had a lot of good experiences in baseball."

"But you'll be remembered for pitching to a midget."

"At least I'll be remembered. It's part of baseball history, Nate —there'll never be another midget in the game.... just Eddie."

"Did you stay in touch with the little guy?"

"Naw.... I haven't seen him since I pitched against him. But when I read about this, I just had to pay my respects, as a good Christian, you know—to a man who was so important in my life."

"Are you still in the game, Bob?"

"Not since '56.... got a calcium deposit on my wrist, and couldn't get my pitch back. I drove up from Cleveland for this—felt kind of.... obligated."

I didn't hear anything but sincerity in his words and his voice; but I would check up on Cain's whereabouts—and see if he'd driven up from Cleveland before or after Eddie's murder.

The petite blonde was standing at the casket, lingering there, staring down at Eddie, weeping softly into her hanky. The two men had gone back out to the alcove.

This left Mrs. Gaedel free and I went over to her, introducing myself.

"Mrs. Gaedel, Bill Veeck sends his condolences," I told her, taking the seat next to her.

A pleasant-looking woman of sixty, salt-and-pepper hair in a bun, Mrs. Gaedel sat and listened as I told her how I'd been involved with Eddie in his famous stunt. I left out the part about the college girls in the lounge car.

"Mr. Veeck was wonderful to Eddie over the years," she said, her voice bravely strong. "Gave Eddie so much work. Eddie supported me, after his father died, you know."

"Eddie kept busy."

"Yes. TV, movies, stage.... He lived with me, you know—had his little apartment with its little furnishings in the attic.... ceiling so low I had trouble cleaning up there, but he loved it. That's where I found him.... in bed...."

I slipped an arm around her as she wept.

Then after a while I said, "You spoke to Mr. Veeck on the phone, I understand."

"Yes—this morning."

"I'm a private investigator, Mrs. Gaedel, and Bill asked me to talk to you about these.... doubts you have, about the circumstances of your son's death."

"Oh! Are you willing to look into that for me?"

"Bill has hired me to do that very thing, as long as we have your blessing."

"Of course you have my blessing! And my eternal thanks.... What do you want to know, Mr. Heller?"

"This is hardly the time, Mrs. Gaedel. I can come to your home, after the service sometime, in a day or two perhaps—"

"No, please, Mr. Heller. Let's talk now, if we could."

I was turning my hat in my hands like a wheel. "Actually, that would be wise, if you're up to it. The sooner I can get started—"

"I'm up to it. Start now."

We were interrupted several times, as Eddie's friends paid their respects. But her story was this: Eddie had been drinking heavily lately, and running with a rough crowd, who hung out at the Midgets' Club.

I knew this bar, which was over on Halstead, and dated back to the '40s; it had begun as a gimmick, a bar where the customers were served by midgets, mostly former members of the Singer Midgets who'd played Munchkins in *The Wizard of Oz*. An area was given over to small tables and short stools, for midget clientele, and eventually the midgets essentially took over. But for the occasional tourist who stopped by for the oddity of the joint—to pick up the trademark halfbooks of matches, see a few framed *Oz* photos, and get some Munchkin autographs—the Midgets' Club became the cultural center of midget activity in Chicago.

"I thought the Midgets Club was pretty respectable," I said.

"It is—Elmer St. Aubin and his wife still run the place. But a rough element—carny types—hang out there, you know."

"That blonde you were talking to. She doesn't seem part of that element."

"She isn't, not all. That's Betsy Jane Perkins... she worked with Eagle's Midget Troupe, does a lot of television, personal appearances, dressed and made up like a doll... the 'Living Doll,' they call her."

"Were your son and Miss Perkins good friends?"

"Oh yes. He'd been dating her. She was wonderful. Best thing in his life... I was so hopeful her good influence would wrest him away from that bad crowd."

"Do you suspect anyone in particular, Mrs. Gaedel?"

"No, I... I really didn't know many of my son's friends. Betsy Jane is an exception. Another possibility are these juvenile delinquents."

"Oh?

"That's what I think may have happened—a gang of those terrible boys may have gotten ahold of Eddie and beaten him."

"Did he say so?"

"No, not really. He didn't say anything, just stumbled off to bed."

"Had he been robbed, mugged? Was money missing from his wallet?"

She shook her head, frowning. "No. But these juveniles pick on the little people all the time. If my son were inebriated, he would have been the perfect target for those monsters. You should strongly consider that possibility."

"I will. Mrs. Gaedel, I'll be in touch with you later. My deepest sympathies, ma'am."

She took my hand and squeezed it. "God bless you, Mr.

Heller."

In the alcove, I signed the memorial book. The crowd of midgets was thinning, and the blonde was gone.

Nothing left for me to do but follow the Yellow Brick Road.

The Midget Club might have been any Chicago saloon: a bar at the left, booths at the right, scattering of tables between, pool table in back, wall-hung celebrity photos here and there, neon beer signs burning through the fog of tobacco smoke, patrons chatting, laughing, over a jukebox's blare. But the bar was sawed-off with tiny stools, the tables and chairs and booths all scaled down to smaller proportions (with a few normal sized ones up front, for tourist traffic), the pool table half-scale, the celebrity photos of Munchkins, the chatter and laughter of patrons giddy and high-pitched.

As for the jukebox, Sinatra's "Tender Trap" was playing at the moment, to be followed by more selections running to slightly dated swing material, no rock or R&B—which suited me, and was a hell of a lot better than "Ding Dong the Witch Is Dead."

I had known the club's proprietor and chief bartender, Pernell "Little Elmer" St. Aubin, since he was, well, little—a child entertainer at the Midget Village at the Chicago World's Fair back in '33. He'd been tap dancing and I'd been busting pickpockets. Elmer had been in his teens when he appeared in *The Wizard of Oz,* so now —as he stood behind the bar, polishing a glass, a wizened Munchkin in an apron—he was probably only in his mid-thirties. But as was so often the case with his kind, he looked both older and younger than his years.

I selected one of the handful of somewhat taller stools at the bar and said to Elmer, "For a weekday, you're doing good business."

"It's kind of a wake," Elmer explained. "For Eddie Gaedel. People coming over after visitation at Keurtz's. You knew Eddie, didn't you?"

"Yeah. I was over there myself. Paying my respects, and Bill Veeck's."

Elmer frowned. "Couldn't Veeck make it himself?"

"He's pretty sick. So was Eddie ornery as ever, up to the end?"

"Christ yes! I hated serving that little bastard. Sweet enough guy sober, but what a lousy drunk. If I hadn't been secretly watering his drinks, over the years, he'd have busted up the joint long ago."

"I hear he may have been rolled by some juvies. Think that's what killed him?"

"I doubt it. Eddie carried a straight razor—people knew he did, too. I think these young punks woulda been scared to get cut. Funny thing, though."

"What is?"

"His mama said that straight razor didn't turn up in his things."

I thought about that, then asked, "So how do you think Eddie died?"

"I have my own opinion."

"Like to share that opinion, Elmer?"

"The cops weren't interested. Why are you?"

"Eddie was a friend. Maybe I'm just curious. Maybe there's a score to settle."

"Are you gonna drink something, Heller?"

I gave the Munchkin a ten, asked for a rum and Coke and told him he could keep the change, if he stayed chatty.

"Eddie was playing a puppet on a local kid's show," Elmer said, serving me up. "But he lost the gig 'cause of his boozing. So lately he was talking to some of my less classier clientele about going out on the carny circuit. Some kinda sideshow scam where they pretended to be Siamese triplets or something."

"Work is work."

"See that little dame over there?"

Every dame in here was little, but Elmer was talking about Betsy Jane, the Living Doll in her blue satin prom dress. I hadn't spotted her when I came in—she was sitting alone in a booth, staring down into a coffee cup cupped in her dainty hands.

Elmer leaned in conspiratorially. "That's Betsy Jane Perkins, the actress—Eddie was crazy about her, and she felt the same about him. She was trying to straighten him out, and I think she might've succeeded, if it hadn't been for that ex-husband of hers."

"Yeah?"

"Guy named Fred Peterson. He's a shrimp."

"A midget?"

"No, a shrimp—a 'normal'-size guy who stands just under five feet. He's a theatrical agent, still is Betsy Jane's agent; specializes in booking little people. Makes him feel like a big man, lording it over us."

"He is a regular?" I swivelled on the stool and glanced around. "Is he here?"

"Yes, he's a regular, no, he's not here. He wouldn't pay his respects to Eddie, that's for goddamn sure."

"Why?"

"Lately Fred's been trying to get back in Betsy Jane's good graces, among other things. Why don't you talk to her? She's a sweet kid. I think she'd do anything to help out where Eddie's concerned."

I took Elmer's advice, and my rum and Coke and I went over and stood next to the booth where the painfully pretty little woman gloomily sat. She looked up at me with beautiful if bloodshot blue eyes; her heavy, doll-like makeup was a little grief-smeared, but she was naturally pretty, with a fairly short, Marilyn-ish do.

"Miss Perkins, my name is Nate Heller—I was a friend of Eddie Gaedel's."

"I don't remember Eddie mentioning you, Mr. Heller," she said, almost primly, her voice a melodic soprano with a vibrato of sorrow.

"I'm an associate of Bill Veeck's. I escorted Eddie to that famous game in St. Louis back in '51."

She had brightened at the mention of Veeck's name, and was already gesturing for me to sit across from her.

"I saw you at the funeral parlor," she said, "talking to Helen."

"Helen?"

"Mrs. Gaedel."

"Yes. She feels the circumstances of her son's death are somewhat suspicious."

The blue eyes lowered. "I'd prefer to reminisce about Eddie and the fun times, the good times, than..."

"Face the truth?"

"Mr. Heller, I don't know what happened to Eddie. I just know I've lost him, right when I thought..." She began to cry, and got in her purse, rustling for a handkerchief.

I glanced over at Elmer, behind the bar, and he was squinting at me, making a vaguely frantic gesture that I didn't get. Shrugging at him, I returned my attention to the Living Doll.

"You'd been trying to help Eddie. Encourage him to stop drinking, I understand. Not run with such a rough crowd."

"That's right."

I'd hoped for elaboration.

I tried venturing down a different avenue. "I understand some j.d.s have been preying on little people in this neighborhood."

"That.... that's true."

"Eddie might have been beaten and robbed."

"Yes... he might have."

"But you don't think that's the case, do you?"

Now she was getting a compact out of her purse, checking her make-up. "If you'll excuse me, Mr. Heller—I look a fright."

And she went off to the ladies' room.

I just sat there and sipped my rum and Coke, wondering if I would get anything out of Betsy Jane except tears, when an unMunchkin-like baritone growled at me.

"You got a fetish, pal?"

I turned and looked up at the source of the irritation, and the reason for Elmer's motioning to me: he was short, but no midget, possibly five foot, almost handsome, with a Steve Canyon jaw compromised by pugged nose and cow eyes; his hair was dark blonde and slicked back and he wore a mustache that would have been stylish as hell if this were 1935. Deeply tanned, his build was brawny, his hairy, muscular chest shown off by the deep v-neck cut of his pale green herringbone golf shirt, his arms short but muscular.

I said, "What?"

"You got a scratch to itch, buddy?"

"What the hell are you talking about?"

He leaned in, eyes popping, teeth bared, cords in his neck taut; he reeked of Old Spice. "You some kind of pervert, pops? Some kinda letch for the midget ladies?"

Very quietly, I said, "Back off."

Something about how I'd said it gave him pause, and the clenched fist that was his face twitched a couple times, and he and his Old Spice aura backed away—but he kept standing there, muscular arms folded now, like a stubby, pissed-off genie.

"And you must be Fred Peterson," I said.

"Who wants to know?"

Not offering a hand to shake, I said, "My name's Heller—friend of Eddie Gaedel's, and Bill Veeck's."

He blinked. "What, you were over at the funeral home?"

"That's right."

"Paying your respects."

"Yes. And looking into Eddie's murder."

He frowned; then he scrambled across from me into the booth, where Betsy Jane had been sitting. "What do you mean, murder?"

"He was beaten to death, Fred. You don't mind if I call you

'Fred'... ?"

His hands were folded, but squeezing, as if he were doing iso-metrics. "The cops said it was natural causes. Why's it your busi-ness, the cops say it's natural causes?"

"I'm a private investigator, working for Veeck. When I get enough evidence, I'll turn it over to the cops and see if I can't change their minds about how 'natural' those causes were."

He leaned forward, hands still clasped, a vein in his forehead jumping. "Listen, that little prick had a big mouth and a lot of ene-mies. You're gonna get nowhere!"

I shrugged, sipped my rum and Coke. "Maybe I can get some-where with Betsy Jane."

The cow eyes flashed. "Stay away from her."

"Why should I? She seems to like me, and I like her. She's a cute kid. She interests me...kind of a new frontier."

"I said stay away."

"Who died and appointed you head of the Lollipop Guild? I'm going to find out who killed Eddie Gaedel, and have myself some tight little fun along the way."

And I grinned at him, until he growled a few obscenities and bolted away, heading toward the rear of the bar, almost bumping into Betsy Jane, coming back from the restroom. She froze seeing him, and he clutched her by the shoulders and got right in her face and said something to her, apparently something unpleasant, even threatening. Then he stalked toward the rear exit.

Her expression alarmed, she took her seat across from me and said, "You should go now."

"That was your agent, right?"

"... right."

"And your boyfriend?"

"No... husband. Ex-husband. Please go."

"Jealous of you and Eddie, by any chance? Did you go to him with the idea for a new act, you and Eddie as boy and girl livin' dolls?"

She shook her head, blonde bangs shimmering. "Mr. Heller, you don't know what kind of position you're putting me in...."

I knew that her ex-husband didn't want any man putting this doll in any position.

But I said, "I think for a little guy, your ex-husband and current agent has a tall temper. And I think he's goddamn lucky the cops didn't investigate this case, because he makes one hell of a suspect in Eddie's death."

She began to weep again, but this was different, this was more than grief—there was fear in it.

"What do you know, Betsy Jane?"

"Nuh... nothing... nothing...."

"Tell me. Just tell me—so that I know. I won't take anything to the police without your permission."

Damp eyelashes fluttered. "Well... I... I don't know anything, except that... on that last night, Fred was... nice to Eddie and me."

"Nice?"

"Yes. He'd been furious with me, at the suggestion that Eddie and I would work as a team, livid that I would suggest that he, of all people, should book such an act.... We had two, no three, terrible arguments about it. Then... then he changed. He can do that, run hot and cold. He apologized, said he'd been a jerk, said he wanted to make it up, wanted to help. Sat and talked with us all evening, making plans about the act."

"Go on."

"That's all."

"No it isn't. I can see it in those pretty eyes, Betsy Jane. The rest... tell me the rest."

She swallowed, nodded, sighed. "They... they left together. Eddie lived close, you know, easy walk home to his mother's house —Fred was going to talk business with him. They went out the back way, around midnight. It was the last time I saw Eddie alive."

The alley behind the bar, bumped up against the backyards of residences, would be as good a place as any for an assault.

She was saying, "But I can't imagine Fred would do such a thing."

"Sure you can."

She shook her head. "Anyway, Eddie was no pushover. He carried a straight razor, you know."

"So I hear. But I also hear it wasn't among his effects."

"Oh. Eddie had it that night. I saw it."

"Yeah?"

"He emptied his pocket, looking for change for the jukebox... laid his things right on this counter, razor among them. We were sitting in this very booth... this was... our booth."

She began to cry again, and I got over on her side of the booth, slid an arm around her, and comforted her, thinking that she really was a cute kid, and midget sex was definitely on my short list of things yet undone in a long and varied life.

But more to the point, what had become of that razor?

If Fred had attacked Eddie out back, maybe that razor had been dropped in the scuffle—and if it was back there, somewhere, I'd have the evidence I needed to get the cops to open an investigation.

"Betsy Jane," I said, "we'll talk again ... when you're feeling up to it."

"All right... but Mr. Heller... Nate... I am afraid. Terribly afraid."

I squeezed her shoulder, kissed her cheek. "I'll make the bad man go away."

She put her hand on my thigh—her little bitty hand. Christ, it felt weird. Also, good.

Nodding to Elmer, I headed toward the rear exit, and stepped out into the alley. The night was moonless with a scattering of stars, and the lighting was negligible—no street lamps back here, just whatever scant illumination spilled from the frame houses whose back yards bordered the asphalt strip. A trio of garbage cans—full-scale, nothing midget about them—stood against the back of the brick building, and some empty liquor and beer cartons were stacked nearby.

Not much to see, and in the near-darkness, I would probably need my flashlight to probe for that missing straight razor. I had just decided to walk the several blocks to the side street where my car was parked, to get the flash, when a figure stepped out from the recession of an adjacent building's rear doorway.

"Looking for something?" Fred Peterson asked, those cow

eyes wide and wild, teeth bared like an angry animal, veins throbbing in his neck, one hand behind his back. Though he stood only five foot, his brawny frame, musculature obvious in the skin-tight golf shirt, made him a threatening presence as he stepped into the alley like a gunfighter out onto the Main Street of Dodge.

I was thinking how I should have brought my gun along—only usually, attending midget funerals, it wasn't necessary.

"Get some ideas," he said, "talking to Betsy Jane?"

He was standing there, rocking on legs whose powerful thighs stood out, despite the bagginess of his chinos.

Shrugging, I said, "I thought Eddie mighta dropped something when you jumped him."

Peterson howled as he whipped something from behind him and charged, it was a bat, he was wielding a goddamn baseball bat, and he was whipping it at me, slicing the air, the bat whooshing over me as I ducked under the swing. Screw baseball, I tackled him, taking him down hard, and the bat fell from his grasp, clattering onto the asphalt. I rolled off him, rolling toward the sound, and then I had the bat in my hands, as I got up and took my stance.

That's when I found that straight razor I'd been looking for, or rather Fred Peterson showed me what had become of it, as he yanked it from his pocket and swung it around, the meager light of the alley managing to wink off the shining blade.

I didn't wait for him to come at me: I took my swing.

The bat caught him in the side of the head, a hard blow that caved his skull in, and by the time Peterson fell to his knees, his motor responses were dead, and so was he. He flopped forward, on his face, razor spilling from limp fingers, blood and brains leaching out onto the asphalt as I stood over him, the bat resting against my shoulder.

"Strike zone my ass," I said to nobody, breathing hard.

Finally I went back into the Midget Club, carrying the bloody bat, getting my share of my looks, though Betsy Jane had gone. I leaned on the bar and told Elmer to call the cops.

But the little bartender just looked at me in amazement. "What the hell did you do, Heller?"

"Somebody had to go to bat for Eddie. Call the goddamn cops, would you, please?"

No charges were brought against me— my actions were clearly in self-defense—and Eddie Gaedel's death is listed to this day as "natural causes" on the books. Though I shared with them everything I knew about the matter, the police simply didn't want to go to the trouble of declaring Eddie a murder victim, merely to pursue a deceased suspect. Poor Eddie just couldn't get a fair shake in any of the record books.

A few days after the cops cleared me, Veeck spoke to me on the phone, from a room in the Mayo clinic.

"You know, ten years ago, when I sent Eddie Gaedel into that game," he said, reflectively, "I knew it would be that little clown's shining moment... What I didn't know was that it would be mine, too! Hell, I knew it was a good gag, that the fans would roar, and the stuffed shirts holler. But who coulda guessed it'd become the single act forever identified with me?"

"We're any of us lucky to be remembered for anything, Bill,"

I said.

"Yeah. Yeah. Suppose Eddie felt that way?"

"I know he did."

For years after, Helen Gaedel remembered me at Christmas with cookies or a fruitcake. Betsy Jane Perkins was grateful, too.

Veeck expressed his gratitude by paying me handsomely, and, typically, fooled himself and all of us by not dying just yet. The man who invented fan appreciation night, who provided a day care center for female employees before the term was coined, who was first to put the names of players on the backs of uniforms, who broke the color line in the American League, and who sent a midget up to bat—and who also bought back the Chicago White Sox in 1975 —lived another irascible fifteen years.

And wasn't that a hell of a stunt.

AUTHOR'S NOTE: Fact, speculation and fiction are freely mixed in this story. My thanks to George Hagenauer, my longtime research associate on the Nathan Heller novels, who knew Bill Veeck. Newspapers of the day were consulted, and a number of books, including *Bill Veeck: A Baseball Legend* (1988) by Gerald Eskenazi; *Munchkins of Oz* (1996) by Stephen Cox; *The Story of My Life* (1989), Hank Greenberg; and *Veeck - As in Wreck* (1962; revised 1976), Bill Veeck with Ed Linn.

TWO-BAGGER

by Michael Connelly

T he bus was forty minutes late.

Stilwell and Harwick waited in a six-year-old Volvo at the curb next to the McDonald's a block from the depot. Stilwell, the driver, chose the spot because he was betting that Vachon would walk down to the McDonald's after getting off the bus. They would begin the tail from there.

"These guys, they been in stir four, five years, they get out and want to get drunk and laid in that order," Stilwell had told Harwick. "But something happens when they get off the freedom bus and see the golden arches waiting for them down the block. Quarter Pounder and fries, ketchup. Man, they miss that shit in prison."

Harwick smiled.

"I always wondered what happened with real rich guys, you know? Guys who grew up poor, eatin' fast food, but then made so much money that money doesn't mean anything. Bill Gates, guys like that. You think they still go to McDonald's for a grease fix every now and then?"

"In disguise maybe," Stilwell suggested. "I don't think they

71

drive up in their limos or anything."

"Yeah, probably."

It was new partner banter. It was their first day together. For Harwick it was also his first day in GIU. Stilwell was the senior partner. The *veterano*. They were working one of his jackets.

After forty-five minutes and no bus, Stilwell said, "So what do you want to ask me? You want to ask me about my partner, go ahead."

"Well, why'd he bug?"

"Couldn't take the intensity."

"Since I heard he went into special weapons I assume you're talking about your intensity, not the gig's."

"Have to ask him. I've had three partners in five years. You're number four."

"Lucky number four. Next question, what are we doing right now?"

"Waiting on the bus from Corcoran."

"I already got that part."

"A meth cook named Eugene Vachon is on it. We're going to follow him, see who he sees."

"Uh huh."

Harwick waited for more. He kept his eyes on the bus depot a half a block up Vine. Eventually, Stilwell reached up to the visor and took a stack of photos out from a rubber band. He looked through them until he found the one he wanted and handed it to Harwick.

"That's him. Four years ago. They call him Milky."

The photo was of a man in his early thirties with bone-white hair that appeared to be pulled together in back in a ponytail. His skin was as white as a new lampshade and his eyes were the light blue of washed-out denim.

"Edgar Winters," Harwick said.

"What?"

"Remember that guy? He was like an albino rock star in the seventies. Looked just like this guy. He had a brother, Johnny. Maybe he was the albino."

"Missed it."

"So what's Milky's deal? If you're on him, he must be Road Saints, right?"

"He's on the bubble. He was cooking for them but never got his colors. Then he got popped and went to The Cork for a nickel. He's got to crack an egg now if he wants in. And from what I hear, he wants in."

"Meaning whack somebody?"

"Meaning whack somebody."

Stilwell explained how the Gang Intelligence Unit kept contacts with intelligence officers at prisons all over California. One such contact provided information on Vachon. Milky had been protected by incarcerated members of the Road Saints during his five-year stay at Corcoran State Penitentiary.

As a form of repayment for that protection as well as a tariff for his admittance to formal membership in the motorcycle gang turned prison and drug organization, Vachon would perform a contract hit upon his release.

Harwick nodded.

"You're the resident expert on the Saints, so it goes to you. Got that. Who is the target?"

"That's the mystery we're going to solve. We're going to follow Milky and see if we can find that out. He might not even know himself right now. This could be an in-house thing or a sub-contract job the Saints took on. A trade-off with the blacks or the *eMe*. You never know. Milky might not have his orders yet. All we know is that he's been tapped."

"And we're going to step in if we get the chance."

"When we get the chance."

"When we get the chance."

Stilwell handed the whole stack of photos to Harwick.

"That's the Saints' active membership. By active I mean not incarcerated. Any one of them could be the target. They're not above going after their own. The Saints are run by a guy named Sonny Mitchell who's a lifer up at Ironwood. Any time anybody on the outside acts up, talks about changing the leadership, maybe bringing it outside the walls, then Sonny has him cut down. Helps keep people in line."

"How's he get the word from Ironwood to Milky over at Corcoran?"

"The women. Sonny gets conjugals. He tells his wife, probably right in the middle of giving her a pop. She leaves, tells one of the wives visiting her man in The Cork. It goes like that."

"You got it down, man. How long've you been working these guys?"

"Coming up on five years. Long time."

"Why didn't you ever rotate out?"

Stilwell straightened up behind the wheel and ignored the question.

"There's the bus."

Stilwell had been right. Milky Vachon's first stop after getting off the bus was the McDonald's. He ate two Quarter Pounders and went back to the counter twice for ketchup for his french fries.

Stilwell and Harwick went in a side door and slipped into a booth positioned behind Vachon's back. Stilwell said he had never met Vachon but that he needed to take precautions because it was likely Vachon had seen his photo. The Saints had their own intelligence net and, after all, Stilwell had been assigned full time to the gang for half a decade.

When Vachon went to the counter for ketchup for the second time, Stilwell noticed that there was an envelope sticking out of the back pocket of his blue jeans. He told Harwick that he was curious about it.

"Most of the time these guys get out, they want no reminders of where they've been," he whispered across the table. "They leave letters, photos, books, everything behind. That letter, that must mean something. I'm not talking sentimental. I mean it means something."

He thought a moment and nodded to himself.

"I'm gonna go out, see if I can set up a shake. You stay here. When he starts wrapping up his trash come on out. If I'm not back in time I'll find you. If I don't, use the rover."

Stilwell called sheriff's dispatch and had them contact LAPD to send a car. He arranged to meet the car around the corner from the McDonald's so their conference wouldn't be seen by Vachon.

It took almost ten minutes for a black and white to show. The uniform officer pulled the car up next to Stilwell's Volvo, driver's window to driver's window.

"Stilwell?"

"That's me."

He pulled a badge out of his shirt. It was on a chain around his neck. Also hung on the chain was a gold 7 about the size of a thumbnail.

"Ortiz. What can I do for you?"

"Around the corner my partner's keeping an eye on a guy just off the bus from Corcoran. I need to shake him. He's got an envelope in his back pocket. I'd like to know everything there is to know about it."

Ortiz nodded. He was about twenty-five with the kind of haircut that left the sides of his head nearly shaved and a healthy inch of hair on the top. He had one wrist on the top of the wheel and he drummed his fingertips on the dashboard.

"What was he up there for?"

"Cooking crystal meth for the Road Saints."

Ortiz picked up the rhythm with his fingers.

"He going to go easy? I'm by myself, in case you didn't notice."

"At the moment, he should be easy. Like I said, he just got back on the ground. Just give him a kick in the pants, tell him you don't want him on your beat. That ought to do it. My partner and I will have your back. You'll be safe.

"Okay. You going to point him out?"

"He's an albino with a pony tail. Like that Edgar Winters guy."

"Who?"

"Never mind. You can't miss him."

"All right. Meet back here after?"

"Yeah. And thanks."

Ortiz pulled away first and Stilwell watched him go. He then followed and turned the corner. He saw Harwick standing on the curb outside the McDonald's. Moving north on foot a half a block away was Vachon.

Stilwell pulled to a stop next to Harwick and his new partner got in the Volvo.

"I was wondering where you were."

"Forgot to turn on my rover."

"Is that the shake car just went by?"

"That's it."

They watched in silence as the black and white pulled to the curb next to Vachon and Ortiz stepped out. The patrolmen signaled Vachon to the hood of the cruiser and the ex-convict assumed the position without protest.

Stilwell leaned across to the glove compartment and got out a small pair of field glasses and used them to watch the shake-down.

Ortiz leaned Vachon over the hood and patted him down. He held him in that position with a forearm on his back. After checking him for weapons and coming up empty, Ortiz pulled the white envelope out of Vachon's back pocket.

With his body leaned over the hood, Vachon could not see what Ortiz was doing. With one hand Ortiz was able to open the envelope and look inside. He studied the contents for a long moment but did not remove them. He then returned the envelope to the man's back pocket.

"Can you see what it is?" Harwick asked.

"No. Whatever it was, the cop looked at it in the envelope."

Stilwell continued to watch through the field glasses. Ortiz had now let Vachon stand up and was talking to him face to face. Ortiz' arms were folded in front of him and his body language suggested he was attempting to intimidate Vachon. He was telling him to get off his beat. It looked pretty routine. Ortiz was good.

After a few moments Ortiz used a hand signal to tell Vachon to move on. He then returned to his car.

"All right, you get back out and stay with Milky. I'll go talk to the cop and come back for you."

"Gotcha."

Ten minutes later the Volvo pulled up next to Harwick at the corner of Hollywood and Vine. Harwick climbed back in.

"It was a ticket to a Dodgers game," Stilwell said. "Tonight's game."

"In the envelope? Just a ticket to the game?"

"That's it. Outside was his address at Corcoran. With a return that was smeared. Not recognizable. Postmark was Palmdale, mailed eight days ago. Inside was just the one ticket. Reserve level, section eleven, row K, seat one. By the way, where is Vachon?"

"Across the street. The porno palace. I guess he's looking for—"

"That place has a back door."

Stilwell was out of the car before he finished the sentence. He darted across the street in front of traffic and through the beaded curtain at the entrance to the adult video arcade.

Harwick followed but at a reduced pace. By the time he had entered the arcade Stilwell had already swept through the video and adult novelty showroom and was in the back hallway slapping back the curtains of the private video viewing booths. There was no sign of Vachon.

Stilwell moved to the back door, pushed it open and came out into a rear alley. He looked both ways and did not see Vachon. A young couple, both with ample piercings and drug-glazed eyes leaned against a dumpster. Stilwell approached them.

"Did you just see a guy come this way a few seconds ago? White guy with white hair. An albino. You couldn't miss him."

They both giggled and one mentioned something about seeing a white rabbit going down a hole.

They were useless and Stilwell knew it. He took one last look around the alley, wondering if Vachon had merely been taking precautions when he ducked through the porno house, or if he had seen Stilwell or Harwick tailing him. He knew a third possibility, that Vachon had been spooked by the shake-down and decided to disappear, was also to be considered.

Harwick stepped through the back door into the alley. Stilwell glared at him and he averted his eyes.

"Know what I heard about you, Harwick? That you're going to night school."

He didn't mean it literally. It was a cop expression. Going to night school meant you wanted to be somewhere else. Not the street, not in the game. You were thinking about your next move, not the present mission.

"That's bullshit," Harwick said. "What was I supposed to do? You left me hanging. What if I covered the back? He could've walked out the front."

The junkies laughed, amused by the angry exchange of the cops.

Stilwell started walking out of the alley, back toward Vine where he had left the car.

"Look, don't worry," Harwick said. "We have the game tonight. We'll get back on him there."

Stilwell checked his watch. It was almost five. He called back without looking at Harwick.

"And it might be too late by then."

At the parking gate to Dodger Stadium, the woman in the booth asked to see their tickets. Stilwell said they didn't have tickets.

"Well, we're not allowed to let you in without tickets. Tonight's game is sold out and we can't allow people to park without tickets for the game."

Before Stilwell could react Harwick leaned over to look up at the woman.

"Sold out? The Dodgers aren't going anywhere. What is it, beach towel night?"

"No, it's Mark McGwire."

Harwick leaned back over to his side.

"All right, McGwire!"

Stilwell pulled his badge out of his shirt.

"Sheriff's deputies, ma'am. We working. We need to go in."

She reached back into the booth and got a clipboard. She asked Stilwell his name and told him to hold in place while she called the stadium security office. While they waited, cars backed up behind them and a few drivers honked their horns.

Stilwell checked his watch. It was forty minutes until game time.

"What's the hurry?"

"BP."

Stilwell looked over at Harwick.

"What?"

"Batting practice. They want to see McGwire hit a few fungoes out of the park before the game. You know who Mark McGwire is, don't you?"

Stilwell turned to look at the woman in the both. It was taking a long time.

"Yes, I know who he is. I was here at the stadium in eighty-eight. He wasn't so hot then."

'The series? Did you see Gibson's homer?"

"I was here."

"So cool! So was I!"

Stilwell turned to look at him.

"You were here? Game one, ninth inning? You saw him hit it?"

The doubt was evident in his voice.

"I was here," Harwick protested. "Best fucking sports

81

moment I've ever seen."

Stilwell just looked at him.

"What? I was here!"

"Sir?"

Stilwell turned back to the woman. She handed him a parking pass.

"That's for lot seven. Park there and then go to the field level gates and ask for Mr. Houghton. He's in charge of security and he'll determine if you can enter. Okay?"

"Thank you."

As the Volvo went through the gate it was hit with a volley of horns for good measure.

"So you're a baseball fan," Harwick said. "I didn't know that."

"You don't know a lot about me."

"Well, you went to the World Series. I think that makes you a fan."

"I was a fan. Not anymore."

Harwick was silent while he thought about that. Stilwell was busy looking for Lot 7. They were on a road that circled the stadium with the parking lots on either side denoted by large baseballs with numbers painted on them. The numbers didn't seem to be in an order he understood.

"What happened?" Harwick finally asked.

"What do you mean what happened?"

"They say baseball is a metaphor for life. If you fall out of love with baseball you fall out of love with life."

"Fuck that shit."

Stilwell felt his face burning. Finally, he saw the baseball with the orange seven painted on it. A dull emptiness came into his chest as he looked at the number. An ache that he vanquished by speeding up to the lot entrance and handing the lot monitor his pass.

"Anywhere," the monitor said. "But slow it down."

Stilwell drove in, circled around and took the space closest to the exit so they could get out quickly.

"If we catch up with Milky here it's going to be a goddamn nightmare following him out," he said as he turned the car off.

"We'll figure it out," Harwick said. "So what happened?"

Stilwell opened the door and was about to get out. Instead he turned back to his partner.

"I lost my reason to love the game, okay? Let's leave it at that."

He was about to get out again when Harwick stopped him once more.

"What happened? Tell me. We're partners."

Stilwell put both hands back on the wheel and looked straight ahead.

"I used to take my kid, all right? I used to take him all the time. Five years old and I took him to a world series game. He saw Gibson's homer, man. We were out there, right field bleachers, back row. Only tickets I could get. That would be a story to tell when he grew up. A lot of people in this town lie about it, say they were here, say they saw it..."

He stopped there but Harwick made no move to get out. He waited.

"But I lost him. My son. And without him... there wasn't a reason to come back here."

Without another word Stilwell got out and slammed the door behind him.

At the field level gate they were met by Houghton, the skeptical security man.

"We've got Mark McGwire in town and everybody and their brother is coming out of the woodwork. I have to tell you guys, if this isn't legit, I can't let you in. Any other game, come on back and we'll see what we can do. I'm LAPD retired and would love to—"

"That's nice, Mr. Houghton, but let me tell you something," Stilwell said. "We're here to see a hitter, but his name isn't McGwire. We're trying to track a man who's in town to kill somebody, not hit home runs. We don't know where he is at the moment but we do know one thing. He's got a ticket to this game. He might be here to make a connection and he might be here to kill somebody. We don't know. But we're not going to be able to find that out if we're on the outside looking in. You understand our position now?"

Houghton nodded once under Stilwell's intimidating stare.

"We're going to have over fifty thousand people in here tonight," he said. "How are you two going to—"

"Reserve level, section eleven, row K, seat one."

"That's his ticket?"

Stilwell nodded.

"And if you don't mind," Harwick said, "we'd like to get a trace on that ticket. See who bought it, if possible."

Stilwell looked at Harwick and nodded. He hadn't thought of

that. It was a good idea.

"That will be no problem," said Houghton, his voice taking on a tone of full cooperation now. "Now this seat location. How close do you need and want to get?"

"Just close enough to watch what he does, who he talks to," Stilwell said. "Make a move if we have to."

"This seat is just below the press box. I can put you in there and you can look right down on him."

Stilwell shook his head.

"That won't work. If he gets up and moves, we're a level above him. We'll lose him."

"How about one in the press box and one below—mobile, moving about?"

Stilwell thought about this and looked at Harwick. Harwick nodded.

"Might work," he said. "We got the radios."

Stilwell looked at Houghton.

"Set it up."

They were both in the front row of the press box looking down on Vachon's seat. It was empty and the National Anthem had already been sung. The Dodgers were taking the field. Kevin Brown was on the mound, promising a classic matchup between a fast ball pitcher and McGwire, a pure-bred slugger.

"This is going to be good," Harwick said.

"Just don't forget why we're here," Stilwell replied.

The Cardinals went down one, two, three and left McGwire waiting on deck. In the bottom half of the first the Dodgers did no better. No hits, no runs.

And no sign of Milky Vachon.

Houghton came down the stairs and told them the ticket Vachon was carrying had been sold as part of a block of seats to a ticket broker in Hollywood. They took the name of the broker and decided they would check it out in the morning.

As the second inning started Stilwell sat with his arms folded on the front sill of the press box. It allowed a full view of the stadium. All he had to do was lower his eyes and he would see row K, seat one of section eleven.

Harwick was leaning back in his seat. To Stilwell, he seemed as interested in watching the three rows of sports writers and broadcasters as the baseball game. As the Dodgers were retaking the field, he spoke to Stilwell.

"Your son," he said. "It was drugs, wasn't it?"

Stilwell took a deep breath and let it out. He spoke without turning to Harwick.

"What do you want to know, Harwick?"

"We're going to be partners. I just want to... understand. Some guys, something like that happens, they dive into the bottle. Some guys dive into the work. It's pretty clear which kind you are. I heard you go after these guys, the Saints, with a vengeance, man. Was it meth? Was your kid on crank?"

Stilwell didn't answer. He watched a man wearing a Dodgers baseball cap take the first seat in row K below. The hat was on backward, a white pony tail hanging from beneath the brim. It was Milky Vachon. He put a full beer down on the concrete step next to him and kept another in his hand. Seat number two was empty.

"Harwick," Stilwell said. "We're partners but we're not talking about my kid. You understand?"

"I'm just trying to—"

"Baseball is a metaphor for life, Harwick. Life is hard ball. People hit home runs, people get thrown out. There's the double play, the suicide squeeze and everybody wants to get home safe. Some people go all the way to the ninth inning. Some people leave early to beat the traffic."

Stilwell stood up and turned to his new partner.

"I checked you out, Harwick. You're a beat-the-traffic guy. You weren't here. In eighty-eight. I know. If you were here, you gave up on them and left before the ninth. I know."

Harwick said nothing. He turned his eyes from Stilwell.

"Vachon's down there," Stilwell said. "I'm going down to keep watch. If he makes a move, I'll tail. Keep your rover close."

Stilwell walked up the steps and out of the press box.

McGwire struck out at the top of the second inning and Brown easily retired the side. The Dodgers picked up three unearned runs in the third off an error, a walk and home run with two outs.

All was quiet after that until the fifth when McGwire opened the inning with a drive to the right field wall. It drew 50,000 people out of their seats. But the right fielder gloved it on the track, his body hitting hard into the wall pads.

Watching the trajectory of the ball reminded Stilwell of the night in '88 when Kirk Gibson put a three-two pitch into the seats in the last of the ninth and won the first game of the series. It caused a monumental shift in momentum and the Dodgers cruised the rest of the way. It was a moment that was cherished by so many for so long. A time in L.A. before the riots, before the earthquake, before O.J.

Before Stilwell's son was lost.

Brown carried a perfect game into the seventh inning. The crowd became more attentive and noisy. There was a sense that something was going to happen.

Throughout the innings Stilwell moved his position several times, always staying close to Vachon and using the field glasses to watch him. The ex-convict did not move, other than to stand up with everybody else for McGwire's drive to the wall. He simply drank his two beers and watched the game. No one took the seat next to him and he spoke to no one except a vendor he bought peanuts from in the fourth.

Vachon also made no move to look around himself. He kept his eyes on the game. And Stilwell began to wonder if Vachon was doing anything other than watching a baseball game. He thought about what Harwick had said about falling out of love with baseball. Maybe Vachon, five years in stir, was simply rekindling that love. Maybe he missed baseball with the same intensity he missed the taste of alcohol and the feel of a woman's body.

Stilwell took the rover out of his pocket and clicked the mike button twice. Harwick's voice came back quickly, his tone clipped and cold.

"Yeah."

"After the eighth you better come down here so we can be ready when he leaves."

"I'll be down."

"Out."

He put the rover away.

Brown let it get away from him in the seventh. St. Louis opened with two singles to right, spoiling the perfect game, the no hitter and putting the lead in jeopardy with McGwire on deck.

With the runners at the corners Brown walked the next batter, bringing McGwire to the plate with the bases loaded. The Cardinals would gain the lead and the momentum if he could put one over the wall.

Davey Johnson trotted out to the mound for a conference with his pitcher but the manager appeared to give only a quick pep talk. He left Brown in place and headed back to the dugout accompanied by a chorus of applause.

The crowd rose to its feet and quieted in anticipation of what would be the confrontation of the night. Stilwell's rover clicked twice and he pulled it out of his pocket.

"Yeah?"

"Do you believe this? We gotta send that guy Houghton a six pack for this."

Stilwell didn't reply. His eyes were on Vachon, who had stepped away from his seat and was coming up the stairs to the concessions level.

"He's moving."

"What? He can't be. How can he miss this?"

Stilwell turned his back and leaned against a concrete support column as Vachon emerged from the stairs and walked behind him.

When it was clear, Stilwell looked around and saw Vachon heading toward the lavatory, making his way by several men who were rushing out in time to see McGwire bat.

Stilwell raised his rover.

"He's going to the bathroom just past the Krispy Kreme stand."

"He's had two beers. Maybe he's just taking a leak. You want me down there?"

As Stilwell replied a huge noise rose from the crowd and then quickly subsided. Stilwell kept his eyes on the entrance to the men's room. When he was ten feet from it, a man emerged. Not Vachon. A large white man with a long dark beard and a shaved skull. He wore a tight T-shirt and his arms were fully wrapped in tattoos. Stilwell looked for the skull with halo insignia of the Road Saints but didn't see it.

Still, it was enough to slow his step. The tattooed man turned to his right and kept walking. Harwick's voice came from the rover.

"Say again. The crowd noise blocked you out."

Stilwell raised the radio.

"I said get down here."

There was another short burst of crowd noise but not sustained enough to indicate a hit or an out. Stilwell walked to the lavatory entrance. He thought about the man with the shaved skull, trying to place the face. Stilwell had left his photos in the rubber band on the Volvo's visor.

It hit him then. Weapon transfer. Vachon had come to the game to get instructions and a weapon.

Stilwell raised the rover.

"I think he has a weapon. I'm going in."

He put the rover back into his pocket, pulled his badge out of his shirt and let it hang on his chest. He unholstered his .45 and stepped into the restroom.

It was a cavernous yellow-tiled room with stainless steel urine troughs running down both sides until they reached opposing rows of toilet stalls. The place appeared empty but Stilwell knew it wasn't.

"Sheriff's Department. Step out with your hands visible."

Nothing happened. No sound but the crowd noise from outside the room. Stilwell stepped further in and began again, raising his voice this time. But the sudden echoing cacophony of the crowd rose like an approaching train and drowned his voice. The confrontation on the baseball diamond had been decided.

Stilwell moved past the urinals and stood between the rows of stalls. There were eight on each side. The far door on the left was closed. The rest stood half closed but still shielded the view into each stall.

Stilwell dropped into a catcher's crouch and looked beneath the doors. No feet could be seen in any of the stalls. But on the floor within the closed stall was a blue Dodgers hat.

"Vachon!" he yelled. "Come out now!"

He moved into position in front of the closed stall. Without hesitation he raised his left foot and kicked the door open. It swung inward and slammed against one of the interior walls of the stall. It then rebounded and slammed closed. It all happened in a second but Stilwell had enough time to see the stall was empty.

And to know that he was in a vulnerable position.

As he turned his body he heard a scraping sound behind him and saw movement in the far reach of his peripheral vision. Movement toward him. He raised his gun but knew he was too late. In that same moment he realized he had solved the mystery of who Vachon's target was.

The knife felt like a punch to the left side of his neck. A hand then grabbed the back collar of his shirt and pulled him backwards at the same moment the knife was thrust forward, slicing out through the front of his neck.

Stilwell dropped his gun as his hands instinctively came up to his torn throat. A whisper then came into his ear from behind.

"Greetings from Sonny Mitchell."

He was pulled backwards and shoved against the wall next to the last stall. He turned and started to slide down the yellow tiles, his eyes on the figure of Milky Vachon heading to the exit.

When he hit the ground he felt the gun under his leg. His left hand still holding his neck, he reached the gun with his right and raised it. He fired four times at Vachon, the bullets catching him in a tight pattern on the upper back and throwing him into a trash can overflowing with paper towels. Vachon flopped onto the floor on his back, his sky blue eyes staring lifelessly at the ceiling, the over-turned trash can rolling back and forth next to him.

Stilwell dropped his hand to the tile and let go of the gun. He looked down at his chest. The blood was everywhere, leaking between his fingers and running down his arm. His lungs were filling and he couldn't get air into them.

He knew he was dead.

He shifted his weight and turned his hips so he could reach a hand into the back pocket of his pants. He pulled out his wallet.

There was another roar from the crowd that seemed to shake the room. And then Harwick entered, saw the bodies on opposite sides of the room and ran to Stilwell.

"Oh, Jesus. Oh, Jesus."

He leaned over and studied Stilwell for a moment, then pulled out his rover and started to yell into it. He realized he was on a closed frequency, quickly switched the dial to the open band and called in the officer down report. Stilwell listened to it in a detached way. He knew there was no chance. He dropped his eyes to the holy card he held in his hands.

"Hang in there, partner," Harwick yelled. "Don't go south on me, man. They're coming, they're coming."

There was a commotion behind him and Harwick turned around. Two men were standing in the doorway.

"Get out of here! Get the fuck out! Keep everybody back!"

He turned back to Stilwell.

"Listen, man, I'm sorry. I fucked up. I'm so fucking sorry. Please don't die. Hang on, man, Please hang on."

His words were coming out like the blood flowing from

Stilwell's neck. Non-stop, a mad torrent. Desperate.

"You were right, man. You were right about me. I-I-I lied about that game. I left and I'm so sorry I lied. You've got to stay with me. Please stay with me!"

Stilwell's eyes started to close and he remembered that night so long ago. That other time. He died then with his new partner on his knees next to him, blubbering and babbling.

Harwick didn't quiet himself until he realized Stilwell was gone. He then studied his partner's face and saw a measure of calm in his expression. He realized that he looked happier than at any other time he had looked at him that day.

He noticed the open wallet on the floor and then the card in Stilwell's hand. He took it from the dead fingers and looked at it. It was a baseball card. Not a real one. A gimmick card. It showed a boy of eleven or twelve in a Dodgers uniform, a bat on his shoulder, the number 7 on his shirt. It said "Stevie Stilwell, Right Field" beneath the photo.

There was another commotion behind him then and Harwick turned to see paramedics coming into the room. He cleared out of the way, though he knew it was too late.

As the paramedics checked for vital signs on his fallen partner, Harwick stepped back and used the sleeve of his shirt to dry the tears on his face. He then took the baseball card and slipped it into one of the folded compartments of his badge case. It would be something he would carry with him always.

STRIKE ZONE

by K.C. Constantine

The thing is, until the last 14 months or so, all these years I've truly enjoyed coming to work. I liked driving in, knowing where I was going, knowing what I was going to do, especially in the heat of the late summer, like today, when the fog's low in the hills and the dew's all over the grass and trees, and the sun's bouncing off the dew. Looks like diamonds sparkling out there.

Today was anything but. I saw the same things driving in I've been seeing every August morning, the fog, the dew, the sun on the grass and leaves, but today I couldn't get the sour aftertaste of coffee out of my mouth. It affected what I was seeing. The coffee tasted terrible as soon as I drank it, and I knew I hadn't made it any different from any other day.

Soon as I got here, even before I put my feet on the gravel, I tossed the dregs of that last mug. Truth is, I wasn't able to finish any of the cups I filled, and I'd made the pot at about quarter to four, which is when I hung up from talking to Joe Markousek. Then, when I had to step out of the cruiser and felt the gravel under my shoes, which I've been feeling for years, it didn't feel anything today like it's felt all those other mornings. Tell you the truth, I never paid attention to how gravel felt until this morning. Suddenly No. 2B Driveway Gravel's real important. Suddenly it's not just the name of something I put on a requisition to the Streets and Roads Committee. Suddenly it's not just the stuff Roadway Stone and Gravel dumped and spread all over our parking lot three months ago. Suddenly it's the same-size stuff they spread all over the Circle Bar's parking lot. And suddenly it's not just golf-ball-size rocks anymore. Suddenly it's missiles. And when I couldn't postpone it any longer, when I knew I had to go inside, I grabbed all my gear and my briefcase, shoved the door shut with my ankle, and walked in and my gear felt like it weighed about half a ton.

Joe Markousek had the bad luck to catch a lot of the physical hell last night— not most of it, but enough of it, and he looked it. I didn't want to ask him how it went down, or how it was going down, or how he was doing. I didn't want to ask him anything. There was a scratch under his left eye and a scrape on his left jaw, but it wasn't those things so much as his general appearance that bothered me. He just looked worn down to a nub. For a couple seconds he had trouble looking at me. Couldn't blame him for that, God knows.

"Morning, Joe. I'm not gonna ask how you're doing cause I can see how you look. Where is he?"

"You think I don't look so good, wait'll you see Frank. Got a busted collar bone and a big cut over his left eye. Sixteen stitches. And his insurance don't kick in for another twenty-eight days, and he wanted me to make sure I told you about that. That's what he was bitchin' the most about in the ER waitin' for 'em to work on him."

"Oh, well, that's the easiest thing to solve. Supervisors ain't gonna give him static over that. And if they do, which they won't, I'll take care of it myself, and don't worry about telling him, I'll tell him first chance I get."

"He's in Three."

"Wake up yet?"

"If he is he's not making any noise. 'Course, what's he gonna say? He don't remember nothin'? Sorry. Shouldn't've said that, Chief."

"No, no, that's alright, I understand. You write it up yet?"

He handed over a clipboard with the report on top. "I was waiting till you come in before I started typing."

I was already reading and didn't hear the rest of his complaints about how he wished he'd taken typing in high school and how if he'd known how much typing he was going to do as a cop he most certainly would have taken it. I'd heard it before, lots of times. That wasn't my problem. My problem was right there in my hands. And down the hall in Number Three lockup.

I had to sit down to finish reading it. Thought my knees were going to give out. Once I started to ask Joe if the numbers were right, if he was sure he hadn't made any mistakes, but he answered me before I even got the question half started.

"They're right. Been over 'em I don't know how many times. Checked with Frank and both the firemen—who're also worryin' about insurance by the way, especially the one with his knee messed up."

I put my briefcase and my mug on my desk, took off my duty

97

belt and hung it in my locker, and locked it. Couldn't put it off any longer. I'd screwed around long enough.

I grabbed the key ring from Joe, and headed for Number Three. I was seriously hoping I didn't throw up before I got there, and I wished I'd brought some Titrilac or some Tums or something like that. Shouldn't've have drunk the coffee. Coffee's great except when you're upset. Then it just makes your upset worse.

He was still dead away when I got there, his mouth hanging open, his bare feet over the end of the bunk. He wasn't snoring exactly, but he was breathing heavy. And he smelled too. So that's what tequila and beer smell like the morning after. That's what it said on page three of Joe's report he'd been drinking in the Circle Bar. Or so said witness Jack Page, the bartender. Oh, Lord. Here we go.

"Alright, John, time to wake up." I raked the key ring across the bars.

He sat up with a lurch into about a half-crunch before he put up his right arm to ward off the light, and I couldn't help thinking, boy, if only it was as simple as telling him to put down his arm, the time had come for him to see the light. But that was dumber than dumb, and I'm glad I didn't say it.

Then he saw me and groaned and swung his feet down onto the floor real slow. He was wincing and grunting, and I almost felt sorry for him.

"Wonderin' when you was gonna get here." His voice was all morning-after growly. He rubbed his face with both hands. Then he shivered once, and stood up, all six feet five of him, shuffled over to the bowl, undid his fly, and peed for what seemed like five minutes.

I could smell his urine even from where I was outside the bars.

"You weren't wonderin' anything of the sort," I said. "You don't remember last night, and soon as they brought you in, you passed out, and I know you didn't wake up till just now, so don't give me that you-were-wonderin'-when-I-was-gonna-get-here crap."

"I was dreamin' it," he said, shaking himself and zipping up. He sat down with a thump on the bunk and buried his face in his hands. "Any coffee?"

"Not for you."

"No? Why'n the hell not?"

"Cause we got things to discuss, that's why."

"I could discuss 'em a lot better if I had some coffee."

"Well if you'da been drinkin' coffee last night 'stead of what you were drinkin' we wouldn't have to be discussin' anything now."

"Aw, don't start, okay?"

"Don't start? What do you think you're doin' here, son? This ain't your usual drunk and disorderly. You stepped way over the line this time. I'm not gonna be able to talk anybody out of this, any of it."

"Oh right, yeah, what'd I do this time, bust a coupla street lights? Bend a stop-sign pole over? What misdemeanors did I commit, Chief, Sir?"

"Watch your mouth, boy, and I'll tell you what misdemeanors you committed. And what felonies too. So just wipe that attitude off your face and listen up—"

"Felonies?! Oh balls, I didn't commit no felonies, that's bullshit. Who says?"

99

"I said watch your mouth. And if you're not gonna watch it, then maybe you oughta just shut it and listen up. I got a lotta reading to do here."

"Huh? You serious? Good god, look at you, you're serious. Aw shit. Alright, c'mon, I know you can't wait, what'd I do, let's hear it, c'mon."

"You can stop right there, you know I can't wait. You're not gonna turn this around on me. This is all you, son, none of this is me."

"Whatever. Well c'mon, let's have it, stop fuckin' around and get it over with. I know you're enjoyin' this. Every time you said, boy, this hurts me more'n it hurts you, I knew you were havin' yourself a good old time."

I let that go. Much as it hurt, I let it go. "You want to hear it, brace yourself. We'll start with the generalized charges first, then I'll break 'em down. Assault, criminal mischief, disorderly conduct, public drunkenness—"

"Aw, hey," he said, laughing, "you're leaving out the numbers, c'mon, I want the whole treatment, fair's fair, I deserve no less than anybody else gets in your lockup. C'mon, give me the numbers, you know what I'm talkin' about, Title 18, Pennsylvania Consolidated Statutes, Crimes and Offenses, c'mon, Chief, Sir, read 'em out, I wanna hear 'em."

"Joke if you want to," I said. "But you hurt some people last night. Up to now you're the only one been hurt—aside from your mother. But last night—"

"Up to now *I'm* the only one been hurt?! Oh, man, that's too cool for words. I'm the only one. Nobody else, huh? Nobody else maybe in the near vicinity is maybe takin' just a little bit of pain out of this, huh? Anybody maybe we both might know getting just a little bit of pain and satisfaction here, huh?"

"—as I was sayin', last night you moved on from public drunkenness and disorderly conduct to felony assault. You wanna hear the numbers, okay, I'll give 'em to you. Simple assault, Section 2701, paragraph A, sub paragraph 1, causing serious bodily injury knowingly or recklessly under circumstances manifesting extreme indifference to the value of human life, five counts—"

"Jesus, you got 'em memorized."

"Aggravated assault Section 2702—don't interrupt me. You wanna hear it, then close your mouth and open your ears. Section 2702, paragraph A, subparagraph 3, causing serious bodily injury to a police officer making or attempting to make a lawful arrest—"

"You got 'em memorized, no shit," he said, shaking his head.

"No. Not before this morning I didn't. But I've been up since three-thirty, which is when Joe called me. And I've read 'em over plenty of times, so I guess I'm close to memorizin' 'em. Did you hear me say five counts?"

"Five! Huh? There's only four cops in the whole damn township and that's countin' you, what're you talkin' about, five counts!"

"The two officers who responded had to have help subduin' you. That's how the two firemen got involved. And the reason the firemen were there, in case you can't remember that either, the firemen got called out when one of the guys whose window you busted while he was trying to drive away from you, and since you wanna hear the numbers, that's Section 2705 reckless endangerment, and Section 2707, propulsion of missiles into an occupied vehicle—you like the sound of those numbers, huh? That last one's a first-degree misdemeanor. Reckless endangering, that's a second-degree misdemeanor. Aggravated assault under A-1 and A-2, that's a second-degree felony. Under A-3, that's a first-degree misdemeanor. You still wanna hear the numbers, huh?"

He didn't say anything. He just looked at me. I was hoping it was starting to sink in, but I knew better.

"I misspoke," I said. "Two counts against police officers, I don't know how the DA's office is gonna treat the assaults against the firemen, since neither one's a duly sworn officer."

"You said five," he said. I could barely hear him.

"Yeah. Well the fifth count's the bartender. When he came out to see what you were up to, you let him have one in the ribs, hunk of gravel about the size of a golf ball. Busted one of his ribs and, uh, I can't make out here whether this is a seven or a nine, but it's at least seven stitches. Have to ask Joe about that. And one of the fireman, he just got a split lip and a busted little finger, but the other one, you dislocated his kneecap when you kicked him. He's gonna miss maybe six weeks, seven, who knows, maybe eight weeks of work account of you. And naturally you don't remember kickin' him, right?"

No answer. Was I right to keep on hoping that any of it was sinking in?

"Propulsion of missiles into an occupied vehicle? What missiles?" So instead of thinking about what I was hoping he'd be thinking about, he'd been thinking about something else.

"Rocks. Gravel. The whole parkin' lot around that bar is nothin' but gravel. Says here the bartender said they just had it covered fresh about a month ago."

"And I'm supposed to've been propelling these missiles into occupied cars?"

"That's what the witnesses say. All thirty of 'em. Guys came runnin' out of the bar when one of 'em heard glass breakin'. You were out there, windin' up, givin' it your best fastball into their side windows. So naturally they started takin' off, what'd you expect? And witnesses say you were chasing 'em out of the parkin' lot, pitchin' that gravel at 'em as they went by, at least three of 'em anyway, and one of them was the one hit that pole, got him so rattled, probably he was half drunk too, I don't know, I haven't read that report yet, that's a separate one. You don't know how lucky you are you didn't cause somebody's death last night. That bartender, twelve, fourteen inches higher, you'da hit him in the face, you wanna think about that?"

"Twelve inches higher? You're kiddin' me, right? I spent the last five years learnin' how to throw low, cause the goddamn zone kept goin' lower and lower. In high school—"

"Oh here we go," I said, and I couldn't hold my head up any more. Chin just fell down against my chest. Jesus, was he ever gonna get up off the strike zone?

"Yeah, right, you don't wanna hear it. Nobody wants to hear it."

"Nobody wants to hear it cause that's all you talk about. People get fed up listenin' to somebody talks about the same thing all the time—you think you wouldn't?"

"—in high school, umps called the zone the way the rule book says, middle of the chest to knees. Get out in OB, it isn't middle of the chest any more, uh-uh, no, man, it's the belt—"

"What it says, and you know this as well as I do, is it's a horizontal line at the midpoint between the top of the shoulders and the top of the uniform pants, so just stop it right now —"

"Naw I'm not gonna stop it. You're the one made me read the goddamn rule book. I didn't wanna read the goddamn rule book, nobody else I knew read the goddamn rule book, just umpires, they're the only people I ever heard of read the goddamn rule book —except you! Told me you wanna play the game, you gotta know the rules, bought me the goddamn rule book, gave me tests on the goddamn thing—"

"Cut it out, John."

"No, I ain't gonna cut it out. You bought me the book, you made me study it. Well I studied it, goddammit. I read it, I studied it, but when I got into OB, the zone wasn't what the book said it was. And then you watch that goddamn Glavine pitch, the plate's not just a plate. He gets the right suit back there, plate Glavine gets is half a plate bigger'n everybody else's plate—"

"Stop it, John. I mean it, stop it right now."

"No I ain't gonna stop it. Fair's fair. You told me a hundred times, a thousand times, ten thousand times! You told me no rules, no game. You started tellin' me that before I went to school. And I believed you. I believed every word you told me, Chief, Sir. But you didn't tell me the zone I'd be pitchin' to in OB didn't have nothin' to do with the one that's in the book, that's the one thing you forgot to tell me. Oh and there was one other little thing you forgot, didn't you? One other little detail just slipped your mind, right, Chief, Sir?"

"John, I don't know how many times I have to tell you I don't know why your father left, son. And neither does your mother. And since nobody knows where he is, it's way past time you quit askin' that question."

"That's what you say. That's what you always said. Soon as you got around to tellin' me I wasn't your son. I understand what you were sayin', Chief, Sir. I'm not talkin' about that. What I wanna know is do you understand what I'm sayin' now? Do you understand when I tell you that when I used to tell the blue suits I was entitled to the same size plate as Tom Glavine, that fair's fair, and that if it was a strike for Glavine when he put it out there eight inches off the black it shoulda been a strike for me when I put it out there eight inches off the black, I mean fair's fair. The man who said he was my father told me so.

"But they'd tell me the plate's only seventeen inches wide, and that's not countin' the black, and if I wanted a strike, I was gonna have to put it over the white, that's where the zone was, and I'd tell 'em yeah, that's right, except when I throw one up there across the middle of their chest, then it's a ball, it ain't a strike up there no more, uh-uh, it's gotta go low, down there below the belt, so I don't know why you're thinkin' I should be worryin' whether I hit that bartender in the face, 'cause there's no way I'm hittin' him in the face, I was goin' low, Chief, Sir. Yeah, right, the white and the black, the right and the wrong, the good and the bad, a rule's a rule, and without the rules there's no game, no rules, no game, how many thousand times did you say that to me, huh? You tell me I can't remember what happened last night, I'm tellin' you you can't remember how many times you told me no rules, no game. C'mon, take a guess, how many times, huh? Guess if you can't remember. Anybody can guess.

"That's what that goddamn Barnwell told me right before he released me. Said, son, you gotta have an idea out there, you can't just guess it up to the plate, gotta have an idea where you want the ball to go, got to vis-you-a-lize, that's what he said, yes sir, Chief, Sir, sounded just like somebody else used to tell me to vis-you-a-lize, got any idea who that might be, huh? Chief, Sir? Can you viz-you-a-lize who that might be?" He finally had to quit talking because he was running out of breath.

"John, you were released a year ago in June. It's August. I've told you and told you and told you you can't keep dwellin' on that, you have to move on with your life—"

"Move on where, Chief, Sir? Huh? Move on where, where am I supposed to move on to? And what am I supposed to do when I get there? They don't want me in the American Association, they don't want me in Triple-A, they don't want me in Double-A, they don't want me in A ball, or Venezuela or Puerto Rico, they don't even want me in the Mexican League. And you know why, Chief, Sir? Cause I can't get it over the white. I can't even get it over the black on the edge of the white. But when I throw it out there far enough so they can't get wood on it, I say to myself, if Tom Glavine can have a plate that's twenty-five inches wide, why can't I? Ain't fair fair for everybody?"

"John, we've been over this and over this till I'm out of words to say to you, son. I don't know why Tom Glavine gets a wide plate. I've told you I've seen him pitch some games on TV where he doesn't get the wide plate, I've seen games where he gets the same size plate as everybody else. And even if there are some umps that give him a wide plate, maybe all the other pitchers in that league are askin' the same question you're askin', I don't know, how'm I supposed to know that? Maybe other umpires are askin' the same question, or maybe the umpire in chief or whoever it is bosses the umpires in the National League, maybe he's askin' the same question, but it doesn't make any difference to you, son, not any more. Even if I did know the answer to that question it wouldn't make any difference to you, not now. I mean, my god, look at you. You put on fifty pounds since you got home. Do you seriously think there's a team anywhere that would hire you now? Do you think you could pitch now? You're so outta shape, I mean, do you think you could even walk out on the mound and pick up a resin bag without tippin' over? Boy, you got a gut on you bigger'n a quarter keg."

"Yeah, that's right, Chief, Sir, tell me how I look."

"John, stop it! I mean it, stop feelin' sorry for yourself. You have hurt people! Some of them very bad, you have destroyed people's property, my god, boy, you broke twenty-seven car windows last night. If you didn't do anything else, just think of the cost of that. And who do you think's gonna pay for that? Me and your mother, I guess you think, huh? Well we're not, John. Not this time. I can't stop you from turnin' into who you're hell bent on turnin' into, a self-pityin' drunk, a public nuisance. Which if that's all it was would be bad enough, but last night you went way past public nuisance. Last night you turned into a violent drunk. And other people are paying for your violence. But your mother and I are not gonna pay for it, I promise you that. Those other times, over my objections, she paid. But no more. This time, I promise you, this time it's you who's gonna pay."

"Playin' by your rules now, right, old man?"

"Not mine, son. Commonwealth of Pennsylvania's rules."

"Oh yeah. Right. Old Title 18, Crimes and Offenses. No rules, no game, right?"

"That's right, son. No rules, no game. Break the rules in this game, they don't just tell you to take a shower. All those people whose windows you broke? My guess is most of 'em have five hundred deductible, which means they're gonna want somebody to pay for the new glass and the installation, and that's not gonna be your mother, I forbid that. She loves you with all her heart, but you notice she's not here."

"I did notice that little fact, yes I did."

"Well, it wasn't because I told her she couldn't see you. She didn't because it was her choice not to."

"Thanks for tellin' me, Chief, Sir. Makes me feel a whole lot warmer and fuzzier inside."

"Watch it, John. I won't tolerate you bein' disrespectful to her, whether she's present or not."

"Why'd she marry you? Just tell me that."

My chin fell on my chest again. How many times was I supposed to answer that question? How many times in this life do you have to explain your behavior when it wasn't a criminal act? Where's it written that you have to explain the good things you do? Because if I ever did a good thing in my life it was marrying this boy's mother. When I was released, I knew exactly what I wanted to do. I never hesitated, I never screwed around, I never got drunk and laid around for months and months. When my career was over in OB, I came back here, and as soon as I got over my probationary period with the department, the very next day I proposed to her. It was one of the best decisions I ever made. Well, two of them actually. Except he's never forgiven me for adopting him. Taught him how to throw a curve, slider, a change-up. Didn't teach him that fast ball. That came from God. But I taught him everything else about pitching. Taught him how to hold runners on. Taught him everything he knows about the game. And then to have him turn out like he's doing, to have him just go nuts over where the zone is, I mean I just don't understand that. I know I did something wrong, I mean common sense tells me I must have, but I don't know what it is. I really don't.

I didn't even try to answer him. I just stood up and walked back out to the duty room. I'm through trying to answer him about that. What am I supposed to say to him? That he's turning out just like his old man? That it doesn't matter where his old man is, everything he taught you by running away is sticking to you a lot better than anything I ever taught you? I'd be wasting my breath. He doesn't want to hear that, not any of it.

Told Joe he could quit struggling with the typewriter and go home. Told him I'd type up his report for him, soon as he told me whether it was seven stitches or nine in that bartender's ribs. Then, after I finished typing it, I called the DA's office. That was the hardest call I ever had to make to that office. And then I picked up the phone and called his mother. I didn't want her hearing any of this from anybody but me.

She didn't say much. Didn't have to. I could hear her fighting back the tears. All she wanted to know was how I'd feel about her paying for his lawyer. I said I wouldn't interfere in that. She thanked me for that. I said she didn't have to, but she said it again. Just as long as she knew I meant what I said about us not paying any of the damages or fines or costs this time.

Soon as I hung up, I started wondering how I was going to feel tomorrow morning driving in. I wondered how the sun was going to look on the dew on the grass and leaves. I wondered if it was still going to look like diamonds. But I knew it wasn't. And I knew I had to quit standing around wondering about such things. There was work to do, and nobody but me to do it, and one of the first jobs I had was figuring out who was going to relieve me this afternoon. Joe was dog tired, Frank was still in the hospital, and Teddy, god, I forgot that Teddy was up in Cook's Forest with his in-laws till Friday. Hadn't even been thinking about him at all. Good Lord, that meant I either had to stay here with John all day and night until he posted bail or else I had to turn him loose. And who was going to buy the bond except his mother and me?

I've heard it said so many times that if it was only between right and wrong, good and bad, life would be as easy as playing baseball. Days like today, I wish all I was doing was pitching, trying to find the strike zone. I remember how I used to think how hard that was some days, just getting the ball over the plate. And when I was out there trying, the zone went clear up to the top of the letters and if you threw it there and they didn't hit it, by god, you got the call. But compared to now, this minute? I can't believe I was ever that dumb. Cause right now, I can't think of one person in this whole township I can pick up the phone and call to relieve me at three o'clock.

And now he's starting to holler for coffee.

A FAMILY GAME

by Brendan DuBois

T he June day was surprisingly muggy and hot, especially out in
the baseball field behind the Morton Regional High School,
where there was no shade and the sun beat down so hard that
Richard Dow could feel its strength through the baseball cap he was
wearing. The cap was yellow with a blue "P" in the center, just like
the caps of the dozen boys who were on the field or in the dugout
this day who played for the Pine Tree Rotary youth team. He stood
by first base, the team's assistant coach, and he looked over at the
scoreboard, kept current by a young girl using a piece of chalk
almost the size of her fist. Pine Tree Rotary 1, Glen's Plumbing &
Heating, 0. Two out, the bottom of the sixth. The game was almost
over. Just one more out.

He rubbed his hands together. A boy from Glen's Plumbing &
Heating was on third base. He didn't know his name. But he certainly knew the name of the boy pitching this afternoon's game: Sam
Dow, age 12, who was one out away from earning Pine Tree's first victory this season. They were 1 and 5, but nobody on the team counted that solitary victory: it had been a forfeit, when the other team—

Jerry's Lumberyard—didn't make it to the game because the coach's van had struck a moose on Route Four.

"C'mon, Sam!" he called out, slapping his hands together. "One more out, you can do it! Just one more out!"

Sam ignored him. Good boy. Focus on the hitter, standing there with his helmet and blue and white uniform, bat looking so large in his small hands. The attendance was good for a warm summer day in Vermont, with a smattering of parents and friends and relatives in the stands behind home plate. Someone in the stands was smoking a large cigar, and a brief breeze brought the scent over, and Richard was surprised at the hunger he felt at smelling it. God, how long had it been since he had a really good cigar...

Richard looked over in the stands again, saw his ten-year-old daughter, Olivia, carefully keeping score in a large, looseleaf binder. He waved at her but she, too, was ignoring her father, keeping focused on the job at hand. And that's what their mother Carla was doing this early afternoon as well, working at the local travel agency.

Sam wound up and the ball flew fast for such a young boy, and the batter swung just as Richard heard the satisfying thump! as the ball landed in the catcher's glove. The umpire did his sideways dance and said, "Strike!" and there were a few cheers and groans, but no jeers. The umpire today was Denny Thompson, the town's fire chief, and he had a good eye and for an umpire, was pretty reasonable.

"C'mon, Sam," he whispered, "one more strike. You can do it." He rubbed his hands again, looked over at the few boys of Pine Tree who weren't on the field, now leaning forward on the badly-painted green bench in the dugout. He could sense their anticipation, their youthful hunger, to feel—just once—what it would be like to win. That's all, pretty simple stuff, but for an eleven or twelve year old boy, getting that first win meant everything. It had been a long time since Richard had been this young, but he remembered. He always remembered.

There. Another windup from his boy, the blur of the ball, and —
Crack!

Richard snapped his head, tracking the flying ball, it was well-hit, pretty well-hit but wait, it's arcing over, it's just a pop-up fly, great, a pop-up fly, that's it, it's going to happen, we're going to win, it's going to happen...

Then Richard noticed the slow-moving legs of the Pine Tree Rotary boy backing up in right field, one hand shading his eyes, the other hand holding up the open glove, his arm now wavering, trembling, moving back and forth like a semaphore signaler. Leo Winn. The youngest player on the team, and Richard just whispered again, "C'mon, Leo, you can do it buddy, just catch the ball, just like practice, nothing to it, nothing at all."

The ball plopped into his glove and before the cheers could get any louder from the Pine Tree players and fans, young Leo, still moving backwards, tripped and fell on his back, the ball flying free into the freshly-mown grass, the cheers and shouts now coming from the other team, as Pine Tree players and fans, including Richard, fell silent, as they lost once again.

After the ceremonial end-of-the-game line-up, when the players stood in line in the field and shook each other's hands, murmuring "good game, good game," Richard was in the parking lot of the school, one arm over Olivia's shoulder, the other over Sam's. Olivia was carrying the score book under her arm and said, "Sam, that was your best game ever. Three strikeouts and only one hit. And that was scored as an error."

"Yeah, I know, I know, I was there, okay?" Sam replied. "What difference does it make? We still lost."

Richard hugged his boy's shoulder. "You did well, Sam. Even Leo."

"Dad, he's no good," Sam complained.

"He's not as good as you, but he's still out there, practicing and playing," Richard said. "That counts for a lot. He could have given up a long time ago. But he didn't."

Sam didn't say a word, and Richard knew the poor guy was struggling, over showing emotion at having lost yet again, yet determined not to say anything that could lead to dreaded tears pouring out. For twelve-year-old boys, sometimes showing tears was worse than anything else.

Olivia spoke up. "Look, there's the other team. Going out for ice cream."

"Well, we can go, too," Richard said, seeing the smiles and happy faces of the other boys, trooping into open car and minivan doors.

"Dad..." Sam said. "No, let's just go home. It doesn't count. They're going for ice cream 'cause they won. Losers don't get ice cream after a game like ours."

Richard was going to say something but he noticed something going on over near the school's dumpster. He pulled out his car keys, passed them over to Sam. "Here, go in and get the car opened up. I'll be right along."

Sam said, his voice now not so despondent: "Can I start it up?"

"Yes, but move it out of park and I'll ground you 'til you're thirty."

His two kids ran ahead to his Lexus, and he dodged around the end of a pickup truck hauling an open trailer with a lawn mower on the back. There came a man's voice, loud and insistent, "... dummy, how in hell could you drop that ball? It was an easy out!"

Richard froze at what he saw. George Winn, landscaper in town—among other things, some legal, some not so legal—had his boy's T-shirt twisted up in a large fist, and was shaking the poor guy, back and forth. Tears were streaming down his face and his ball cap was on the ground. George was huge, with a beer gut that poked out from underneath a dark green T-shirt, and a beard that went halfway down his chest. The hand that was wrapped around the boy's T-shirt was stained with dirt and grease. Richard stepped forward. "Hey, George, lighten up, okay? It's just a game."

George turned, his face looking surprised, like he could not believe anyone would approach him for something so insignificant. "Hunh? What did you say, Dick?"

Richard hated being called Dick but let it go for now. "George, c'mon, it's just a game. Your kid did all right."

George let loose of his son's shirt, and the boy quickly went

117

over to pick up his hat. The older man stepped closer and Richard caught a whiff of beer. "You looking for trouble, Dick?"

His hands seemed to start tingling, like they were being suddenly energized by the adrenaline. Richard recognized the sensation, tried to dampen it. "No, I'm just telling you that your kid's a good player. Hey, he's a trooper. Why don't you—"

George came over, punched a finger into Richard's chest, making him step back. "No, he ain't no trooper. He's a loser, writer-man, so back off. Unless you want to settle this, right here and now."

A horn honked, and he recognized the tone. His kids were in the Lexus, urging him to hurry up so they could get home. A door slammed and he saw the small figure of Leo, in the front seat of the truck. Richard stepped back, made sure his back wasn't turned to George.

"No, I don't want to settle this, right here and now."

George snorted in satisfaction. "Good. Then why don't you go home to your kiddie books and leave me and my boy the frig alone."

Richard walked over to his Lexus as the truck backed up and roared away, the front right fender brushing his pants leg as it bailed out of the parking lot. He got to his Lexus and sat still for a moment, as Sam talked more about the game and Olivia asked what he thought would be for dinner tonight, and it was like their voices were coming at him through thick cotton, for the only voice he could really make out was George's.

Dinner that night was the usual rolling chaos of dishes being prepared, voices being raised, the television set on and the phone ringing, with boys and girls calling for Sam and Olivia—and was it a genetic quirk amongst children everywhere, Richard thought, that they always called at dinner time?—and he managed to give Carla a quick hug and kiss as she heated up a tuna fish casserole.

"Besides losing, how was the game?"

"Great," he said. "Sam pitched well. Got three strikeouts. Your day okay?"

"Unh-hunh," she said, handing over a head of Romaine lettuce to him. "Wash this up, will you?"

"Sure," he said, looking over at the trim figure of his blonde-haired wife, her tight jeans and black flat shoes, and the light blue polo shirt that had white script on the left that said Central Street Travel. The casserole smelled all right but he remembered a number of years ago, when Carla would prepare dishes like baked ziti and manicotti and a lobster fettucine... my, how good that had been. But all those food dishes had been left behind, years ago, when they had come to Vermont.

Olivia was at the kitchen counter, drawing a horse, and piped up, "I think Daddy almost got into a fight today."

That got Carla's sharp attention. "He did, did he?"

He started running the cold water, started washing the lettuce leaves. "No, he didn't. It wasn't a fight, it was just a discussion."

"That true, Olivia?" Carla asked, her voice still tense.

"Dunno, mom," she said, still working on her horse. "The car doors were closed, but the other man was pushing his finger into daddy."

"Oh, he was, was he," she said, her brown eyes flashing at

him. "I thought you said things went great."

"They did," he said, washing another leaf of lettuce.

"And who was this guy, and what was going on?" she demanded.

"Nothing much," Richard said, patting dry the leaves of lettuce on a stretch of paper towel. "We were just talking about the game and about sports dads. That sort of thing. He got a little heated up, and that was that. I just tried to remind him that it was just a family game. That's all."

"No trouble then," she asked.

He smiled at his demanding wife. "No trouble."

Some hours later he woke up in bed with Carla, staring up at the ceiling. He rolled over, checked the time on the red numerals of the nearby clock radio. It was 1 a.m. Time to go. He slowly got out of bed, sitting up and letting his feet touch the floor, hoping he wouldn't disturb his wife. But Carla was too good.

She gently touched his bare back. "What's up, hon," she whispered, shifting closer to him in the darkness.

"Nothing much," he said, leaning over to a chair, picking up his pants and a pullover.

"Getting dressed?"

"Unh-hunh."

"What's going on?"

"Gotta see a guy about something."

"Something bad?"

He reached behind him, stroked her face. "No, nothing bad.

Just seeing a guy about something. No big deal. I'll be back in an hour or so."

"'kay," she murmured. "You be careful, and you come back to us. *Capisce?*

"Capisce," he said, leaning over to kiss her forehead.

A half hour later he was on the other side of town, at a small dirt park near the wooden covered bridge that spanned the Bellamy River. He shifted in his seat, wincing some at the uncomfortable feeling of the 9 mm. Browning pistol, stuck in his rear waistband. It was a quiet night and he leaned his elbow outside the open window. The night sound of crickets and frogs were pleasant enough, but he remembered other night sounds as well. Traffic, always moving, always going. Horns and sirens and brakes squeaking. Music and the rattle-roar of the subway and people talking, shouting, laughing. And behind it all, the constant hum of an island filled with millions of people, always moving, always dealing, always doing something. That sense of energy, of being plugged in, of being part of something, God, he missed it as much as the faraway scent the day before of the cigar...

Lights coming across the bridge. The headlights flashed twice and then the lights dimmed as the car pulled up beside him. He stepped out and kept the hood and engine block between him and the visitors.

"Richard?" came the familiar voice from the dark car. One Charlie Moore, and once again, he wished he could be in a place where he would never hear that voice again.

"The same," he said, relaxing, bringing his hand to his side from where it had been, at the rear of his shirt.

"Glad to see you," he said. "Have a visitor here. Do you mind?"

"Do you care if I mind or not?"

A laugh. "Nope, I guess not."

The footsteps came towards his Lexus, and a voice cautioned, "Watch it, light coming on." He moved his head away and a small battery-powered lamp was turned on, and was then placed on the hood of his car. In the small but bright light he made out the face of two men, one familiar, the other a stranger. The familiar one said, "Time for introductions. Bob Tuthill, Department of Justice, please meet Richard Dow. Formerly known as Ricky 'the Rifle' Dolano."

Tuthill just nodded. He had on a dark suit, white shirt and red necktie. His companion was dressed more comfortably, in jeans and a black turtleneck shirt. Richard said, "Charlie, what's going on?"

Tuthill spoke up. "What's going on is another trial, set to start in August."

"Where?"

"California. Two days, maybe three."

"Who are you guys after?"

"Mel Flemmi," Charlie said. "Used to be in your neck of the woods, then got into trouble in San Diego. The government needs to prove a pattern of criminal conduct, which is where you come in, testifying about what he did in Jersey. That won't be a problem, will it?"

"Nope," Richard said.

Tuthill shook his head. "Sorry, Ricky, that was—"

"Richard," he interrupted. "The name is Richard Dow. Go on."

Tuthill looked over at Charlie in exasperation and said, "What I was saying is that you answered too quickly. Saying there wouldn't be a problem is a given, 'cause you know where we've got you. Set up in this little piece of paradise is part of the deal, and so is your testifying when we say so. But I don't like the way you answered Mister Moore so quickly. What I need to know is that we're going to have your full faith and cooperation in testifying against Flemmi. Understood?"

Richard folded his arms, feeling his breathing tighten, just like when he was face to face with that moron George Winn, at the high school parking lot. He said, "Look, Mel Flemmi is an animal. I know enough about what he did so you guys could put him away until the next millennium, even without bringing up whatever he did in San Diego. So yeah, I don't have a problem with testifying against him. Little slug, his own teenage niece started doing drugs, started staying out late in the streets, he whacked her, personally. So she wouldn't bring shame to his family. So that's the kind of guy he is and so here's the story, I don't have a problem testifying against him. That good enough for you, Tuthill?"

A little smile came across the man's face. "Nice talk from someone accused of committing eleven murders in his career,"

"Accused," Richard said. "Never convicted."

This time, Tuthill laughed and turned to Charlie. "What is it with these wiseguys? Man, they flip and testify at the drop of a hat. The old timers in my office, they said there used to be a time when guys like this would rather serve ten, twenty or thirty years before being accused of being a rat. They getting soft or what?"

Richard tightened his arms against his chest. "I don't know about any 'they.' All I know is that I found out my boss was cooperating with clowns like you. So I cut my own deal, to protect myself and my family. Loyalty's a two-way street, and I'm not going to Leavenworth for life for some guy who wants to get free on my back."

Tuthill laughed. "Whatever. Moore, I'm ready to go back. Oh, Richard, one more thing."

"Yes?"

Tuthill leaned over the hood of the car. "Some of your compatriots over the years, they've embarrassed the department over side deals they had going on while they were in the program. Your job, what is it? A children's book writer?"

"That's what they gave me," Richard said.

"And the publicity problem... ?" Tuthill asked.

"You should know," Richard said. "I write under a pseudonym. The books are for two and three year olds. Not much chance of many fan letters. There's no photo on the book jacket, it says the author lives in California. The locals, they don't care. This is Vermont. You could sacrifice goats to Lucifer in your spare time, and nobody'd care, as long as you don't keep your neighbors up with the noise."

"How charming," Tuthill said. "Which brings me to my original point. Other guys like you, they've gotten bored with their agreement. They've decided to get back to their original business, like loan sharking and gambling and breaking arms and legs. Which means sleazy defense lawyers get to jump all over their character, and whether or not their testimony is truthful."

"How interesting," Richard said.

"Wait, it gets better. So what I'm telling you is that your friggin' nose better be clean. No violence, no threat of violence, not even a parking violation. This trial is important, quite important, and I'm not going to let some stoolie killer like you spoil it for me. 'Cause if you do, you and your family will be moving. How'd you like to run a pig farm in the middle of Nebraska?"

Richard said, "I like it here. You won't have a problem."

"Good," he said. "Moore, I'm ready to head back."

"Sure," Charlie said. "I'll be right there."

When the sound of a car door being slammed reached them both, Charlie sighed. "Sorry. Young guy, new in his job, wants to make his bones. Sorry about all that yapping and such."

"Not your fault," Richard said, letting his arms relax.

"Still..."

"Yeah?"

"Listen well to what he said, Richard. Except for one little mark against your record since you moved here, you've done okay. Keep it that way, or he will transfer you out to a pig farm. Your wife, your kids, they've adjusted over the years here, haven't they. I don't think they'd like moving again."

Richard said, "You let me worry about my family. And that so-called black mark against my record, that was bogus, and you know it. Besides, I had only been out here a month. I was still adjusting."

Charlie laughed. "You broke the headlights on some guy's car with a baseball bat, and threatened to do the same to his teeth. Doesn't sound too bogus to me."

Richard smiled. "He stole a parking space from me at the shopping center. Look, I've got the message, loud and clear. I'll be a good little boy."

"Okay," Charlie said. "Here, I've got two things for you." Charlie reached into his pocket, took out a computer diskette, which he tossed over to Richard. He caught it with no problem.

"Your next book," Charlie said. "Lulu the Seasick Sea Lion."

"Marvelous. What's the other thing you've got for me?"

"This," Charlie said, handing over a plastic shopping bag, full and bulging. "Some souvenirs from your old haunts. Cheeses and sausages and pepperonis and spices and sauces. A little bit of everything. I figured you still missed some of that old-time food, don't you."

Richard was surprised at how much his mouth watered. "Yeah, you're right."

Charlie picked up the little lamp, switched it off. "Well, don't let it be said that the U.S. Marshall's Office doesn't have a little consideration. I'll be seeing you, Richard."

"Unfortunately, I think you're right," he said, now smelling the delicious scents coming up from the bag. His stomach began grumbling, and he hefted the bag a couple of times as he waited until the other car left the small lot. Richard waited until his eyes adjusted to the darkness, and then he walked a few yards to the beginning of the covered bridge. His feet echoed on the old wooden planks. He leaned over and heard the rushing of the Bellamy River below him, and then took the bag and threw it into the river.

He sighed, rubbed at his face. That was the only way. To follow the rules and survive, and never, absolutely never, dress or smoke or eat or do anything like you once did back home, because they were out there, still out there in the shadows, bent on revenge, and he didn't want to raise a single scent for their benefit.

He looked at the river for a couple of minutes, and then went back to his car and drove home.

At home he was in the upstairs hallway, heading to the bed-room, when he heard a murmuring noise coming from Sam's bed-room. The door was ajar and he could make out a bluish light com-ing from the room. Inside Sam was curled up on his side, his eyes closed, dressed in light gray pajama bottoms. On a dresser at the foot of the bed was a small color TV, and Richard made out a base-ball game being played. He reached up to turn it off when a sleepy voice said, "No, Dad, don't... still watching it..."

"Sam, it's almost three in the morning."

"I know... The Red Sox are in Seattle... it's gone extra innings..."

Richard looked at a little graphic in the corner of the televi-sion picture. "Sam, the score is zero to zero, and they're in the eigh-teenth inning."

"Mom said I could watch the game 'til it was over..."

Richard shut the little TV off. "And I'm saying it's just a game, okay? You need to get to sleep."

No answer. Just the soft noise of his boy, breathing. From the hallway light he made out posters of baseball players up on the walls, all of them Red Sox. He shrugged. He wished the boy would at least follow a winning team, like the Mets or the Yankees, but what could one expect. He bent down to kiss Sam's forehead.

"Just a game, son. Just a game."

In the morning, before she left for work and to bring the kids to a day camp, Carla brought him another cup of coffee in his small office, which was a spare bedroom when they had first moved in. He took the cup and sipped from it, and she said, "So. What went on last night."

Other guys back then, they could spin stories to their wives about being solid waste management consultants, but not Carla. She had entered things clear-eyed and agreeable, and not once had he ever tried to pull something over her.

He put the coffee cup down on his desk. "A trip to California in a couple of months. Another testimony deal. Against Mel Flemmi."

She made a face. "Good. He sure deserves it. What else."

"What do you mean, what else?" he asked.

Carla gently whacked him on the side of his shoulder. "There's always something else with the Feds. What was it?"

He tried a casual shrug. "I've got to keep my nose clean, as always. That way, any defense lawyer won't be able to say I don't have the kind of character to testify truthfully."

"Keep your nose clean..." she said simply. "Does that mean not breaking some guy's headlights over a parking space?"

"It was my parking space, I'd just got here, and it won't happen again."

She leaned over, grabbed his ears and kissed him firmly on the mouth. "Good. 'Cause it ain't no game, Richard. I like it here. The kids like it here. We can continue having a good life here. Don't do anything to screw it up."

"I won't."

"Good. Because if you do, I'll kill you.

He kissed her back. "I have no doubt."

For most of the day, he stayed in his office. He played twenty-three games of computer solitaire, another computer game involving shooting lots of fast-moving monsters—not surprisingly, he scored quite high—and spent a while on the Internet as well, seeing the combined creativity of a number of women who could just barely dress themselves, and got an idea or two for next Valentine's Day.

Then, at about 3 p.m., he popped in the computer diskette, called up a file called SEA LION, and printed out all thirty-three pages. He put the pages in an Express Mail envelope, drove to the Post Office, and sent the envelope to a publisher in New York City. Back home, he made another cup of coffee and waited for Carla and the kids to show up. "Man, writers have it easy," he said.

The next day was a practice one for the Pine Tree Rotary team, and he enjoyed seeing how enthusiastically all the kids took to the field—Patrick and Jeffrey and Alexander and his own Sam and even little Leo, chugging out there on his tiny legs, and all the others. They did some exercises to loosen up, and then some pitching and hitting, and some base running. He took it upon himself to spend some extra time with Leo, tossing up pop flies, and Leo managed to catch fifteen in a row.

Then he took Ron Bachman aside, the town auditor who was the team's manager. "Did you see how Leo's doing?"

"Yep," Ron said, making a note on a clipboard. "Not a single dropped ball. That's what happens when dad's not around. Plays a lot better."

"So tell me, what's the deal with his dad, George. What's his problem?"

Ron looked up from the clipboard. "What do you mean, what's his problem?"

"The way he goes after his kid, that's what."

"Oh, that," he said. "You know, George has got a lot of problems. Drinking and picking fights and being the son of the chairman of the board of selectmen, so he gets a lot of slack cut his way. He's a mean man that takes his frustrations out on his kid. Typical story. Unfortunately, it has to show itself here."

"Yeah," Richard said. "Unfortunately."

Two days later the team went on a field trip to Fenway Park in Boston, an hours-long drive that took three minivans and a number of other parents to act as chaperones. When putting kids in the vans, Richard made sure that Leo was in his van, and he glanced at the boy some while heading into Boston. He half-expected to see a haunted look in the boy's eyes, a troubled expression, but no, there was nothing like that there. Just the excitement of being in Boston and seeing the Red Sox play.

Richard took in Fenway Park as they found their seats. It was an old, tiny park, opened up in 1912, the same year the *Titanic* sunk on its maiden voyage. It had its charms, with the Green Monster out in left field and the intimacy of being close-up to the action, but

Richard wasn't satisfied. It wasn't Yankee Stadium, it wasn't the House that Ruth Built, but he kept his opinions to himself.

All part of his new life.

As the game progressed, he enjoyed watching the kids almost as much as the game itself. They followed each pitch intensely and ate popcorn and hotdogs and drank sodas, and cheered when one of the Red Sox players rocketed a home run over the Green Monster, and booed when the opposing pitcher hit a Red Sox player with a fastball, causing both benches to clear. The game wasn't worth much—an early season bout with the Tigers that the Red Sox managed to lose, 4-3—but it was still fun. He was glad to be here with his boy and was glad not to be in jail, and it even looked like Leo was enjoying himself too, watching the game with wide eyes and grins, seemingly thousands of miles away from his father.

On the way back to Vermont, as Sam rode up front next to Richard, and with most of the boys in the rear seats slumbering, he said, "Dad?"

"Yeah, Sam," he said, feeling a bit juiced after driving through real city streets for a change. Here was real traffic, intersections, lights, people moving in and out. Where they now lived in Vermont, there were two traffic lights, and only a few hundred feet of sidewalk in the downtown. He liked driving in the city and rolled down his window as he drove, to hear the noises, smell the scents out there.

But now they were on a featureless stretch of asphalt, making the long drive back to Vermont.

"About the game," Sam said.

"Go on."

"When the Red Sox hitter got beaned by the pitcher, I was just surprised at how fast the other players came out of the dugout to go after the pitcher. And then, the other team.... well, man, dad, that fight started quick. Why do they fight like that? Couldn't it have been just an accident?"

"Maybe," he said, keeping an eye on both sides of the narrow highway as they headed home, keeping an eye open for deer or moose on the side of the road, ready to trot across and wreck several thousand dollars worth of vehicle parts. "But players like that, it's more than just that. It's a team thing. You stick up for a member of your team, no matter what. And when one of your team members gets hit, or gets in trouble, you help out. That's what happens."

"Oh," Sam said. "Like a family, right? Like you've said before, about me and Olivia helping each other out? Like a family?"

"Sure," he said. "Like a family."

He drove on a few more miles, and looked over at the drowsy face of his boy, remembered a time when he was much younger, and when they all lived in a neighborhood not unlike some of the streets they had passed through on the way to the ballpark.

"Sam?"

"Yeah, dad."

"Besides the game, how did you like it?"

His son moved in his seat, like he was seeking a comfortable position to fall asleep in. "I dunno, what do you mean, how did I like it..."

"I mean the city. How did you like being in the city? You know, all those buildings, all those people. What did you think?"

Sam yawned. "It was too noisy, too dirty. I like it better back home."

"Oh."

He kept on driving, wondering if he should feel angry or glad, that his son— his own boy, raised in New York!—should now hate big cities.

A few days later, the next-to-the last game of the season. Pine Tree Rotary was playing Greg's Small Engine Repair, and Richard was tired and hot and thirsty. The other team had jumped on the boys right away in the first inning, and the score was now 10 to 0. Even his boy Sam, as good as he was, grounded out twice and struck out once. About the only bright spot in the lineup was poor little Leo, who was so small that he confused the opposing team's pitcher, and managed to get on base twice through walks. Even though they were walks, Leo acted like Pete "Charlie Hustle" Rose himself—of course, before getting caught up in that gambling fiasco—and raced to first base, just so damn pleased to be there, out on the bases.

Last inning, and here was Leo. Richard checked his watch and was going to call out to the boy, when somebody with a louder voice beat him to it.

"Leo!" the man bellowed. "You better get a hit or I'll be after you! That you can bet on!"

He shaded his eyes from the glare, knew who had shown up, like a shambling bear wandering into someplace he wasn't welcome. George Winn was at the fence, his fat fingers protruding through the open metal, shouting again. "Leo! You worthless player, you! Get a hit or you'll get one from me!"

Richard yelled out, "Leo, wait for a good pitch, guy, wait for a good one!"

But Leo, his legs trembling, his face red, swung at the first three pitches that came across the plate, and promptly struck out.

He ignored Olivia. He ignored Sam. He ignored the other coaches and players and strode right out to the parking lot again, where George was hauling his kid to his truck, the clothing of the boy's shirt clenched up in his fist. Richard called out, "George, you hold on!"

George spun around, moving surprisingly fast for such a large man. He propelled Leo forward with one hand and said, "Wait in the truck! Now!"

Leo ran ahead and Richard came up to him, saying, "George, you can't yell at your boy like that, he's doing the best he can, and yelling like that—"

And George stepped forward and punched him in the chest. Richard staggered back, the force of the blow bringing back hordes of muscle memories from times past, when he had faced down and put down bigger and badder guys than this, and his fists clenched up and he was spotting his move, what he should do to put this bullying jerk down, but thinking, now, he was thinking about Carla and the kids and—

The next punch struck his jaw, and then George grabbed him and he fell to the ground, and the kicks began, one after another, and

Richard curled up and protected his kidneys and groin and face as much as possible, until there were other voices, other shouts, and the kicking and punching stopped.

Later that night, in bed, Carla was next to him, gingerly wiping down his face again with a wet cloth. Her face was hard and set, and he couldn't tell from one moment to the next who she was most angry with, and he just kept his hands still and let her work and talk.

"You think I like having the children see you, their father, in a brawl right in their own school parking lot?"

It hurt to talk, so he kept his words to a minimum. "Wasn't a brawl. I didn't touch the guy."

"Well, he sure as hell touched you," she said. "Poor Olivia and Sam were crying so much, I thought they'd never stop."

"They're okay."

"Yeah, but you're not. And remember what those Feds told you, about keeping your nose clean? Is this how you're doing that?"

"Didn't file a complaint," he said. "No cops."

She wiped him down again, and he winced. Even with the painkillers, it was going to be a long night.

"Doesn't matter," she said. "Word gets out. And poor Sam... he thinks the whole team should get together and go on over and burn down George Winn's house. He thinks they should stick up for you. Is that right?"

"Nope."

"You're damn right," she said, getting up from the bed, walking into the bathroom and back out again with a fresh washcloth.

135

"But our family... that's something else. I don't like what happened, not one bit. Are you going to do something about it?"

He thought for a moment. "Yeah."

She wrung out the cloth over a small metal bowl. "Are you going to tell me?"

"Not yet," he said. "Not yet."

"When?" she asked.

"Soon," he said.

The next day, in his office, playing computer solitaire and wincing in pain as he moved the fingers on his right hand, the phone rang.

"Is this Richard?" came the vaguely familiar voice.

"It is," he said. "Who's this?"

There came a slight chuckle. "Let's just say it's one of the two gentlemen you spoke with the other night."

He sat up straighter in his chair. "You shouldn't be calling. It's not part of the agreement. It's not part—"

"Look, pal, here's the only agreement I care about, and that's that you testify in August, and that you stay out of trouble. Right now, you're batting five hundred, and I don't like it."

"I don't understand what you mean," Richard said.

"Wasn't there a fight yesterday? In the parking lot of a school? Right after a baseball game with your kid?"

He winced again as his hand clenched the phone tighter. "It wasn't my fault. He picked the fight, not me. There was no complaint filed with the cops."

Another chuckle. "Yeah, I heard you didn't even put up a fight. Man, you must really like that place to put up with crap like that. So here's the facts, one more time. You're right on the edge, my friend. Right on the edge. One more little problem, and I don't care whose fault it was, who threw the first punch, you're still coming out to testify. But you'll come back to that pig farm in Nebraska."

Richard didn't even bother replying, because the caller had already hung up.

He sat back in his chair, looked at the little computer mouse next to the computer, and in one flurry of a motion, tore it from his desk and threw it across the room.

Two days after the phone call, he was in the kitchen when Sam came tearing through. He wanted to call out to Sam, to tell him to slow down, but instead he said, "Hey, bud. What do you have going on today?"

Sam went to the refrigerator, opened up the door, and started chugging down a couple of swallows of orange juice. His mother would never let him get away with doing anything like that, but he knew his father would. What a kid. Sam put the juice away and said, "Not much. Some fishing later with Greg over at the river."

"Want to catch a late afternoon matinee?" he asked.

Sam smiled. "Just the two of us? What would Mom and Olivia think?"

"Mom's at work," he said, "and Olivia's over with some friends, staying through 'til dinner. I'll leave a note for your mom. It'll be fine. Come on, you've got a big day tomorrow. Last game of the season."

Sam slammed the door of the refrigerator. "When?"

"Right now."

"Cool, dad," he said.

The movie theater was on the outskirts of town, in a little shopping mall, and the cool interior felt comfortable. He let Sam pick the movie and it was a live-action film based on a popular comic book series Richard had never heard of. Most of the audience were kids about Sam's age, with a scattering of parents like himself, there to chaperone and make sure the little ones didn't walk out and sneak into an R-rated film. He sat in a row next to a guy he knew, some clerk at the hardware store named Paul, who was there with a boy of about eight or nine.

He checked his watch as the movie droned on with punches and gunshots and buildings blowing up. He looked at the smiling faces of the young boys, illuminated some from what was up on the screen. Smiling and young and full of energy and life. He wondered how Leo was doing, if he was dreading tomorrow's game, the last game of the year, the last chance to win one before the season was over, one more time out there in the field with his father watching and shouting at him.

One more time with his watch. Time. He leaned over to Sam and whispered, "I'm going to get some more popcorn. You want another drink?"

"Unh-hunh," Sam whispered back, attention still focused on

the screen.

Richard got up, stepped on Paul's foot—"Jeez, excuse me"— and walked out of the dark theater.

Later that night, he was in the living room, trying to judge which one of Olivia's drawn horses was the best one—"for a contest the library's holding, dad, and the deadline is tomorrow!"—when the doorbell rang. Olivia looked up at him and then Carla appeared in the entranceway to the kitchen, slowly wiping a salad bowl from dinner. He looked down at Olivia and said, "Right away, squirt. Go see your mom."

"But, dad..."

"Now, please," he said, and Carla added, "Olivia, listen to your father. He'll finish with your horses later."

He went to the door, wiped at his hair for a moment, remembered the many other times when he had answered evening doorbells like this one, so he wasn't surprised when he opened the door and saw the town's police chief there.

"Mister Dow?" he said quietly. "Ted Reiser. Chief of police."

The chief was about ten years older than Richard, heavyset with a black moustache and a chubby neck that spilled over the collar of his white uniform dress shirt. A gold star was in each of his collar tabs, and Richard thought the chief—who was boss of a whole six officers—looked slightly ridiculous.

"Sure," Richard said. "What can I do for you?"

The chief looked past Richard, and said, "Can I come in for a moment?"

"Absolutely, come on in," he said, and the chief came in and took a seat on the couch, balancing his gold-brimmed hat on his knees. Richard sat down and said, "If you'd like, can I get you a drink, or—"

Reiser raised his hand. "Sorry, no. Look, I'm sorry, but this is an official call. I'm investigating something that occurred earlier today. Something I'm afraid that might involve you."

He made a point of folding his hands together and leaning forward in his chair. "One of my kids? Did they do something?"

The chief ignored the question, went on. "George Winn. I take it you know him."

"Sure. I coach his kid in the baseball league."

"You've also had words with him, plus one altercation. True?"

Richard nodded. "True. I try to help out his boy, and George thought the kid would work best under threats."

"But there was an altercation, nearly a week ago."

"I didn't hit him, not once. Can you tell me what's going on?"

The chief sighed. "George Winn was attacked and severely injured today. An intruder broke into his home, struck him from the rear. No description of the attacker, but I'm afraid I'll have to ask you what you were doing at about 4:45 p.m. today."

"Why?"

"Please, Mister Dow. You were in a fight with him last week. I need to know this."

"Should I be getting a lawyer?"

That got the chief's attention. "Do you think you need one?"

"No," Richard answered.

"Then why don't you tell me where you were this afternoon."

Richard shrugged. "All right. I was at the movies with my boy Sam, at the River Mall theater. The picture started at 3:30, got out at 5:30."

"Do you have any proof?" the chief asked.

"Sure." He dug into his pants pocket, past his handkerchief and change. "Look. Ticket stubs for the both of us."

"Anybody see you at the theater?"

"Um, a kid named Larry who took my money."

"Anybody else?"

"Let's see... oh, sure. Paul, who works at Twombly's Hardware. He sat next to me. In fact, I stepped on the poor guy's toes when I left to get some popcorn about halfway through the movie."

The chief moved his hat in a semi-circle. "Did you know what time it was?"

"Nope."

"And what time did you get back into the theater?"

Richard looked at the chief, tried to feel what was going on behind those unblinking eyes. "I'm sorry, what did you say?"

Now it was time for the police chief to lean forward. "You said you left the theater to get some popcorn. And what I want to know is, how long were you out there?"

"Two minutes, maybe three."

"And did anybody see you come back into the theater?"

"Yeah, Paul did, I'm sure."

"Oh, you are, are you," the chief said. "And why's that?"

Richard looked at the chief calmly. "Because when I tried to get past him and sit next to my son, I accidentally poured a cold

141

drink on his head. That's why."

Another sunny day, hot but the air was dry, with little humidity. Richard was back at his position near first base, waiting. It was the bottom of the sixth inning and the score was tied, zero to zero, but his boy Sam was on third base. He rubbed his hands together, could feel the anticipation in the air, as the next Pine Tree Rotary batter came to the plate, little Leo Winn, holding his baseball bat strong and true.

The stands were nearly full and there was Olivia, keeping score again with the large notebook on her tiny lap. Today Carla had taken the afternoon off and she was there as well, and he waved at them both, but neither waved back, as they were talking to each other. Maybe later, he thought.

He wiped his hands on his pants legs. It was a beautiful day, the best so far this summer, and there was the first pitch...

Thump! as the ball went into the catcher's mitt. Denny Thompson was umpiring again today, and he slowly got up. "Ball!" came the shout.

"Good eye, Leo, good eye!" Richard called out, and he looked up in the stands again, and sure enough, there was Leo's dad George, sitting there stiffly. Richard thought about waving at George but decided that would be pushing it.

Another pitch, and this time Leo swung mightily at it, and missed. Another thump! of the ball into the glove.

"Strike!"

Richard clapped his hands. "That's fine, Leo, that's fine.

You're doing all right," and even his teammates in the dugout joined in, calling out to Leo, encouraging him, telling him to take his time, to swing at a good pitch. It was a good sound, a wonderful sound, made even better by the fact that no one was shouting insults, no one was shouting threats. Like he had mentioned the other night in the van to his son, sometimes a team was like a family, looking out for each other. Richard looked up in the stands again, and there was George, sitting still, sitting quiet.

He clapped his hands again. "Come on, Leo, the next one's yours!"

But of course, George had no choice, for George was sitting there, jaw wired shut, after somebody broke into his house and smashed his jaw with what the police believed to be a length of lead pipe. Funny how things happen, Richard thought, and then he looked over at Carla, and waved at her.

And she raised her arm and waved back, and even at this distance, he could see the slight pain in her eyes, for she had quite the workout the previous day, and wielding a lead pipe with such a slender arm could cause some soreness. He smiled as the other team's pitcher began his windup, remembered the meeting last week with the two Feds, and how even to this day, they couldn't figure out why he had gotten away with eleven killings in his previous life. It was simple, really, if you looked at it as a game, as a family game, and he waved once more at his lovely wife.

The pitch flew by and this time, oh, this time, there was a powerful crack! as Leo swung his bat and the ball flew up and out, heading so far out into the sky, and the people in the stands began cheering as little Leo chugged up the baseline, his face so alive and excited, and true enough, this was just a game, but it was the best damn game in the world.

CHICKASAW CHARLIE HOKE

by Elmore Leonard

This time Vernice started in on Charlie while he was making their toddies, what he did every evening Vernice worked days. Charlie said, "Take a load off your tootsies, honey, and let me wait on you."

She eased into her La-Z-Boy to sit there as she always did, leaving a space between her round thighs. Vernice was in her forties, younger than Charlie by ten years, a big redhead with the whitest skin Charlie had ever seen on a bare-naked woman. She started in by saying Carlyle, her brother-in-law, hired a family to work his soy beans and now had a job at the Isle of Capri dealing blackjack. It was always someone she knew, the manager of some podunk motel now a pit boss at Bally's. She'd mention the casinos were always looking for help or desperate for it.

Charlie would say to her, "Honey, I'm not just help." This time he said, "Honey, can you see me dealing cards?"

"Carlyle says between tips and wages he can make up to a thousand a week."

"Those people do that kind of work are ro-bots," Charlie said, pouring bourbon over crushed ice, adding sugar now, an orange slice and a maraschino cherry. "Be a waste of what I'm good at."

"What, talking to people?"

"Talking, referring to my career, sure."

"You could tend bar."

Charlie smiled over at her, Vernice in her pink waitress outfit she wore at the Isle of Capri coffee shop. He said to her, "'Can you see me in a little red jacket and bow tie? A grown man my size grinning for tips?" Charlie was six-four and would put his weight at around, oh, two-forty if asked. He had a gut that wasn't too noticeable on his frame. He had a nose he said was his Chickasaw Indian heritage and eyes like a hawk; he'd set the palm of his hand above his eyes and squint to demonstrate. Seeing himself in one of those little red jackets caused Charlie to shake his head.

He said, "I don't work for tips—" without thinking and wanted to grab the words out of the air. Shit. Like a ball you throw to curve low and away and the son of a bitch hangs letter-high on the batter. He stepped over to Vernice with her drink. "I know what you're thinking, that I don't work, period, but you're too nice a person to hurt my feelings."

"What you do," Vernice said, "is talk."

"Yes, I do."

"Tell baseball stories over'n over."

"Honey, baseball's my life."

"Oh? And what's it pay now, fifteen years later?"

This didn't sound like his honey speaking. It was now sixteen years since he'd played ball, but he didn't correct her.

Now she said, "'Tell me what I'm getting out of this arrangement?"

He wasn't certain what she meant, but said the first thing in his mind. "You get *me,* you get my companionship—"

"I get to hear you talk," Vernice said, "is what I get. I get to fix you supper, I get to loan you money... "

She paused to think of something else and Charlie said, "Till I get fixed. I didn't quit that bingo hall cause I don't like to work. I told you, how'm I gonna talk to a bunch of old women don't even know who I am? I need the right spot's all. Come on, you know me by now. How long we been together?"

He thought she might say too long, though it'd only been a couple months. No, this time she went right to the point saying, "I made up my mind. I'd like you out of the house, Charlie, by the end of the week. I can't afford your companionship any longer'n that."

He thought of a remark he could make if this was one of their usual arguments—Vernice fussing at him for not taking the trash to the dump and his saying, "Oh, I'm sorry, I didn't notice you broke your leg." He could say something about her calling this RV in a trailer park on the outskirts of Tunica, Mississippi, the South's Casino Capital, a "house." He could say, "Oh, that's what you call this tin box waiting on the next tornado?" But this wasn't an argument where you could say what you wanted and then take the trash to the dump.

She was giving him a deadline at the worst time, broke and needing a place to live; so he had to be nice. This wasn't hard because he did like Vernice, her usually quiet way, her pure-white body, her housekeeping. He told her one time cleanliness was a rule

147

with the Chickasaws: a woman who didn't keep her house clean was marked, had her arms and legs scratched with dried snake teeth. It was true. He'd give her Indian lore and she'd roll her eyes. Or she'd say he was no more Indian than she was and Charlie would say, "Then how come they called me Chief all the years I played ball?"

Vernice brought him back to right now saying, "By week's end, Charlie. I'm sorry."

He turned to the counter and took time to screw the cap onto the Early Times bottle. He turned back to her saying, "'What if I'm offered a position by then?"

"I love your choice of words, a position."

"As a celebrity host. What some of us do when we retire."

"Shake hands with the slot players?"

"Take care of the high rollers, honey, see they're comped to whatever they want."

"Like girls? You gonna be a pimp, Charlie?"

He let it go by. "Or I could set up the entertainment, special kinds of events."

"Well, let's see," Vernice said, "Andy Williams is at Harrah's, George Jones at Bally's. One of the Righteous Brothers is opening at Isle of Capri, taking over from that Elvis impersonator." She said, "If all ten casinos can get any big-name entertainers they want...? You see my point?"

She must've seen it as a stopper, a question she could ask without even a smarty tone to her voice. Charlie said, "I got an idea I haven't told you about." Her or anyone at all while he watched the new hotel going up, from bare iron to stone, with a big goddamn wigwam made of concrete rising a good three stories above the entrance. He said, "You know there's a new one opening next week. They got the sign up now, Tishomingo Lodge & Casino, Tunica, Mississippi."

It gave Vernice pause. "You been over there?"

"I'm seeing the fella runs it, Billy Darwin from Atlantic City, young guy. He was running Spade's and the people here waved enough money at him he moved to Tunica. I've seen him around— little guy, has hair like Robert Redford."

Vernice said, "Tishomingo, that's Indian."

"Chickasaw. Tishomingo was the big chief the time they got shipped off to Oklahoma. Follow me now," Charlie said. "Where was I raised? In Corinth. And where's Corinth? Clear across the state but only fifteen miles from the Tishomingo county line, where the Chickasaws came from originally. Some never went to Oklahoma and're still around there. See, but Indians don't have nothing to do with the hotel. I think the owners just like the name."

He watched Vernice thinking about it sipping her toddy, then begin to nod. "You're gonna tell this hotshot from Atlantic City you're a Chickasaw Indian—"

"I am, honey, part. I've told you that."

"And you expect having a few drops of Indian blood'll get you a job—I mean, a position?"

"I find out this fella has run a sports book, loves the game of baseball and has a head fulla stats. What I'm saying, I expect he could also know who I am."

"You're kidding," Vernice said, "aren't you?"

Being hurtful now as well as ignorant. It gave Charlie that urge to bear down and he said off the top of his head, "I'll bet you anything you want I get the job. How much?"

Vernice smiled, but it was like she felt sorry for him. She said, "Charlie, you ever get hired as a celebrity host I'll lose twenty pounds and go to work as a Keno runner."

Sitting there like a strawberry sundae in her La-Z-Boy, knees apart—the woman's know-it-all tone of voice moved his irritation up a couple of notches and he said, "I was you, honey, I'd make it forty pounds."

She was having fun now and ignored the remark. "You're gonna tell this man you're a full-blooded Chickasaw."

"And played ball."

"Gonna paint your face and put on a war bonnet?"

"No," Charlie said, "I'm gonna tell this fella runs the place I'm a direct descendant of the man they named it for, Tishomingo himself."

Vernice said, "And you know what he'll say?"

Billy Darwin said, "Well, Chief, if I thought it mattered, can you prove it?"

This was in front of the Tishomingo Hotel & Casino as Darwin came out of his Jaguar in leisure attire and Charlie introduced himself.

"During my playing days," Charlie said, "the Tishomingo Times in Oklahoma'd run stories about me and mention my lineage. I never left Tishomingo County till I was signed by the Baltimore organization."

"You played ball, uh?"

"Eighteen years. I phoned for an appointment, your girl put me down for 2 P.M. So while I been waiting an hour and a half," Charlie said, trying not to sound too irritated, "I been studying your wigwam"—the three stories of concrete coming to a point above the entrance—"trying to think if Chickasaws ever lived in wigwams, with or without all different colored neon running up it, and it come to me that we never did."

Billy Darwin said, "That's what you want to see me about?"

"I thought I'd mention it. No, I'm here seeking employment as a celebrity host."

"As a relative of Tishomingo or a former ballplayer?"

"I can handle either, talk the talk."

When Billy Darwin shrugged and walked away, going into the hotel, Charlie was right behind him, passing through a room the size of a ballpark where they were laying carpet. On the escalator going up to the mezzanine Charlie said to the back of the man's silky sportshirt, "I was with five Major League organizations and pitched in a World Series."

Billy Darwin tossed his Robert Redford hair and looked over his shoulder as he reached the mezzanine.

"What year?"

"Eighty-four."

"Tigers over the Padres in five," Darwin said.

He kept walking and Charlie followed him through a reception area walled with murals, Plains Indians and buffalo, where some guys in suits were waiting, looking up to be noticed as Darwin went past, now into an office where a good-looking dark-haired woman sat behind a desk. Darwin stopped to ask her, "'Carla, who was my two o'clock?"

She looked down at her pad and said, "Mr. Charlie Hoke. He wanted me to note, 'Former big leaguer.'"

Darwin turned enough to look at Charlie.

"How do you spell your name?"

Charlie told him.

Darwin said, "'You sure it's not H-o-a-x?"

Charlie said, "Billy"—hanging on to his irritation—"while you were playing stickball in the alley I was with the Orioles, the Texas Rangers, the Pittsburgh Pirates, the De-troit Tigers, Baltimore again, got traded back to De-troit in '83 and finished my eighteen years of organized ball with the Tigers in the '84 World Series. I went in what became the final game in the fifth and struck out the side. I got Brown and Salazar on called third strikes. I hit Wiggins by mistake, put him on, and I got the mighty Tony Gwynn to go down swinging at sixty-mile-an-hour knucklers. I went two and a third inning, threw twenty-six pitches and only five of 'em were balls. I hit Wiggins on a nothin' and two count, my only mistake, went to shave him with a fastball and come a little too close. I've struck out Al Oliver, Gorman Thomas and Jim Rice. Also Darrel Evans, Mike Schmidt, Bill Madlock, Willie McGee, Don Mattingly, and I fanned Wade Boggs twice in the same game—if those names mean anything to you."

Billy Darwin said, "Come on in," and led Charlie into an office big enough to hold a dance in and not even remove the desk, which by itself was a size. Darwin took his place behind it and began fooling with his computer, working the mouse, the PC and a phone the only things on the desk. Charlie got tired of standing and took one of the ranchhouse leather chairs without being asked. Looking at Darwin close he saw the man was about forty, had that young-looking hair and appeared to be in shape. Charlie heard the computer making different noises like static on a radio, then was quiet and pretty soon Darwin went to work on the keyboard, typing and looking at the screen, which Charlie couldn't see.

He finally asked Darwin what he was doing and was told, "Looking you up on CNNSI dot com."

"I'm in there?"

"It says you're six-five and weigh two-twenty."

"I've shrunk," Charlie said, "I'm only six-four now."

"But you've put on some weight.

"Couple pounds."

Darwin was looking at the screen again. "The year you were with Detroit..." He stopped. "You only pitched those two and a third innings, allowed one hit, struck out five and walked two." The man sounding surprised as he read it off the screen.

"I only walked one. I told you I hit Wiggins? Come inside on him too close. See, I was never afraid to throw inside. You'd see these batters sticking their butts out ready to bail."

"But the only time you went up to the Majors," Darwin said, "was in '84."

"I was up with other clubs but never used."

"And the only game you pitched in," Darwin said, "was in the World Series," the man still sounding surprised. "When did you strike out Mattingly, Madlock, all those guys you mentioned,

153

Gorman Thomas?"

"You want," Charlie said, "I can go down the list. I got Mattingly when I was with Toledo in Triple-A and Don was with Columbus then. I recall I was playing A ball with Tulsa, a game against Shreveport I got Darrel Evans swinging. Madlock, let's see, I was with Oneonta, that's also A ball, and I believe he was with Pittsfield. I know Mike Schmidt was with Reading when I fanned him and I was playing Double-A with Altoona, back then throwing ninety-nine-mile-an-hour fastballs. I also held the record in the Eastern League for hitting the most batters."

Billy Darwin didn't look surprised anymore, sitting there deadpan, like he was looking at all these baseball facts sliding around in his head.

"Eighty-one I was back with De-troit, sent down to the Mud Hens and struck out Willie McGee. As I recall he was with the Louisville Riverbats. Who else you want to know? Oh, and I was in that longest game ever played that went thirty-two innings. You ever hear of it?"

"Pawtucket and Rochester," Darwin said, "yeah, '81."

"You know your baseball. Baltimore was giving me another shot, this time with Rochester, Triple-A, and I struck out Wade Boggs both times I faced him. The game lasted eight hours and seven minutes before they called it at four-oh-seven the next morning, Easter Sunday. Guys came home and caught hell, their wives thinking they were out all night fooling around."

"They finished the game sometime in June," Darwin said, "but I don't recall who won."

154

CHICKASAW CHARLIE HOKE

"I don't either," Charlie said, "I was gone by then." He grinned at Darwin. "I remember Wade Boggs saying, 'A game like this, you can have a bad week in one night.'"

Darwin was staring at him again and Charlie put on a serious look as Darwin said, "'You spent your entire fucking career in the minors except for one game."

"I was up by the end of August that time. With other clubs too, but was mostly used for batting practice. I had all the pitches, even a split-finger that worked sometimes. I'd throw knucklers, give the boys a chance to see if they could hit junk. Or I'd come inside hard, get 'em to develop the nerve to hang in there."

"You were up several times—why didn't you ever stay?"

"I was wild my first, say, five years, I have to admit that. But being a southpaw with a blazing fastball, shit, there was always a club wanted to have a look at me. Then there was a period I might've been cuttin' up too much. I was having fun. Wherever I was I got my picture in the paper for one thing or another, like brawls they'd say I started. I'd hit a batter and he'd stand there giving me the evil eye. What I'd do, I'd hold my glove down by my leg and give him a motion with it like I'm saying, 'Come on. You think I hit you on purpose?' He'd come tearing at me and the benches'd empty. Seventy-three, or it might've been '74, I won the big league bubble-gum blowing contest." Charlie raised his hands like he was holding a basketball. "Goddamn bubble was this big, I swear."

He knew he had Darwin's attention, the way the man was staring at him, but couldn't tell what he was thinking.

"On the road for something to do, I'd catch balls dropped

from the roof of hotels—put on one of those big mitts catchers use for knuckleballers? It always drew a crowd, only management never cared for what they called showing off. That's the kind of thing I'd get sent down for—don't come back till you grow up."

"I got a guy," Darwin said, "wants to dive off the roof of the hotel. What you said reminded me. He calls up, says he's a professional high diver and wants to know how many floors we have. I told him seven. He goes, 'I'll dive off the roof into nine feet of water.' And he'll bring his own tank."

"I'd like to see that," Charlie said. "How much's he want?"

"Five bills to go off twice a day."

"Sounds cheap enough for a death-defying stunt."

"Said he worked in Acapulco."

"Shit, I'd hire him. He likes high risk, he's no doubt a gambler. Pay him and win it all back at your tables."

Charlie noticed Billy Darwin's keen, appraising look and pulled out another idea that might impress him. "Set up one of those radar guns they use to see how hard the ball's thrown. Put in a pitching rubber and a bullseye sixty feet away, a buck a throw. Anybody can throw a hardball a hunnert miles an hour wins... how much would you say?"

"Ten grand," Darwin said without even thinking about it.

"You have that on a sign by the radar cage," Charlie said. "Another one, it says 'Beat the Big Leaguer and win a hunnert bucks.' These strong young boys come along and look me over. 'Hell, I can take that old man.' Five bucks a throw - you could make some money off me."

Darwin kept staring at him. "'You can still throw?"

"I can get it up to around eighty."

"Come on—an old guy like you?"

"Hell, I'm only fifty."

Darwin looked at his screen again. "'Born in August of '46, you're pushing fifty-five."

"I can still throw harder'n most anybody wants to try me."

"You think," Darwin said, "you could strike me out?"

"You play much?"

"High school and sandlot, couple years of industrial ball."

"You bat right or left?"

"Left."

"Yeah, I can strike you out."

Darwin paused, thoughtful, and then asked him, "What've you been doing the past sixteen years?"

"Well, I distributed whiskey—ran it across the line from Alabama—something I did as a kid and picked it up again. Mississippi'd become wet by then, but there still those that prefer shine."

"Have you ever been arrested?"

"You're not supposed to ask that."

"Have you?"

"Lemme put it this way," Charlie said, "I've never done state time, or have any intention of gaining employment to rip you off—if that's what you're thinking."

"The possibility crossed my mind," Darwin said. "You married?"

"Divorced, a long time. I have a couple of daughters, both in Florida, five grandchildren." Charlie said, "Is this the job interview?"

Darwin had that thoughtful look again. "You really think you can strike me out?"

Charlie shrugged this time. "Step up to the plate, we'll find out. You want to put money on it?"

The man kept staring. Finally he said, "'How about this? I whiff, you're my celebrity host."

Charlie jumped on it. He said, "Hell, I'll strike you out on three pitches," and wanted to snatch the words back as he heard them. He saw Darwin smiling for the first time.

"I'll bet it was your mouth," Billy Darwin said, "kept you in the minors more'n your control." Not a half hour with Charlie Hoke and starting to sound like him a little. Darwin said, "You're a gamer, Charlie. I'll give you four pitches."

Charlie set it up. He called Vernice at the Isle of Capri coffee shop, told her please not to ask any questions and let him talk to Lamont, one of the busboys. Lamont Harris was the catcher on the Rosa Fort high school baseball team. Charlie knew him from going over there this past spring to help the pitchers with their mechanics, hit fungoes and throw batting practice now and then. He told Lamont to meet them at the field after work, bring a couple of bats, a glove, his equipment and, hey, the oversized catcher's mitt Charlie had sold him for ten bucks.

By five-thirty they were out on the school's hardpack diamond playing catch. Charlie took his warmup pitches, throwing mostly sliders and knucklers, while Billy Darwin in his sunglasses, his silky shirt and sneakers, stood off to the side watching and swinging a bat. Lamont strapped on his protection and Charlie motioned him out to the mound. He told Lamont, a big seventeen-year-old he'd played catch with all spring, "'Use the knuckleball mitt."

"That's all you gonna throw?"

"He'll think it and want to look the first one over. While he's looking," Charlie said, "I'm gonna throw it down the middle of downtown."

And that's what he did, grooved it. With that popping sound of the ball hitting the catcher's mitt, Lamont called, "That's a strike," and Darwin turned his head to look at him. When he was facing this way again, swinging the bat out to point it at him, Charlie said, "You satisfied with the call?"

"It was a strike," Billy Darwin said, swung the bat out again, brought it back and dug in, Charlie observing the way he crowded the plate.

This time Charlie threw a slider, a two-bit curveball that came inside and hooked down and over the plate and Darwin swung late and missed. But he hung in, didn't he?

Okay, with the count nothing and two Charlie was thinking about offering a big, sweeping curve, lefty against lefty, throw it behind him and watch him hunch and duck as the ball broke over home plate. Or, hell, give him a knuckler, a pitch he'd likely never seen. Get it anywhere near the plate he'll swing early and miss it a mile. Charlie gripped the ball with the tips of his gnarled fingers, his nails pressed into the hide, went into his motion, threw the floater and watched Darwin check his swing as the goddamn ball bounced a foot and a half in front of the plate.

"He came around on it," Charlie said.

Lamont was shaking his head saying no, he held up.

"We don't have a third base ump to call it," Charlie said, but I'm pretty sure he came around."

Billy Darwin said, "Hey, Charlie, you threw it in the dirt, man. Come on, throw me a strike."

Shit. What he needed was a resin bag.

Darwin was swinging the bat now and pointing it way out past Charlie toward the Mississippi River, then took his stance, digging in, and Charlie wasn't sure what to throw him. Maybe another slider, put it on the inside corner. Or show him a Major League fastball—or what passed for one sixteen years later. Shit. He felt his irritation heating up and told himself to throw the goddamn ball, fire it in there, this guy won't hit it, look at him holding the bat straight up behind him, waving the fat end in a circle. Jesus, a red bat, one of those metal ones they used in high school. You can't strike out a guy waving a tin bat at you, for Christ sake? Charlie went into his motion and bore down, threw it as hard as he could and saw the red bat fly up in the air as Billy Darwin hit the dirt to save his life.

Vernice, making the toddies this evening, said, "I don't understand why you threw it at him."

"I didn't; it got away from me is all. I should've taken time to settle down, talk to myself."

"But you lost your temper," Vernice said, handing Charlie his drink, "and your chance of getting that position."

"I ain't finished the story," Charlie said, in the La-Z-Boy where Vernice in her sympathy had let him sit. "I started toward him as he's brushing himself off. He says to me, picking up the bat, to stay out there and you bet I stopped in my tracks, in my goddamn wingtips. Now he's swinging the bat to show me where he wants it, belt high, and says, 'Lay one in right here.'"

Vernice said, "He wasn't sore at you?"

"Lemme finish, okay? I laid one in and he hit it a mile out to right center. He says, 'There. Just so you know I can hit a baseball.' Then he says, 'You own a suit?' I told him of course I owned a suit. He says, 'Put it on the day we open, and wear a tie.'"

Vernice seemed puzzled. "He hired you?"

"Yes, he did."

"Even though you knocked him down?"

Charlie said to her, "Honey, it's part of the game".

SACRIFICE HIT

by John Lescroart

I t wasn't just the Dodgers wearing arm bands.

Every man, woman and child in the crowd of four hundred people at the Dolan City Championships wore a ribbon of black to commemorate the death last Thursday of the Dodger bench warmer (and occasional right fielder) Vaclav Placin, from a rattlesnake bite. It seemed even more tragic that Vaclav, a twelve-year-old emigre from the atrocities in Bosnia, had only been in the country for six months. This was to be his first full season of baseball, his first year in America.

There was even short-lived talk of canceling Sunday's game, but in the end, the Board decided that too much was riding on its outcome. After all, this was for the Little League championship, the American League pennant winning Yankees against the National League's Dodgers.

With about fifty thousand full-time inhabitants and another fifteen thousand college students during the school year, Dolan was a medium-sized town in many respects. But as a Little League base-ball talent ground it had achieved a status that nearly rivaled that of legendary Taiwan. Three times in the past seven years, the Dolan All-Stars had made it to Williamsport for the Little League World Series, and two years ago had taken home the trophy. Visitors taking the downtown exit off the freeway were greeted with a huge banner spanning Main Street, proudly proclaiming Dolan to be the home of the 1999 Little League World Series Champions.

A big deal. A very, very big deal indeed.

As anyone who knows Little League understands, the team that goes to the Regionals and Sectionals and so on—and eventually, if it keeps winning, to Williamsport and the Little League World Series—is an All-Star team made up the best players from all the teams in a given city or region. Dolan had seven teams of twelve players in each of its two leagues—the American from east of Main, the National from the more affluent west side.

Many aficionados of the game believed that the secret to Dolan's extraordinary success in baseball was due to the town's truly unusual lack of support for any other organized sports. While most towns of any size in California boasted every type of children's sports team imaginable—AYSO and Select soccer, roller, field and ice hockey, water polo, swimming, Pop Warner football, girls' softball—Dolan's city fathers and mothers had decided long ago that theirs was going to be a baseball town.

So there wasn't a soccer or hockey field within the city limits. Kids who wanted to skate had to go down the road to the Vacaville rinks or up to Sacramento. The public pools were too small to make laps worthwhile. By contrast, the Little League's Main Diamond at Dolan Playparks, where the "major leaguers" played their games, was the cornerstone of a five-acre baseball theme lot at the corner of 10th and Main.

The field was a slice of Norman Rockwell Americana - a perfectly groomed and landscaped cinder and grass diamond with twelve rows of grandstands, covered against the Central Valley heat, extending past the dugouts along both foul lines. The outfield fences at each of the five diamonds at the Playparks were covered with advertisements of local merchants. If you wanted to have a profitable business in Dolan, you either sponsored a team outright or you put your company name on the fence at one of the fields. The waiting list for a place on the fence at the Main Diamond was about four years long.

The four other diamonds at the complex - A, B, C, and D— were home to the games of the younger Little Leaguers, mostly nine- and ten-year-old kids at the "Double-A" or "Triple-A" level. These fields, too, were nicely maintained, but they backed up against the parking lot and then the railroad tracks, an unkempt area of high weed and spear grass, rocks and broken bottles. The true showplace was the Main Diamond.

The game this Sunday would not decide which players would be All-Stars. But it would determine one crucial element of the tournament team, which in turn was the sum of all of Dolan's Little League hopes for the year: the manager of the City Champion team went on to coach the All-Stars.

This year, this day, the battle was to be joined between teams managed by two men—Bob Trewitt and Gary Fallon—who had grown up together in Dolan, played ball together in high school, played against each other in college, even dated some of the same women.

Seven years before, when Trewitt's oldest son was twelve, Bob had managed the Dodgers to the City Championship, then taken Dolan's All-Stars all the way to Williamsport, only to be defeated by Taiwan, 6-5. To that date, this was the farthest that the city had ever progressed. In '96, Trewitt got another group of All-Stars to the show, only again to fall short.

Then, finally, in '99, Gary Fallon had a twelve-year-old son who played for the Yankees and became an All-Star. Fallon had won the City Championship, then managed the All-Stars all the way to the National Championship.

In almost any town in America, there will always be a few men managing Little League teams who to the average onlooker would appear close to insane. They would exhibit a certain lack of perspective in the importance to which they assigned children's baseball. In Dolan, these men who were fanatic almost to the point of lunacy were mild-mannered compared to Trewitt and Fallon. They sometimes at least gave lip service to sportsmanship, as opposed to winning. Trewitt and Fallon suffered from no such crisis of focus. They wanted to win and made no bones about it. That's what the game was about, and the only thing it was about.

Both of them had computer printouts of every player who'd tried out, and stats for the past years of achievement back through when the kids were five years old and picking flowers in the outfield during t-ball games. The bad behavior of both men in their respective quests for baseball dominance was legendary, but last year alone supplied a couple of typical instances.

In one incident, Trewitt's son Kevin—batting clean-up for the Dodgers—was coming up to the plate with men on second and third and two outs. Kevin was batting about .550 and the other team decided to walk him intentionally and take its chances with the next batter. This was only smart baseball. Trewitt, however, had become so enraged at his opposing manager's "chicken shit" strategy that he marched his team off the field and forfeited the game.

In Fallon's case, an umpire had called one of his Yankee players out at the plate, ending the game on a close play that would have tied it up in the sixth (or last) inning. Fallon charged from the dugout, all but frothing out the mouth, and after administering a blisteringly obscene tongue-lashing to the sixteen-year-old umpire, got himself ejected from the game. Later that night, as the umpire was leaving the lot, Fallon ran him down in his car. Luckily the poor kid only broke his leg. Fallon claimed it had been an accident, he hadn't seen the dark umpire's suit, and so on. The victim never brought charges, but rumor had it that he was bought off—after all, this was the year after Fallon had brought home the World Championship. The man was a hero.

It might stand to reason that two such idiots would never be entrusted with the care of the bodies and souls of young athletes again - and indeed, a few parents in Dolan pulled their kids out of Little League because these men were allowed to continue as managers. But their defenders countered that both these guys were fierce competitors, that was all - great coaches who could turn mediocre players into competent starters, talented kids into superstars. The normal rules simply shouldn't apply.

Although Jim Wright, Dolan's mayor and president of the Little League Board, was unambiguously delighted that this year, one of the two best coaches the town had ever produced was guaranteed to be the All-Star manager, he knew that politically the road would be smoother if he could talk Trewitt and Fallon into making a gesture to sportsmanship.

At nine o'clock on the first Sunday in March, the fourteen major league managers met at Dolan High for the annual draft. At this meeting, Wright told both men that they would need to compromise their draft picks slightly for the good of the program. This was non-negotiable. They would do it or they wouldn't manage.

There were two high-visibility young players who were nowhere near the quality of the rest of these two men's other draft picks, but both of them would symbolize the Little League's commitment to the right kind of values—he game wasn't just about winning, but about sportsmanship and inclusion. So one of these men was going a pick a girl, Annie Lodge, and the other would get a foreign kid who had never played baseball, Vaclav Placin.

They flipped a coin. Fallon got Annie for the Yankees, and Trewitt and the Dodgers got Vaclav.

At noon, an hour before game time, it was already 93 degrees. Michael Tully picked up his black armband, tied it on, then stopped by the snack bar. He chatted for a few minutes with Dorothy Moore, the very attractive volunteer and recent divorcee who ran the booth, and then bought himself a bubble-gum flavored sno-cone.

The first bite was so good, he hurried the next mouthful of ice, swallowed it too fast, and suddenly his head felt as though an ax had cleaved it north to south. He leaned back against one of the struts of the grandstands and brought a hand up to his forehead, thumb on one temple and forefinger on the other, squeezing hard.

"Brain freeze?"

He managed to open an eye to a vision of smiling loveliness. In another couple of seconds, miraculously, the pain had passed and he willed himself to look again. She was still there, a short woman with some Latin blood, slender and buxom—maybe not yet thirty—with long, shining dark hair.

Tully blinked, blew out a quick breath. The short-lived pain was gone, but it had been awesome. He brought himself back to the woman in front of him. "I'm sorry, what did you say?"

The green eyes held laughter and empathy. "I said 'Brain freeze.'" She pointed to his forgotten sno-cone. "You can't eat those things too fast, they'll kill you."

"Getting killed might be better."

"Less painful in any event. Anyway, that's why I came over. You looked like you were going down." She extended her hand. "I'm Maggie Chabon."

No ring on her left hand, he noticed. "Michael Tully." He raised his eyes to indicate their surroundings, the already substantial crowd. "You got a boy playing today?"

The question seemed to surprise, then amuse her. "Oh. No. My older sister Theresa.... my nephew is on the Yankees. Joey

169

Gorda? Shortstop? I just came down to cheer on the team. How about you?"

"I'm in your boat," he said. "No kids, which I suppose is a good thing, considering I'm not married." He hadn't planned to blurt out that information, but once he had, he found himself feeling okay about it.

Something else about his answer—beyond his marital status—had obviously piqued her interest. "So you're just a fan?"

"Everybody in Dolan's a fan. You've got to be if you live here. It's in the city charter."

"But you haven't been to too many games this year. Maybe this is your first one." She didn't phrase it as a question.

He narrowed his eyes at her. "What makes you say that?"

"You'd have known about sno-cones. Brain freezes. Besides," she added, "I'm here all the time and I haven't seen you before."

"Maybe you just didn't notice."

A spark flashed in her eyes. "No, I notice things. I would have noticed you and you haven't been here."

He gave it up. "Okay, you got me. This is the first time since I played here myself as a kid." He hesitated. "So what else do you notice?"

"About you?"

He nodded. "Sure, about me. Why not?"

Crossing her arms, she backed up a step and looked him frankly up and down. "Not too much, to tell you the truth," she began. "You live with a brown, short-haired dog and you're something of a sensualist. Oh, and you're a left-handed, color-blind jogger who cuts his own hair. Beyond that, not much. Except of course that you're a policeman."

He took a careful bite of his sno-cone, keeping his eyes on her face. He sensed that she wasn't showing off. Her expression was matter-of-fact, with no trace of gloating, although she'd gotten everything right. "That's pretty impressive," he said.

She shrugged. "As I said, I notice things." Suddenly she became more serious. "Which means you're not really here to root for anybody, are you? You're here about Vaclav."

They made their way over to some picnic tables under a small grove of shade trees, down the right field line from the Main Diamond.

"There's really no trick to it," Maggie was saying. "You've got brown dog hairs on your shirt near your collar. You're wearing shorts, and I see both by your legs and the wear in your running shoes that you put some pretty good mileage on them."

"Okay."

"As far as sensual, the sno-cone. Once you tasted it, obviously into it, wanting more so much your brain froze over it. Then left-handed? You're wearing your watch on your right wrist. Color-blind?" She smiled. "Well, it's a nice shirt but we're not really in the Christmas season yet. And finally," she touched her own hair, "you missed a couple of your blind spots back here. Not that it's really so noticeable. All in all, it's a pretty decent haircut."

"Thanks, I think." Tully had discarded the remainder of his sno-cone and now was sitting in dappled sunlight on a picnic table, elbows on his knees, his hands hanging down in front of him.

He squinted at Maggie Chabon with a keen interest, "How about the cop thing?"

Her expressive face arranged itself into an attractive moue. "Well, that was a bit of a cheat. You introduced yourself and I happen to read the papers. Michael Tully is the Chief of Police. I figured that had to be you."

"As a matter of fact," he said, "there are two other Mike Tullys in Dolan. One's a student at the college and the other is my dad. So you got a little lucky."

"I'll take that," she said easily. "I'd rather be a little lucky than a little smart any old day."

"From what I've just seen," Tully replied, "you don't need much help on the luck front."

On the Main Diamond, someone was doing a sound check with the loudspeaker system and judging from all the feedback, it wasn't going well. The Yankees had taken the field, the boys at their positions, taking infield or shagging flies. Maggie followed Tully's glance over to the field. They both watched as the shortstop ranged far to his left, behind second base, scooped a hard, low roller and gunned a strike to first. The boy let out a jubilant cry. They could see his grin as he hustled back to his position. "That's Joey," she said, puffed with pride.

"Good looking kid. Nice play."

From the outfield, a booming adult voice carried over to them. A trim middle-aged guy was hitting fly balls from the foul line to a group of kids clustered by the center field fence. He yelled after every hit. "Run, you baby. You're not going to *win* if you don't *hustle*. I want to see sweat, I want to see *desire.*" He hit another fly ball and one of the boys charged but couldn't get to it—the ball dropped in front of his outstretched mitt. *"You're doggin' it, Brandon, god... dang it! Give me twenty pushups, then take a lap. Anybody else want to run with him? Then catch the dang ball!"*

"That gentleman," Maggie said in a disapproving tone, "is Gary Fallon, Joey's coach."

"I know." Tully let out a sigh.

"What?"

"It's just that the game itself is so pure," he said. "All the kids really want is to have fun. And that's what seems to get lost after the adults get involved. Then it's all win win win."

She studied his face. "You're thinking about Vaclav?"

He put up a guarded expression. This was his job now. "You read minds, too?"

"Only on selected occasions."

Tully remained inside himself for another moment. Then he met her eyes. "I hope you're doing something with this talent of yours."

She flashed him a wistful expression. "I teach kindergarten. I really like it," she added quickly. "The kids are so.... so pure as you say at that age...."

"But?"

She shrugged. "I thought if I got to them early enough, I could get them in the habit of noticing, of soaking up the world around them, loving life. I wanted to inspire them."

173

"Past tense?"

She shook her head. "Oh, no. I still feel that way, at least most of the time, I think. It's just now I've been doing it for six years, and I've had to get more realistic, or cynical. Or both." A sigh. "There's just so many other issues closer to home for most of them. They come to school without breakfast, their shoes aren't tied, they haven't had baths, their clothes are filthy. Not all of them, of course, but enough. And it's my curse. I notice."

They had made their way over to the grandstands, which were beginning to fill up. Maggie and Tully individually knew many of the fans, and the walk through the seats was slow and convivial. The old small-town feel permeated the day—all of the black arm bands notwithstanding. Whole families had come out to the ballyard together, their coolers filled with sodas and sandwiches and beer. The sound system was up and running by now, and music through the ages—from the marches of John Philip Sousa through the Village People's "YMCA"—blared from the loudspeakers.

The Yankees had given up the field and now sat in their dugout. Tully noticed Fallon pacing in front of the team, gesticulating with a manic energy. Mayor Jim Wright was holding a conference of some kind with a knot of the league's supporters behind home plate. On the diamond, the Dodgers were taking infield. Their manager, Bob Trewitt, kept up a steady, macho, just-this-side-of-vulgar chatter as he slapped shots to each position, rockets off his bat that most of the boys managed to field cleanly.

In the top row of the grandstands, out of earshot from the

next nearest fan, Tully brushed away some sunflower seed shells and made a space for him and Maggie to sit. And then, suddenly, he simply ran out of words. Maggie watched his face settle into a hard frown as he stared at the field, at everything going on down there.

"Michael?" She lightly touched his leg.

He turned to her, stone-faced, and shook his head. "I'm missing something."

"The paper said it was an accident."

"Yes it did."

"And yet you're here?"

He nodded heavily, "After school on Wednesday, Vaclav was out exploring in the field behind his house with one of his friends, Paul Moore, and they pulled up a rock and found a snake coiled under it. It might have been a baby rattler, with no rattles yet."

"Might have been?"

"We'll get to that."

"And the babies are more poisonous than the adults, aren't they?"

"Well, the poison's the same potency, but adults control how much of it they release with each bite. The young ones haven't learned how to do that, so they tend to squirt it all out, a huge dose, easily enough to kill a child. So anyway, these kids got hold of an old shoebox and put the snake in it, then had a discussion over who'd get to take it home the first night."

"And who won?"

"Paul did. He had a sleepover with another friend planned for the next night, Thursday, and his friend's mom wouldn't want him to

175

bring a snake, so Vaclav said okay, why not. That's Paul at third base down there for the Dodgers." He pointed. "That's his mom, Dorothy, on the field now with Jim Wright. The blonde."

"Sure," Maggie said without much enthusiasm, "I know her. She's very pretty, isn't she?"

"Yes she is. Anyway, I talked to her on Friday. On the Wednesday, when she found out her son had brought home a snake in a shoebox, she wanted to take a look at it."

"I don't blame her," Maggie said. "I would have done the same thing."

"She told me that the snake was a common garter, not a rattler. And she ought to know, she sees a lot of snakes."

"Why is that?"

"Because she volunteers at the Whole Earth Science Center. You know, the interactive place, out in the flats." He gestured apologetically. "I realize it's just hearsay and she might have been wrong, but still."

Maggie nodded, processing it all carefully. "And Vaclav got it next?"

"Yeah. The next day, Thursday, Paul Moore brings it to school for show and tell. It doesn't look like a rattlesnake to their teacher, Mr. Wallace, either."

"Al Wallace?"

He nodded. "You know him?"

"Sure, the assistant coach for the Dodgers." It was Maggie's turn to point. "That's him hitting fungoes down the left field line. His boy Lucas is their catcher."

Tully's eyes had turned to slits. "He never mentioned he was involved in Little League when I went to his class."

This wasn't a huge point to Maggie. "Maybe he assumed you already knew, since every other male in town seems to be. Anyway, so what did he say about the snake? The one Paul brought in?"

"Well, he admitted that he's no expert, but to him it was a garter snake. They passed it around the class, twenty kids held the thing, no problem."

"Twenty kids?"

Tully nodded. "Imagine. So now it's Thursday afternoon, and Vaclav brings the box with him to Little League practice..."

"Which was where?"

"Right here. Both teams that day—the Yankees had an hour at the batting cages while the Dodgers worked out on the Main Diamond. Then they switched."

"So the box was here? In one of the dugouts?"

A nod. "For the first hour, then I guess Vaclav took it with him over to the batting cages. And then when he brought it home, it had a rattler in it. Not a garter snake."

"Maybe after practice he went exploring again and found a different snake." Maggie gestured to the parking lot behind them. "There's all kinds of junk back there by the train tracks. And it's been so hot. There must be lots of snakes, maybe even out sunning themselves."

"Maybe there are," Tully conceded, "but Vaclav didn't do that. He stayed around the cage, finished batting practice, then Trewitt drove him home, along with a few of the other kids."

"Who? Do you know?"

Tully shot her a look, then reached into his breast pocket and extracted a small spiral notebook. He flipped a few pages, then read, "His own son, Kevin Trewitt, Damon O'Brian, Benjamin Weiss, and Vaclav. All Dodgers."

"Did any of them open the box? Or look in it?"

This brought a gentle smile. "I may not notice things the way you do, Maggie, but I can ask the right questions."

"I'm sorry," she said. "I didn't mean...."

"No, that's all right." He touched her knee for half an instant with his fingertip. "I think we make a good team. But none of the boys touched the box, which they might have done except that Trewitt's kid Kevin spilled his sno-cone getting into the front seat and Trewitt gave them all a lecture on being aware of their surroundings and developing a winning attitude. I guess on the theory that a Hall of Fame second baseman or whatever would never be so clumsy as to drop a sno-cone. I don't think I like him."

"Trewitt?"

"Trewitt. He's so ticked off at his son that he drops him off at his own house before any of the other kids. So the ride home for the rest of them is a little tense, as you can imagine."

Maggie was chewing the inside of her cheek. "Did Vaclav have one?"

"Have one what?"

"A sno-cone."

Tully narrowed his eyes at her. "As a matter of fact, he must have had a few of them. At the autopsy, his tongue was still purple from the dye, and there was still traces in his stomach. Why?"

"I'm not sure," Maggie said. "Just another fact, that's all."

But the accretion of facts didn't seem to lead to any solution, and Tully shook his head dejectedly. "It doesn't make any sense. That's what I can't figure. Something about it doesn't smell right, but there's no motive. There's just no reason for it to be anything but an accident."

A muscle worked in Maggie's jaw and for a long moment she stared straight ahead into nothingness. "Well, maybe there is, although it's..."

"What?"

"No, it's too far-fetched. It would be too weird."

"What?" Tully repeated.

When Maggie finally spoke, her voice was low, conspiratorial. "Just Joey—my nephew? And his mom. My sister. They said right from the start that they didn't think it was an accident."

"Did they give you any reasons?"

Maggie was sitting in the same posture as Tully—elbows on her knees, hands clasped in front of her. "When Joey first heard about Vaclav dying, he said, dead serious, 'I bet somebody on the Dodgers killed him.' And Theresa was like 'Come on, Joey, you can't joke like that. Nobody would have a reason to kill Vaclav.'

"But it bothered her so much she called and told me about it that same night, asked me if I thought it was possible. I told her I didn't think so. I mean, a rattlesnake bite. How can that be intentional? But Theresa asked me if I would come over and talk to Joey. So I did."

"And what did he tell you?"

"Just that he heard his coach—our quiet friend Mr. Fallon over there—telling one of the ladies at the snack bar that if he had Vaclav on his team, three automatic outs, he'd put a hit on him. Fallon was laughing about it. Call it a sacrifice hit. Give him up for the good of the team."

Tully cut her off. "That is truly sick. But beyond that, I don't get it. What's three automatic outs?"

"Little league rules," Maggie explained. "Since there are only nine positions, every player can't play a position in the field every inning. But you've got twelve kids on each team and you've got to let everybody on the roster get their at-bats, regardless of whether they play the field that inning."

"Okay."

"Okay, so a kid like Vaclav before this year had never played the game and wasn't too coordinated to boot. It was really a little pathetic. I don't think his dad should have forced him to play, at least not at this level. But he wanted him to be an American. Well, long story short, it turns out he didn't get one hit all year, never even touched the ball, not so much as a foul tip."

"Ouch."

"No kidding. According to Joey, Vaclav single-handedly made the Dodgers suffer both of their losses in the regular season, because of which they almost didn't make it to the Championship Game today."

"How did he do that again?"

"Evidently the poor kid struck out three times *with the bases loaded* in each of the only two games the Dodgers lost this year."

Tully whistled softly, remembering his own, sometimes awful playing days. "Six strikeouts with the bases loaded?"

Maggie nodded. "He never learned how to swing the bat, Michael. Joey's Dodger friends told the story that in practice once Vaclav actually dribbled one that went fair and he started running toward *third base*. It was the saddest thing."

"So what's this three outs?"

"Well, if Vaclav was here today, in the normal course of the game, he'd probably come up at least three times in six innings, as he did in both games the Dodgers lost. And every time he got up, he'd make an out. Automatic. So the fact that he's not here strengthens the Dodgers' lineup considerably. Those three outs he won't make could easily be the difference between who wins the City Championship, or doesn't."

"And you think someone would kill a little boy for that reason?"

She thought about it for a long moment. "Complete maniacs though these guys are, I don't know if I can imagine it, if I could take it that far. But Joey seemed to have no trouble with the concept. 'Would Mr. Trewitt kill somebody to get to manage the All-Stars?' he said to me.

'There's a big "Duh," Aunt Mag.'"

Down on the field, some angry voices started to carry up over Bobby McFerrin's voice exhorting everybody not to worry, to be happy. Tully and Maggie stopped their discussion and directed their attention down to the ruckus.

The mayor and his knot of Little League supporters and volunteers were still around home plate with the umpires, but now both managers, Trewitt and Fallon, had joined the group. And Fallon was obviously in a high rage. "I don't see how you can force me to play all my players when they didn't bring their full team."

The mayor responded in measured tones. "The boy died, Gary. Jesus Christ."

"And I'm sorry for him, I truly am. But the point remains that I'm stuck with my handicap player"—this was Annie Lodge, sitting within earshot of this exchange in the Yankee dugout—"and the Dodgers don't have theirs. It's patently unfair and I'm formally objecting and playing this game under protest."

Up in the front row of the stands on the Dodgers' side, one of the dads got to his feet and bellowed. "Get a fuckin' life, Gary! Quit your belly-achin'!" Another fan on the Yankees' side screamed back. "Hey, watch the language, dickhead! There's kids here." The first cat-caller swore again and flipped off the second one, and people—mostly men, but a few women—on both sides started getting to their feet, the sweet family feel of the day gone ugly in a heartbeat.

"I think this is my cue." Tully's voice had a resigned edge, but there was flint under it. "Care to join me?"

"No. You go ahead," she said. "I want to see about something."

He would have asked her what it was, but the situation was deteriorating rapidly down below.

Tully ran down the bench seats, crossed behind the Dodger dugout, and pushed open the gate that led onto the field. He had his badge out, holding it up over his head as he approached the home plate area. They had a second microphone plugged in and set up for pre-game announcements, and Tully strode right up to it and sig-naled the sound man in the booth, motioning again with his badge.

The music went off, leaving a vacuum of silence.

Tully heard his own breathing, loud, in the newly-live mike in front of him. He was angry and frustrated at the crowd, at the stu-pidity and lack of perspective of these parents, and was tempted to go into cop mode and give a lecture on the rules: no drinking, no pro-fanity, no fighting. Maybe even call the whole overblown exercise off, with the excuse that it was disturbing the peace. But he couldn't do it. All that came out were the words: "Let's show a little respect for these great kids."

He nodded to the sound man and the music came up again almost immediately—Don McLean's original version of "American Pie." Tully turned and walked back toward home plate, where most of the people gathered there began offering him some embarrassed words of thanks. He made some awkward, "somebody had to do it" remarks. All he wanted to do was get out of there and back in the stands, where he and Maggie could continue what they'd begun.

But looking up, he saw her coming onto the field now, through the gate beside the Yankee dugout, on the right field side over by the snack booth. She was carrying what looked like a flat-tened piece of cardboard in her hand. And there was no trace of the dazzling smile he'd first seen less than an hour before. In fact, her face looked grim and ashen.

He took a few steps toward her. "Maggie, what ... ?"

No one else was paying them any mind. She came so close that for a second he almost felt that she was going to kiss him.

183

Instead, she looked up into his face, her jaw set, and spoke in a rasping voice through clenched teeth. "Deputize me," she whispered.

"What?"

"I know what happened," she said urgently. "Vaclav was murdered. I know how, and I know who did it. And I can prove it. Right now."

Tully looked into her stunning brown eyes. In them he saw neither guile nor bravado, but an intelligence and a certainty—a depth of character and good judgment. He suddenly knew he was fated to be with her, that this would be the first of many decisions they would make together as a team, perhaps as a couple. "Please," she said again. "Trust me."

He hesitated for a last second, then nodded. "Raise your right hand," he said solemnly.

In the grandstands, the large gallery grew increasingly restless at the unexpected delay. The game was due to begin in less than five minutes, and they hadn't even begun the official announcements over the loudspeaker—the introduction of the teams, the managers, the sponsors. With the crowd of mucky-mucks clustered around home plate, it was beginning to look as though they would have to re-draw the chalk lines for the batter's boxes. And now the Chief of Police, standing next to an attractive young woman, was getting everybody's attention for what looked to be another round of delay and discussion.

"Let's play ball!" someone yelled, and the cry was taken up around the stands.

Tully stood out between home plate and the pitcher's mound and flashed his badge at the broadcast booth again, and again an abrupt silence ensued, oppressive in its own way as a thermal inversion. Over the bowl of the field, under a bright blue sky and a brutally hot sun, the Chief of Police waited for the commotion in the grandstands to die down, then spoke in his quiet and authoritative way.

"This is Deputy Maggie Chabon. She's been working on the case of Vaclav Placin, and I'd like you to give her your complete attention for a few minutes please."

"What case?" Fallon yelled. "The kid got snake bit, that's all." He turned to his assistant coach and, *sotto voce,* said, "I'm getting damn tired of hearing about this kid."

Mayor Wright began to put in his own two cents. "Maybe this isn't the right time, Chief. We've got this game. . ."

"Excuse me!" Maggie stepped in front of Tully. "This is the best time, Mr. Mayor, the only time. Everybody's here, and we're talking about bringing a killer to justice."

Audible all the way to the stands, this announcement created a stir both on the field and off. "What did she say?" "A killer?" "Who got killed?" "Who is that woman?"

Maggie all but ignored the outburst. Her hands, with the flattened piece of cardboard in them, were clasped behind her back. She took a few more steps toward home plate, waited for the noise to subside slightly, then addressed the knot of people surrounding the mayor.

"I'd like to talk about the events of last Thursday, when Vaclav Placin died, but first...." Turning to Tully, she asked him to

185

call the teams out of their dugouts and onto the field. The Chief of Police hoped she knew what she was doing, but he'd already committed himself this far, and if he was going to jump into this quagmire, it was going to be with both feet.

Within a minute, the Dodgers and the Yankees were lined up along both baselines.

Maggie took in the situation and nodded with satisfaction. "Thank you." She turned to the Yankee side. "And now I'd like to ask you, Gary Fallon, if you ever mentioned what you'd do if you had a kid like Vaclav on your team in the Championship Game, a kid who couldn't hit, who was good for three automatic outs. Didn't you say you'd have him killed?"

Fallon reacted as though he'd been hit. "Hey, that was a joke. I didn't mean—"

"As a joke, it was in the worst possible taste. And I didn't ask you if you meant it, I asked if you said that you'd kill Vaclav if he was on your team."

Fallon took off his Yankees hat and wiped the sweat from his brow. "I might have."

Jeers and catcalls erupted from the stands.

Maggie turned to the Yankee team, strung out along the first base line. "Did any of you kids hear your coach make this kind of remark at the snack bar?"

No one on the team was anxious to rat on their manager, but Joey—Maggie's nephew—finally screwed up his courage and raised his hand, and it was followed by half a dozen others.

"All right." Maggie half turned to the third base side. "Mr.

Trewitt, is that where you got the idea?"

Trewitt's face flushed deeply under his sunburn. "I didn't get no idea," he said. "I never would do anything like that. I'm here to coach these boys. Vaclav was a good kid. I'm sorry about what happened to him."

"But you did drive him home that Thursday, didn't you?"

"Yeah. I drove home a bunch of my players. So what?"

"And you took your son home first, because he spilled a sno-cone in your car."

Tully knew these facts as well as Maggie, but couldn't see where she was going with them. He threw her a worried glance, but she only nodded confidently. Mayor Jim Wright took a step toward the mound and addressed himself to Tully. "I really don't see what this is about. Chief Tully, when did this woman become a deputy?"

"Recently," Tully replied easily. "Give her five more minutes." A warning to Maggie as well. She'd better make her point.

Clearing her throat, Maggie fought down a spell of nerves. She'd never done anything like this before, and though she knew where she wanted to go, she was fumbling with the route. "Mr. Trewitt, where did your son get the sno-cone?"

The Dodger manager snorted. "Is this is a joke. Where do you think he got the damn sno-cone? He got it at the snack bar!"

"So the snack bar was open that Thursday?"

"Must have been, huh?"

An awkward laughter rolled across the crowd, but Maggie ignored it. "It must have been, yes," she said. "But the schedule is posted on the bulletin board just over there, and it wasn't a game day, so it wasn't supposed to be open that day."

"That's right." Dorothy Moore stepped out of the pack and spoke up. "It was another scorcher like today, and I knew both teams would be down here practicing, so I came down and opened up so they could get some drinks and snacks."

Tully hated to do it, but it was beginning to look as though he'd made a mistake giving Maggie this chance. He started to interrupt again. "Maggie, I'm afraid there's no . . ."

"There is!" She whirled down the third base line again. "Mr. Wallace, did you see the garter snake that Paul Moore brought to school on Thursday?"

The question held no threat, and Wallace stepped up and answered calmly. "Yes."

"Do you remember the box that he brought it in?"

Wallace thought a moment. "I think so, yeah. It was just a blue shoebox, kind of beat up. He punched some holes in the lid and wrote his and Vaclav's name on the side in magic marker."

Maggie moved closer to him. "Did you see that box during baseball practice here that day?"

"Yeah, sure. Vaclav had it on the dugout bench. Then when we went over to the batting cages, he brought it with him."

"He brought it with him," Maggie repeated. "And Mr. Trewitt—" She was now all but on top of the knot of people around the plate. "It's my understanding that Vaclav wasn't much of a hitter. Did you spend a lot of time with him in the batting cage that day?"

Trewitt considered, then replied. "Yeah. With all my guys. That's why we get the cages."

Maggie whirled and faced the Dodger players. "You boys, is that true? What your manager is saying? If Vaclav spent a lot of time taking batting practice in the cage on Thursday, just raise your hands."

She waited. Everyone waited. No hands went up and finally, finally, Trewitt relented. "The kid couldn't hit. I'm sorry, but that was it. I'd spent hours on him all year, and nothing took. I didn't want to waste the cage time."

Maggie nodded. "So you didn't spend time with him in the batting cage after all. Instead," she spun again, "Vaclav hung out for an hour in the shade by the snack bar, eating sno-cones, didn't he, Mrs. Moore?"

The pretty woman looked to Trewitt, down to the ground. "Yes."

"Then why didn't you contradict Mr. Trewitt just now when he told me that Vaclav was at the cages practicing?"

"I don't know. I didn't..." She stopped. "What difference would it make?"

"All the difference," Maggie said evenly. She turned up the baseline to the Dodger side, walked until she was abreast of Dorothy's son, and brought the flattened piece of cardboard around for him to see it. "Paul, do you recognize this? It's got your name on it. And Vaclav's."

The boy's eyes were those of a deer in headlights. Mr. Wallace came down from the other end of the line of players and stopped in front of her. "This was the box the snake was in," he said.

"Yes, it is," Maggie agreed.

Tully had come up beside her. "Where did you find this?" he asked.

She didn't turn to him, but to Dorothy Moore. "Where it had to be. Where Mrs. Moore had to get rid of it. Back over by the tracks. She couldn't use her home or any of the dumpsters here in case the police decided to check. So she just flattened it and ran it over by the tracks. With the rest of the debris over there, she thought no one would ever notice."

"That's not true!" Dorothy Moore was standing flat-footed, shell-shocked. "Why are you saying all this?"

And finally, the human enormity of the crime and her accusation of Dorothy Moore did seem to hit Maggie for the first time. Her shoulders slumped and she sighed, then walked up and stood in front of the pretty woman. "Gary Fallon gave you the idea, didn't he? And you thought about it and realized that if you could give that gift to Bob Trewitt—give him the City Championship—that he'd love you for it. He might even leave his wife...."

"No," Dorothy said. "It wasn't...."

"Yes it was." Maggie spoke gently, but did not yield. All around her, the silence was profound. "You were the only one who could get access to a baby rattlesnake on short notice. You admitted to Mike Tully that you knew snakes very well. You knew that Vaclav was going home with the snake that Thursday night, the same night you arranged for your son to be gone, the same night that your lover Bob Trewitt dropped off Vaclav on his way to the rendezvous you'd arranged at your house."

"No, that's not true. Bob and I..."

Trewitt took a step toward them both. "Dorothy, don't say anything. She's tricking you."

Maggie's voice was firm. "No, I'm not tricking anybody, Mr. Trewitt. Mrs. Moore is the only one who could have done this. All she had to do was what she did do—take one of the young rattlesnakes from the Science Center, put it in one of her own shoeboxes from home, then arrange to come and open the snack bar, where she knew that Vaclav would be hanging out, probably alone most of the time."

"No! I didn't.... you can't prove....."

"Dorothy, shut up. This can't be true," Trewitt explained to everyone. "She has nothing."

"I have all I need." Maggie turned to Tully. "You've got the other shoebox, the one that held the rattlesnake, don't you, Michael?"

Tully appeared grateful for something to say. "It's in evidence down at the station."

Maggie nodded. "Any forensics report will place that box in your possession, Mrs. Moore. The shoes that came in it are probably still in your closet."

Now Dorothy Moore's expression began to show a trace of fear. "No, Paul must have put the garter snake in a new box before he brought it to school."

His face a mask of confusion, her own son piped up. "No, I didn't, mom. I didn't do that."

Al Wallace was up with them, shaking his head. "He didn't, Dorothy," he repeated. "Paul had the box this woman is holding."

"How can you know that for sure, Al?" Dorothy shot the question back at him.

But he remained unruffled. "Because I wrote our classroom number on it, and here it is." He held up the cardboard. "E-Five."

Mrs. Moore's eyes darted back and forth, rested on her lover. She stammered. "Bob....I never thought it would kill him, just make him sick for a few days."

He stared open-mouthed at her in disbelief "Jesus!" He turned to Maggie and Tully. "I didn't know anything about this. I swear."

"Bob, don't desert me now. Please. I knew how much you wanted to win this game, to get another shot at Williamsport. It was all for you."

Trewitt swore again, kicked the dirt at this feet, brought his eyes up to stare at her in disbelief. "You *killed* a kid for me." He turned away in disgust.

Maggie ignored him and came back to her suspect. "How did you explain it to Vaclav, Mrs. Moore? Did you ask to see the snake, then tell him the old box had a hole in it? Or did he just not notice since the new box was close to the same color?"

Mrs. Moore's face had gone vapid and slack. A madwoman in panic. She spit out her lines. "He was a twelve-year-old boy. They don't notice anything. Everyone knows that. He didn't even look at it."

At which point Michael Tully stepped forward and placed her under arrest.

The Yankees won the Championship Game, 6-4, when Annie Lodge, batting in the number twelve position, delivered three doubles in her three at-bats, driving in all the runs scored by her team.

Though she wasn't chosen for the ALL-Stars, she was the Championship Game's Most Valuable Player.

When Michael Tully opened the door to the police station, having spent the better part of the day in the interrogation and booking process with Dorothy Moore, Maggie Chabon was waiting for him. She appeared fragile herself, and somehow shaken. As though they'd been friends forever, and might someday be more, they fell into an embrace.

When they separated, he looked down at her. "Technically," he said, "you're still a deputy. Now I know you've probably been a fine kindergarten teacher—hell, maybe the best ever kindergarten teacher—but maybe you'd want to consider a career move. I'm pretty confident I know where you could find some meaningful work."

"Do you think so, really, that I could do it? It's a lot more real than I ever thought."

"Oh, it's real all right. But this is where your talent lies. And here's an opportunity, listen up: knock knock. I just have one question," he added, "How did you know?"

Her eyes shone with humor. "When you've eliminated all the other possibilities, then whatever remains, however improbable, must be the solution."

Tully broke a thin smile. "It seems to me I've heard that somewhere before."

"I wouldn't be surprised. So in this case, Dorothy Moore was the only place where all the pieces fit—knowledge of the various timetables, access to the snake, the whole magilla. When I realized Trewitt and she were having an affair—"

"How did you know that, by the way?"

She shrugged. "That's why she'd arranged her son Paul to have a sleepover that night. It's also why Trewitt dropped his own son off at his house first, then volunteered to take Vaclav home—he lives a stone's throw from Mrs. Moore, remember? So it was obvious, actually, right?"

"Sure," Tully said, "obvious."

"Anyway," Maggie concluded, "after that, the whole thing fell together. It had to be her. I just needed to find that first shoebox, the last damning bit of evidence. And it was pretty close to exactly where it had to be."

"Had to be, huh?"

The amazing smile he'd first seen earlier that day was back again. It looked as though it was here to stay. "Well," she said, "it was, wasn't it?"

ROPA VIEJA

by Laura Lippman

The best Cuban restaurant in Baltimore is in Greektown. The natives think this makes perfect sense. They don't care what anyone else thinks.

It was the fourth day of August and Tess Monaghan was a block away from this particular restaurant when she felt that first bead of sweat, the one she thought of as the scout, snaking a path between her breasts and past her sternum. Soon, others would follow, until her T-shirt was speckled with perspiration, and the hair at her nape started to frizz. She wasn't looking forward to this interview, but she was hoping it would last long enough for her Toyota's air conditioner to get its charge back.

The Cuban Restaurant. Local lore about the place—and there had been much as of late—held that another name was stenciled over the door on the night of its grand opening. Havana? Plantain Plantation? Something like that. Whatever it was, the daily paper, the *Beacon-Light,* had gotten it wrong in the review and the owner had decided it would be easier to change the name than get a correction. After all, it had been a favorable review, with raves for the food and the novel-for-Baltimore gas station setting. If people wanted to think it was, simply, The Cuban Restaurant, it would become just that.

Live by publicity, die by publicity. That's what Tess Monaghan wanted to stencil above her door.

She slid her car into an empty space next to the old-fashioned gas pumps where attendants had so recently juggled a nightly crush of Mercedes, Cadillacs and Lincoln Navigators. Inside the cool dining room, a sullen bartender was wiping down a bar that showed no sign of having held a drink that day, and two dark-haired young waitresses stood near the coffee pot, examining their manicures and exchanging intelligence about hair removal. One preferred wax, the other swore by laser. If Tess had been there for lunch, that conversation would have killed her usually unstoppable appetite. But she wasn't, so it didn't.

She found the owner, Herb Marquez, in an office behind the bar. The glass in front of him might have held spring water, or it might have been something else. Whatever it held, the glass was clearly half-empty, at least in Herb Marquez's mournful eyes. His round face was as creased as a basset hound's, his gloom as thick as incense. Even his moustache drooped.

"You see that?" He waved a hand back at the empty dining room.

"I saw."

"A week ago, maybe—*maybe*—you could have gotten a table here at lunch if you were willing to wait 20, 30 minutes. We don't take reservations at lunch. At night—two weeks to get a reservation, three weeks on a weekend. That may happen in New York, but not in

Baltimore, almost never. I been in the restaurant business 40 years—I started as a bus boy at O'Brycki's crab house, worked my way up until I could open my own place, serve the food my mama used to make, only better. And now it's over because people think I poisoned the most popular guy in Baltimore."

"Most popular?" Tess had a reflexive distaste for all hyperboles. "Bandit Gonzales isn't even the most beloved Oriole of all time. He's just the flavor of the month."

It was an unfortunate choice of words. Herb Marquez winced, and he must have been thinking about the flavors he had served Bandit Gonzales, that subtle blend of spices and beef that went into *ropa vieja*. Literally, old clothes, but those old clothes had been credited with creating a new man out of the aging pitcher, who had been having the greatest season of his life.

Until last Sunday, when a sold-out crowd in Oriole Park at Camden Yards—not to mention the millions of fans who had tuned into the Fox game of the week—had watched him throw three wobbly pitches to the first batter, fall to his knees and give new meaning to the term "hurler."

"Well, I'd put him in the top 3," Marquez insisted. "After Cal Ripken Jr. and Brooks Robinson."

"And Boog," Tess said. "Boog Powell is still popular with fans, if only because of his barbecue stand at Camden Yards. Frank Robinson, of course. Maybe that catcher, the one who always led, 'Thank God I'm a Country Boy' during the seventh-inning stretch. Then there's Jim Palmer.

"Okay, fine, he ain't even in the top five, all-time. But he's the

197

only bright spot in the Orioles' piss-poor lineup this season and he thinks, and everyone else thinks, that he spent 24 hours puking his guts out because of my goddamn food. It was in all the papers. It was on 'Baseball Tonight.' Those late-night guys make jokes about my food. And now this guy's talking lawsuit! Like I got anything for anyone to take. I'm ruined."

He gave that last word its full Baltimore pronunciation, so it had three, maybe four syllables.

"Do you have an umbrella policy?"

"Yeah, sure. I'm so careful my liability policies have liability policies."

"So what do you care? Besides, I can't really see how Gonzales was damaged. I mean, other than the throwing-up part. I did hear he heaved so hard he broke a couple blood vessels under his eyes, but those heal. Trust me."

"He was on the last year of a three-year contract and had an endorsement deal pending. Local, but it was some guy who has a lot of those SUV franchises. Now he doesn't want him. Who does? The only endorsement Bandit is going to get is for Mylanta."

"Still, that's the insurance company's problem. Not yours. That's why you pay them premiums."

"Yeah, they'll take care of their money," Marquez said, "but they'll leave me and my reputation for dead. I gotta prove this wasn't my fault, if I ever want to get my business back."

"How can I help you do that? I'm a private investigator, not a health inspector."

Herb Marquez got up and walked over to the door, closing it

after a quick glance at his still-empty dining room.

"I don't trust no one, you understand? Not even people who worked for me four, five years. This is a jealous town, a jealous business. Someone wanted to hurt me, and they did it by pissing in Bandit Gonzales's dinner."

Tess made a face and a vow: She was never going to eat out again as long as she lived.

"Not literally," Marquez amended. "But someone doctored that meat. Forty people ate from that same pot of ropa vieja on Saturday, and only one got sick. It's not like I made it special for Bandit."

"You told the press you did."

"Yeah, well, it sounded nice. I wanted him to feel special."

Tess wasn't much of a baseball fan, but it occurred to her that a 35-year-old man with Latin lover good looks who earned $6 million a year for throwing a ball 95 mph probably felt a little too special much of the time.

But all she said was: "I pulled your inspections at the health department after you called me. You've had your problems here."

"Who hasn't? But there's a big difference between getting cited for a cook who's caught without a hairnet and serving someone rancid meat, or whatever it is people think I did. If I hadn't run out of the stuff, I could get it tested, prove it was fine when it left here. But it was gone, and the pot was washed before he tried to start that Sunday afternoon."

"Did he get take-out or did he eat here?"

"We delivered it special to him, whenever he called. That's

why I sent for you. Your uncle tells me you do missing persons, right?"

She didn't bother to ask which uncle, just nodded wearily. She had nine. each one capable of volunteering her for this kind of favor. Everyone in her family was promiscuous with her time.

"I had a busboy, Armando Rivera. He came from the Dominican. Claimed he played baseball there, I don't know. I do know he was crazy for the game, belongs to this informal league that plays in Patterson Park on weekends and evenings. This guy begged me for the right to take the food to Bandit. So, I let him."

"Every time?"

He nodded. "When he was on the road, we Fed-exed it to him. I'm guessin' Armando delivered the food to the guy at least six times. You see, the first time he came in, it was coincidental-like, the night before Opening Day, and he was homesick for the food he grew up with in Miami—"

"I know, I know," Tess said, and she had to restrain herself from making the kind of rotating wrist movement that a television director made to indicate a performer should speed up. Marquez was like a moony-eyed teenager, telling the story of his first love—basking in the details, thrilling at the mention of the cherished one's name.

"So he ate it the night before every start," Marquez finished, deflated. "And he told reporters about it, and people began coming here, because *ropa vieja* was the fountain of fuckin' youth. My food rebuilt that guy's arm, no less. And now lie thinks it ruined him. But I don't think it was the food. I think it was the bus boy."

"Armando Rivera." Tess had been a reporter before she

became a private investigator, and she knew how to sift the relevant details out of the tortured, mis-told narratives she heard every day. "Do you have an address for him? A phone?"

"He didn't have a phone."

"Okay, but he had to have an address. Don't you need that to do the paperwork for his W-2?"

Marquez hunkered down, like a dog prepared for a scolding. "He didn't have one of those either. See, that's why I have to work with you, instead of the cops. Look, the restaurant business has its own version of don't ask, don't tell. Armando Rivera showed up here this winter, saying he had lost his green card. I paid him in cash, he did his job. He was a good worker. At least, he was, until he walked out of here Saturday night with Bandit's food and never came back."

"No address, no phone, no known associates. How am I supposed to find him?"

"Hell, I don't know. That's why I need a private detective. He lived somewhere in East Baltimore, played ball in Patterson Park. Short guy, but strong looking, very dark skin."

"Gee, I guess there aren't too many Latinos in East Baltimore who fit that description." Tess sighed. This was going to be like looking for a needle in a haystack. No—for a single grain of cayenne in the *ropa vieja*.

Tess could walk to Patterson Park from her office, so she leashed her greyhound and headed over there as the sun was setting. It was uncomfortably muggy, and she couldn't believe anyone would be playing baseball on such a night, but a game was under way on the diamond, with more than enough men to field two teams.

And they were all Latino, Tess realized. She had noticed that Central and South Americans were slowly moving into the neighborhood. The first sign was the restaurants, Mexican and Guatemalan and Salvadoran, then the combination tiendas-farmacias-video stores soon followed. She had begun to hear snatches of Spanish on the streets, although her high school-rusty skills were not up to the task of grasping more than a word or two.

But to see 20, 30 men, gathered in one spot, calling to one another in a language and jargon that was not hers, was quite extraordinary. It meant stodgy Baltimore was capable of changing, and not always for the worse.

The players wore street clothes and their gloves were as worn as their faces, which ran the gamut from pale beige to coffee-dark. But these men were good, too, better than the over-competitive corporate types Tess had glimpsed at company softball games over the years. Their lives may be hard, but that only increased their capacity for joy. They played because it was fun, because they were good at it, and it pleased them to be good at something. Again and again, she watched the softball soar to the outfield, where it was almost always caught *Muchacho, muchacho, muchacho.* The center-fielder had an amazing arm, capable of throwing out a runner who tried to score from third on a long fly ball. And these guys were really fast, Tess noticed. They were wiry and quick, as drunk as six-year-olds on their own daring.

When the centerfielder was called out at third trying to

stretch a double, the players quarreled furiously, and a fist fight almost broke out. Silly to care so much about a game, Tess thought, and she was relieved when the combatants backed down.

The last out and dusk came almost simultaneously and the men gathered around a cooler, pulling out the cheapest local beer, Carling Black Label. Strictly illegal, but Tess imagined the cops in Southeast District had more important concerns than a few postgame beers. She sauntered over, suddenly aware there were no women here, not even as fans. The men watched her and the greyhound approach, and she realized she would not have any problem getting them to talk to her.

Getting them to speak truthfully, about the subject at hand—that was another matter.

"Hablan engles?" she asked briskly.

Almost all of them nodded, but only one spoke. "Si," said the centerfielder, a tall, broad-shouldered young man who wore a striped T-shirt and denim work pants. "I mean—yes, I speak English."

"You play here regularly?"

"Yes." She saw his face closing off, and realized that a strange woman, speaking in curt, officious tones, was not going to inspire confidence in this group.

"I have an uncle who owns a couple of restaurants in the area, and he's looking for workers. He's in a hurry to find people. He wanted me to spread the word, interview people at my office a few blocks from here. I'll be there from 9 to 5 tomorrow, if people want to stop by."

"We all got jobs," the spokesman said. "And not just in restaurants. I'm a——" he groped for the English word, and couldn't manage it. "I fix cars."

"Well, maybe some of you want better jobs, or different ones. Or maybe you know some people who are having trouble getting jobs—for whatever reason. My uncle's relaxed about some things. Here's my card. As I said, I'll be there tomorrow."

She handed him what she thought of as her "neutral" business card, a plain rectangle that listed only her name, address and office number, but made no mention of what she did there. The centerfielder took it noncommittally, holding it by a corner as if he planned to throw it down the moment she walked away. But Tess saw some bright eyes in the group, and hoped someone might take the bait. She left them to their Carling Black Labels. Conscious of their stares, she tried not to twitch too much when she walked away, but one hip was higher than the other, and she always wiggled a little, in spite of herself.

"Hey, lady," the spokesman called after her.

"Yes?" she turned expectantly, pleased the results were so swift.

"If your uncle plans on cooking tu pero, your dog, he better put some meat on it first."

Even the men's laughter sounded foreign to her ears. But it wasn't mean, or cruel. And she liked the implication that she didn't need any meat on her bones. She didn't.

The next day, she kept the office hours she had promised, but with little hope of visitors. She used the time to read everything she could about the "nausea incident" and was stunned by the sheer volume of baseball information on the Internet. She wandered into site after site, taking strange detours through stats and newspaper columns and something called "roto," which she thought might be about rotator cuff injuries, but turned out to be a site dedicated to rotisserie baseball, the fantasy league. There was simply too much information for her to make sense of, so she called her father, the biggest baseball fan she knew.

He couldn't have been happier if she had called to say she was going to marry a lawyer, move to the suburbs, have 2.2 children and a mini-van.

"You're working for Bandit Gonzales?" Patrick Monaghan asked breathlessly. It was the only time Tess had ever heard that starstruck note in her father's voice.

"Not exactly," Tess said. "But I need to understand why some-one might have wanted to make him sick last weekend."

"Hey, if I had thought of it, I might've poisoned the guy, although I'd rather make the owner throw up. In fact, I'd like to run the whole management staff over with my car, but I think it's too late to save this season."

"You're a fan, why would you want to hurt Gonzales?"

"I wouldn't, but his illness couldn't have been better timed in some ways. He got sick on July 30th."

His expectant silence told Tess this should have meaning for her, but it didn't.

"So?"

Mock-patient sigh. "July 31st is the trade deadline."

205

"Let me repeat: So?"

"Jesus, what do you do, just read the news sections of the paper? July 31st is the last day to make trades without putting guys on waivers. Teams like the Orioles, which ain't going anywhere, start dumping high-priced talent for prospects. The Mets—" as was his custom, her father appeared to spit after saying that team's name, for the 1969 Mets-Orioles World Series had been very hard on him. "The Mets were going to take Bandit to shore up their pitching roster. The Mets! I know it would be nice for Bandit to play for a team that was in the chase for the pennant, but I couldn't bear it, and I wasn't the only one.

"You mean other fans felt the way you did?"

"Jesus, the least you could do is listen to Oriole Baseball on WBAL. I thought I raised you better than that. Anyway, after he puked and checked himself into the hospital, the Mets got cold feet. They didn't want to take the chance it was something serious, and they were under the gun because of the deadline."

"Dad, I know you were joking about poisoning Bandit's food—" at least, Tess hoped he was. "But would someone have had something to gain from keeping him off the Mets?"

"The Atlanta Braves."

"Seriously, Dad."

"I was being serious." He sounded a little hurt.

"What about Bandit himself?"

"Huh?"

"Is there a reason he might not have wanted to go? Was there a downside to his contract with the Mets?"

"You're the private detective," her father said, still injured. "You find out. Go talk to him."

"Just go over to wherever Bandit Gonzales lives and say, 'Hey, by the way, did you make yourself puke?'"

"Yeah. Yeah." Her father's voice had a note of urgency she had never heard before. "But before you ask him that, would you get him to sign a baseball for me?"

The tricky part of looking for something is that sometimes you find it. Once Tess fixated on the idea that Bandit Gonzales was in the best position to doctor his own food, she quickly discovered all sorts of reasons why he would do it. Gonzales had bought property in the so-called Valley, not far from where Cal Ripken Jr. lived. He had taken out various construction permits and a behemoth of a house was under construction. Another hunch kicked in. Back downtown, at the state office building, she found he had recently incorporated. A check of newspaper archives indicated he was mulling a post-baseball future that included real estate ventures and other business deals. He had started a charity, too, and had a nice large endowment.

And opening a restaurant. They had even registered a name: Bandit Gonzales's Cuba Cafe.

He lived at the Harbor Court, a luxury hotel-condo that rose just a few blocks from Camden Yards. The water view was the expensive one, the ballpark view the one expected of a player. Bandit had both, in a corner unit that provided a broad expanse of harbor across the east-facing main rooms, and a sliver of ballpark from the master bath. Tess knew because she faked a need for the bathroom upon arriving, then quickly searched Bandit's medicine cabinet for Ipecac, or anything else that could produce vomiting on demand. She didn't find it, but that didn't change her mind. She went back to the living room where a bemused Bandit, unused to people making demands of him, was waiting. Well, waiting wasn't exactly right. He was sliding back and forth on an ergometer, a piece of work-out equipment that Tess knew better than she wished. A sweep rower in college. she still worked out on an erg. If you did it right, if you let the erg take you as far as you could go, you didn't need bad meat to make you throw up.

"You said you were from the health department?" He had no trace of an accent, but then—his family had migrated to Miami before he was born.

"No, not exactly. But I am looking into.... the incident."

Bandit didn't look particularly embarrassed. Then again, he had given interviews naked, so maybe throwing up in front of people wasn't such a big deal after all. He continued to slide in his seat on the erg, up and back, up and back.

"So for who?" he asked after a few more slides.

"Did you know," Tess sidestepped neatly, "that Johns Hopkins is doing all this research into new viruses? We're talking parasites, the kind of things you used to have to go to Mexico to get, showing up in food on this side of the border. I guess NAFTA had farther-reaching ramifications than we ever dreamed."

He stopped moving on the erg. His complexion had definitely taken on a greenish cast. "Really?

"Really."

"How can you know if you have a parasite?"

"I dunno," Tess shrugged.

"But you work for Hopkins."

"I didn't say that." And she hadn't.

"Still, you're looking for this parasite, right? You think I might have it?"

Another shrug.

"Fucking Jesus, Joseph and Mary." He bent forward, his head in his hands. He was a good-looking man, with bright brown eyes and glossy blue-black hair, and young by the world's standards. His flan-colored legs, left bare by filmy shorts, were thickly muscled, while his arms were long and slender, not as defined. Yet there was something odd about baseball, Tess decided. Because Bandit's sport considered him old, he was aging faster than a non-athlete might. His face was lined from years in the sun, his hair a little thin, as if his cap had rubbed bits of it away around the crown.

"Did you do it yourself," Tess asked, "or did you have help?"

He lifted his face from his hands. "What do you mean? Why would I give myself a parasite?"

"I don't think you intended to give yourself a parasite. But I think you sought someone's help last weekend because you didn't want to go to the Mets, and leave a city where you were planning on a future."

"Huh?"

"Or maybe it's as simple as your desire to open up a restaurant that will rival the one you made famous. I can see that. Why should someone else get rich because you eat there? If someone's going to make money off you, it should be you, right?"

"I was going to talk to Herb about a partnership in that," Bandit said, and he looked as if he might believe his own story. "I just didn't get around to it."

"Still, you weren't planning on leaving here anytime soon. You were building a house. You had a local charity. You were trying to put down roots."

Bandit began to massage his left arm, rubbing it with the unself-conscious gesture that Tess had seen in other athletes, and even dancers. They lived so far inside their bodies that they seemed to see them as separate entities.

"You don't know much about baseball, do you?"

"I know enough."

"What's enough?"

"I know that the Orioles won the World Series in 1966, 1971 and 1983. I know the American League has the DH. And I'm vaguely familiar with the infield fly rule."

Now Bandit was working his knees, rubbing one, then the other. They made disturbing popping sounds, but Bandit didn't seem to notice. He was like a guy tinkering on a car in his driveway, not because it needed work, but because that's what he did in his spare time.

"I'm guessing you don't know much about the *business* of baseball. Yeah, I was going to be sent to New York, in exchange for prospects. But my agent had let the Orioles owner know I'd be happy to be signed again when my contract was up at the end of the season. And I wasn't going to hold him up for a multi-year contract. Just one more year, at a good price. It was a good deal for everyone. Now I'm tainted as the meat that Herb sent over here. Look, I know he didn't do it on purpose, but he did it."

"Did you eat anything else that day?"

"No, because I felt pretty punky when I got up that morning. I shouldn't have tried to start, but I kept thinking I was going to get better."

It was Tess's practice to give out as little information as possible, but she needed to dish if she was going to get anything out of this interview. "Herb thinks the delivery guy might have done it."

Bandit rolled his shoulders in a large, looping shrug. "Then he shouldn't have sent someone new over here. Manny was a good guy. I signed a ball for him once. We spoke Spanish sometimes. The new one was kind of a jerk, his attitude came in the door about three feet in front of him. It was like he thought it was some damn social call, and he expected me to get him a beer, sit down and watch some television with him. He acted like he owned me. I couldn't get away from him fast enough. I thought maybe he was a little retarded."

"Retarded?"

He mistook her echo for a rebuke. "Oh yeah, you're not supposed to say that anymore. But, I mean, he was over 40 and he was a delivery boy. That's kind of sad, isn't it? And a real motor-mouth. Like I say, he was driving me nuts. It was 11 p.m. I just wanted to eat my supper and go to sleep, get ready for my start the next day."

"Does Harbor Court have a video system, for security?"

Another Bandit-style shrug, but forward this time. Tess wondered if he knew this movement made him look as if he were about to heave.

"I dunno. I don't think so. What good would it do? You think he spit in my meat on the elevator or something?"

Really, she was going to be a vegetarian before this was all over.

"Do people have to sign in? Log in their license plates?"

"The doorman's cool about my deliveries. He always let Manny leave his car in the drive, because he was in and out fast. Hey—" he noticed she was moving toward the door. "Don't you want a photo or something?"

"Maybe for my dad. His name is Pat."

He walked over to a sleek modern desk and extracted a glossy photo of himself from a thick folder, signed it with a practiced hand.

"And for you?"

"I gave up keeping scrapbooks after I was forced to step down as the president of the John Travolta Fan Club, West Baltimore chapter. *Saturday Night Fever* era, not *Pulp Fiction.* It was all quite sordid."

Bandit gave her a quizzical look, like a god who had just discovered the world he inhabited was polytheistic. "If I told you I had an ERA under 4, would it mean anything to you?"

"No, but I would pretend that it did."

The doorman proved to be a nosy little gossip of a man. Tess wouldn't want to live next door to him, but she wished every investigation yielded witnesses like this one. He not only remembered the motor-mouth delivery boy, he remembered the car he drove, a

Porsche 911, fairly new.

"You gotta be kidding," Tess said. "A Porsche?"

"Would I make that up? Guy got out in a rush, handed me his keys like he expected me to park it for him. I told him to just go up, I'd watch his precious wheels. Hey, get this—he even had vanity plates—ICU."

"As in Intensive Care Unit?"

"Maybe. Although in my experience, doctors drive Jags, while the lawyers who sue them pick Porsches. Hey do you know the difference between porcupines and Porsches?"

"Yes," Tess said, leaving before he could deliver the punch-line. She avoided lawyer jokes, on the grounds that they were just too easy.

Everything was too easy. Or so she told herself when she ran the plates, and found they belonged to Dr. Scott Russell, who kept an office in a glossy new professional building. Too easy, she repeated, when she drove to the address and saw the Porsche parked outside. Too easy, she thought, as she sat in the waiting room and pretended to read *People* magazine, watching a white-jacketed doctor come and go, chatting rapidly to his patients. He had a smug arrogance that would be charming in doctor, but off-putting in a delivery boy. A motor-mouth, the doorman had said. As if he expected me get him a beer, Bandit had said. The doctor, dressed as a delivery boy, had not been ready to surrender his place in society.

The only surprise was that he wasn't a surgeon, but an opthamologist in one of those new-fangled LASIK centers, a successful one judging by its clogged waiting room. "ICU"—now she got it. And wished she hadn't.

By 2:45, after several surgeries, which had been broadcast live on a large-screen television in the waiting room much to Tess's discomfort, the busy buzz of the "Visual Liberation Services" had shifted into low gear. Tess approached the desk and asked for Dr. Russell.

"It's almost 3 p.m.," the receptionist said nervously. "He never takes appointments at 3 p.m. on Wednesdays."

"I'm not here for an appointment. And if the doctor doesn't want to see me now, I'll come back with the Baltimore City Police faster than one of your lasers can slice open an eye."

"But it's almost 3 p.m. and it's *Wednesday*," the receptionist repeated.

"I don't see the significance."

"It's deadline. He's never to be disturbed just before deadline. The last girl who went in there after 2:30 on a Wednesday got fired."

"Luckily, I don't work for him."

Tess began walking toward the doctor's office, curious to see if anyone would try to stop her. The receptionist simply watched in horror, as if she were heading into the lion's den.

When she pushed open the door to Dr. Russell's office, he was on the phone, one of those hand-free headsets, his back to her as he leaned back in the window, feet on the windowsill.

"—no, no, Delino is good, I swear. You always think I got inside information because I'm a doctor. I might know if his eyes were bad, but I don't know anything about his back. I just don't need run production as much as I need pitching, so I'm willing to unload him for a closer. Look, you're not even in the hunt, so what do you care? It's bad sportsmanship to turn down a trade just because you think it's going to hurt me."

"Hey," Tess called out, trying to make herself heard over his rapid-fire speech. "I see you. Get it?"

He turned around, his features almost contorted with rage. He had a narrow face, with a pointy chin and eyes so tiny that Tess wasn't sure he was suitable for his own surgery. "I am BUSY," he said. "I know everyone who comes in here thinks I have to do every step of the process, but really, the other doctors here are quite competent to do intake."

"I've got 20-20 vision," Tess said. "And I'm here because a doorman with awfully good vision saw your car last Saturday night, when you dropped off some food at Harbor Court. Here's a tip: If you want to pull off felonies, try not to do it in Porsches with vanity tags."

"I've got to call you back," he said into his headset, switching it off. Then to Tess, not so loudly, but just as quickly: "Felony—what felony? The guy's fine. So he threw up a little, big deal. No one was hurt. I love Bandit Gonzales. I'm counting on him to post another win when he starts tomorrow night. I mean, I put everything on the line for this guy. And I'm a doctor, I knew what I was doing."

"I'm not sure he sees it that way."

"Look, I was in a desperate spot. It's August, and I'm in first place, but only by a few points. I'm talking $5,000. That's a lot of money."

In fact, $5,000 was, Tess knew from reading the literature in the lobby, what Visual Liberation Services charged for 20-20 vision, an operation that took almost 15 minutes to perform.

"I'm not sure I'm following you.

"I'm in roto," the doctor said. "Rotisserie baseball. I've been in the 'No Lives' league for almost 15 years and I've never fucking won. Never even ended in the money. Bandit Gonzales changed that for me. I picked him up cheap, in our draft. No one expected him to have a good year, and he ends up 11-3 in August. It was genius on my part, I tell you. Genius. But if he goes to the Mets—" He was getting visibly agitated, shaking and sweating, swinging his arms.

"I still don't get it."

"We're an American League-only roto. When our players get traded to the National League, that's just our dumb shit luck." Turning quite red, he jumped up from his chair, stomping in a little circle around his desk. "Do you understand? I could still win, as long as Gonzales stayed in the American League. If the trade had been the Yankees or the Mariners, I would have been fine. But it was the Mets! The Mets, the Mets, the fuckin' Mets. All my life, since 1969, I've hated the Mets and they're still finding ways to screw me."

He was now hopping around the room, like Rumpelstilskin in his final rage, and Tess wondered if he would simply fly apart. But all he did was bang his knee on his desk, which forced him to sit down and rub it.

"How much did you pay Armando Rivera to give you the bag and disappear?"

"Two thousand dollars."

"So you'll really only win three, if you win. I don't know roto.

Do they throw you out for felony assault?"

Russell looked thoughtful. "I dunno. They haven't thrown me out for lying and cheating. But then—that never got me anywhere. That trade I was just about to make, when you came in? I do know the Orioles team doctor, and I do know Delino's probably on the DL. But I had to do it by 3, so you fucked me over good. I hope you know that."

Two days later, Tess went back to the baseball diamond, saw the same men in their nightly game. The weather wasn't cooler, exactly, but it held a promise of fall, as August often does. They played even better in the slightly sharper air, perpetual boys of summer.

Between innings, she signaled to the centerfielder, who loped over warily.

"What's the score?" she asked.

"Quatro-tres," he said. "Four-three. But I think I will get a home run at my next at-bat. Maybe I'll call it, like your Babe Ruth did. That would be something, wouldn't it?"

"You know a guy named Armando Rivera? Dominican, plays ball here sometimes?"

"Maybe."

"Well, tell him Herb Marquez said all is forgiven. But also tell him that Marquez didn't know he got paid for letting the guy borrow his jacket and his order. He might want to keep that secret, seeing as how things worked out, the guy going to jail and all. Luckily, Mr. Laser Vision never really looks at anyone. He couldn't pick Armando

217

out of a line-up."

"Okay." He turned to go.

"By the way—" he turned back, hopeful. "What did you do with the $2,000?"

"I don't know what you're talking about. I'm a mechanic."

"Okay, you're a mechanic. But remember, whatever you do— it's only a game."

"At least I play," he said. "I don't move men around on paper, like little dolls, and pretend that I own them."

He ran back to home plate, with a springy, athletic stride that Tess envied. The days were getting shorter, and so were the games. They'd be lucky to get nine innings in tonight.

THE SHOT

by Mike Lupica

"**Y**ou know it would kill him," she was saying, "if he even knew we were together."

Tommy Maywood sipped some of his beer. "What doesn't kill him?" he said. "I was out in the bullpen the other night, just shooting the shit after assface pinchhit for me? Soon as I get out there, Delroy hits the home run to win the game, and everybody goes crazy because the goddam ball practically lands at our feet. And your husband? The tragic figure? He walks past us, up to the wall, so he can see the pitcher better. Watches him all the way until the kid is gone into the third base dugout. You ask anybody out there. Christ, it gives us all the fucking creeps, like he was in some kind of trance or something."

Jenny Marr said, "It doesn't take much."

"Are you kidding?" Tommy said. "A stiff breeze is usually enough."

She reached over, picked up the cigarette he had going in the ashtray, and took a drag of it. "You never did seem to understand," she said, "that it was a hell of a lot more fun being you."

219

"Yeah, yeah," he said. "He never gets to live it down. But you know what? I never lived up to it after that, not really."

It was always about him. What was the old joke? Enough about me. What do you think about me? It actually made Jenny smile.

"What's so funny?" he said.

"You," she said. "Or your pain. I can't decide which."

"Aw, c'mon, Jen," he said. "He's got to let it go. Eventually you've got to let shit go, don't you? Or does he plan to stay this fucking depressed for the rest of his fucking life?"

"So far," she said, "so good."

"He ever ask about us?" Tommy said idly, not looking at her, watching the girl serving them drinks lean over the table next to them.

"Never."

"You ever get the idea that he suspects?"

"He's in his own world sometimes." She shrugged. "Most of the time."

"Anyway," he said, "you've got to help me out here, because you're probably the only one who can sell this to him. It'll be worth it, believe me. Joey? My agent? He says we could make a million just over the winter, and that's before he even talks to the book guys."

Jenny said, "I read somewhere that one of the local sportswriters is planning a book about it. On account of next year being the anniversary."

"Plan this," Tommy said, making a motion like he was grabbing himself under the table. "If he doesn't have the guy who hit it and the guy who threw it, he's got shit."

Jenny watched him, full of his latest money grab, because it was always about the money with him; he was on fire with it, the way he would be when they were all kids in Norfolk—Triple-A adults, Bud used to call them, almost ready for the bigs, and he'd convince them to drive up to New York after a day game on Sunday, hitting the George Washington Bridge about 10 o'clock, partying all night, even on a Sunday, crashing at this cheap Holiday Inn over on 57th Street, Bud and Jenny in one room, Tommy and whichever girl he'd picked up along the way going at it in the room next door. Even at 20 he had them fooled with his Opie looks, red hair and freckles: the Kansas City boy in the big city. He'd smile and say, I've got to have my strange, meaning strange pussy, as if that explained everything, all the girls. Bud said one night, in front of him, that Tommy needed to get his ashes hauled the way the rest of us needed oxygen.

"....only the best card shows," he was saying. "Then fifty grand, to split, for some speeches and personal appearances. He says we should work up a little act, like Branca and Thomson finally did. You know who Branca and Thomson are?"

Jenny said, "The first shot 'heard round the world.'"

"When they were old," Tommy said, "they'd go to golf tournaments and dinners and Branca, acting pissed off, would sing, 'Because of you...' And then Bobby Thomson, all happy, would come in with '...there's a song in my heart.' I saw them at the Boston baseball writers' dinner one time. Crowd ate it up."

Jenny said "You want to have one more? I should be getting back soon."

221

Tommy reached over with one hand and covered hers, gestured to the waitress with the cute ass with the other.

"Listen," he said. "I know it's sucked being him, even if he did end up with you. But for Chrissakes, Jen, we're moving up on ten fucking years. Isn't there some kind of statute of limitations on feeling this goddam sorry for yourself?"

Bud Marr, his dumb floppy fishing cap down over his eyes, watched them hold hands from across Madison.

"I'm going out for a walk," she said. "If you get hungry, why don't you just order in Chinese or something?"

"When do you think you'll be back?"

"I might go to a movie. That chick flick with Emma Thompson you said you'd only see at gunpoint"

He'd waved goodbye from behind the sports section of the *Times.*

"Love you," she'd said.

He waited until he heard the elevator doors close, then took the steps from the fifth floor of the old brownstone on E. 69th two at a time. He saw that she hadn't taken a cab, was walking west. He gave her a block lead and than started following her.

When he saw it was Tommy Maywood waiting for her at the outdoor table, he wasn't even surprised. Maybe this was exactly the way it was supposed to work out. A destiny deal, him coming back to New York, ending up with the goddam Mets. Maybe this was exactly the way it was supposed to end.

He watched them get another round and left, not even caring

if they left together, because if it wasn't this time it would be the next time. He walked back to the apartment they were sub-leasing for the rest of the season and found the tape he'd hidden from her, in the equipment bag he'd brought back from Japan. He poured himself a Scotch, shut off all the lights in the living room, set all the locks so he'd hear her keys in all of them—that way she couldn't surprise him when she finally did come home. Put the tape in the VCR and hit the play button.

Tomorrow he'd follow through with Shaheen, the backup shortstop, about how you went about getting a gun.

Jenny would go through his shit from time to time, looking for one more tape that she hadn't burned or thrown in the garbage, losing it sometimes, saying he was starting to scare her that he'd gone flying past what the doctors called clinical depression to some morbid place where the doctors couldn't reach him and neither could she.

The first year after, before he hurt his arm, he'd bullshit the reporters when they'd have the nerve to ask him about it, joke that there was no reason for him to watch a tape of the game.

"Why should I?" he'd say. "The damn thing ends the same way every single time."

That was before everything in his life became bullshit, even Jenny now.

He'd edited this one down to just the bottom of the ninth, coming in where Costas was saying, "Joe, this has a chance to be the most dramatic ending in baseball history."

And Morgan saying, "Only if Haywood hits one out."

"People have always said that nothing could ever come close to Bobby Thomson's home run off Ralph Branca in '51."

"And nothing will if Bud Marr can keep his friend in the ballpark here."

"Not just friends," Costas said, "close friends, from college at the University of Miami right through the minors, until Marr was traded to the Red Sox two years ago."

Getting closer all the time, Bud thought.

"Bottom of the ninth, Game Seven, the Red Sox this close to their first world championship since 1918," Costas said now. Bud knew the rest of this solo by heart, all about all the waiting in Boston, all the disappointments, Costas going on about a mythical place called Red Sox Nation, from Block Island to Kennebunkport, so he hit the mute button as they came in for a closeup of his face, with the stupid little goatee he was wearing that year, the one Jen thought was so cute.

Costas was talking about how the Sox had blown a three games to one lead in the Series, how the Mets had come back to win both the last two games in extra innings, how Bud Marr had been the starter and winner in Game 1 and Game 4 and now was being asked to get the last out of the Series, out of the bullpen, in Game Seven, with Boston trying to hold on to a 7-4 lead. Normally it would have been their closer, Sammy Cardenal, facing Tommy Maywood with everything on the line, but Cardenal had hurt his shoulder on the play before, a collision at first base.

And Cody, the setup man, had made such a mess of Game 6

that the manager, that hothead Mazzo, had screamed in the club-house later that Cody would never pitch another fucking game for the Boston Fucking Red Sox.

Mazzo had told Bud to warm up when the inning started, just in case, and now the Mets had one run in and the bases loaded and on the tape, you could see Mazzo stuffing the ball in Bud's blue Rawlings.

"You got the best arm I ever saw, son," Mazzo said that night. "And, by God, I know it's got one out left in it."

"You got one out, don't you?"

Bud saw himself grinning on the TV, everybody would talk about that later, tying to look brave even though he knew he didn't have shit, his arm was dead in the bullpen and everybody out there knew it. He shot one of Mazzo's dumb-ass lines back at him as a way of answering the question.

"Does a Pope shit in the woods?"

He put the sound back up now, for the good parts, rubbing his fingers gently over the tattoo of Jen's name, on the inside of his right wrist.

Costas: "Bud Marr looks like twenty-five going on fifteen, doesn't he, Joe?"

Morgan: "Maybe that's why he doesn't ever seem to get tired. The guy threw a hundred and twenty-seven pitches just three days ago."

Strike one, ball one, ball two.

There was a shot of the crowd at Shea Stadium, everybody on their feet, the announcers actually shutting the fuck up for a moment. He closed his eyes, even though he could still see every-thing that was happening on the screen. Him looking around at all the runners. They'd cut to the Mets dugout right after that, almost all of them on the top step. Then to a shot of Mazzo in the Sox dugout, down at the end of their bench, apparently thinking no one could see the cigarette he was trying to hide.

Now Bud opened his eyes, for the quick shot of Jenny in the stands, wearing her hair longer that year, her eyes wide, her hands under her chin, as if praying.

Then back to the shot from the centerfield camera, Bud going into his full windup, Parker, the catcher, settling up outside.

Costas: "Here's the pitch."

Which wasn't even close to being outside. Which was letter high and flatter than home plate. Tommy used to call them mattress pitches when they were in the minors, stealing the line from Reggie Jackson.

Mattress pitch 'cause you laid all over the sonofabitch.

Bud Marr hit the mute button again, so it was all some kind of spooky silent film now, everything that happened next, all the quick cuts from the field back to the insanity in the stands. There was the Red Sox rightfielder, Pokey Moon, No. 28, back as far as be could go, right hand on the blue wall, setting himself for a leap he thought he could make and then knew would be a waste of time. Then a shot of Tommy, rounding first, realizing the ball was gone, throwing his arms up in the air, jumping for joy.

Then the picture of Bud Marr himself, one of the most famous pictures in baseball history, on his knees behind the pitcher's mound, still staring at the rightfield wall while all hell broke loose around him in the infield, the Mets running past him as if he wasn't there, following Tommy Maywood around the bases, while that stupid giant funhouse apple they had behind the outfield wall at Shea rose up as the fireworks went off.

Sound up.

"....the second shot in the city of New York 'heard round the world,'" Costas was shouting.

Bud drank some Scotch and watched as Tommy Maywood started to make it from third to home, through his own teammates and some of the fans who'd made it past the cops and horses.

He heard Jenny's key then, first in the middle lock, then the deadbolt.

"No movie?" he said, back on the couch, tape stuffed safely back in the bag.

"I decided it would be too depressing."

She was wearing a white man's shirt that looked as clean and pressed as when she'd gone out, tight jeans, those chunky black Doc Martens she liked. She still smelled of cigarette smoke.

He looked at her, how put-together she was, and wondered if they'd had time for a fast one somewhere, maybe Tommy's apartment over on 81st. Picturing the two of them together the way he had for a week since Tommy's phone number had accidentally shown up on their caller I.D. before Jenny had rushed out one afternoon forgetting to delete it.

He had put the Braves game on. "What'd you do?"

She was making herself busy, opening a bottle of

Chardonnay. "Barnes & Noble. Latté at Starbucks. It's only taken a few weeks, I'm back to being a yuppie princess." She sat down at the other end of the couch. "What about you?"

"Been watching the History Channel. Great orators week. Fight them on the beaches. Fight them in the National League East."

They sat there, all the usual silence between them, now this lie squeezed in there, too, the silence as big as the fucking ocean. It had been growing, they both knew it, through all the shit years, the first surgery, the rehabbing in the minors, the knocking around from team to team, finally Japan. And the three-months at Silvermine, up in Connecticut, a vacation only he and Jen knew about, the Silvermine Care Center, when the shrink she made him start seeing in Minneapolis started talking about clinical depression and even that bipolar thing Mike Tyson had, which sounded to Bud like the the main event. You've got to examine your growing need for an audience with these episodes, the shrink said.....

"I was thinking," he said, "I'm gonna talk to Tommy tomorrow, tell him what the hell, we should all get together."

He just wanted to see what happened if he brought his name into the room with them.

"Really?" she said, giving him a surprised took with her eyes, then looking away as she rearranged the pillows behind her.

"Yeah. Maybe next week after we get back from St. Louis. I think there's a day game on Wednesday, against the Expos. Get some dinner, have some drinks and some laughs. Be like old times."

"You said you two had been pretty much avoiding each other since your first day back."

"We have," he said. "But I've been thinking about that, too." He grinned. "There's just too much between us to just ignore it. Don't you think?"

He picked up his glass, leaned forward, clicked it with hers.

"To old times." he said.

"You really want to do this?" Jenny said, watching him.

"Yeah," Bud said. "I do." He smiled and said, "I really want to do this."

The backup shortstop, Shaheen Cadberry, acted surprised when Bud had first asked him about the gun. Not that he wanted one, Shaheen said, just that he didn't have one already.

"How do I go about finding a gun?" Shaheen had said in the clubhouse that day, both of them there before anybody else. He had made his high-pitched voice deeper, talking loudly, imitating Bud asking him the question.

Bud jerked his head around, making sure they were still alone, that none of the clubhouse guys were around.

Shaheen smiled, showing off the two gold teeth he had in front, one on top, one on the bottom. "Relax, baby," he said. "I'm just playin' which you." He had his hair in cornrows, and what looked like about half the diamond district on 47th St. around his neck. "How do you get a fuckin' piece? Sheeit, next you'll be asking me how to find you some beef, even with that fine-lookin' wife a yours at home."

In the time Bud had been away from the big leagues, beef was how a lot of the young guys talked about girls now, except for

229

Tommy, who still called it strange. Constantly. Even back in the minors they'd all imagined Tommy Maywood with this incredibly long checklist, types of women he wanted to screw in his life before his dick fell off. They'd be in some bar in some jerkwater minor-league town, and Tommy would leave with a female cop, or emergency-room nurse or aerobics instructor or local anchor girl, and the rest of them would laugh and make a checking-off motion, like, okay, now he can move from cops or anchor girls to the next category on the list. Once even a girl in a wheelchair, in Syracuse...

"...you need this for *now,* you don't mine my askin'?" Shaheen had said.

"Protection," Bud said.

Shaheen laughed, a he-he-he sound. "'You know what they say, Bud Man—"

"What do they say?"

"A .22 a lot safer than a rubber."

Bud had laughed along with him then, not wanting to sound too anxious.

That was last Friday. In the clubhouse now, Shaheen pulled Bud aside and said, "I talked to Jesus. He was down in Atlantic City, on some personal, but he back now."

"Jesus?" Bud said, pronouncing it the way Shaheen had, "Hay-soos."

"I tol' you about Jesus last week," Shaheen said. "He's the one who can usually get you a piece in thirty minutes or less, else it's free, like your Dominos." Shaheen nodded. "He said he might meet us after the game. I let you know."

Bud went over to his locker and changed into a grey Mets t-shirt, the logo still looking as if it should belong to somebody else, his running shoes, black Nike running shorts, went outside to do what he usually did in the afternoon before a night game, run some laps around the ballpark, the tacky orange-and-blue all around him, wondering how he could have ended up here with that dink, knuckle-curve he'd taught himself in Japan for fun, at least until they put him into that blowout against the Yomuri Giants and nobody could hit the fucking thing.

He ran along the blue outfield walls, in front of the place in dead-center where the apple still was. Every time it came up, like some weird jack-in-the-box he imagined grinning at him, he thought about watching it the night of Tommy's home run, staring at it, like he was hypnotized, still on his knees, until Gary Cabrera, the Red Sox first baseman, picked him up, saying, "You got to get out of here."

Looking at him with the same kind of pity people had ever since, even in Japan.

Goddam, he hated that apple.

Nine years, less two months, he thought, running easy now, nothing ever wrong with his legs, amazingly clear-headed, seeing the whole thing play out, knowing what he had to do as well as he knew the tape of the bottom of the ninth. Nine years of being treated like the worst bum in baseball, worse than Branca, even worse than Bill Buckner, the poor crippled bastard who'd let that ball roll through his legs when the Red Sox had blown the World Series back in 1986.

Branca was a sweetheart, he'd met him once in spring train-

231

ing, Vero Beach, when the Dodgers were giving him a look. They were sitting in the little clubhouse there, in the middle of the whole complex, like some kind of happy-making Magic Kingdom of baseball when Lasorda was still the manager, and finally Bud opened up to him a little bit about it, trying to explain how he had this radar finally, knowing when strangers were going to bring it up, when they weren't.

"It's not what they say," the old man said. Branca was bigger than he looked in pictures, but had this sweet way about him, gentle almost. "It's what they don't say that kicks the shit out of you."

Bud asked him what he told the ones that did something.

"That it was one pitch in one ballgame played a hell of a long time ago," Branca said.

Nine years going on ten. Old Dodger fans, the ones from '51 still alive, never got over Branca the way Red Sox fans never got over Buckner. Only he was worse than Buckner now with Red Sox fans, Hitler, Bud used to tell himself, to the other guy's Mussolini. The game was already tied when the ball went through Buckner. As bad as it was, it was still just the ending to Game Six, the Red Sox had a chance in Game Seven. There was no chance after Bud threw his mattress pitch to Tommy Maywood, with the Sox one out away.

He ran in front of the rightfield wall, where Pokey Moon had waited to make his leap. Did he read somewhere that Buckner and Mookie Wilson were making appearances together now? Buckner even signing "Oops" or "Sorry" on pictures of him reaching down for the ball? How pathetic was that?

Did he need the money that much?

Sorry? Bud was sorry every day for nine years, even in Japan,

232

kids waiting outside the ballpark in Tokyo, all over the league with perfect photographs of him on his knees. Of course it was a thousand times worse in the States. Branca was right. It didn't matter whether they said something or not. But he'd know when they were going to say something. He'd see it in the way they'd come up to him shy-like, a little tip of the head, not thinking there were sirens going off..

You're probably tired of hearing this.

Oh no, he'd want to say, I fucking live to talk about it.

Or: You're not going to believe this, but I was sitting out in rightfield that night.

No kidding. Really? That's fascinating. Did you keep the ticket stub?

Bud always wanted to say, Oh, so you're one of the eight-hundred thousand people who were at the game.

Sometimes he'd run into beered-up Red Sox fans in a bar, the assholes who were never going to let it go, the kind who'd tell him that he'd ruined their lives.

Sometimes Bud, in a quiet voice, just because he couldn't walk away every time, would say, "No, just my own."

He had won twenty-one games his first year with the Red Sox, nineteen the World Series year. The next spring he tried to throw everything 200 mph and blew out his elbow. Sat out a year. The Red Sox released him and then came the bullpen tour. Cubs and Astros and Brewers. Dodgers for about twenty minutes before he blew out the shoulder once and for all and had the rotator cuff surgery. Shoulder surgery. That's when the phone stopped ringing for good.

He finally signed with the St. Paul Saints, an independent team, got lit up one night, went back to the motel on the other side of the river, had an episode. There had been other ones before it, one at a hotel in Houston, one in the garage of that house he and Jen rented in the valley when he was with the Dodgers. But Minneapolis, that was the worst one yet, the one that officially put him at Silvermine, which he always thought sounded more like a country club than the nut-house.

He spent the rest of the season there. Jenny would come on weekends. It was that time, in there, when he was sure she started seeing other guys. One of the therapists asked how Bud knew and he said, "She finally seems happy again...."

"Hey," a voice said from behind him.

Bud had stopped in left-center, hands on his knees, feeling the dull ache that had been there for a couple of weeks, the one that made him sure that this time the shoulder was going for good.

It was a groundskeeper, a thin old black guy, wearing a faded New York Giants cap, the same "NY" logo the Mets used.

Bud said "Hey yourself."

"Member me?"

"Don't tell me, you were here that night."

He was in his 60s, maybe even older than that. He nodded and said, "I'm the one picked up the ball."

Bud did remember. "You're the one who gave it back to Tommy."

The man put out a hand. "Winston Maurice."

Bud said, "How you doin', Winston?"

"Tired a doin'. This is my last summer. Retirin' to North Carolina, where I come from. Plan to sit on my porch, only listen to baseball when I want to, on the radio, like I did when I was a boy."

Bud said to Winston Maurice, "You coulda retired a long time ago, if you'd sold that ball to some rich nitwit instead of just handing it over."

"S'pose so," the old man said. "But I feel the same way now I did then. It just wouldn't've felt right, getting' rich off what happened to you." He took off the Giants hat, showed off snow-white hair against skin the color of coal. "Read somewheres once that nobody even knows what happened to that ball Bobby Thomson hit. Just disappeared. That always seemed to me the way it should be.

"Anyways," he said. "You gots work to do. I just wanted to say hello, tell you I'm glad you made it back."

Even the nice ones wanted to talk about it.

"One more shot," Bud Marr said.

He made a gesture that took in the whole ballpark.

"One more shot," he said, "at the scene of the crime."

He ran hard across the wide expanse of the outfield, all the green, towards the first base dugout. Maybe Shaheen had firmed it up with Jesus for after the game, so Bud could take care of his personal once and for all.

"Excuse me?" Bud said.

"We tour," Tommy said. "What that's rap singer? Eminem? We're the M&M of baseball. Marr and Maywood. I'll give you top billing."

They were in the players lounge, across from the trainer's room. Tommy had shown up late, as always, a couple of minutes before batting practice was supposed to start, looking as if he hadn't slept. Or maybe he was late today because Jen had waited for Bud to leave for the park, earlier than usual that day, about one-thirty in the afternoon.

Bud said, "We go on a tour? You and me?"

Tommy nodded, excited, the words tumbling out of him, as if he wanted to explain it to Bud all at once. "One last score, for both of us," he said. "And it's not like we can't use it. I watch you rubbing your arm when you think nobody's watching. Besides, it's not like those rotten melons you're throwing up there are going to get you five more years up here..."

"Thank you," Bud said.

Tommy acted as if he didn't hear. Two things I've never done well, he told Bud once, listen and give a shit.

"But you know something? You're probably going to last longer than I am. You see the way I've been swinging the bat? Some nights I can't catch up with dink fastballs, in the 80s. The Mets extending my contract for next year is a mercy deal, just because of the anniversary." He took a deep breath. "We only do the top shows. Joey—my agent?—he's talking to *Sports Illustrated* about an exclusive, to run sometime before the actual anniversary. We agree as part of the contract not to give interviews to anybody else. Joey thinks we can parlay that into a book deal, maybe even an HBO movie." Tommy lit a Marlboro Light, Jenny's brand.

"You're serious," Bud said.

"Serious as a hard-on."

"You want us to be a team now?"

"Listen to me, will you? Before you go all wounded-soldier on me. You never made any, money, not after... Not after. I've pissed most of mine away. Joey really thinks that over the next year, we can clear a million apiece, maybe two, if we play this thing right. He's even talking to ESPN about a radio show."

"So I can take calls from all the ones who want me dead."

Tommy waved smoke away, exasperated. Bud noticed how old he was starting to look around the eyes, how tired, even as he was trying to be the peppy schemer he was when they were riding buses. He looked older than thirty-eight. What was the line from the Indiana Jones movie? It's not the years, it's the mileage.

"God almighty, Bud," he said. "Don't you get it? We've always been a team, whether you wanted it that way or not. Whether you were even fucking talking to me or not. It's the way things fell. The way things are. It's not about fair or unfair, just the way they are. You throw it, I hit it. Mookie hit that dribbler, Buckner did the wicket deal. Why don't you put it to work for you, instead of letting it eat you up every day of your goddam life?"

"Let me think about it, okay?" Bud said.

"Just don't take too long, Joey says he wants to start booking some of this shit now."

Bud grinned, more to himself, thinking this actually played right into it.

"I'll tell you what," he said. "Let's you and Jenny and me go out and kick this thing around. Next week maybe, after we come back from St. Louis. There's an afternoon game, I checked. We'll have

237

dinner and then bounce around uptown, like the old days. Jenny was just saying that she hasn't seen you since we've been back, she'd love to get together."

Tommy looked off. "I'll bet she's as pretty as ever,"

"Prettier."

"It's a date," Tommy said.

Bud said, "Don't worry, I'll set the whole thing up."

He actually got into a game the next night, against the Cubs, before he and Shaheen drove over to the Bronx, a place called Jimmy's, to meet Jesus. Bud asked why he even needed to go, why Shaheen couldn't take the money and pick up the gun for him, but Shaheen said Jesus had his ways. Bud had heard some of the Spanish guys talking about Jimmy's and actually wondered what it was like inside, but he just waited in the passenger seat of Shaheen's car, a neat little BMW. Even guys like Shaheen Cadberry, who maybe got into forty games a year, maybe a few more as a defensive replacement, got to act high-priced, bigtime, even if they were bare-ly making the major league minimum the way Bud was.

Shaheen talked the whole way over from Shea about that night's game. The Mets had been behind 7-1 when Bud got the call in the top of the third; he figured it was just going to be more mop-up shit. But then he got out of second and third, one out, without the Cubs scoring any more runs. He threw his slop pitch to strike out their big home run guy, Agape, and the crowd got into it a little bit, and for the next three innings, it was like the old days for him, put-ting the ball where he wanted to even if there wasn't much on it, holding them to just one more hit while the Mets started to come back. Tommy finally started a three-run rally in the ninth with an infield single, and the Mets won it, 8-7, Bud getting the win.

Bud actually got into Shaheen's replay of the night, laughing in the front seat, having finally convinced him to turn off the rap station.

"So funny?" Shaheen said.

"This could be like one of those DisneyWorld commercials," Bud said. He imitated a deep-voiced announcer the way Shaheen had imitated him the other day. "Hey, Bud Marr, you've just won your first game in two-and-a-half years. Where you goin'?'" Then Bud said, "I'm goin' to Jimmy's to get a gun!"

They were there about ten minutes when Shaheen's cell phone chirped. He started talking and as he did, a black Mercedes pulled up in front of them, on the side street behind Jimmy's, parallel to the Deegan.

A guy who had to be Jesus got out, a real fat guy in a baggy linen suit, topping the outfit off with a white Panama hat, as if he were playing the bad ass in a movie.

Shaheen and Bud got out of the BMW. Jesus came right over to them and gave Bud a hug; as he did, Bud could feel him slipping the gun into the pocket of his windbreaker.

Bud had brought a lot of cash, because Shaheen had told him to. He asked Jesus how much and was told a grand.

"Wow," Bud said.

"Is for everything," Jesus said in a thick accent, smiling in the streetlights. He poked Shaheen. "Parts, labor, 'specially that I don' talk if this bad boy ends up someplace it's not 'sposed to."

239

"Way my dick does," Shaheen said, and they both laughed.

Bud patted the side pocket of the windbreaker. "I've never used one of these."

Jesus said, "Is like one of those cheap Kodaks they give out on Camera Day at the ballpark. Point an' shoot."

Shaheen said that he and Jesus were going inside, to have a drink and check out the beef, did Bud want to join them? Bud said no thanks, he'd seen all these cabs lined up out front, he was just going to head home, put some ice in a drink and behind his shoulder.

Jesus said, "I make one suggestion?"

Bud said, sure.

"Don't even try to spot your fastball no more. Spleet-finger, regular, don' matter. You threw Maywood a curve that night, you'd be on your way to the Hall of fucking Fame by now."

Bud thanked him for the advice. On the way home, he found himself wishing that Jenny had been at the game, remembering how she used to come all the time, even when he wasn't starting, how she'd be waiting for him just inside the players' entrance when he'd finished showering....

It was nearly one when he let himself into the apartment. He tiptoed into the bedroom, not wanting to wake her.

She wasn't there.

The note was on the pillow, her side of the bed.

"Girls night out," she said. "From the gym? I'll try not to wake you. Love, Me."

He went into the living room, sat on the couch, suddenly feeling the gun. He took it out and looked at it now, surprised at how shiny it was, how small. Jesus had let him take it out, fast, on the street, just to show him there were bullets already in it, how to make sure the safety was on.

"Twenny-two," he'd said. "Like your old number."

Bud fixed himself a drink. He latched the door this time, so she'd have to ring. If she asked why, he'd tell her he'd done it when he came home, thinking she was asleep, and forgot. He went and got the tape, put it in the VCR and turned on the set, hitting the mute button and fast-forwarding to where Tommy was digging in at the plate.

Tommy, then Jen's face, then him on the mound.

He had the gun in his right hand. He checked once more to make sure the safety was on, then went into his full windup, facing the TV screen.

"Here's the pitch," he said, in the quiet of the apartment, the trigger feeling as good and natural to his touch as the seams of the ball.

They got one of those minivan cabs for the ride out to Shea. Jen carried the two bottles of champagne the bartender at Dakota, up on Third, had given them after they'd managed to scrape Tommy off the two night attendants from United who'd insisted on buying him one last drink.

Nice party, Bud thought, as they took the exit to Shea off the Grand Central, Jen with the champagne, Tommy with the glasses, me with the gun.

He was trying, had been trying all night actually, to act as giddy as they were, even as he only drank half as much, if that. As they'd come over the Triboro he'd been reminding them of the pizza party they'd had at Shea the first September they'd gotten called up, before he got traded away to the Red Sox in the big deal that winter.

"We could only aford beer then," Bud'd said, actually getting into it now, for his own reasons, feeling the brightness in him start to build, like the arc-lights at the top of the stadium slowly going on, one after another. "Moet tonight," he said.

"Moet?" Tommy said, giggling. "Didn't he pitch for the Sox in the old days?"

They had the driver let them off near the Diamond Club entrance, on the first base side, then Bud walked them around to the door near the Press gate that he knew would open with a good shove. It had always amazed him, back to the minors, how easy it was to get into an empty ballpark, day or night, if you just knew how. He'd hung around after everybody was gone the night they'd gotten back from St. Louis, knowing this was the week, walking around a lit-tle bit, inside and out, seeing that there was only one security guy in a room near the groundskeeper's office, more interested in getting back to his old black-and-white reruns on Nick at Nite.

When Bud and Jen and Tommy got out on the field, they saw the blue tarp covering the infield, and noticed that the lights were at about half-power up at the top of the place, like some kind of weird halo, one of those auras Delroy, their third baseman, was always talking about,

"....so we came out here, like we're doing now, and we did it right here in the dugout," Tommy was telling Jen, as if she were just another one of his teammates wanting to hear who he did it with, and where, and how.

"An intern?" Jen said, trying to act interested

"She's on camera now," Tommy said, and giggled again. "Wish like hell she had been that night."

They came out on the field and Jen and Tommy spread a blanket at the base of the mound. Bud got above them and sat on the pitching rubber, hearing Shaheen's annoying voice inside his head, wondering now if the gun he was pulling out of his pocket was safer than this rubber, pointing the gun right at Tommy Maywood as he said, "Did you and Jen ever do it at the ballpark?"

Tommy spit out some champagne, the way a comedian would, because he always thought he was such a fucking comedian. "Where'd you get that thing, Guns R Us? You gonna shoot us with it?"

"No," Jen said quietly.

Tommy looked at her. She wasn't looking at the gun, just staring calmly, seriously, at Bud's face.

"You're not, are you, Bud?"

He shook his head. "Nope."

"Well then what's the goddam toy gun for?'

"You want to tell him or shall I?" Jen said.

"Gonna shoot myself," Bud said, "while you two watch."

"Wait," Jen said. "I get it now. One last shot heard 'round the world."

"Something like that," Bud said.

"Could somebody please explain to me what the fuck is going on here?" Tommy said. "This is a joke, right? You think there's something going on? Between Jen and me? You know what, man? I wish. For nearly twenty years." He started to get up, acting sober now. "This is too weird."

Bud stood up with him, pointing the gun at him again, at the polo pony that he had on every shirt he owned. "Sit down," he said.

To both of them he said, "I saw you together."

"The other night?" Jen said. "He wanted me to help convince you to go on a tour with him this winter."

Tommy started to say something, not wanting to listen, even now. Jen's voice, the sharp one Bud knew,... said, "Shut up, Tom. Okay?"

She hadn't moved, arms still hugging her knees, completely still. "Is this the one you go through with, honey?"

"What's that supposed to mean?" Tom said.

Bud and Jen both looked at him. He couldn't shut up, there was no point in even trying.

Jen said, "Bud has these little episodes every so often. That's what we call them. His episodes. Usually they're just for my benefit. I'm an audience of one. I'm the only one who sees the big show. The psychiatrists keep telling us it's more of a female trait, these fake suicides."

"Don't," Bud said.

But she told Tommy now, about the time in Houston when he took the pills, just not enough pills to do the job. Then there was the time in LA, in the cute house on the cute sitcom street in the valley, when he left the engine running in the garage, knowing she'd find him in time. And in Minneapolis, when he'd actually gone as far as cutting a wrist, the scar covered by the tattoo now...

"You don't know what it's like," Bud said in a dead voice.

"The hell I don't." Jen snapped at him, making even Tommy jump. "Is this the part where you tell me all you've gone through every day for the last nine years? About what it's been like to live with one lousy stinking fat pitch? Well, I've lived every goddam day of it, too. Sometimes I feel like I'm the one who threw that goddam ball."

Bud nodded at Tommy. "He's just the latest."

"There haven't been any," she said. "You know there haven't been any."

"I want to do it this time," Bud said.

"You know what I want?" Jen said. "I want you to take Tommy's deal. Take the money. Take it all and then we'll find a place where people don't give a damn about you or baseball."

"So I become more of a joke than I already am?" Bud said. "So they can line up to feel sorry for me?"

Jenny Marr said "You want to make somebody pay? Make them pay whatever they do at those stupid shows for your auto-graph. Five bucks a pop. Ten. A hundred. Whatever it is. Don't make yourself pay anymore. Stop making me pay, for God's sake. Make *them* pay."

"No!" he yelled.

Winston Maurice would tell people later, the ones he told anyway, that he liked to jump out his skin, hearing one gunshot from the outfield, then another, then another.

Winston lived right up the street from Shea, in the walkup on Roosevelt Ave. Some nights, if he couldn't sleep, he'd take what he called his constitutional, walk up to the park, walk around a little bit, take off his shoes and feel the grass he'd helped work on, go back home and sleep then, maybe after a little taste.

He was over in the visitors' dugout, having a smoke, when he heard the shots. He thought about going down the runway, but decided to go straight across the field, because it sounded like the shots came from the wall behind dead center. Winston didn't have time to be scared, just opened the door and saw Bud Marr with the gun in his hand, Tommy Maywood and some pretty girl he seemed to recall he knew from somewheres next to Maywood.

Crazy damn ballplayers...

"One more," Bud said, and then Winston saw him aim and fire his little gun right at the apple that came up after a Met hit a home run, paint and plastic and even some plaster scattering everywhere.

"You kill it?" Winston Maurice said, as they all noticed him standing there.

"Nah," Bud said. "But at least now I can afford to fix the stupid thing." He handed the gun to Winston and said, "Here's one more souvenir you don't want."

The three of them walked out into centerfield and Winston heard Bud say to Tommy Maywood, "You said we start in Kansas City....?"

THE POWER

by Michael Malone

I t all started with one of Badger's screwy theories, which he told me the first night we met. I'd noticed the little weirdo in the crowd at the Mick Bar because he had on a hat and not many men wear hats indoors in the South anymore. Or outdoors either. Not many men wore hats up North even back in the seventies, which is when my dad went bust with his hat store on East 34th. My dad loved hats more than money, as he proved time and again. What happened to him taught me a lesson: Between love and Chapter Eleven there's a short straight line. It was a lesson reinforced by my ex-wife and her lawyer. Ever since my divorce I don't give love the time of day. As far as I'm concerned, you can take love and hand it back to the French along with the snails and the Jerry Lewis movies.

But because of my dad, I spot this guy Badger in his classic folder Panama with the dropped brim and I notice he's reading. Skinny and squirmy, he's at the bar, bits of newspapers all over the counter and sticking out of the pockets of a nubbled mohair jacket that he'd probably pulled from a bin at a thrift store. He was flicking his cigarette ashes into an empty longneck and reading *The*

Dialogues of Plato in a paperback so old the price on the cover was fifty cents.

Badger isn't all that bad-looking and only maybe ten, twelve years older than I am, but his outfit made him look older, a good fit with the Mick, which is a fifties retro sports bar named after Mickey Mantle. I happen to be a sports agent or believe me I wouldn't hang at the Mick, but it's where sports people pass the time down here in this Carolina town I'm stuck in. It's loud and smoky and not cheap, in a worn-out building with a brick front the color of tobacco, always crowded because it's across the street from the old stadium. Tap Upchurch, the guy that owns the place, got sent up to the Yankees for a single season back in the late fifties. He never made it off the bench so he moves down South and opens a bar named "The Mick" after his hero Mickey Mantle, who I guess spoke to him a couple of times. He's got a bat that Mantle hit one of his nine grand slam home-runs with and a towel Mantle wiped his face on. He keeps this towel in a plastic case above the bar because he loves Mantle so much.

Since 1959, farm team players have hung out at the Mick wait-ing for the big time to come save them. These days a few women show up alone and turn out to be stringers for ESPN, but mostly it's the same old Mick full of men, the same old-timers bragging about the same old memories to the same old bartender. It's got boiled eggs floating in pickle brine and a Wurlitzer jukebox with Rosemary Clooney hits and a cigarette machine telling you to buy unfiltered Camels for 25 cents a pack even though the machine now charges over three bucks for cigarettes and doesn't sell Camels anymore anyhow. Of course plenty of people in North Carolina still smoke, claiming they're helping out the economy, and I admit I started back myself when I got down here. But most local smokers don't sit around in noisy sports bars wearing Panama hats and reading Plato. So I pick Badger out of the crowd right away, and before long he's telling me this theory of his about Marilyn Monroe and The Great DiMaggio.

Later I find out that Badger is kind of the mascot of the Mick and uses it like a temp service, picking up odd jobs from the regulars. Ten years ago he moved down here alone from New York where Tap thinks he was some kind of a teacher until he'd "run into personal problems" and lost his job. Tap didn't know the details, didn't know Badger's real name. Nobody did. When Badger's not running errands, he sits around reading ancient philosophers and asking other customers questions about the meaning of life—he calls it "the fundamentals." That's why he's called "Badger"—because of how he latches onto things and won't get off them. He'll keep after you like you were a slot machine and he couldn't stop pulling the handle. These are not questions like "Think the Braves can take the Series?" These are more like "Is the entire universe just a dream of love in the mind of God?" Well, a lot of people don't want to be bothered trying to answer this type question over a beer in a loud bar, so there was an empty stool on either side of Badger when I saw him that first time.

I figure it was because of my dad's loving hats so much that I sat down next to him and said, "Nice Panama." Or maybe it was because I hadn't been back South all that long and didn't really know anybody in town except these two clients of mine who play triple A ball and one of them doesn't drink and the other one's on lithium but not enough of it. Or maybe it was because Badger was reading a paperback, which my mom was always doing before she died. Anyhow, the little weirdo lets go with this huge smile when I sit down beside him and then out of the blue he asks me if I believe in irresistible impulse.

I said, "For example?"

He said, "Jimmy Stewart, remember, defending Ben Gazzara for killing the bartender in *Anatomy of a Murder.*"

I said, "Didn't it turn out that guy pulled a fast one on Jimmy Stewart and there was nothing irresistible about it at all?"

He said, "Jump back Jack," which maybe meant, "Point well taken." Then he turned and tapped the magnet pin-up of Marilyn Monroe that was stuck to the old cigarette machine behind him. Marilyn looked right at home in the Mick with her big red fifties mouth and her white fifties dress blowing up around her thighs from the whoosh of the Manhattan subway she was standing on.

I said, "Marilyn Monroe."

He said, "Yeah. Irresistible impulse. Happened to Joe." Then Badger tells me his theory that Joe DiMaggio murdered Marilyn Monroe because even after she'd broken his heart he couldn't stop loving her and went crazy whenever he saw her with another man. And this was because Marilyn Monroe had been, quote, "at the height of her power" when Joltin' Joe had fallen for her and so there was nothing he could do to resist his feelings. Badger told me he could produce "a labyrinth of circumstance" to back up this theory and he started smoothing out clippings from his pockets that I guess were going to prove his point. He had a couple of baseballs in his pockets too and they rolled down the sticky bar counter at Tap Upchurch who rolled them back without looking up. Later I found out Badger gets the players to sign these balls so he can sell them in front of the stadium across the street—except if he can't find the players he just signs them himself.

Instead of doing the smart thing—excuse myself and leave— I buy him a beer and say how I'd recently read a book claiming it was the Kennedys who'd done away with Marilyn Monroe. Badger was ready for that one. "Yeah, I read that too, and you know how those rumors got started?"

I took a stab at it. "J. Edgar Hoover?"

"Nah. DiMaggio started them. He had pals in the L.A. police that helped him plant the evidence against John and Bobby, the whole rat pack. Because deep down in a synergistic sense they did kill her and Joe knew it." Badger snatches my lapel so tight he wrinkled the wool. "Joe was a gentleman, a great human being, and why shouldn't he hate those smug bastards? They treated the woman he loved like a goddamn hooker. Am I right, Ricky?" His eyes were hot as a gas pilot.

Curiosity dragged me in. "Why are you calling me Ricky? My name's Jordan."

He patted my face in an admiring way. "I look at you, I see Ricky Ricardo. I mean when he was nice and young, nice-looking guy before Lucy plowed him under. Hey, Ethel, hey, Ed, where'd Lucy go?"

But I still don't hop off that stool. I guess it's like my mom used to tell my dad about all his businesses going bust, "Carino, you never know the time to say good-night." Instead of heading for the exit, I ask Badger why DiMaggio's plan hadn't worked. I mean if the baseball hero was so tight with the L.A. cops, why hadn't they ever accused the Kennedys of killing Marilyn Monroe? Because nobody had even suspected the Kennedys until they'd been dead for thirty or forty years. Badger patted my hand like we were a couple of close friends, when he didn't even know my name, which by the way is Jordan Cole, Jr. "You oughta know better than that." He shot his eyebrows up and down, like why couldn't I see the obvious? "The Kennedys had the wherewithal to make problems disappear. Like Mary Jo in the back of that car, you know what I mean?"

Well, my dad didn't like the Kennedys either because he always blamed JFK's hair for destroying the hat business, so maybe that's why I ordered Badger another longneck. I told him it was a little funny to me that somebody who worshipped the Great DiMaggio the way he did should accuse the man of murder. Badger came back to his opening remark. "Irresistible impulse. We can't blame Joe."

"Are you blaming Marilyn for getting herself murdered?"

He thought about this a while, then shook his head. "We can't blame Marilyn. My friend, never underestimate the cosmic power of love. Plato had the skinny on that." He tapped his paperback. "*Symposium.* There's nothing you can figure out that Plato wasn't there first. All the Greeks knew what love could do."

"Cosmic power of love?"

"When a woman like Marilyn's at the height of her power, it's like an earthquake. Buildings are going over."

I said, "Niagara Falls."

He smiled from ear to ear. "Babaloo!" Then he slid a few newspaper clippings towards me. "On a lesser plane, now, on a *much lesser* plane from Marilyn and the Yankee Clipper, it was the same thing with O.J. and Nicole." He tapped at an article with a headline about the O.J. Simpson murder trial. "Same thing, right?"

"I'm not sure I follow you."

He gave me an impatient punch on the arm. "Nicole. Extremely hot. She was at the height of her powers too."

"So O.J. couldn't help it?"

"Nobody can help it. Like Medea tells Jason. Euripides—" Badger waits, so finally I nod like I know what the hell he's talking about. His eyes flare up. "She tells him, she's out of control, 'With more love than sense, I left my home for you, I killed for you, and you dare to leave me, basest of men?'!"

"Medea had a rough time, sounds like."

He folds his clippings carefully. "Jane Russell said it all, Ricky. When love goes wrong, nothing goes right."

I agreed with that much. "You're right, love's a troublemaker," I told Badger. "Love and I have nothing to do with each other personally."

"You never know," he warns me and tips his hat.

So that was back in April. Now it's August and career-wise everything's going great. I'm sitting in the Mick talking over a big new contract with my hyperactive client, the AAA pitcher named Ronny Lamar Rome, and with us is naturally Badger. By now he's like my shadow. Okay, maybe he's a little weird but at least you can mention the Eighth Avenue Line or the West Village or the Belmont track without getting a blank stare. Over the last few months, I've bought him a few beers and a few meals and sent a few errands his way, and the result is he hangs around me like he had emphysema and I was a tank of oxygen. After he got bounced from his apartment and moved to a one-room, I let him store some stuff in my garage and since that time Badger's got it in his head we're really close friends. I hear him telling regulars in the Mick how I'm his "best bud." Well, I figure, what's the harm. He doesn't have any family; at least if you ask he won't answer your question but points up at the sky like they'd all gone to heaven at some point. He thinks the two of us have a lot in common: we've traveled (a lot of folks in this town haven't even been out of the state), we watch movies on TV (what else is there to do around here?) and we're both, according to him, "unshackled by natural bonds to tellurian gravity"—whatever that means. Badger's brainy. I mean he can read Plato in Greek. I've seen him with the books.

In May I took a trip to Madrid. My mom was born in Mexico and my dad met her in Madrid when she was on vacation there and he was stationed in Spain and falling in love with hats. They were always talking about falling in love in Madrid. So I figured what the hell, might as well see what the place looks like. While I'm there, Badger calls me long distance from a pay phone with a bag full of quarters and tells me these museums to go to. So while I'm changing planes in London I buy him this tee shirt that says "MIND THE GAP" and he says he can't get over how I remembered him. He wears the tee shirt all the time. He's got it on tonight along with the brown Borsolino fedora I gave him out of a box of my dad's unsold hats I've got stored in my garage. One of these days I'll take them to the thrift store.

This night in August it's about ten p.m. when the pitcher Ronny Lamar Rome moves off to get his Polaroid taken with some drunk frat boys. Badger's gassing on about how baseball's the only thing in America that's like Greek plays. "Baseball and the ancient Greeks understand the nemesis of inevitable chance. The fate of who you love. Oedipus marries his mother, what does he know?" I'm nodding like I couldn't agree more but about to wrap things up when out of the blue he plucks hard at my sleeve and points to the door. I look over and see Angie Schuelenmeyer standing there. Badger shakes his head, pretty agitated. "Hey, Jordan, 'member my telling you how there's love goddesses wreaking havoc on the earth?"

I said, "Not really."

"Sure you do, you figured the Kennedys killed Marilyn—"

"—No, I didn't say—"

"And I explained it was Joltin' Joe. 'Cause when women are at the height of their powers, hang on, boys, you're taking a ride on the Atom Smasher. You remember the Atom Smasher at Rockaway's Playland?"

"Not really. Rockaway Beach? Queens?"

"Yeah, Woodyallenville, I grew up there. Love's a roller coaster and you can't get off."

So then he starts in on Marilyn Monroe and the Yankee Clipper again; by this time I'd heard a hundred different versions of his screwy theory on "the cosmic force of love power," but DiMaggio murdering Marilyn was his favorite. "Irresistible impulse," I said.

He smiled. "Babaloo! Well, Angie over there "—he jerked his

head at the door—"She's got the power."

I looked again at the woman coming into the Mick. "You know that's Zane Schuelenmeyer's wife."

"I sure do. Like you said, Niagara Falls. Five point five billion gallons of water could land on your head every hour, you dally too long with the Maid of the Mist."

"What are you talking about?"

Badger gets his gas-pilot intense look. "Jordan, you need to point out the post-lapsarian implications of big falls to Ronny Lamar Rome, otherwise...." Suddenly the little weirdo picks up an imaginary club and starts bashing in an imaginary somebody on the table-top. He doesn't stop till I shake his arm. It was a pretty good imitation of a homicidal maniac completely losing it. You can see why a lot of people in the Mick just steer clear of him.

I ask him, "Is something going on with Ronny and Angie?" He just points.

I watch my star pitcher Ronny Lamar Rome wheel around from the frat boys and follow Angie doing her "keep your eyes on my hip bones slipping out of their sockets" type walk she has, which she does all the way over to our booth where she stops and looks right through me. (What else is new?) Then Ronny slides back into the booth and she scoots across the vinyl after him and runs her hand up his leg. Right away I can tell I've got a situation on my hands. The fact that all of a sudden I can't see Ronny's hands and that Mrs. Schuelenmeyer is moving around on him like she's riding a mechanical bull indicates to me that the situation is by no means a new one. I don't need Badger whispering "Jump back, Jack" in my ear to let me know I have somehow dropped the ball and need to pick it up fast and throw it out of the park because the ball is in the nature of a crate of TNT with a quick fuse.

Here's the deal. Devil Rays brass is flying into Raleigh-Durham to finalize on the two Triple-A clients I represent. This deal is totally greenlighted except the brass wants to watch my two guys in one last game before we sign. Naturally, one of my two guys is Ronny Lamar Rome, the pitcher with the 1.85 ERA who's now got his hands under the skirt of Zane Schuelenmeyer's wife. Naturally Zane Schuelenmeyer is the other guy. The only way it could be worse is the way it is: Zane Schuelenmeyer was the catcher when this pitcher threw three shut-outs and two no-hitters this season. The only other way it could be worse is that I suddenly see Zane walking into the bar. Which I do. This is a bar where everybody knows everybody, right? It's not like there's more than one baseball hang-out in this boonie town, so where else did Angie think her husband was going to come looking for her?

If Zane makes it to the booth, even he's bound to notice that his wife is by now pretty much doing a slow dance on his friend Ronny Lamar Rome's lap. But I luck out. Like he was stealing second, Badger shoots across the room and gets himself in the doorway between Zane and the booth. He pulls the big catcher off to a corner where he can't see what the rest of us are seeing, and keeps him there autographing baseballs while I try to reason with the lapdancing wife.

Angie's one of those red-haired Southern girls. She's got, well Badger later called it an "indiscreet" face. Plus, a long full body it's

257

hard to look away from. She's got attitude too. So when I say, "Angie, you wanna climb off Ronny? I see Zane headed this way," she tells me, "Jordan, all you see is your fifteen percent of Zane headed this way." Okay, I *am* counting on those commissions and god knows I've earned them. But at least maybe she thinks about her eighty-five percent and she gets off Ronny's lap.

Tonight Angie's wearing a kind of retro-fifties outfit like she'd coordinated herself with the Mick Bar—a red halter top with white pedal pushers and white sandals with stiletto heels. She leans that halter over into Ronny's face as she swings out of the red vinyl booth. "I need to go to the toytoy," she tells him like it was an invitation to heaven, then she walks away doing some kind of salsa dance to Rosemary Clooney singing "Mambo Italiano." Ronny had leaned out of the booth so far to watch her go, he was defying gravity. He would have been in the Ladies Room with her in a flash if I hadn't grabbed his wrist (non-pitching arm) with both my hands and twisted.

"Oww," he says surprised.

"Ronny, you do know that's Zane's wife?"

"Angie, yeah, so?" He shrugs, ruffling his hair, which is dyed a greenish yellow and styled like he'd slept on it wrong and just woke up. On the looks scale, Ronny Rome is definitely at the "extremely hot" end of things. He claims to have slept with a thousand women and I'd believe him if I thought he could count that high. He has an easy strut to his walk and big brown sleepy eyes that he uses on females so fast that sometimes the one coming to his front door and the one leaving it run into each other and I have to "handle" the crossover for him.

"Yeah, so, Angie," I say. "Look at me, Ronny, you're pitching tomorrow. Zane's catching and the two of you are gonna play so fantastically that these gentlemen flying up from Tampa are actually going to give you millions of dollars. Millions, Ronny. Of which I am going to take fifteen percent plus the seventeen thousand you already owe me."

"Whatever."

"Angela Schuelenmeyer is off limits banned no-no taboo. You get it?"

He smirks at me. "Hey, talk to her, she's free white and twenty-one."

I smirk back. "No. She's not free, she's married. And she's twenty-seven. And Zane's your friend. More important, listen to me, he's your catcher."

"Whatever." Ronny's not listening. He's running his tongue around the lip of his glass like it was Angie Schuelenmeyer.

"Where's Kristi, Ronny?"

"Who?"

Kristi was his last girlfriend. Last and obviously past. She's a local model. In the outfield at the stadium, there's a big billboard of Kristi lying on wall-to-wall carpeting she wants you to buy. Just a few months ago, Ronny asked me to set up a date with her and I had. Like Badger says, there's a lot to being an agent.

I knew I needed to move fast. Now, unlike most of this boonie town (where Time doesn't stand still, it lies down and takes a nap), I can move fast. Maybe I was born in the South, but my dad took us to New York when I was nine, to see if men would buy more hats up North. They wouldn't. But I grew up in Manhattan, midtown, off Lex, right above my dad's third COLE HATS store that went bust. I picked up a lot of speed there. My mom always said New York wasn't as fast as Madrid or Mexico City either. I don't know about that, but compared to down here, Manhattan is one big blur going by. I never would have come back down South if I'd had any choice because, like my mom said, this place is slow as syrup, and likes it that way. She says she would have lost her mind down here if it hadn't been for all the books. Some rednecks treated her like crap because she was from Mexico and had an accent. The hell with them.

My whole goal in life is to get back to New York. Like I said earlier, I'm a sports agent—you know, like Jerry McGuire, except do I have Cuba Gooding, Jr. dancing in the end zone? No. I've got Ronny Lamar Rome disappearing underneath a bar booth with his catcher's wife. I deserve better. I'm good at my job. In fact, according to my ex-wife the tennis star I'm better at my job than I am at my life. I give everything I've got to my clients. Last year, I kept my bulimic ice skater on the circuit even after her shoplifting hit the tabloids. (It was Godiva chocolates; they caught her in the store with a twelve-pound Millennium "Ultimate Party Favor" in her duffel bag. $375.00 retail.)

Last year was a bad time. My whole life went south and I had to follow it. My mom died. Two months later my dad took off after her like he was running for a bus. She was the only thing he loved more than hats. My wife left me and the agency's new boss Emili—with an "I"—Miller-Roth tells me we're downsizing and I'm getting transferred to our branch office covering the South. This woman actually said to me she figured I wouldn't mind leaving New York because of my "recent broken ties"—by which she meant not just my mom and dad dropping dead but my wife divorcing me because she's having an affair with Emili Miller-Roth. On a scale of one to ten, the whole year was in negative-one-thousand for Jordan Cole, Jr.

But I need the job so I go South in my dad's old apple-green Pontiac that I've still got the New York plates on. One night I come out of the Mick and some A-hole's slapped a bumper sticker on it saying "WE DON'T CARE HOW YOU DO IT UP NORTH." Well, Bubba, you ought to care! Wake up and smell the double espresso—not that you could ever get one around here—or the *Times* either.

I work hard, handle the Nascar racers and the bass fishermen and the stunt artist that jumps his dirt bike over eighteen-wheelers when he isn't in jail. Then a few months after I get to Carolina I meet these two new triple-A players, Schuelenmeyer and Rome, at their agent's funeral. From then on I'm counting the days till I fly to Manhattan and tell Miller-Roth I no longer work for her lousy agency because I'm the competition. I quick sign the pitcher and catcher on the side, figuring the minute I sell them to the majors, I'm on the plane to JFK.

Zane Schuelenmeyer, the catcher with the wife, is batting .413. Ronny Lamar Rome, the pitcher with the wife on his lap, can throw a fast ball 105 miles an hour. With Zane catching, Ronny sometimes gets seventeen-eighteen strike-outs a game. The problem is, without Zane catching, Ronny is just as likely to rip a base bag out of the dirt and chuck it at the umpire. He takes more handling than the bulimic ice skater, which is saying something.

Ronny's always calling me. "Jor, I need you to handle this thing for me, okay?" Usually he wants me to get rid of a girl. It's too bad he didn't call me the first time he laid eyes on Angie Schuelenmeyer. I could have told him that back in Georgia his buddy Zane, the best catcher in the minors, put a shortstop in a wheelchair for life because this guy got his hand inside the top of Angie's bikini at somebody's pool party. A wheelchair for life. I mean, they were both slinging their fists and everybody said it was an accident, but hey that doesn't make the guy a shortstop again.

Zane's a Georgia boy from a town with a smaller population than the last apartment building I lived in when I lived in New York. What Einstein had in brains, Zane's got in body, and sort of vice versa. He's six-foot-five, two-thirty, pumped—and he didn't buy his muscles at a drugstore either, he worked on them. He doesn't drink, smoke, or take any kind of pills except vitamins. He's got no bad habits I know of except his wife. Zane and Angie got married in high school. They have exactly zero in common except they both think she's the hottest ticket in town. In which opinion obviously they're not alone.

Thank god Angie's made it into the toy-toy when Zane finally spots me, Ronny and Badger in the booth and ambles over. I say, "Hey there, Zane, big game tomorrow, right?"

But he clearly could care less about his future in the majors and has nothing but Angle on his mind. "Y'all seen Kitten?" He calls his wife Kitten, and I guess you can call a Bengal tiger "kitten" if you want to.

Badger suddenly pipes up. "Matter of fact your wife was in here looking for you, Zane."

"She was?" The catcher frowns and I stop breathing.

262

"Yeah, Angie got worried waiting at home for you so she came here. She said if we saw you to tell you she went back to the house. Right, Jordan and Ronny?" After this amazing lie, the nut smiles at Ronny Lamar Rome, so there's nothing I can do but jump in and say, "Yeah, that's right, isn't it, Ronny?" and stomp my loafer into Ronny Lamar's instep to shut him up. The pitcher had his mouth open and could have said anything.

"Kitten went on back home, Ronny?" asks Zane slowly.

"Wherever," Ronny shrugs without looking at him.

"Well, I guess she better be there. I'm going on back then," Zane tells us; thank god before the door to the Ladies Room opens and Angie mambos out of it. But instead of leaving, he just stands there frowning. Zane's got a big handsome freckled face that's almost always squeezed into that frown, like the world's going by him too fast. Weird, because a 100 mph fastball doesn't bother him at all. He can catch one. He can hit one. Two weeks ago he hit a grand slam off a fast ball. But Angie has a different kind of speed.

I hop up and yank at the catcher. "Come on, Zane. Badger, let's walk Zane out."

After we hustle Zane Schuelenmeyer outside the Mick and I shove him into his white Caddy and wave him off, I slam Badger against the brick wall. "Are you psychotic? Suppose Zane'd started to wonder why Angie was looking for him in a bar when he doesn't drink?"

Badger laughs richly as he hugs me. "I love you, my friend, but you gotta understand character. Zane doesn't hypothesize."

I shake him again. "Suppose Angie'd walked out of the john?"

He wiggles loose and picks up the Borsolino, smoothes the brim. "She did. She went out the back. Zane was talking to you. She's meeting Ronny, at the Marriott."

I stare at him horrified. "Who the hell told you that?"

"Cogito ergo sum, Ricky," he grins.

I grab a fistful of his London Underground tee shirt. "Don't mess with me, Badger."

He puts his hand around my fist and pats it. "She slipped a Marriott card key down Ronny's shirt on her way to the can."

I stare at him some more. He nods.

"Shit!" I say.

He points at his tee shirt. "Time to Mind the Gap, right?"

Once when Badger was grilling me about the philosophy of a sports agent (like I have time to ruminate on a philosophy while I'm lugging a 55-inch TV over to Ronny's mother's or taking some bass fisherman's large-mouth to the taxidermist), I told him an agent does what's written on that London tee shirt. "Mind the Gap." A good agent minds the gap between his client and his client's best interests. And he does it not out of love but because he takes fifteen percent. A gap is when clients do things that hurt them—like eat chocolates, like make a play for their catcher's wife in a sports bar where everybody knows them. Things like that. When the gap widens so much nothing can bridge it, your client falls through. Deal falls through. You don't go to New York.

"Game's over," I say and light up a Marlboro. I admit I felt defeated.

Badger mooches from my pack and lights up too. "You oughta

quit smoking, Jordan," he says to me. "A guy with his life ahead of him."

"What life?"

"You're still in love with that girl, the tennis player. Maybe you could get her back."

"Badger, don't go there. And you don't want to force me to choose between you and cigarettes. Zane gets home, she's not there, game's over."

"That's no tautology," Badger says, god knows what he means half the time. Then he shows me this damn Swiss army gizmo he carries around with everything on it from a little ruler to a big knife. "I don't want you to worry. I ripped up his back tire while you were getting him in the car. He'll be a while getting home. Babaloo." I swear, I was almost glad I'd put up with the little weirdo all this time. I told him to quick take my car to the Marriott and get Angie to go home before Zane gets back there. I'd waylay Ronny.

So we do that. I tell Ronny that Angle can't meet him tonight and Ronny throws a ketchup bottle at the wall 95 mph and knocks off the Mickey Mantle bat and gets ketchup all over it so Tap Upchurch has a fit and throws him out. I ride with Ronny home to his contemporary off in the woods with its deck out over a deep lake. He calls the place the sex shack and he's built it in the middle of nowhere because he likes his privacy so he can "do it naked under the stars." He tells me I'll have to fix it so he can sleep with Zane's wife without Zane's noticing. "I gotta have her," he tells me. "I'm totally in love here." I take his car and the keys to his truck so he can't leave the house. (It's not like you can whistle down midnight taxis in boonieville.)

Badger's waiting for me at my place to tell me how he intercepted Angie at the Marriott and followed her back home with some baseballs for Zane to sign so he was there when Zane drove in after he'd finally gotten his tire changed. Badger said Angie did a good job following his lead, claiming how she'd been out earlier looking for Zane at the Mick. So all's well except Badger also tells me that to get Angie to leave the Marriott, he had to give her a note he wrote in Ronny's handwriting (which he was good at from faking all the baseball autographs) going on about how much he loved her but their love would have to wait till tomorrow. This upset me. "Tomorrow? The Tampa scouts are coming to the game tomorrow! Couldn't you have said, "Our love will have to wait till Friday, our love will have to wait till Never?"

"Love," says Badger, "is the Euclidean lever that moves the planet earth."

I threw him out of my house.

Naturally I'm up all night worrying about whether Zane Schuelenmeyer has found that love letter from "Ronny" and slaughtered Angie while she slept, which would mean he wouldn't be available for tomorrow's game, and probably neither would Ronny Lamar Rome who'd probably be slaughtered in his bed too, and there goes my little midtown office with the sign I've already done the layout on: "The Cole Agency. Tomorrow's Stars Today." At four a.m. I even drive over to the Schuelenmeyers' brick colonial in the Colony Club Estates but there're no police cars or ambulances in the driveway.

Well, like they love to say down here, tomorrow is another

day. Pre-game practice starts. Zane shows and so does Ronny because Badger takes him back his car and his keys, and so do the two big shots from the Devil Rays who treat me like dirt but what the hell, they sign with me or they don't sign. Zane, frowning, asks me if I think anything funny's going on with his wife Kitten and I say absolutely not, he can trust me on that. Zane hits a homerun in the first that he dedicates to his Kitten (he dedicates all his homeruns to her or his mother or to Jesus Christ), and a triple in the third that bounces off Ronny's ex, Krista, where she's lying on the wall-to-wall in the big centerfield billboard. Ronny has eleven strike-outs by the fifth. These Tampa guys have got the caps off their signing pens.

And that's when Badger starts grabbing at me and pointing. I turn and see Angie striding through the stadium with her red hair bouncing in the sun. Her eyes are so green you can see them twenty rows away. She's got a man's white shirt tied under her breasts and her tan stomach bare above this short white skirt. She walks like girls in an old print my dad kept on the wall of his hat store on 34th—one of those Depression pictures of Manhattan working girls strolling down the sidewalk, out on the town, all of them wearing hats. You could see their strong thighs under their thin dresses. Angie had that kind of feel to her, an overflowing kind of feel, like you could pour her out like honey warmed on the stove.

She's headed for the dugout where Zane's picking up a bat and Ronny Lamar Rome is sitting on the bench blowing big pink bubbles of gum and then slowly sucking them back through his lips like they were Angie Schuelenmeyer.

Before she gets down to the dugout, half the stadium is look-

267

ing at her, including the Devil Rays brass. They want to know who is she? "Zane Schuelenmeyer's wife," I explain while kicking at Badger who naturally is stuck to my side like a bare sweaty leg to a leather car seat. Today he's wearing a black homberg of my dad's and a tee shirt with Aristotle on it. He holds the homburg on with both hands and shoots off in that fast ferret way of his. He stops Angie when she's still a good fifty feet away. I see her hand Badger a note as she points to Ronny. Ronny spots her and starts crawling over the back of the dugout to get at her. And do what? He's in the middle of a god-damn ball game!

Zane notices Angie and strikes out on three pitches, with two outs and two men on. She leaves the stadium while he's swinging away, and when he's done he hurls his bat into the dugout, maybe at Ronny's head. Inning's over and Ronny and Zane have to take the field. Ronny slings a warm-up pitch right at Zane and smacks him in the face mask with a curve ball. "What's the problem?" asks the top Tampa guy.

"No problem," I guarantee and excuse myself. As I climb the bleachers, ahead of me I see my future disappearing like the Manhattan skyline on a foggy night. "What's the problem?" I ask Badger, snatching the note from Angie out of his hand and reading it. It's addressed to "Baby Big Boy" and it's pure porno passed off as ever-lasting love. It instructs Ronny to come straight home to his lake place after the game where she'll be lying waiting on his bed. "Don't shower," it says, "I love your pitching smell."

I kill myself hopping over bleachers to chase Angie down before she can take off in the new powder blue BMW convertible that Zane will actually be able to afford if I can get these goddamn contracts signed. Badger's right behind me when I throw myself in front of her car (which is a lot nicer than the old apple-green Pontiac of my dad's that I'm still driving). At least she stopped. I try not to shout. "Angie you wanna use your head? You want Ronny ending up in a wheelchair like that shortstop in Georgia?"

Angie looks at me. There's a first. She says, "Come here, Jordan."

I step around to the driver's door. It's hard to explain but there's so much brightness to her, she's hard to look at. She says, "I need you to do me a great big favor."

I scowl at her. "What?"

All of a sudden she reaches up, pulls me down by my tie and kisses me on the mouth. I jerk away like I've been electrocuted, which is what it felt like. She says, "I need you to be nice and take care of Zane, okay? I'm leaving him for Ronny."

I'm having trouble breathing. "You can't. You'll blow this deal and you'll be getting eighty-five percent of zero on either one of these guys."

"Hey," she says like she's made it up, "Money can't buy happiness."

"Angie, neither can Ronnie Lamar Rome. Trust me on that."

She stares at me some more. "Anybody ever tell you you look like the guy on *I Love Lucy?*"

It wasn't what I expected. "Yeah," I say, "Badger."

She smiles over at Badger and gives him a wave. "Badger's a brain, okay. But you know what, Jordan, for a good-looking man, you don't have a clue." She pulls sunglasses out of her cleavage and puts them on.

"What are you talking about?"

She laughs and starts her engine. "See what I mean?"

I guess she would have run me over if I hadn't vaulted out of the way. She drives across the parking lot at fifty mph and slams to a stop in front of the Mick. One for the road, I guess.

I just stand there wondering what she and Ronny think her husband's going to be doing while she's sniffing the pitcher's armpits out at his sex shack beside the lake. I jump when Badger gives me a pat on the shoulder from behind. He can sneak up on you like he did it for a living. "I told you Angie had the power," he says. "It's Joltin' Joe time. Two guys on the track and here comes the Silver Comet. Head-on collision, my friend, jump back. They're all in the grip."

I light a cigarette to make myself breathe. Okay, Badger was right. Something had to be done. I think fast and come up with a plan. Badger will handle the Angie end, I'll take care of Zane and Ronny here at the stadium. I explain what we need to do.

Fortunately, while Angie's porno ramblings to Ronny "Baby Big Boy" Rome go on for four pages of personalized lavender stationery, all that the last page says is, "Win win win!!! Your prize is waiting on your bed—Love kisses love 4ever! A—"

On the other side of this page I get Badger to write the beginning of a note in Angie's handwriting and address it to Zane. He does a great job, you can't tell the difference.

Zane honey—

'Member Tabby, my old best girlfriend from high school? Her Mama called me—Tabby just got hurt pretty bad totaling her car so I'm driving to Tenn. to see her—She's in the I.C.U. Don't worry about me. I'll get back as soon as I can. I'll call—(over)
Win win win!!! Your prize is waiting on your bed—

Love kisses love 4ever! A—

I reason this way. Zane won't remember Angie's old friend who moved to Tennessee (it was actually Badger who dreamed up the name Tabby), but he'll figure that over the years his memories of poor old Tabby have slipped through his porous brain. And there'll be no way for him to trace her since Tennessee is large and she has no last name or even real first name. As for the prize waiting on the bed—which is no doubt the naked Angie sprawled out at Ronny's sex shack panting for the sweaty pitcher's return—I'll substitute a different kind of trophy and leave it on Zane's own bed. There's a lot of stuff from my marriage packed away in boxes in my garage and somewhere in it is a loving cup inscribed "World's Best Husband." My tennis star wife gave it to me four years ago (obviously this was before she divorced me to move in with Emili Miller-Roth). That cup'll make a great prize for Zane.

I'll say this for Badger, he just says "Yes." I tell him if we pull this plan off, I'll give him ten percent of my fifteen. He tips the black homburg but shakes his head. "I don't care about money. I care about love. You're my best friend, Ricky, babaloo!" And he hugs me. Well, Jesus, but still...

So Badger shoots off in my car. The idea is for him to race over to my place in the Pontiac, pick up the trophy, zip to the

Schuelenmeyers' colonial in Colony Club Estates, break in, and plop the WORLD'S BEST HUSBAND cup down in the middle of their king-sized bed. (I warn him to watch out for Angie's Lhasa Apso, Lover.) Then he has to barrel across town to the bypass and show up at Ronny Lamar Rome's lake house. His job there is to convince Angie to leave town for a week, how he does it I leave up to him—he can tell her how Ronny's waiting for her in Atlanta, tell her her mother's dying, tell her whatever he wants, just get rid of her.

By the end of the week I'll have the two contracts signed with the Devil Rays, and by that time Ronny (who's got a serious case of what they currently call attention deficit disorder) will probably have forgotten all about Angie because I will have fixed him up with one of the hot bimbos he was pestering me to fix him up with before Angie swung into view.

As soon as Badger drives off, I run back into the stadium where Ronny has gotten himself out of the sixth, but not without let-ting two runs score, so now the game's all tied up. I tell the Devil Rays big shots that my boys are saving the best for last. They look skeptical. I get Ronny off by himself in the dugout and slip him the first three pages of Angie's sex-memo. He's looking at that lavender paper like it's lined with cocaine and he's Darryl Strawberry. I tell Ronny how I handled things for him with Angie. She loves him too but she can't come to his house. She'll be waiting for him at the Marriott instead, in a hot tub suite in his name.

"I want her to come to the lake," he says.

"Too risky. And she wants you to stay away from Zane. Oh and the other message." I tell him Angie says if Ronny can get twenty strikeouts in this game, she'll be the angel flying him up for his first look at Paradise tonight at the Marriott. (You have to talk to Ronny like a country western song.) "Hey damn thanks, Jor." He grins and smacks me on the back. I point out that to get twenty Ks, he has to strike out nine more batters in the remaining three innings. "Okay," he shrugs.

Then Zane comes back from the locker room john and I get him off by himself. He wants to know where Kitten went and what she was handing to Badger? I give him the last page of Angie's lavender stationery with the news about Tabby's terrible car crash. "Angie didn't want to bother you during the game. She asked Badger to give you this." I have to be patient while Zane studies the note, which he does frowning and moving his lips. Then he reads aloud, "Tabby, my old best girlfriend from high school," and shakes his head puzzled. "Tabby? What friend Tabby?"

I try to be helpful. "Tabby?... Oh wait, that's right, I remember Angie telling me one time about an old friend of hers named Tabby. Seems like she said she moved to Tennessee or something."

Zane thinks as hard as he can, a painful sight. "...Yeah, Tabby, yeah, I kinda remember." His big freckled face goes all sad and sweet. "Poor Kitten. Her friend Tabby got in a car accident and she's gone driving off to Tennessee to see if she can help out."

I squeeze his forearm which feels like a piece of the Alaska pipeline.

"That's Angie for you," I say. "Always thinking of others."

He frowns. "...Yeah. She's got a heart big as...as...big as—"

I help him out. "She's got a big heart."

Slowly he smiles. "She sure does."

"You're a lucky man having such a big-hearted wife."

"You know what, Jordan, I'm gonna hit another homerun and dedicate it to Tabby's pulling through."

"Zane, that's a great idea."

I climb back into the grandstand and sit down beside the Tampa brass, the bald one looks at his watch. "Where you been the last twenty minutes?" he wants to know.

I tell him, "Minding the gap."

Zane Schuelenmeyer hits a double in the eighth and a grand slam homer in the ninth, his second of the season. He's four for four. He catches a pop-up unbelievably far back in the stands (the crowd's on its feet) and he throws out on a steal the only guy that gets on base in the last three innings....

As for the other nine guys that come up to bat against us, Ronny Lamar Rome strikes them all out for a grand total of twenty Ks. He throws five fast balls in a row that clock over a hundred. This game widens his strikeouts-to-walks ratio to eight to one, which is up there with Pedro Martinez. He gets a standing ovation when he leaves the mound in the ninth.

The Devil Rays sign.

We celebrate at the Mick. I don't see Badger but my dad's old green Pontiac is parked out in front of the bar with the key in the ignition. Still no Badger when I take Zane home. Zane's upset when he sees Angie's packed her bag (in a hurry too) and taken her Lhasa Apso, Lover, off with her. But he bursts into tears when he sees the WORLD'S BEST HUSBAND loving cup on his bed. "She's the sweetest girl in the world," he tells me. I agree.

Of course Ronny Lamar Rome gets upset when the world's sweetest girl is not waiting naked in his hot tub suite at the Marriott that I reserved for him. He throws his shoe through the television. But I'm at the Marrlott just a few minutes later with room service and an exotic dancer named Sierralyn, who's as close to a life-sized Barbie doll as it's possible to get and still walk upright. I had to pay a limo service three hundred bucks to drive her in fast from Charlotte, which is where Ronny first saw her last spring in a cage at the Inferno Club. I tell Ronny I know he's serious about Angie, but she just couldn't take the chance of Zane's getting wind of their love. Give it time and in the meanwhile be nice to Sierralyn, who drove all the way from Charlotte to congratulate him. I leave them with Ronny showing her how he can pop open a champagne bottle with one thumb.

If Sierralyn doesn't work out, I've got Kaylee, a Tampa TV personality, on a back burner.

Everything is going great. The next morning I'm getting calls from talent that a month ago wouldn't use my back to wipe their cleats on. I quit Emili Miller-Roth by fax. She calls me personally (there's a first). My wife's left her too. It was a good day for Jordan Cole, Jr.

Then a week goes by and Zane's flipping out because Kitten hasn't gotten in touch with him at all and he's supposed to leave for Tampa today. I lie and claim that Angie called me from Nashville and told me she couldn't reach Zane because there must be a problem with his answering machine. I promise him she's fine.

Then I go seriously looking for Badger. I haven't seen him since I sent him to Ronny's lake house to do something about Angie and I'm beginning to think I need to know what he did. I ask around in the Mick, but nobody's seen Badger since the afternoon of the "big game" (as it's now referred to, the game that sent Rome and Schuelenmeyer to the majors), when somebody remembers seeing him in a booth with Angie Schuelenmeyer. Meanwhile Tap Upchurch doesn't care what happened to Badger because his autographed Mickey Mantle grand slam bat is missing from over his bar and it was worth, he says, eighteen thousand dollars. While I'm trying to get Badger's home address out of Tap, Zane all of a sudden runs into the Mick. He's looking for me. With a frown, he shows me this note postmarked Nashville that he just got from "Kitten."

The note says that Angie and her dog and "Tabby's mom" are taking Tabby "up North" because there's a plastic surgeon "up there" who's the only one who can "do something" about Tabby's face, which according to the note was "ruined" when she went through the windshield of her car. (The note is actually on Angie's lavender stationery so I figure Badger must have stolen some out of her bedroom when he planted the loving cup on the bed.) I have a little trouble breathing as I read this forgery, which Zane takes to be sympathetic on my part. I think fast. I advise him to fly to Tampa tomorrow as planned and let me locate Angie for him. I say there's no knowing exactly where "up North" she's taken Tabby for plastic surgery, but I predict she'll call home as soon as she possibly can. I hope he's had his answering machine fixed. He says he's got voice mail now. He frowns. "She oughta keep on calling."

"Angie probably just doesn't want to leave Tabby's side," I suggest. "You know how warm-hearted she is."

Zane frowns deeper. Sooner or later even he's gonna notice something's weird.

Something's weird, all right. When I get home that night, there's a letter for me from Badger—also postmarked Nashville. In it he sends congratulations, he read in the paper that I got a great deal for Schuelenmeyer and Ronny with the Devil Rays and he knows how much those contracts meant to me. In a PS, he says that Angie won't be a problem. Then he adds, "I'm headed out West. If you need to, tell the authorities I stole the car. But if you can avoid it, I'd appreciate it. Remember: Some people go over the Falls and survive. Your friend, Gabriel Dawson."

Three days later I'm packing up my house for the move to New York. I'm still worrying where the hell is Angie, what does the weirdo mean: if you need to, tell them I stole the car? And that stuff about surviving the Falls? Plus, it's the first I've heard of Badger's real name, which rings a tiny bell but I can't think why. Then that night I get a heartsick phone call from Zane Schuelenmeyer, who's crying into the receiver; he needs me down in Florida right away. Angie's left him. I say, "How do you know?" He tells me—from a letter in her car. I'm an agent; he's my second biggest commission (Ronny's the biggest); I hop on a plane the next day.

In Tampa here's what I find out. Yesterday morning Zane wakes up at his rental and finds his wife's powder blue BMW convertible parked in his driveway. In it there's a letter from Angie taped to the steering wheel. (Except I know it's not from Angie, it's from

Badger. Of this, I suddenly have no doubts at all because in it Angie is claiming she has an "irresistible impulse" to be on her own.) The letter explains how she's brought back the convertible BMW to Zane's house because she didn't feel like she had a right to keep it. She claims she got the address from me. She goes on about how she'd meant to explain everything in person to Zane but she lost her nerve before she could knock on the door. So she walked to the station and took a bus "out West." She hopes someday Zane will forgive her and understand why she has to have her freedom. That's why she's leaving him. There's nobody else, nobody. And never was. It's a personal thing. When Zane is ready for a divorce, go ahead and get one with her blessing. And please go on with his life and become a super star. She'll be pulling for him. It's signed, "Love kisses love 4ever, Kitten and Lover." The car is otherwise clean and empty.

Zane has gone completely to pieces at his wife's leaving him (and taking their dog), but fortunately there's a three-day break before he has to play against the Red Sox and we're able to put him back together. Ronny Lamar Rome is actually a big help. Ronny manages to keep his mouth shut about being so in love with Angie himself that he was trying to steal her away from his best friend. He keeps telling Zane it's the best thing for him and Angie both until Zane starts to believe it. Meanwhile Ronny confides in me that it's now clear to him why Angie never showed at the Marriott to take him to Paradise. She got on "some type of woman kick" about personal identity and is probably now "drivin' around the country like goddamn Thelma and Louise." He actually believes that Angie's left Zane because she has to have her freedom, but I'm getting a different idea.

Flying back to Carolina from Tampa, I keep thinking over the screwy theories I've heard from Badger in the past year, about the cosmic power of love, how DiMaggio killed Marilyn and the rest. I'm up all night thinking. The next morning I go to my garage and pull down the boxes I let him store there. Two of them are full of old out-of-date clothes. Inside the third box are mostly philosophy books, including five copies of a book by Gabriel Dawson, Ph.D., that's called *Agape and Filia in the Dialogues of Plato* and was published by some college in the midwest about fifteen years ago. (Later on I look up the Greek words on the Internet and find out they mean "Love and Friendship," which I guess Badger had a thing about figuring out.)

Underneath the books I find some letters from a woman named Nina, plus lots of black and white photographs—the kind actors use for auditions—of a really good-looking woman with a sexy smile. At the bottom of the box is a yellowed New York tabloid folded over. I see a young Badger staring out at me from the first page, which I read. I remember where I heard his name before.

After a while, I go to my computer, get on the Web, key in "criminalrecords.com." I ask about Gabriel Dawson in the State of New York. They fill in some details and lead me to others. Badger's wife's name was Nina. She was an actress. Or wanted to be. She was sleeping with a bartender in the restaurant where she worked, on 92nd Street near where Badger had just gotten a job teaching philosophy. When the guy brought her home at three a.m. one night, Badger was waiting on the apartment steps. He beat them both to death with a piece of lead pipe he picked up out of the garbage on the sidewalk. The guy that came along and pulled him off them cracked Badger's skull open with a tile pipe to calm him down.

The next twenty years Badger spent in a hospital for the criminally insane upstate. That's where he finished the book on Plato. At his trial, the prosecutor had fought the temporary insanity plea; he thought it was a bunch of bull to claim Aphrodite made you do things against your will. But apparently the jury decided (like a lot of regulars at the Mick decades later) that the way Badger talked about the power of love meant that he was crazy. They decided he hadn't premeditated anything, that he had murdered under an irresistible impulse.

So I think awhile and I bag the photos and letters and the old newspaper and take them to the dump with my trash. Mind the gap, right? Nobody's ever going to think of Badger. And there's no way they can say I did it; you can't get from the stadium to Ronny's and back in twenty minutes, much less kill somebody while you're gone. (And I've got the Devil Rays brass checking his watch, saying, "Where you been for twenty minutes?")

The rest of Badger's things I box back up to go to New York along with my dad's hats and my mom's books in Spanish and the leftovers of the marriage that my wife didn't want. Okay, these boxes are kind of my family, I guess, if that doesn't sound too weird, and I might as well hang onto them, what the hell.

Back in my living room, I unpack a nice crystal glass and pour myself a drink from one of the bottles of good scotch that the Tampa brass sent me. I sit and think through what must have happened when I sent Badger to take care of Angie Schuelenmeyer. I shouldn't have said, "take care of," maybe. I figure Angie's down there at the bottom of the lake off the deck of Ronny's sex shack and she's been down there around three weeks. And Mickey Mantle's autographed bat that Tap Upchurch says is worth eighteen thousand dollars, I figure that's at the bottom of the lake too. Maybe Angie gave Badger a hard time about her plan to leave Zane for Ronny that afternoon and brought back bad memories, or maybe it was just the way she looked at the height of her powers. Or maybe it was just because he didn't want to let me down.

Badger must have driven the powder blue BMW convertible to Nashville (and sent the cards from there to Zane and me, and then driven to Tampa where he left the car in Zane's driveway with the good-bye letter. I don't know what he meant by heading "out West," but if he went to California, there're so many crazies out there he'll fit right in.

A few days after I looked through his belongings, I got a good-bye letter of my own from Badger, postmarked Tampa, Florida. I think he sent it from the bus station because inside was a strip of four photos, the kind you get made in the machines they have in stations, where you sit on a seat and look at a mirror. In each shot Badger's got on a different one of the hats of my dad's that I gave him. The brown Borsolino fedora. The Dobbs felt wide brim. The Harris Tweed trilby. The plaid golf cap. In each shot Badger has that huge smile he had when I first sat down beside him at the bar of the Mick.

. And he's holding Angie's little dog Lover in his arms.

The letter's not very long.

Jordan,

I want you to know I love you, my friend. You treated me with kindness. You were generous. If I went too far to repay you, I apologize. But maybe someday she'll come back to him. Love is the lever. Go to New York. Tennis is a good game to watch there.

Gabriel Dawson

I keep the strip of photos but I burn the letter. Right, sure, Badger. You don't come back from the bottom of a lake.

The night before I fly to Manhattan, I drop by the Mick to say so long to some of the regulars. I get a shock. They're having a sort of good-bye party for me, balloons, cake, a photo of the Mick with their signatures all over it. They give me a great big cheese in the shape of North Carolina and throw in a lot of ribbing about me being a big cheese now and looking down on the good old boys. They joke about how I'll never come back to town. But it's probably true. I never will. Then somebody asks me about Badger and I hear myself saying he sent me a postcard a few days ago explaining that he's moved to Chicago because he's got family there and they got in touch with him after all these years. The regulars say they're surprised to hear it. They didn't think Badger had anybody but me.

They talk about him for a while. All his weird theories about love power and how he read books in Greek and always had a hat on because he had some kind of scar on his head that must have embarrassed him. They want to know if I ever got Badger's real name and his story out of him. I say I never did.

I'm leaving when I notice Tap Upchurch has now got a base-ball signed by Ronny Lamar Rome on a stand above the cash regis-ter. I figure the autograph's in Badger's handwriting. I'm looking at it when Tap comes over and points out that the Mickey Mantle auto-graphed bat is back on the wall next to the towel in the plastic case. Tap says a few days ago he was cleaning and he found the bat rolled under the bar into a far corner. He must just not have seen it before. It's fine, he says, except for that stain from the ketchup bottle that Ronnie Rome threw at it the night before the big game. He asks me, "Remember that night, Jordan?" I say I do, but I'm not really listening. I'm wondering am I all wrong and Badger never touched that bat? Could Ronny be right, it was a woman thing with Angie? Did maybe Badger get her into a deep discussion that afternoon here at the Mick or maybe out on the deck at Ronny's sex shack and did she maybe decide to go be free on her own? Is it possible they drove out of town together in her blue convertible, talking about fundamentals?

I'm waving good-bye when Tap stops me and reaches under the bar. He thinks he oughta give me something, since didn't I give it to Badger in the first place? He pulls out the black homberg, the hat that Badger was wearing the last time I saw him, when I asked him to go take care of things.

I ask him where he got it.

Tap shrugs, "I found it on the floor behind the bar, go figure how it got there."

"Go figure." I take the hat from him, straighten the brim, brush the crown. Tap says, "Boy, Jordan, that little nut used to say some weird shit, didn't he?"

I say, "Hey, what do we know, maybe the entire universe is just a dream of love in the mind of God." I fit the homberg on my head and head for New York.

HARLEM NOCTURNE

by Robert B. Parker

Mr. Rickey was wearing a blue polka dot bow tie and a gray tweed suit that didn't fit him very well. He took some time getting his cigar lit and then looked at me over his round black-rimmed glasses.

"I'm bringing Jackie Robinson up from Montreal," he said.

"The other shoe drops," I said.

Mr. Rickey smiled.

"I want you to protect him," he said.

"Okay," I said.

"Just like that?" Rickey said.

"I assume you'll pay me," I said.

"Don't you want to know what I'm asking you to protect him from?"

"I assume I know," I said. "People who might want to kill him for being a Negro. And himself."

Rickey nodded and turned the cigar slowly without taking it from his mouth.

"Good, " he said. "Himself was the part I didn't think you'd get."

I looked modest.

"Jackie is a man of strong character," Rickey said. "One might even say forceful. If this experiment is going to work he has to sit on that. He has to remain calm. Turn the other cheek."

"And I'll have to see that he does that," I said.

"Yes. And at the same time, see that no one harms him."

"Am I required to turn the other cheek?"

"You are required to do what is necessary to help Jackie and me and the Brooklyn Dodgers get through the impending storm."

"Do what I can," I said.

"My information is that you can do a lot. It's why you're here. You'll stay with him all the time. If anyone asks you, you are simply an assistant to the General Manager. If he has to stay in a Negro hotel, you'll have to stay there too."

"I got through Guadalcanal," I said.

"Yes, I know. How do you feel about a Negro in the Major Leagues?"

"Seems like a good idea to me."

"Good. I'll introduce you to Jackie."

He pushed the switch on an intercom and spoke into it, and a moment later a secretary opened the office door and Robinson came in wearing a gray suit and a black knit tie. He was a pretty big guy and moved as if he were working off a steel spring. He was nobody's high yellow. He was black. And he didn't seem furtive about it. Rickey introduced us.

"Well, you got the build for a bodyguard," Robinson said.

"You, too," I said.

"Well, I ain't guarding your body," Jackie said.

"Mine's not worth ten grand a year," I said.

"One thing," Robinson said, and he looked at Rickey as he spoke. "I don't need no keeper. You keep people from shooting me, good. And I know I can't be fighting people. You gotta do that for me. But I go where I want to go and do what I do. And I don't ask you first."

"As long as you let me die for you," I said.

Something flashed in Robinson's eyes. "You got a smart mouth, " he said.

"I'm a smart guy."

Robinson grinned suddenly.

"So how come you taking on this job?"

"Same as you," I said. "I need the dough."

Robinson looked at me with his hard stare.

"Well," Robinson said. "We'll see."

Rickey had been sitting quietly while Robinson and I sniffed around each other. Now he spoke.

"You can't ever let down," he said. He was looking at Robinson, but I knew I was included. "You're under a microscope. You can't drink. You can't be sexually indiscreet. You can't have opinions about things. You play hard and clean and stay quiet. Can you do it?"

"With a little luck," Robinson said.

"Luck is the residue of intention," Rickey said.

287

He talked pretty good for a guy who hit .239 lifetime.

It didn't take long to pick up the way it was going to be.

Peewee Reese was supportive. Dixie Walker was not. Everyone else was on the spectrum somewhere between.

In St. Louis, a baserunner spiked Robinson at first base. In Chicago, he was tagged in the face sliding into second. In St. Louis, somebody tossed a black cat onto the field. In Cincinnati, he was knocked down three times in one at bat. In every city we heard the word *nigger* out of the opposition dugout. None of this was my problem. It was Robinson's. There was nothing I could do about it. So I sat in my corner of the dugout and did nothing.

My work was off the field.

There was hate mail. I couldn't do anything about that, either. The club passed the death threats on, but there were so many of them that it was mostly a waste of time. All Robinson and I could do about those was be ready. I began to look at everybody as if they were dangerous.

After a double header against the Giants, I drove Robinson uptown. A gray two-door Ford pulled up beside us at a stop light and I stared at the driver. The light changed and the Ford pulled away.

"I'm starting to look at everybody as if they were dangerous," I said.

Robinson glanced over at me and smiled the way he did. The smile said, *pal you have no idea.*

But all he said was, "un huh."

We stopped to eat at a place on Lennox Ave. When we came

in everyone stared. At first I thought it was Robinson. Then I realized they hadn't even seen him yet. It was me. I was the only white face in the joint.

"Sit in the back," I said to Robinson.

"Have to, with you along," he said.

As we walked through the place, they recognized Robinson and somebody began to clap, then everybody clapped. Then they stood and clapped and hooted and whistled until we were seated.

"Probably wasn't for me, " I said.

"Probably not."

Robinson had a Coke.

"You ever drink booze?" I said.

"Not in public, " Robinson said.

"Good."

I looked around. Even for a hard case like me it was uncomfortable being in a room full of colored people. I was glad to be with Robinson.

We both ordered steak.

"No fried chicken?" I said.

"No watermelon either," Robinson said.

The room got quiet all of a sudden. The silence was so sharp that it made me hunch a little forward so I could reach the gun on my hip. Through the front door came six white men in suits and overcoats and felt hats. There was nothing uneasy about them as they came into the colored place. They swaggered. One of them swaggered like the boss, a little fat guy with his overcoat open over a dark suit. He had on a blue silk tie with a pink flamingo hand-painted on it.

"Frank Digiacomo," Robinson said. "He owns the place."

Without taking off their hats or overcoats, the six men sat at a large round table near the front.

"I hear he owns this part of Harlem," I said.

Robinson shrugged.

"When Bumpy Johnson was around, " I said, "the Italians stayed downtown."

"Good for colored people to own the businesses they run," Robinson said.

A big guy sitting next to Digiacomo stood and walked over to our table. Robinson and I were both close to 200, but this guy was in a different class. He was thick bodied and tall, with very little neck and a lot of chin. His face was clean shaved and sort of moist. His shirt was crisp white. His chesterfield overcoat hung open, and he reeked of strong cologne.

"Mr. Digiacomo wants to buy you a bottle of champagne," he said to Robinson.

Robinson put a bite of steak in his mouth and chewed it carefully and swallowed and said, "Tell Mr. Digiacomo, no thank you."

The big guy stared at him for a moment.

"Most people don't say no to Mr. Digiacomo, Rastus."

Robinson said nothing but his gaze on the big man was heavy.

"Maybe we can buy Mr. Digiacomo a bottle," I said.

"Mr. Digiacomo don't need nobody buying him a bottle."

"Well, I guess it's a draw," I said. "Thanks for stopping by."

The big guy looked at me for a long time. I didn't shrivel up and blow away, so after awhile he swaggered back to his boss. He leaned over and spoke to Digiacomo, his left hand resting on the back of Digiacomo's chair. Then he nodded and turned and swaggered back.

"On your feet, boy," he said to Robinson.

"I'm eating my dinner," Robinson said.

The big man took hold of Robinson's arm, and Robinson came out of the chair as if he'd been ejected and hit the big guy with a good right hand. Robinson was a good-sized guy in good condition, and he knew how to punch. It should have put the big guy down. But it didn't. He took a couple of backwards steps and steadied himself and shook his head as if there were flies. At Digiacomo's table everyone had turned to look. The only sound in the room was the faint clatter of dishes from the kitchen. It was so still I could hear chairs creaking as people turned to stare. I was on my feet.

"Sit down." I yelled at Robinson.

"Not up here," Robinson said. "I'll take it downtown, but not up here."

The big man had his head cleared. He looked at the table where Digiacomo sat.

"Go ahead, Sonny," Digiacomo said. "Show the nigger something."

The big man lunged toward Robinson. I stepped between them. The big man almost ran over me, and would have run over both of us if I hadn't hit him a hell of a left. It was probably no better punch than Robinson's, but it benefited from the brass knuckles

I was wearing. It stopped him but it didn't put him down. I got my knee into his groin and hit him again with the knucks. He grunted and went down slowly. First to his knees, then slowly toppling face forward onto the floor.

The place was like a tomb. Even the kitchen noise had stopped. I could hear someone's breath rasping in and out. I'd heard it before. It was mine.

The four men at Digiacomo's table were on their feet. All of them had guns, and all of them were pointing at us. Digiacomo remained seated. He looked mildly amused.

"Don't shoot them in here, " he said. "Take them out."

I was wearing a Colt .45 that I had liberated from the U.S. Marine Corps. But it was still on my hip. I should have had it out when this thing started.

One of the other men, a thin tall man with high shoulders, said "Outside" and gestured with the .38 belly gun he carried. He was the gunny. You could tell by the way he held the weapon, like it was precious.

"No." Robinson said.

"How about you, pal?" the gunny said to me.

I shook my head. The gunny looked at Digiacomo.

Digiacomo said, "Okay, shoot them here. Make sure the niggers clean up afterwards."

The gunny smiled. He was probably good at it. You could see he liked the work.

"Which one of you wants it first?" he said.

At the next table a small Negro with a thin moustache, wearing a cerulean blue suit, said "No."

The gunny glanced at him.

"You too, Boy?" he said.

At the table on the other side of us a large woman in a too-tight yellow dress said, "No." And stood up.

The gunny glanced at her. The small Negro with the mustache stood too. Then everyone at his table stood. The woman in the too-tight dress moved in front of Robinson and me. Between us and the gunny. The people from her table joined her. The people from moustache's table joined them. Then everyone in the room was on their feet, closing on us, surrounding us, making an implacable black wall between us and the gunny. I took my gun out. Robinson stood motionless, balanced on the balls of his feet. From the bar along the far side of the room came the sound of someone working the action of a pump shotgun. It is a sound, like the sound of a tank, that doesn't sound like anything else. Through the crowd I could see the round-faced bartender leaning his elbows on the bar aiming a shotgun with most of the stock cut off.

The gunny looked at Digiacomo again. They were an island of pallid faces in a sea of dark faces. Digiacomo got to his feet for the first time. His face was no longer amused. He looked at me through the crowd, and at Robinson, and seemed to study us both for a moment. Then he jerked his head toward the big man who had managed to sit up on the floor among the forest of Negro feet. Two of the other men with Digiacomo eased through the crowd and got the big man on his feet. They looked at Digiacomo. Digiacomo looked at us again, then turned without speaking and walked out. The gunny put his belly gun away, sadly, and turned and followed Digiacomo. The other men, two of them helping the big guy, went out after him.

The room was as still and motionless as Sunday in Antarctica. Then Robinson said again, "Not up here," and everyone in the room heard him and everyone in the room began to cheer.

"Lucky thing this is a baseball crowd," I said to Robinson.

He looked at me for a moment as if he were somewhere else. Then he seemed slowly to come back. He smiled.

"Yeah," he said. "Lucky thing."

THE CLOSER

by Thomas Perry

How a man of intelligence like Rudolph Prosser could have been deceived into something as unpromising and self-destructive as owning a baseball team is a question that's puzzled some people, but not me. I was there.

At the time, Prosser had no interest in sports. He was in the resale business. He had part-time associates—young women who wanted a few extra bucks—going around to garage sales and church bazaars on weekends, buying up things that looked interesting, which was his term for old and cheap. On any weekend, they might come back with trinkets, mementos, pictures, clothes, pieces of luggage designed to hold things nobody wears anymore, tools for doing things nobody does anymore, or assorted objects of a decorative nature.

If you went into Prosser's office on a weekday, he would be sitting with one of their finds on the bare table in front of him. He would glare at it as though he were trying to see through it. He would walk around the table and squint at it. He would turn away and look out a window for a minute, then suddenly spin and see it as though it had just appeared there by surprise. He would lean back in his swivel chair, and turn the object over and over in his hands. After a time, he would say out loud what it was. "This is the cane that George Gershwin carried to the first performance of 'Rhapsody in Blue.'" "This is a ribbon cut as a souvenir from the dress that Catherine the Great wore to her first dance in St. Petersburg." "This is the vest that Leon Czolgosz wore when he shot President McKinley."

Later he would dig up books of pictures from the library and make copies of the pictures for proof. You could look, and Gershwin was wearing a tuxedo and carrying a cane, and yeah, it could have been the same shiny plain black cane. You couldn't prove it wasn't. And there would be a drawing of a guy shooting McKinley, and sure as hell, everybody in it was wearing a vest. Prosser would put all these things in a big cabinet with glass doors on it, and collectors would come and buy them. The trade in sacred relics has never been the province of skeptics: everybody wants to believe. The collectors are usually people who have a whole lot of fresh money, and are busy trying to look as though they didn't earn it, but found it lying around the family mansion, where it's been for many generations. Their only fear is that the supply of historical oddities will get used up before they get enough of them. So Prosser was doing fine.

But Prosser was now holding cash, so the old upper crust, the ones whose families bought their respectability a long time ago, could pull the reverse scam on him. They would bring him the same sorts of stuff—whatever they found in an attic or basement—and serve it to him with a sauce of nonsense. "My grandmother was

Eleanor Roosevelt's best friend at school. Many years later, she gave grandma this cigarette case. It seems that George Bernard Shaw gave it to Winston Churchill. Churchill only smoked cigars, so he passed it on to Franklin, who smoked cigarettes. When Franklin died, Eleanor gave it to my grandma." Prosser never believed a word of this stuff, but he was a captive. The scammer would have a famous name: probably his grandmother really did go to the same school as Eleanor Roosevelt. Prosser's ambition required that he have good relations with these people, and they knew it. He couldn't say, "Your granny's a liar," and expect to be invited to her summer house in the Hamptons. He couldn't say that he didn't want the priceless family treasure, because not wanting it was the same as saying it wasn't real. He couldn't say he couldn't afford it, because money was his only claim to legitimacy. So he always said, "Amazing. What a find," and he said it while he was writing a check.

But Prosser's real talent was defending himself—ducking a punch and redirecting the force of it to open a door for him. He would wait until the seller was gone, then sit down and type up the story exactly as it had been fed to him, with all of the real names and fake events and dates that he'd just heard. What it did was give this piece of trash a genuine provenance, transforming it from a mere thing into an old and valuable thing that used to belong to the famous. Prosser was not the one claiming anything: he was only recording the testimony of the heir of a great family.

It began to happen to Prosser more and more often. On the afternoon when Wilfred Sternham called and said he was going to stop by Prosser's office to talk about something important, I think

Prosser was expecting to be sold his third set of George Washington's false teeth or his fourth pair of Ben Franklin's spectacles. The Sternhams were an old family that had a long history in Delaware before one of them moved to California to sell spoiled food to miners during the gold rush. But the truth was worse than an old set of spectacles. What Sternham was selling was the California Coyotes.

Sternham was still rich, but he was leaking money. His grandfather had built Coyote Stadium in the same shoddy way he had built half the apartment buildings in Southern California. He'd always started with a set of plans that got him permits, then rolled them up and put them away while the building was adlibbed by a crew of laborers he trucked in from Tijuana at night. The stadium had already outlasted all of the apartment buildings, but it was crumbling. Wilfred the Third couldn't afford to fix it up at modem labor prices, and modern building codes would have sent him to prison. So every year he spent hundreds of thousands just having guys go around with buckets of epoxy, gluing chunks of concrete back where they'd fallen off.

But his big expense was his payroll. He had a handful of players who had put in a few great seasons, but none of them lately. In the field they were semi-retired. They'd catch a fly if it was high enough so they could walk under it. They'd pick a grounder if it was going to hit them in the balls anyway. To balance them, Sternham filled in with eager rookies, all of them so young that when a grown man talked to them, he couldn't tell whether they were dumb or not. The only bright spot, speaking athletically, was Marcus D. Walsh. He was the finest young pitcher since the first time somebody got the gruesome idea of wrapping a dead horse's skin around a ball of string and hitting it with a stick. He even had the ideal look of a pitcher: tall and rangy, with hair that couldn't be cut so it didn't stick out under his cap and a face so ugly that even his normal, businesslike stare could loosen a batter's bowels. In a fit of optimism, when Sternham was still deluding himself into believing that all the Coyotes needed was pitching, he had signed Walsh for two million a year. That was much less than he was worth, but it brought the total payroll for the twenty-five man roster to just over nine million. The ticket sales for the previous year had been three and a half. When the word got out among people who knew Prosser that he had bought the California Coyotes, there was a certain amount of disbelief, followed by a lot of speculation about how Sternham could have fooled him.

But I knew that Prosser was not buying a hopelessly bankrupt baseball team with a ruined stadium because he thought it was something else. Within a day or two he began, after his own fashion, to pay attention to it as a business. He took out a big insurance policy on the players, with a special Marcus D. Walsh Rider that had a pay-off commensurate with Walsh's value if he had been made of pure plutonium and had the Hope Diamond stuck up his nose. Rudolph Prosser buying an insurance policy meant something. You can run a baseball franchise, a circus, or a government for a very long time on credit, but insurance is a serious business run by adults. Either your premium is paid in advance, or you're not a customer.

When Prosser took over it was already time for the All-Star

break. Only two Coyotes were picked to play for the National League. Actually, it was one—Marcus D. Walsh. The other was Bart Floyd, the only catcher in the league that was used to predicting where Walsh's junk pitches were going to break, and having his mitt there in time to keep the umpire from getting hurt. That afternoon, Walsh was supposed to pitch the first three innings. He cheerfully went out to the mound and celebrated the eternal values of the great American pastime by throwing two and a third innings of perfect baseball—seven strikeouts—against the best hitters the American League had. Pulling him out was a direct order from the Commissioner, because the television network warned him they were losing their audience. The viewers who weren't really baseball fans but had just tuned in out of curiosity had gotten the erroneous impression that because nothing was happening, nothing was happening. Walsh's pitching had a bad effect even on the announcers. They had used up their superlatives after two innings, and were forced to repeat all the same ones for the rest of the game.

The season started up after the All-Star break, and the Coyotes were doing a bit better than usual. Whenever Walsh pitched, the other side did lousy, and if a few of the Coyotes could hit anything, they won. That alone gave them about quarter of their games, and they won a few more on other teams' late-season injuries and sheer fatigue. The Coyotes' older players didn't work hard enough to get tired or hurt, and the rookies didn't know what those words meant.

During this part of the season, Prosser was trying to work out a way to make some money on the team—at least enough of it to keep from getting shut down before he could sell out. Because he was dishonest by preference and long practice, he was not without ideas. But the first thing he needed to do was hire a ringer.

The guy's name was Alvin Rollins. Or that was the name I was told he was born with. But you never know with a ringer, and that's precisely the point, isn't it? Alvin Rollins had a talent, and he had taken it all the way from a practical skill to a vice, and maybe occasionally, beyond that to a delusion. People said he had been trained as an actor, but that wasn't because it was true. It was because that's the kind of thing people say. They always try to explain away somebody else's ability with training, to imply that they could have been just as good at it if they'd had the years of instruction and practice. The truth was that the only kind of instruction Alvin Rollins had was the kind where you try to fool somebody, and if you fail, they kick your ass for you.

He did have lots of practice. Every time there was a guy in the papers who did something he admired, he would pay a lot of attention to the articles. Next week, sure enough, he would be out there in the world, presenting himself as the doctor who invented some vaccine to cure a disease. He almost never even looked like the guy, as anyone would know if they compared him with a picture of the real doctor. But who carries around a picture of some doctor? That would be sicker than impersonating the guy. All Alvin had to do was look and act like the kind of doctor who might have invented a vaccine.

When he was being a ringer for somebody, he threw himself into it. I ran into him one time when he was pretending to be the conductor of the Philadelphia Symphony Orchestra, and asked him why he bothered. He said, "Well, the money isn't great, but it's been grat-ifying to spend my life making the kind of music I love, and working with so many talented musicians." I wasn't sure if he had forgotten I knew him, or if he'd forgotten he hadn't been within a thousand miles of Philadelphia. But it was neither. He just stayed in character like that, relentlessly, until he decided to be somebody else. He did it without knowing more about the person than what had been in the papers. He didn't bother to find out more. He would just act like him-self as that person—do what he would do if he had actually been born as that person.

Of course, what he was doing was practical. He was using the unused portions of a person's reputation to get free meals, trips to pleasant places, gifts, loans, sometimes mutually-satisfying relation-ships with women. He was robbing the other guy, but he also wasn't. He took things the real guy probably wouldn't have wanted. And he wasn't crazy. He might make you forget who he was, but he didn't forget, and if he needed to get out fast, he did.

The summer when Prosser got in touch with him, he was already in his prime. He could be anybody whose face was not com-pletely familiar. There's some percentage of the population at any given time that doesn't know, for instance, who the Vice President is—can't name him, can't identify his picture. For those people, Alvin would have been a more-than-adequate Vice President. And he would have done it without pay, just for what he could pick up on his own.

Prosser may have been the first one ever to give Alvin any of his own money to do an impersonation. It wasn't big money, of course. He just helped Alvin apply for credit cards in the name Rudolph Prosser. There was a federal law that limited Prosser's liability for what anybody charged to him fraudulently to fifty bucks on each card. But the money the cards brought Alvin was potentially a big number. This arrangement also gave Prosser an excuse to have Alvin come to his office and spend time listening to Prosser's voice and learning how he dressed and carried himself. I guess he didn't want Alvin to embarrass him.

A couple of days later I saw Alvin, because I was supposed to put him on a plane to join the team in Houston. His clothes, his manner, his posture, his walk were right. He didn't look like Prosser. But he looked like he was a human being who occupied the same space in the food chain—the way all game show hosts do, or all dark-haired actresses who tempt the hero, but don't get to marry him. And his voice was better than that. It was perfect. If he had called me on the phone, he would have fooled me. He was ready, and it was a good thing, because that was the right time for Prosser to put his ringer in: as soon as he took control of the team, and before anybody in baseball had ever seen him. While everybody had their eyes on Alvin, Prosser could place his bets.

Betting on baseball is a peculiar activity. Given teams of reasonably equal ability, what you are betting on is who the pitchers will be that night, and that's information that's printed on the sports page in advance. If it were a simple question of betting on a good pitcher against a bad pitcher, it would be hard to find anybody who would take your bet. You would be limited to betting against that small segment of the population who sees a dog chasing a car, and bets that the dog will catch the car, kill it, and eat it. The bookmakers solve your problem by adjusting the odds to compensate for risk, and console themselves for whatever their own problems are by taking ten percent vigorish. Their labors enabled Prosser to make some money on the Coyotes.

Prosser won his bets in a number of ways. Sometimes he would list Walsh as the starting pitcher, place a bet against the Coyotes, and then pull Walsh before the game so his team would lose. Sometimes he would list another pitcher—say, Tyler Tyler, the frighteningly inaccurate fastballer, or Eduardo Martinez, the oddly-named Canadian pitcher who could throw equally badly with either arm—and bet on the Coyotes, then put Walsh in as a reliever. Walsh would come in, throw pitches that either wobbled erratically or came across the plate so fast that they were mainly heard rather than seen, and then amble off to the showers while Prosser collected.

Prosser kept the team alive that way through a five-game run against Houston, and a three-game stand in Cincinnati. Obviously, Prosser had no realistic chance of keeping this up very long. Betting by anyone who can influence a professional baseball game is famously illegal, and placing winning bets too often on anything can make the losers suspicious.

Right then, the Coyotes were coming up on a one-game stand against the Florida Catfish. The Cats were the only team I know of ever to be owned by a pro athlete. The owner was Eddie Brand, the P.G.A. golfer, a man who lived for—

Okay, okay. Everything is a matter of proportion and degree, and no person is all one thing or another. So now, will you shut up and let me go on? There are great athletes and great competitors, and they're not the same thing. Brand was an okay athlete: he had to be to make the tour. But he won matches far out of proportion to his skill, because he was the most competitive human being I ever saw. Brand began competing way before the match, as soon as he heard your name. That was when he started figuring out who you were and how he would beat you.

He had to win—to be in the process of winning all day long. If he couldn't get you to do what he did, which was playing golf, he would invent something neither of you did, and beat you at that. I once saw him at breakfast in a hotel in Palm Beach the morning after a tournament, when most of the other pro golfers had left. He couldn't get anybody to go to the putting green with him. Nobody would go to the pool and race him. Finally, he made up a game where you go out on the patio and throw forks at a bagel. Honest to God. The rule was that you had to get it to stick.

Here is all you need to know about Brand: He hadn't just made up that stupid game. He had made it up before, and practiced. Before anybody bet any money, he had already made himself into the world champion of bagel-forking.

I've heard people giving their theories about what the trouble was. Every single one of them is right. Yes, his brain did have a chemical need, a requirement for a lot of extra stimulation before it released enough norepinephrin to give him a rush. This is common to people who make big bets, climb higher than is good for them, or ride in things that go too fast. And yes, he did have a psychological need to continually prove his worth to himself to make up for some inadequacy. And if you like really simple-minded terms, you could say he was evil. He made himself feel good by making other people feel bad. Any way you want to talk about these things, they made him a hard man to beat: you couldn't rattle him, get him to quit, or hope for mercy.

Prosser had only been winning bets for a couple of weeks before he learned that Eddie Brand had found out how he was breaking even. Brand made a couple of thinly-veiled comments where he knew Prosser—actually Alvin Rollins—would eventually hear them. He even said some things at a benefit dinner to a Coyote named Abie Grelton. You might remember him from the days when he played for Atlanta. You sure as hell wouldn't remember him from his time with the Coyotes.

Brand's hints made Prosser do some figuring. What Brand wanted was to win his game against the Coyotes. He wanted his Florida Catfish to take the World Series, and he knew that the last remaining obstacle to getting into the Series was being a game behind the Cincinnati Reds. Prosser also judged that Brand was bright enough to know that Prosser didn't care about winning games. That was for kids. Prosser was interested in winning money.

Brand and Prosser began to bump into each other by accident more and more often. This was, of course, not Brand and the real Prosser, but Brand and Alvin. The real Prosser was not available to travel around the country watching games or going to charity dinners. He was busy trying to keep enough money coming in to meet his payroll.

After a few of these coincidental encounters, it became clear to the real Prosser what Brand was trying to do: he wanted to establish an understanding between them, an agreement. Prosser didn't let the conversation take place. But two days before the game with Florida, Prosser, in the person of Alvin, was seen by Brand's surveillance men giving money to a swarthy man in a panama hat, who then placed some large bets against the California Coyotes. That was me.

What happened next confirmed one of my beliefs about Brand. He could not bear to see anybody engage in anything like a competition and not jump in to beat him. He had never, since he had bought the Florida Catfish, placed a bet on a game. He knew it would get him kicked out of baseball for life. But as soon as he knew Prosser was about to win a bet, he couldn't help placing a bet on Florida against the Coyotes too. If that was where Prosser's money was, then Florida was a sure thing. Being Brand, he not only had to have his Florida Catfish win the game against the Coyotes, but he had to win more money than Prosser did betting that they would.

But Brand faced a couple of problems. One was that Prosser's bets had been placed before his. Prosser's bets, he figured, must be so big that they changed the odds. If Brand was to bet the same way, he had to bet more money just to get the same winnings. When he started betting, the odds were already eight to five that Florida would win. He had to bet twice as much as Prosser to beat his take, so he bet three times as much. Then he worried that his people hadn't seen all the bets Prosser might have placed, and made it five times as much. But he was dealing with a sure thing, a fixed game, and it was hard to stop betting. I'm not sure what he bet after that. It had to be a fortune, because it put him into debt and kept him worried. It ate at him and tormented him.

Part of him believed everything was going to proceed as he expected. Walsh would be listed as pitcher. At the last minute, Prosser would change the roster. The pitcher for the Coyotes would be some dope, who would lose. Great. But Brand knew baseball could be more complicated than that. The dope the Coyotes put in to lose might throw the game of his life. Half the Catfish lineup might catch the flu. Anything could happen. Brand chewed on the problem for another day. Then he hired George Decker as his closer.

In his early years, Decker was known primarily as a marksman, so I know you're assuming what I'm going to describe is him sitting in a building a quarter mile from the stadium with a thirty-ought-six and laying the crosshairs on the crown of Marcus Walsh's hat. Decker could certainly have done that if Brand had asked. But he was capable of something more subtle, too. I heard he got Paul McConnell by injecting poison into an orange while it was still on the tree in his back yard. He just knew McConnell wanted his own organic oranges every day because he didn't want to eat food with bug spray on it. Decker did people with knives a couple of times that I know of, but of course, nobody who's done that once does it again unless he really has to. He ran over at least one guy with a car, and drowned some others. He was not a man who was ever at a loss. He could kill you with your own shoelaces.

Brand had bet heavily that Prosser was planning to lose the game, and that he would succeed. If that didn't happen, Decker could help. Killing anybody on the field would stop a game. If he stopped the game before the end of the fifth inning, the game didn't count. If he stopped it any time after the fifth, it counted. So if things were going so badly early in the game that Brand wanted to call it off, he could. If Brand's team was ahead later in the game and he wanted to end it then, he could do that. Decker's job was to be nearby with his cell phone turned on and in his pocket, watching the game like the closer in the bullpen, waiting for Brand to call him in to end it.

The first two series earlier in the season had been split even, one for the Coyotes and one for the Catfish. Actually, what happened was that the Coyotes got lucky on the first stand, and the forces of physics reasserted themselves during the second one. Brand hated giving up a hit, let alone a run, and losing the first three-game stand in May made him crazier than usual. When his Catfish won the second stand, the sun looked brighter to him, and his food tasted better.

The final game was played on an uncharacteristically beautiful Florida evening. Normally, Florida is a hateful, pestilent place with air so thick with humidity you can faint blowing up a balloon, and get a hernia lifting it afterward. We stood up for the national anthem in daylight, with the sun guttering beyond the Gulf of Mexico, and the stars already visible in the east, floating in that special blue that glows. When the ump dusted the plate and yelled, "Play ball!" the Coyotes went back into their dugout. The first three came out carrying bats, but they needn't have bothered. It was wasted weight. When they were through doing nothing as the ball sailed past, they got their gloves and trotted out to the field. But the one who came out with them to the mound was not Marcus D. Walsh. The announcer said, "Pitching for the Coyotes is....Ernesto Martinez!" I looked more closely, and it was no mistake. It was the ambidextrous hurler from North of the Border.

I caught a glimpse of Eddie Brand, sitting up behind the glass in his owner's box. He was smiling. The grin didn't get any smaller for the next three innings. Martinez threw right-handed against left-handed batters, and left-handed against right-handed batters, so the ball would naturally swoop in at them. It didn't swoop. It just hung until the bat punished it. So Martinez would throw to each batter next time up with the other hand. It didn't do him any good. They liked everything.

It was not until the bottom of the fourth that Eddie Brand lost his composure. He happened to be looking at the box that was reserved for dignitaries from the visiting team's organization, when the announcer pointed out that the owner of the California Coyotes had just arrived and taken his seat. I don't know if the announcer knew Prosser by sight, or just figured that must be who it was. But I saw Brand the moment when he heard it. He stared, he squinted, he scowled, and then he picked up a pair of binoculars. The man he was looking at was not the man he knew as Rudolph Prosser. His suspicion grew to worry, then consternation. He had been studying the wrong man, drawing conclusions about his character, establishing unspoken understandings about what was supposed to happen in this game. When he considered the nature of the silent agreement he had made, and the fact that he had made it with an impostor, he began to sweat.

But he looked at the field, and his eyes argued with him. His Catfish had two runs. The Coyotes had no runs. Maybe the ringer was working for Prosser just to handle his bets, and had been acting in accordance with his wishes. After all, Walsh had been scheduled to start the game, and he had been scratched at the last minute. And that was what Brand wanted.

Brand was not uncomfortable with pressure. He sat back in his upholstered seat in the owner's box and considered. The game was going just as it was supposed to be. His team was winning. It was the bottom of the fourth, and the Coyotes were scoreless. He thought long and hard, and then he picked up the cell phone he carried and called his closer.

I could see him doing it, and so could everyone else. Prosser and I were probably the only ones who knew the name of the man on the other end, or what Brand could have been saying. He wanted to take the element of pure chance out of the game. He wanted Decker to get ready and stand by. If the Florida Catfish held their lead at the end of the fifth, he wanted Decker to end the game. All Decker had to do was drop someone on the field. Anyone would do—the umpire was always a favorite with the crowd, but the choice wasn't important. The reason you hire a professional is that they don't care who they kill.

But as soon as Brand put in the call, Prosser put in a call of his own, to his manager, one-legged Doc Crandall. In a moment, Crandall was limping toward the mound. He held his right arm in the air and tapped it with his left, and the bullpen opened. Marcus D. Walsh trotted out from behind the fence to take Martinez's place. He threw his seven warm-ups, then nodded to the umpire. The batter came to the plate, swung at the first pitch, and popped up to the second baseman. The second batter struck out on four pitches, and the third tapped a dribbling ground ball back to Walsh, who made a slow toss to first to retire him. Walsh was out of the inning on seven pitches. It was an ugly sight to Eddie Brand, certainly, but not terribly worrisome in any practical way. The Catfish had a two-run lead. In one more inning, Decker would shut the game down.

The top of the fifth inning was not what Brand had expected. It might have been that the arrival of Marcus Walsh gave the Coyotes confidence. It might have been the odd combination of players on the Coyote team. There were three old professionals who were near the end of their days and lived on the fact that their nervous systems had done nothing for about thirty years except direct their arms and legs in a few set motions involved with catching, throwing, or hitting a baseball. The rest were rookies, and very emotional. They were half-crazy to hit every pitch. When they hit one, and the ball was in the air, they were so eager that they looked like they wanted to outrun it and catch it in their teeth like young dogs. In the top of the fifth they seemed to be able to smell tension in the air, and it affected them. Chip Hrsinka was up first, and he slammed a line drive over third base that put him on second. Roy Moulger, the old Red Sox third baseman, came out as always and did the least that he deemed necessary, which this time was to tap a Texas Leaguer only a few inches over the first baseman's glove and along the right field line. This easily scored Hrsinka, who came home standing up, looking as though he wanted to round the plate and dash the circuit of bases again just out of excitement. Then a kid named Billy Stupak, a rookie from Minnesota who had the vacant, pale eyes of a future serial killer, got possessed by the spirit and hit a home run. At that point, Brand was on the phone to Decker again, frantic to call him off. If Decker killed somebody on the field now, the game would be in the books as a loss.

In the sixth inning Decker was in a seat beyond the outfield holding a popcorn bag that probably had a silenced pistol inside it, and the cell phone in his breast pocket where he could be sure to hear it ring.

The Coyotes held on. In the seventh, he was along the first base line right behind the first base coach. Since he spent the whole inning there, he didn't care which coach was going to get it. Or maybe it was one of the umpires, who was about as close, and of a size that would have made him impossible to miss.

It was the bottom of the eighth when Eddie Brand decided he had to make something happen. Walsh had been pitching for the Coyotes as though he knew how important this game was, and the Catfish couldn't hit anything. Brand ordered Axel Poole to lean into the plate and take one for the team. Poole did it. Only, because it was Marcus Walsh throwing, Poole got lifted off his feet as though he had been blown away from the plate by lightning. Afterward they couldn't even stand him up. Brand put in a pinch runner, Zipper Moore, to take his base. The next Catfish batter, Ervin Dumas, popped up. The right fielder for the Coyotes was Spokane Arkwright, the old Cardinals player. He went to step under it as he'd done maybe a hundred thousand times, when Carmine Tularemia, the eighteen-year-old Dominican center fielder, got all wild-eyed and ran like a gazelle across the field, dove, and collided with him. The ball bounced.

Zipper Moore, the Cat pinch runner, took second, and Ervin Dumas crossed first.

But the play wouldn't die. Tularemia snatched up the ball, and hurled it to the shortstop to hold the base runner on second. Only the man he threw it to was a shortstop of his imagination, who must have been about twelve feet tall, and quite a jumper. The ball sailed over Porky Thomas's head. If it had gone into the seats, the damage would have been limited. But it hit the fence and dribbled away. Zipper Moore, the pinch runner, rounded third. The Coyotes' third baseman, Roy Moulger, had tired himself out getting a hit and running the bases today already, so it took him a few huffing waddles to get the ball. He lifted it and threw, like an old pro, right on target toward home. Only the second runner, Ervin Dumas, came around third when Moulger wasn't expecting to see him, because he had just seen Zipper Moore come by there. The throw hit Dumas in the back of the head as he rounded third, and dropped him on his face in the dirt. After he was revived and all this got sorted out, the rule is that a man hit by a thrown ball went to the next base. In this case, the base was home. It was Catfish four, Coyotes three.

At this moment, I thought I knew exactly what was happening in Eddie Brand's mind. Two of his best men were too injured to play. The Coyotes seemed to have gotten used to his best pitchers around the top of the fifth. And though his team had squeaked ahead for the moment, the lead had only been accomplished by having a player step in front of a fastball, a feat no other player was likely to repeat. The Catfish still couldn't hit Walsh's pitching with their bats, and they knew it. They were ahead, but they were standing around looking dazed and demoralized, while the worst that could be said of the Coyotes was that they were showing excessive energy and spirit. Brand knew that very shortly his team's lead was going to disappear. Before that happened, he wanted this game over. He had his phone in his hand, and he was calling in his closer.

I looked at the spot where I had last seen Decker. He was gone. So I looked at the owner's box to watch Brand behind the glass to see if I could figure out who, exactly, was going to get it. I guessed that Brand would be staring down at the man he was telling Decker to kill. Since Brand was the sort of man he was, I figured Marcus D. Walsh was about to wind up, step toward the plate, release a pitch, and follow through right into the ground. But I couldn't be sure, because Brand finished his call and sat calmly up there in his air-conditioned glass box, looking straight ahead.

I waited. There were no loud noises. The Coyotes got through the bottom of the eighth, and came to bat. I kept waiting for the shot. It had to come soon, before the Catfish lost their slim lead. I began to suspect that Brand was more complicated than he seemed. Maybe he had a way to get back his money whether he won the game or not. Maybe he'd insured his team for even more than Prosser did, and he was going to have Decker kill one of his own players. That way, he would not be a suspect, and he'd clear enough to pay whatever he borrowed and still make more money than Prosser.

I stared at Brand. He was still a statue. The Coyotes came to bat in the top of the ninth. They were in a frenzy. Not only were the batter and the man on deck wearing batting helmets and holding bats, but so were the seven men in the dugout. The first player up was Roy Moulger, who got on base again with another tap that went right over the third baseman's head, not a foot farther than necessary. Then Darren Warren, a Coyote outfielder who was so young that his mother had to sign his contract, hit a double. He ran so fast that he could reach out and pat Moulger on the back, so Moulger ended up on third in spite of himself. All this time, I was waiting and watching Brand. My fascination with him had reached new intensity. He was absolutely unperturbed. Maybe his lust for competition, his love of risk was so uncontrollable that he enjoyed this, and couldn't quite get himself to have Decker end it.

A kid named Corliss came up to bat for the Coyotes. He was in about the same mental state that soldiers are who charge machine-gun nests. The ball came toward the plate, he swung and hit a line drive against the left field fence. For a moment, when the Catfish left fielder was chasing it down, I had a chance to look at the infield. Roy Moulger was trotting along as fast as he felt was required with Darren Warren a pace behind, looking crazy because he couldn't pass Moulger on the base path. Corliss by this time was only a pace behind Warren. As the throw came sailing toward home plate like a meteor, you could see the three of them step on the plate like a six-legged animal—tap, tap, tap—just like that.

Six to four.

I stared at Brand. He didn't move. The Florida Catfish came to bat and Marcus Walsh put them down in order. The game was over. People in the stadium stood up and began to head for the exits. Eddie Brand didn't. One of his people went to his air-conditioned box and rapped on the glass, but Brand didn't answer. The guy went to get a security man to open it up.

Brand was dead.

People didn't wonder much about Brand's death, because it was the sort of game that might kill an owner, and almost nobody knew about the bets or about Decker. Most of the speculation among people who did was about how it affected Prosser. Of course Prosser lost some money: about a million on the bets I placed for him on the Catfish. But he made eight million on the bets he had placed on the Coyotes, five million on the sale of Marcus D. Walsh to the Yankees, and twenty-six million for the California Coyotes on the eve of the playoffs. The price was so high because he didn't mention to anybody that Walsh was not part of the deal.

I ran into Decker in New York a year later, and he told me enough to satisfy some of my scientific curiosity. What happened was Brand's call to Decker at the bottom of the eighth.

Brand told him, "The Catfish are ahead. So kill somebody on the field now, before the Coyotes take the game away from them. Use the noise and confusion to get Rudolph Prosser, too."

Decker said, "Why him?"

Brand said, "Because he stiffed me." And then Brand made the big mistake. He said, "Prosser bet money that the Catfish would win. So I bet the Catfish would win. All that betting jacked up the odds. In order to win enough to make this worth it, I had to bet a fortune. By the time I was done placing bets, the best odds I could get were thirteen to five. It's costing me nearly three bucks to earn one. Now kill somebody quick, before I lose even that!"

Decker hung up. All this time, he'd been assuming that what

317

was motivating Brand was just wanting to win. Now he knew that an unusual sum of money had been bet on this game, and that the odds were lopsided that the Catfish would win. He also realized that he was holding a cell phone that Eddie Brand made sure couldn't be traced to either of them. He dialed the number of the well-known bookmaker Anxious Barlovsky and inquired about the current odds. They had risen to fourteen to five because the Catfish were ahead and it was late in the game.

But Decker had respect for Brand's judgment. Brand had just told him that if something didn't end the game prematurely, the Coyotes were going to take back the lead. He could see as well as Brand could that the momentum was with the Coyotes and the Catfish were in a state of confusion. So Decker placed a wager of his own on the Coyotes. What Brand forgot, momentarily, was that there are two things you have to remember about professionals: they don't care who they kill, and the only reason they kill anybody is the money.

I didn't have the lack of tact to ask Decker how, exactly, he killed Eddie Brand. He certainly didn't tell me. The autopsy said Brand had heart failure, so I figured he must have used one of those drugs that stop the heart. I thought about the different times when I had seen Decker, and where he had been, and so on. I still couldn't figure out how he had gotten an injection into Brand unless he had done it before the game had even begun. Now I think I know: he didn't. All he did was turn off the telephone he had, pop it into a trash bin, and then sit down to watch the rest of the game. I think watching Decker not kill anybody was what killed Brand.

After I talked to Decker, Prosser decided to get in touch with him, and they met. They got along surprisingly well. When Decker left, Prosser gave him a present. It was the bat that Babe Ruth used to hit his first major league home run. People saved a lot of memorabilia from late in Ruth's career, but from the beginning, hardly anything: who knew? It was one of Prosser's most valuable finds.

KILLING TEDDY BALLGAME

by Henry Slesar

I t was either the best job of my life or the worst. You tell me. There I was, sitting in a box at Fenway Park, in a seat reserved for me by Joe Cronin himself. The only time I ever got closer to a ball game was when I played two seasons for the Minneapolis farm club. I hit a decent .300 the first year, .199 the second, which tells you why I gave up baseball and joined the Boston Police Department. I was only thirty-nine when I retired, so I opened up my own P.I. agency and found runaway teenagers, caught errant husbands in *flagrante delicto,* and then landed the best assignment of my career. Or the worst. You call it.

What made it the worst, of course, was right in front of me. Thirty thousand Boston Red Sox fans, a mosaic of faces and sports shirts and strong feelings this way or that way about Ted Williams, despite a record that said he was the best damn hitter in baseball, that he was driving in more runs than anybody for the team for which they were cheering themselves hoarse. How could I know who loved or hated him? How could I spot the potential killer of Teddy Ballgame out of thirty thousand suspects?

But that's what I was there for, to keep The Kid from getting killed. Was it possible? That was the question Joe Cronin asked me when we ran into each other at a Sports Writers Club cocktail party almost two months ago. I was flattered that Joe recognized me, until I realized that he mistook me for Tim McGarrity of the Boston *Globe*. I looked a bit like Tim, but I was cuter. When I corrected him, Joe didn't blink an eyelash. He said: "You're a detective?" I modestly mentioned that I was also an ex-ballplayer. Never mind the record. That lifted his bushy eyebrows even higher. "Hey," he said, "'just the man I wanted to talk to!"

He grabbed my elbow and steered me into a quiet corner. Then he told me what was on his mind. The club had been receiving some threatening phone calls and at least a dozen angry letters, all about Ted Williams. It was no big surprise, of course. Teddy Ballgame had been the Red Sox's most controversial player for a decade. The fans loved him and hated him at the same time. And the sports writers—Joe looked around the room—he was their favorite target and Ted always returned their fire. "Who knows?" he said. "Maybe some of these bozos made those calls." He grinned to show me he was only kidding.

I asked how Ted felt about the threats, and Cronin put a scowl on his big square-jawed face.

"Ted hasn't seen them," he said. "I decided not to show them to him. Ted's got enough on his mind these days. Remember that elbow he cracked last year?"

"All Star game, Comiskey Park. Ralph Kiner."

"Kiner, right. Hit one deep into left center, Ted caught it and

322

crashed his elbow into the fence. Out for two months. It still bothers him, but the fans bother him more, the ones who boo him."

"Ted never helped himself with the fans, did he? At Fenway or anyplace else. I was in Detroit last year. It was the first game of a double-header, and Ted dropped a pop fly. He got booed, of course, and Ted made those donkey ears at them."

Cronin grunted, shifted in his chair. "He also hit a grand slam that day, remember? Didn't help much, since we were losing thirteen zip."

"But that second game," I reminded him gently. "'When Ted made an error and they screamed even louder.... That's when he gave them another gesture. Flipped the bird."

"He apologized for that," Cronin said defensively.

"And that spitting business. Spitting at the fans. That didn't make him any friends. But I think what offended them most was his refusing to tip his cap. Let's face it, Joe. The fans like to cheer for their heroes, but they want something in return."

Cronin was looking depressed.

"What's the use?" he said. "Ted's got a temper, we all know that. But he's also got a heart. Everybody on the team likes him. And God knows we need that big bat of his."

I gave Cronin the best advice I could. Don't sweat the stuff. Every big name gets crank mail. Most threats are empty. Etcetera, etcetera. The manager nodded his head, but I'm not sure my argument had convinced him. Just before someone dragged him away, he said: "What about Eddie Waitkus? Who would have figured that to happen?"

When I got home that night, bragging to my wife Angie about my new best buddy Joe Cronin, she said: "Why didn't you ask him for a job? Maybe we could afford steak instead of franks and beans."

"A job doing what? There's no way I can trace these screwballs. Besides," I said, "I like franks and beans."

I told her the details of our talk, and she stopped me at the mention of Eddie Waitkus.

"Happened a couple of years ago," I said, reaching for the mustard. "Waitkus used to play first base for the Cubs, a real hotshot, good field, good bat. The ladies liked him, but one liked him too much, a woman named Ruth Ann Steinhagen. In '48, Waitkus was traded to the Phillies. A year later, on a day the team played the Cubs, this Ruth Steinhagen showed up at his hotel with a .32 caliber rifle and shot him in the chest."

Angie gasped. "But why?'"

"Because she was a fan," I said with half a grin. "Fans go crazy sometimes. That's what Joe Cronin is afraid of. That the same kind of thing might happen to Teddy Ballgame."

"Who?"

"Ted Williams. It's his nickname. Some kid gave it to him."

On the weekend, I took Angie out to Fenway, and watched Teddy Ballgame smack a home run his first time at bat. The crowd yelled for him to take a bow, but he ignored them as usual. The Splendid Splinter—another nickname—still wouldn't tip his cap for anyone.

When we got home, Angie said: "All those people! I don't see how you or anyone can tell who the crazies are. Why doesn't your friend Cronin hire a bodyguard?"

"Because Ted would never accept one, that's why."

"Then why not ask somebody else to look after him? Somebody close to Williams, like another ballplayer."

Out of the mouths of babes, I thought. And my Angie was some babe.

I put a call through to Joe Cronin. He was too busy to see me personally—the Sox were having a losing season—but he referred me to a batting coach who might be helpful. The coach came up with a name right off the bat. Ha-ha.

"We've got this guy Rafe Connelly, came up from the farm club about six months ago? Plays right field, swings a bat a lot like the Thumper. Ted's his role model, you know?"

"Are they close?"

"Yeah, I'd say so. Hangs around Ted all the time. They talk about hitting for hours. Also, Connelly loves to fish, and that's Ted's hobby."

Sounded good to me. Joe Cronin arranged a private meeting with Connelly, in a coffee shop near the stadium. Rafe was almost as tall and rangy as Ted himself and he was flattered when I mentioned the resemblance. He was four years younger, married but no children, excited by his first opportunity to play in the Big Leagues.

I liked this kid. He was obviously awed by Teddy Ballgame, and when I swore him to secrecy and told him about the threats on Ted's life, he reacted with shocked concern.

"Shouldn't you call the police? I mean, even if they're only crackpots, better safe than sorry, right?"

325

I told him why that wouldn't do any good.

"That's why I need your help, Rafe. You see a lot of Ted, you go on fishing trips with him, you're in a position to see when trouble might come his way."

"You want me to watch his back, is that it?"

"The odds are nothing will happen," I said. "And I don't want you trying to play hero, risk your own life, or your career for that matter. Understand?"

"I sure do," Rafe said. But he looked uncertain.

"Is there a problem?"

"Not exactly a problem. But there's my wife."

"What about her?"

"Caroline hates it when I don't get home in time for her dinner parties, and she gives a lot of them. And Ted, he's always staying late at the stadium..."

"So I heard. And if any of these fruitcakes makes a move against Ted, that might be the time. Look," I said, "'maybe if I talked to Caroline myself...'"

He didn't think much of the idea, but he agreed to invite me over to his place for dinner, me and Angie both, to make it look like a social occasion. Angie beamed when I told her where the Donnellys lived, in a brownstone on Commonwealth Avenue. Swank, it turned out.

Caroline was a piece of work. She was a small woman who stuck her nose in the air to make herself look taller. At the dinner table, we learned the following: (a) that she didn't like leaving the Southern bluebloods of Georgia where her family lived. And (b) that

326

she didn't think much of the game of Baseball and the crude and vulgar types who played it.

"Caroline's only been to two ball games in her life," Rafe said forgivingly. "One in Minneapolis, and one in Boston. Didn't understand either one."

"What I really don't understand is why Rafe took up the game in the first place. He was a banker in Macon when I met him."

Rafe chuckled. "I wasn't a 'banker,' I was a teller. And only because my old man owned the bank and put me in a 'training program.' As soon as he learned that I couldn't count, he let me try out for the local farm team. I batted .340 my first year, had the best slugging percentage, led the league in rbi's.'"

"I refuse to ask what all that means," Caroline said. I looked at Angie, wondering how I was going to bring up the topic we had come to discuss.

It turned out to be easier than I expected. Caroline could care less about her husband's hours; she had just joined a bunch of women's clubs, trying to climb the social ladder among the Boston Brahmins. If Rafe wanted to hang around ball parks to all hours, that was all right with her.

So Teddy Ballgame, without knowing it, had an unofficial bodyguard.

I spent the next couple of weeks chasing a husband who had walked out with the family dog. His wife wanted him back—the dog, I mean. I kept an eye on the sports pages. The Sox were in fifth place, but the Thumper was smacking the ball pretty good.

The day after I reunited wife, husband, and fox terrier I got a call from Joe Cronin. Angie took the message. Cronin wanted to see me.

When I walked in the next morning, he shoved a handful of letters across his battered desk.

"Look at these,'" he said. "More letters for Ted. I intercepted them, and glad I did."

There were four letters, all in the same kind of envelope, all postmarked August 1951, all addressed to "Ted Williams, c/o Boston Red Sox, Fenway Park, Boston, Mass." Crude block letters. Outside and in. The notes were all brief and to the point.

"You conked your last old lady on the head, Kid, now it's going to be your turn. Make sure your insurance is paid up."

It was unsigned, and so was the next one.

"You big hunk of dirt," it said. *"I'm going to hit a home run on your big head and bury you in right field where you can't hit."*

The third one read: *"You won't be spitting on us any more, Splint. You'll be spitting up your own blood before the end of the season. This is a promise."*

"You don't have to tip your cap, Teddy," the fourth letter read. *"I'll tip it for you. Wait and see."*

I put down the letters and gave Cronin a reassuring smile. "More empty threats, Joe."

"I'm not so sure. There's something different about these letters." He picked up one of them and read: "'No more old ladies'.... Remember that one, Harry? Ted got so sore at the crowd, he threw his bat at them, hit this nice old lady right on the bean. I think Ted was hurt worse than she was. At Christmas he sent her a diamond watch."

"I still don't think it's anything to worry about. And don't forget Rafe Donnelly. He's agreed to keep an eye on Williams."

"That's fine," he said. "But it's not enough. I'd feel better if you kept an eye on him, too... What would you say to three hundred bucks a week? And a season pass?" I had to glue my pants to the chair to keep from sliding off.

I took the assignment, as impossible as it was.

I never even met Teddy Ballgame. I didn't follow him around, carrying a firearm in case of trouble. I couldn't alert the Boston police and ask for round-the-clock surveillance; they didn't have that kind of manpower, even if they believed the threats were genuine. Me, I wasn't sure. But I knew one thing. I didn't want to open the Boston *Globe* some morning and read that Teddy Ballgame was murdered.

I went to every game. I tensed up when Ted came to the plate. He wasn't having his best year, but he was still a formidable figure, batting around .320, but nobody expected him to reach the amazing .406 he put into the record books a decade ago.

I didn't watch him bat. I watched the stands. I was dumb enough to think I could glom a would-be killer in that enormous crowd, the glint of a highpowered rifle, or maybe the gleam in some fanatical eye.

When I glanced back at the game, I saw that the Boudreau Shift was on. Some people were now calling it the "Williams Shift," but it was Cleveland's player-manager Lou Boudreau who first thought of bunching his fielders in right field, aware that Ted Williams rarely hit a ball to left. This time, the defensive tactic didn't work. Ted drove a ball over the second basemen's head.

It was going to be a short season for my season pass. There were only five weeks to go until the Series, and there was no way the Red Sox were going to appear in post-season play.

Joe Cronin wasn't happy about the situation. Not only was his team in fifth place, there was trouble brewing on another kind of playing field, in a place called Korea. Ted Williams faced a call-up; he had trained pilots in World War Two, and they need him again. But right now, I wasn't thinking about the possibility of losing Teddy Ballgame to North Korean gunfire. My concern was some armed lunatic who might come up behind him on a duck blind or fishing hole or dark Boston street.

I was wrong.

When the killer struck, it was after hours at Fenway Park. And the victim wasn't Teddy Ballgame.

It was Rafe Connelly.

The Sox had finished losing a game to Chicago. It was supposed to be a twi-night double header, but it started to rain and they called off the nightcap. An hour after the last disappointed Boston fan had left, while the grounds crew was cleaning up, Ted was still in the Park. He was often there, long after the other players were gone, weighing his bats, checking his equipment. As usual, Rafe Connelly was with him. But Rafe had to leave; his wife had tickets to the Philharmonic. And when Rafe entered the tunnel leading to the locker rooms, someone came out of the shadows and struck him on the back of his head with a baseball bat. Three times, the medical examiner said. Then the assailant had dropped the bat and run.

There was one other clue, but it was no help at all. The killer left a note next to the body, a note written in the same crude block letters as the four notes which preceded it. Only this time, it was more than a threat. It was a farewell.

"Ninth inning, Teddy. Three strikes and you're out."

Try to imagine how I felt. No, you can't. Not even Angie, who knew me inside and out, could understand that I was feeling every blow that killed poor Rafe Connelly. I was the one who convinced him to take the assignment that led to his death. I never considered that he might end up pinch-hitting for Ted Williams when the killer struck.

Yes, Teddy Ballgame had been spared. But a nice kid from Georgia ended his career and his life with only half a dozen times at bat in the record book. He was one for six.

Joe Cronin was in the record book, too. Only player to ever hit five pinch-hit home runs. He probably wasn't impressed by Rafe Connelly's prowess, but he was deeply moved by his violent death.

I wasn't the one who had to inform his wife; to my relief, the Boston Police assumed that responsibility. But Cronin insisted on my presence when he attended a meeting at headquarters that included the Police Commissioner himself.

"Maybe now you'll take this threat seriously," he said. "The killer made a mistake, but he won't make it twice. I say Ted Williams is still in danger from this loony fan, if that's what he is."

There was an officious-looking man behind the desk, and he chilled the atmosphere with his next statement.

"And what do you think the police can do, Mr. Cronin? Keep a twenty-four patrol on Mr. Williams? Dog his footsteps, watch his house? Go to restaurants with him, the movies, the bathroom?"

"I understand he's a fisherman," the Chief of Detectives said. "Fishing is a lonely sport, most of the time. It's part of its appeal. I do some bass fishing myself."

Cronin was getting red-faced. "I'm not talking about guarding Ted night and day. I'm talking about catching this killer before he tries again."

"This much we can promise you," the Commissioner said. "That we'll make every effort to apprehend this criminal. The life of Raphael Connelly has the same value in the eyes of the law as Mr. Ted Williams."

"I agree with that," Cronin said. "But Ted still has his life. I want it saved."

Of course, Teddy Ballgame still knew nothing of his own personal danger. But he was depressed about the death of his friend Rafe.

Two days after the murder, I took my usual seat at Fenway and waited to see if Ted would be affected by it.

He came to bat at the top of the second inning. The Williams shift was on. There were two strikes against him when he leaned into a ball out of the strike zone and drove it over the right field wall. The cluster of players on the righthand side of the diamond couldn't do a thing about it. There was anger in that stroke. Anger and sadness and loss. That was one way Teddy Ballgame expressed his feelings.

That night, I asked Angie if she knew what "the Williams Shift" meant.

"Of course. It's when they move all the outfielders to the right side when Ted Williams is at bat. On account of he always hits the ball that way. Everybody knows that!"

"Not everybody," I said. "Can you hold dinner for a couple of minutes? I need to find something in my den."

That's what we called the spare room. It was filled with books and boxes and files that had never been properly sorted. But it didn't take me long to find the photostated copies of the last four threatening letters Joe Cronin had shown me. The originals were in the hands of the police.

I remembered something about one of them. Something I should have noticed the first time.

"You big hunk of dirt," it said. *"I'm going to hit a home run on your big head and bury you in right field where you can't hit."*

Why didn't I notice it in the first place? *"...right field where you can't hit."*

Every baseball fan in Boston, maybe all over America, even my not-so-savvy wife, knew that Ted Williams sprayed his numerous hits to right field. That's what the Williams Shift was all about. Why did this obsessed fan get it wrong? What did it mean?

I called Vince Savario at police headquarters. We weren't buddies, but he was my last partner before my retirement. We met for coffee and doughnuts, and Vince was eager to know if I had any leads on the Donnelly case. Like every other cop in Boston, Vic would like nothing better than to solve the Fenway Park Murder. He wanted Detective Grade real bad.

He was disappointed when I showed him the letter and explained the problem. "So what?" he said. "Whoever wrote it was just ignorant."

"Whoever clobbered Rafe Donnelly was ignorant, too. He couldn't tell one player from another."

"It was a lucky break for Teddy," Vince said smugly. "Look at it that way."

"You tell Mrs. Donnelly that," I said stiffly. And speaking of stiff, I walked out and let Vince pay the tab.

Walking home, I realized that my sympathy for Rafe's widow hadn't included personal condolences. I knew Angie had sent her a Sympathy card, but in the circumstance it didn't seem nearly enough. I called and asked if we could come over. She wasn't thrilled, but it was understandable. I was the guy who put her husband in harm's way.

She made an attractive widow. Her small, classic features were set off nicely by the lacy black dress she wore. She offered us tea and little crustless sandwiches..

"I know what you're feeling," she said, her blue eyes looking at me solemnly. "But I want you to know that I don't blame you for what happened. Rafe knew what he was doing when he agreed to protect Mr. Williams. I just wish others did, that people would realize he was a kind of hero."'

"It's true," I said. "He was a hero, Mrs. Donnelly. But I'm afraid we can't let the world know about it, at least not until we catch the killer."

"Do you think you ever will? I read that there were almost thirty thousand people in the stadium that day. Any one of them could have stolen a bat and waited in that tunnel..."

"It won't be easy. But we'll do our best."

I was talking as if I was still on the force. I was glad when Caroline Donnelly said she was tiring, and we could get out of there.

On the trip home, Angie said: "How do you steal a bat?"

"What?"

"Don't they lock up the bats and things after a ball game? Could anyone just pick up a bat that's lying around loose?"

"No, of course not."

"Then what did the killer do? Bring a bat with him?"

"I don't know," I said. "But I wish I did."

I had to do a little bobbing and weaving to get to the right person at Headquarters. Every cop I used to know was either retired, transferred, or dead. The best I could do was a young cop named Howie Richards, who remembered his old man talking about me. I took him to lunch at the best restaurant in the Harbor. He ordered a dozen oysters. Then I found out why he agreed to see me.

"You were on the precinct ball team," Howie said. "My father said you were their best batter."

"The team average was .190," I said with a grin. "It wasn't hard to shine in that company.

"He said you used to play with the Red Sox before you joined the Force."

"With the farm club. Never made it to the majors."

"We sure could you use you now. We haven't won a game all

335

season. I'm the team captain, so it's kind of—humiliating."

As casually as possible, I said: "Speaking of baseball, you guys have the weapon that killed Rafael Donnelly, don't you?"

"Sure. It's in the Evidence Room. It was checked out for prints, but there weren't any."

"Any idea where it came from? I mean, did the killer get it out of the supply locker or what?"

"Nobody knows for sure. Our best guess is that he brought it with him. It was a wet night, he could have hidden it under a raincoat." He licked his lips. "Getting back to the team—we've got a game this Sunday, two p.m. at Gahan Park. Why don't you drop by? Maybe you can give us a couple of batting tips."

I had my opening. "Tell you what," I said. "'You let me have a look at that bat, I'll come by and have a look at your team."

It was a deal.

The Evidence Room was dingy and dark, but Exhibit One in the Donnelly homicide was easily located. Richards produced the long plastic bag and then removed the slim ebony bat. The brand name was unfamiliar: *DeMarini*. In the dim fluorescent light it was hard to see the discoloration that might have been Rafe Donnelly's dried blood.

I stared at it for a while, as if hoping it would speak. But all three of us were silent. I shrugged, thanked him, and he replaced the bat in its plastic container.

"Make it around eleven-thirty, Sunday," Howie said. "'The game starts at one. We're playing Ladder Company Number 5, and those guys always cream us." He grinned, and inwardly, I groaned.

There goes my leisurely Sunday morning.

When I told Angie the results of my investigation, she said, "You ought to be happy. You've got the best of both your worlds. Cops and baseball."

That Sunday morning, Angie decided to go with me to Gahan Park. As soon as I saw them on the field, I knew I was going to be very little use to the Precinct players.

It was a softball team.

Okay, maybe softball isn't that much different from hardball, but it was a game I'd never played. From the moment Howie Richards came trotting up to me, bat in hand, I knew I was about to make a damned fool of myself. Not for the first time.

I took a couple of swings, trying to get used to the lighter weight of the bat, trying to remember what it was like to feel the sweet kiss of hide against wood. It was no use. I couldn't tell these guys anything of value. I grabbed the bat by the midsection to hand it back to him. That's when I saw the name.

DeMarini.

It didn't mean too much at first. But then it was like a roaring in my ears. *DeMarini.* Maker of softball bats. Including the one in a plastic bag in the Evidence Room. Whoever the "crazed fan" was who took the life of Rafe Donnelly, presumably in place of Ted, the Kid, the Thumper, the Splendid Splinter Williams, decided to do the dirty deed with the wrong kind of bat.

Ignorance, I thought. That was the word. The key word. The word Rafe had mentioned. Ignorance of the game. Not knowing the difference between Teddy Ballgame's proclivity to hit to right field. Not knowing the difference between a baseball bat and a softball bat.

The starting pitcher showed up at Gahan half an hour later. He was also Captain of the precinct. I took him aside and gave him a tip that had nothing to do with softball.

In the next five days, every sporting goods outlet in Boston and environs was canvassed for information about purchasers of softball bats. It wasn't a hot-ticket item, and women customers were rare enough, so it wasn't too hard to identify the small, intense woman who paid cash and took her purchase with her.

Her name was Caroline Donnelly.

In a way, it was my fault. I gave Caroline the idea the night Angie and I went to dinner at their house, when I told her of the "danger" Ted Williams might be facing from some murderous "fan." She was no dummy, Caroline. She saw possibilities. She saw someone "mistaking" her tall and rangy husband for Ted Williams. She wouldn't wait for it to happen. She would do it herself.

Sure, she'd be a widow. But she would have good reason to be merry. Rafe was the only heir to his father's banking fortune. His widow would be second in line, if something happened to Rafe.

And, of course, something happened. She wrote those four threatening letters, hoping to create the illusion that Ted Williams was the intended victim. The "right field" error was hers. So was the mistake of buying a softball bat instead of a regulation bat.

I wonder if they play ball at the women's prison?

Ted was glad when the case was solved. He never knew the role he played in it. The police were discreet when they briefed the press. There was no mention of the fake threats, no reference to Ted

Williams at all.

It was a good thing. Ted had other things on his mind. The Korean War, for instance. It resulted in his second term of service, this time flying jets. Then his return to baseball, as player and manager. And his fishing. How Teddy Ballgame loved to fish.

PICK-OFF PLAY

by Troy Soos

From where I sat—kneeled, actually, in the on-deck circle near the Beaumont Oilers' dugout—it looked like Archie Hines was out by a mile. The five or six hundred fans scattered about Magnolia Ball Park's weather-beaten grandstand probably saw the play the same way. If so, we were all wrong. The plate umpire's arm was extended toward first base, awarding Hines the bag. The only thing that prevented him from taking it was the fact that he was dead.

I'd been coached since childhood to keep my eyes on the ball, and that's exactly what I had done, watching the Houston Buffaloes' third baseman as he scooped up the two-hopper and threw to first. I hadn't noticed that Hines had never left the batter's box, where he now lay motionless.

As soon as I spotted Hines on the ground, I dropped my bat and ran to him. The potbellied old umpire and the Buffaloes' catcher, masks in hands, were standing helplessly over the young shortstop. Murmurs rippled through the stands, as the fans began to realize that something was terribly wrong. My fellow Oilers and several of the visiting Buffaloes soon joined the circle around the fallen

341

ballplayer. All stood immobile, at a loss for a way to aid him.

The umpire finally grunted, "He ain't movin'." It was one of the few calls he'd gotten right all day. He then spat a shot of tobacco juice toward the backstop. Some dripped onto his ill-fitting blue serge suit as he bellowed to the crowd, "There a doctor here?"

I stared down at Archie Hines, my teammate and roommate. The wiry nineteen-year-old, just off a 1912 season in which he'd led the Texas League in stolen bases, was known for his speed. It seemed he was always in motion, dashing around the base paths or ranging for grounders at short. Now he lay like a pile of dumped laundry, not the slightest twitch from his limbs. Nor from his open, glassy eyes. The only thing moving on his body was the blood that trickled from his crushed left temple and seeped into the clay around home plate.

His very life seemed to be evaporating in the July sun, shimmering off on ripples of steamy air. As I looked at Hines, at his broken skull and his blond hair now stained red, I could almost hear the echo of the ball that struck him, and in my mind's eye I replayed his last at bat.

Hines had led off for us in the bottom of the fourth inning. With a one-strike count on him, Jake Pruett's next pitch came at his head. Hines ducked, and it appeared that he'd evaded the ball—the sharp crack that split the air sounded as if his bat had taken the impact. The ball quickly bounded up the base line, where the Buffaloes' third baseman fielded it. What had confused everyone, I realized, was the terrific distance the ball had traveled. Once more the crack reverberated in my ears, and I could detect the subtle difference in sound of horsehide on bone instead of on wood.

A gangling young man in a straw boater and a seersucker suit hopped the railing and approached the ump. "Perhaps I can help." He had no black bag with him, but I could tell that it didn't matter— nothing in any black bag could help Archie Hines now.

"You a doctor?" demanded the ump.

"No, but my father is."

"My mother was a seamstress," said the ump. "Don't mean *I* can sew a stitch." Then he shrugged. "Go 'head. Take a look at 'im."

The young man bent to kneel, then decided against messing his trousers in the bloody earth. He squatted instead, and took Hines' wrist in his hand, feeling for a pulse. The sad shake of his head indicated that he detected none. Next he looked into Hines' ghostly eyes, while muttering softly to himself. When he picked up the shortstop's cap and placed it gently over his face, the action informed everyone in the ballpark that Archie Hines was dead.

While gasps of disbelief whooshed about the stands, the Houston Buffaloes' first baseman realized that he'd been holding the ball that had killed Hines. He promptly placed it on home plate, as if it had suddenly become hot to the touch.

I backed away from the others, and turned toward the mound. Hulking Jake Pruett, who'd delivered the fatal pitch, stood lazily with his hands on his hips. A smirk creased his unshaven face, and his pale eyes sparkled with amusement.

"You think this is funny?" I yelled at him.

Pruett tilted back his cap at an arrogant angle and the smirk broadened to a grin.

343

"You sonofabitch!" I took off for the mound, determined to change his expression.

A couple of strides from my target, I was tackled from behind and wrestled to the ground. While I struggled to escape and get at Pruett, I noticed the uniforms were home whites—it was my own teammates who were trying to hold me still.

One of them was our catcher, Stump Williams. "It happens, Mickey," he wheezed, while trying to pin my flailing right arm. "Let it go."

"Bastard is smiling. He killed Archie, and he's *happy* about it."

"C'mon, Mick," Williams said. "It was an accident. Can't blame Pruett."

I twisted my head to look at the pitcher. If it was an accident, he showed no signs of regretting the result. Seeing me secure in the clutches of my teammates, he brought a finger to the bill of his cap and touched it like a salute. A salute of triumph.

I renewed my struggles to get at the gloating pitcher while two more Oilers joined the others trying to hold me down.

"Rawlings!" George Leidy barked at me. "Get your ass over here!"

I finally calmed down enough to obey the manager's order. With teammates close on either side of me to make sure I didn't go after Pruett again, I returned to home plate.

Leidy said to me, "Don't go making things worse than they are already." Then he gave Pruett a look that indicated he wouldn't have minded getting in a couple of punches at the pitcher himself.

The players began to mill about home plate restlessly. One of the Buffaloes looked down at Hines and said, "Gonna hafta move him if we're gonna finish the game." I wondered how he could even think of continuing, then realized it could matter to Houston's pennant hopes: They were ahead 5-1 in the fourth inning; if the game was called off, it would have to be played over completely and they'd lose that lead.

The umpire finally conferred with the two managers. He began by pointing out that Hines was entitled to first base but would need a pinch runner if we played on. I glanced at my teammates; not one appeared willing to pinch run for a dead man.

Despite a token protest from the Houston manager, the plate ump eventually decided to call off the game. I'd been in lots of games called because of darkness and rain, and once in North Carolina because of a swarm of bees. This was the first time I'd been in a ballgame called on account of death.

Since Magnolia Ball Park had no changing facilities, I walked the three blocks home in full uniform, having only swapped my spiked shoes for bluchers. As always, I carried my gear—three homemade bats and a Spalding mitt—in a canvas bag slung over my shoulder. What was different was that Archie Hines usually made the walk with me. Today, I carried the glove that he would never use again.

Like many of the Oilers, Archie and I lived at Mrs. Kitzler's boarding house on Hazel Street. I had no intention of finding more permanent housing in Beaumont. To me, the Gulf town was nothing more than a detour on my way back to the major leagues. I had played most of last season as a utility infielder with the World Champion Boston Red Sox, and ached for another shot at the majors. In fact, I paid my rent by the week instead of the month because I kept hoping that I would soon be called to play the rest of 1913 with a big league club.

Back in our room, which Mrs. Kitzler furnished in a style that would be considered stark by most prison standards, I sat on my lumpy iron bed and stared down at Archie's old mitt. I noticed that the palm of the black leather glove was worn clear through, and the seam where the thumb was attached had been crudely resewn at least twice with different colored threads.

Archie Hines was the most frugal young ballplayer I'd ever met. He told me that he grew up in a Pennsylvania coal town, living in a company shanty. Until two years ago, the most money he'd made was $1.50 a day for mining anthracite plus a dollar on Sundays for playing semi-pro ball. Now he was earning an almost princely salary—eighty-five dollars a month, the same as me—but he still refused to pay two bits for a new shirt collar. Instead, he cleaned his old celluloid collars with a rubber eraser. His one suit, hanging on the row of pegs that Mrs. Kitzler called a "closet," was ten years out of style and shiny at the elbows.

I ran my thumb across the repair stitches on his glove, and wished I had thought to buy him a new one. Although I was only two years older than Archie, from the time we started rooming together, he'd looked up to me. I knew it was partly because I had already achieved his dream of playing big league ball. He often pressed me to tell him about playing against Ty Cobb and Walter Johnson and

Joe Jackson—stories I was always happy to repeat—and he'd tell me eagerly how he couldn't wait to face them himself. Also, since I'd traveled more of the country than he had, Archie thought me "worldly" and asked my advice on everything from how to sleep comfortably in a Pullman car to which fork to use in a restaurant. Sometimes when I didn't know an answer, I made one up because I hated to be a disappointment to him.

I'd felt responsible for Archie, and somehow it seemed that I had let him down today by failing to protect him. He was a good roommate—didn't smoke or drink, and most importantly didn't snore—but more than that Archie Hines was a decent kid, and he didn't deserve to die so young.

I wasn't the only one who thought well of Archie. In an oval frame next to the washstand was a photograph of a plain, well-fed girl with a kind face and curly hair. It was Ella, his girl back home and the main reason for Archie's thriftiness: He was saving up to marry her. Archie planned to make the engagement official the day that he made it onto a major league roster, and with his ability, I had no doubt that they would have been engaged soon. Who was going to tell Ella, I wondered, that it was never going to happen now. One pitch, one split second, and everything was changed.

I tried to suppress it, but the image of Archie Hines' final at bat came fresh to mind. Then the memory of Jake Pruett's smirking face. I couldn't reconcile Pruett's expression to the situation. There was no reason to hit Hines—he hadn't been crowding the plate, nor had he been hitting Pruett well enough for the pitcher to want to shake him up. So the pitch must have simply gotten away from him.

But then Pruett should have looked embarrassed at the wildness. Or sorry about the result. Maybe even defiant, as if to say, 'Don't blame me, it happens sometimes.'

I'd seen more than a hundred pitchers over the years, and studied them closely. What I saw of Pruett today stood out as the most peculiar reaction I'd ever seen. I could think of no way that any pitcher would look so satisfied about what had happened to Archie Hines. Perhaps I was missing something, I decided. Perhaps a player who'd seen far more pitchers than I had could explain it to me.

A single bathroom at the end of a dingy hallway was shared by all of Mrs. Kitzler's residents. As I entered, I almost laughed at the sight in the ancient zinc bathtub. Only a face was visible above the surface of the water, like a craggy, leathery island. Towering from the mouth was a lit black cigar, giving the impression of a lighthouse.

"Stump!" I called, but the sound didn't reach his submerged ears. I banged on the rim of the tub and he popped up, the cigar almost falling from his teeth. With his moon face and flattened nose, Williams's head looked like a lumpy catcher's mitt. His body was even less attractive, showing the scars and knocks of twenty years and more than a thousand games.

"You mind if I shave?" I asked. The bathroom was Stump Williams's exclusive domain after a ballgame. In deference to the veteran's age, the rest of the team always let him have a long soak by himself before taking our turns.

"Nah, I don't care," the old catcher growled.

My scant whiskers could easily wait another week, but it

gave me an excuse to be here. "You been in baseball a long time," I said, stirring my shaving brush in the soap mug to work up a lather.

"Yup. And I'm gonna *be* in baseball a long time, too." That was wishful thinking. Stump Williams was sliding back down the ladder of organized baseball; in a couple of years he'd be lucky to be playing semi-pro for a couple of bucks a game.

"You see Jake Pruett much?" I asked. Williams and Pruett were both veterans of the game, I knew, and about the same age.

Williams puffed hard on his cigar a few times until it burned brightly. "For a few years I did. Back when I was with Pittsburgh and he was pitching for Brooklyn."

"What do you know about him?"

He gave me a baleful stare. "Look kid, I been around long enough to know how easy it is to get hurt on a ball field. Hell, I been spiked, beaned, and got broken bones from my nose to my toes. It happens. Leave it be."

I put down the shaving brush, giving up the pretense that I was here for any reason other than to ask him about the man who killed my roommate. "I expect you're right. But I can't leave it be—not yet."

He exhaled a cloud of acrid smoke. "Suit yourself, kid. But I tell you: You'd be better off thinking about tomorrow's game than today's. Archie is dead, and he's gonna stay dead. Don't worry about what you can't change."

I nodded, but pressed on, "So what do you know about Pruett?"

Williams sighed in surrender. "Can't say I knew him well. Didn't run into him off the field much—didn't especially want to.

349

"Why not?"

"Jake Pruett didn't only pitch for Brooklyn. He was born and bred there, and wore it like a badge of honor—thought he had a reputation to uphold, so he always tried to act the tough guy. Always had a scheme going too—cheating at cards, hustling pool, you name it. Oh yeah, and he'd sell 'gold' watches that weren't worth two bits." Williams shook his head. "Pruett was small-time, though, and harmless enough as long you kept a firm grip on your wallet."

"What about on the field? He like to throw at batters?"

"No more'n any other pitcher. The plate was his, and he'd let you know it. Crowd too close, and he'd sit you on your ass. But that's the way the game is played."

"How was his control?"

Williams puffed noisily before answering, "Pruett could put the ball wherever he wanted—fastball and curve both. Never tried a spitter or a shine ball, as far as I know. But even the best pitchers can get wild now and then." He took the cigar in his fingers, but it slipped and fell into the tub with a sizzle and a splash. "Damn!" He groped frantically in the tub and pulled up a soggy mass of tobacco. "Get me another, would you?" He gestured toward his jacket hanging on the back of the door.

I wiped the lather from my hands and dug into his pocket for a fresh cigar and a match. "Why do you think Pruett was smiling the way he was?"

"Hell, I don't know, kid. I wasn't really lookin' at him anyway—I was lookin' at poor Archie. But you can never tell how somebody's gonna react to something like that." He bit the end off the stogie and I lit it for him. Then he submerged himself again, the conversation over.

I still had the image of Pruett's smile in my mind, and still could make no sense of it.

Two days later, I got another look at Jake Pruett's face when I stepped into the batter's box to face him. Texas League officials had ruled that Saturday's game was suspended, so the teams were picking up from where we'd left off. And since local officials had ruled Archie Hines' death an accident, Pruett was free to continue pitching.

Although it was technically the same game, there were some differences from Saturday. One was the size of the crowd. Magnolia Ball Park was packed to overflowing with fans who had come early to pay tribute to Hines in a pre-game ceremony—and with some people, I suspected, who came out of morbid curiosity to see where a ballplayer had been killed. Of course the big difference today was in the lineup. Oyster Joe Martina, a pitcher, had to fill Archie's spot because no other player was willing to take the place of the dead shortstop. In fact, none of us really wanted to continue the game at all, with the memory of the tragedy weighing as heavily on us as the muggy air.

But since the game was to go on, I was going to do my best. As the first up, I tried to shake off all thoughts of Archie, digging my cleats into the clay and twisting the bat handle in my grip. That's when I glanced up to see a thin smile on Pruett's ugly mug. And I knew where his first pitch would be headed. I wasn't sure if it was because I had rushed him in the last game or because I'd dug in a little too close to the plate. Or maybe because Pruett needed to demonstrate that the death of Archie Hines wasn't going to deter him from throwing inside. Whatever the reason, I was going down.

The same umpire from two days ago called "Play ball!" and Pruett peered in for the catcher's sign. He then looked straight at me while he went into a windmill windup. I forced myself to remain fixed in my stance. Just as he had to prove that he was still willing to pitch inside, I had to act like I wasn't going to be scared by what his last inside pitch had done. It took all the acting ability that I had.

Pruett released quickly, snapping off a fastball that headed directly for my left ear. My brain issued the order to duck, but my body froze, unable to obey. At the last instant, I jerked my head back. The ball grazed the bill of my cap, taking it clear off my head, and earning me first base. Although I wasn't hurt, the close call had me shaken. Knowing that the knockdown was coming was what had made it dangerous, I realized. Normally, reflex takes over and the body pulls back immediately. *Thinking* about what to do slows everything down.

Martina trotted to second, and I took first base with some feeling of satisfaction. All Pruett had managed to do was move a runner into scoring position and put me on base.

As the next Oilers' hitter took his turn, I noticed that Pruett's pitch had served a purpose: intimidation. The batter bent in an awkward stance, his rear end partway back to the dugout, obviously ready to hit the dirt. With three feeble swings, he proceeded to fan on three straight tosses. The Oilers who followed him fared no better, all of them tentative at the plate, more interested in their survival than their batting averages.

Throughout the game, I continued to watch Jake Pruett and the Oilers batters closely. Only one of my teammates faced Pruett with no sign of fear: our young left fielder Floyd Geer, who managed to hit a pair of doubles. We couldn't capitalize on Geer's hits, however, and Houston held on for a 7-1 victory. Although the game was a somber one, and a loss for our team, at least this time there were no deaths in the box score.

The smallest moves can sometimes reveal the most about a ballplayer. A pitcher cocks his wrist a certain way, it might mean a curveball is coming. A catcher hoists up on his haunches, it might mean a pitchout. A batter twists his hip a little early, maybe he's about to lay down a bunt. I always watched for these small signs and tried to interpret their meanings. Since nature hadn't endowed me with much natural ability, I had to rely on observation and strategy to have any chance of success. And when I spotted something unusual, it would gnaw at me until I'd figured out the cause.

Floyd Geer's actions today, when he kept digging in against Jake Pruett, were such a case of behavior not fitting the circumstances. Could Geer have been oblivious to the fact that the Oilers' pitcher had killed Archie Hines only two days earlier? Could he have missed seeing Pruett try to stick a fastball in my ear? It simply wasn't possible. Yet Geer had stepped into the batter's box showing as little concern as if he was about to take batting practice. I wanted to know why.

It wasn't difficult to find Geer that evening, primarily because there were so few places we were allowed to go in Beaumont. The Spindletop oil boom a few years back had attracted a rough element to the town, and they'd taken over many of the places typically favored by ballplayers. After a few of the Oilers had been beaten up in saloon brawls and mugged in the red light district, the team's management declared most of the town night spots to be off limits. Church socials, band concerts, and moving picture shows were among the few amusements still permitted us.

Since the nickelodeon was playing the same Bronco Billy pictures that had been running all month, I doubted Geer would be there. And I knew he wasn't one of the players who went for church activities, so I checked the *Beaumont Enterprise* for the concert schedule.

Keith Park was an oasis of cool green in Beaumont, with leafy shade trees, sparkling fountains, and a band shell that had attracted a couple of hundred people to hear the nightly music program. On stage, a brass band honked its way lethargically through a John Philip Sousa march.

I skirted the edge of the crowd and spotted Floyd Geer near a lemonade vendor. The handsome teenager was nattily dressed in white duck trousers and a striped blue jacket. A silk handkerchief bloomed from the jacket's breast pocket and a straw boater topped his pomaded black hair.

Stepping up behind him, I asked, "The one in the pink, or the one in the yellow?" His attention was clearly directly at a couple of young ladies in pastel frocks, and I doubted that he was even aware of the trombone solo being played.

Geer turned to me, his Adam's apple bobbing and his thin face flushing red. "I can't decide. I think I like them both."

I cast an admiring look at the girls. "Well, you got taste. I'll give you that. Can't go wrong with either one of them." I doubted that he would get beyond the looking stage anyway—Geer was the shyest player on the team. "Say," I said, "you sure took the batting honors today."

The young man beamed; there's not a ballplayer anywhere who doesn't like to be complimented on his hitting. He was probably relieved at the change of topic, too. "Yeah, I was seeing the ball real good."

"Showed guts out there. You're the only one who didn't look worried about where Pruett might throw the ball. How'd you do that?"

"Why should I worry? Hell, Mickey, I spent most of my life working on my uncle's farm—milking cows at dawn, slopping the pigs, plowing behind the orneriest mule who ever lived....and always worrying about whether we'd have a good enough crop to tide us over the winter. Compared to that, baseball is easy."

It was a good answer, and I almost bought it. Then a guilty scowl twitched at his face, a small sign something wasn't right. "But Archie Hines was *killed* by a pitch from Pruett," I said. "No way you could ignore what that baseball might do to your skull if it hit you. How did you step in against him so easy?"

Geer hesitated. "I told you."

I snapped at the nervous youngster, "You haven't told me

355

anything. Come on, what's going on?"

He struggled with himself. "If you don't know already, then it don't concern you."

"If I don't know *what?*"

Geer's hand reached for his watch chain and he began toying with the fob. "Hell, I'm not the only one. I know there's others, especially among the rookies. You'll probably find out yourself sooner or later—when he tells *you* to pay up."

"What? I don't—"

"Jake Pruett. Told me I had to give him five bucks a game whenever he pitched. If I didn't, he'd bean me."

Jeez. "And you *paid?*"

"What the hell else am I supposed to do?" His voice had risen to a squawk and he paused a moment to compose himself. "Listen, I face him ten times a year at most. Fifty bucks is worth it to stay in one piece—and to keep playing baseball. One pitch to my head or a broken hand, and I could be back on my uncle's farm." He turned to me with eyes that pleaded for understanding. "I *hate* milking cows."

It was no problem at all to find Jake Pruett. The Hamilton Hotel on Crockett Street was home to most Texas League teams on their visits to Beaumont, and the players could generally be found in the lobby or the barroom.

Pruett, dressed in a loud checked suit, was in the latter. He sat at a small table, his only company a bottle of rye and a shot glass. From what I'd heard of Pruett's personality, it was no surprise that he was by himself. I recognized other Oilers players at the bar, but they gave no indication that they even knew Jake Pruett.

Nor was it a surprise when Pruett tensed at the sight of me. He scraped back his chair, ready to spring up if I made any hostile moves.

I held up my hands, palms out. "Just want to talk to you," I said. That wasn't exactly true; I *wanted* to wring his neck, but for now I would be satisfied with talking.

He wiped the back of his hand across his thin wet lips, making a rasping sound on the unshaven stubble. Pruett's face was as chiseled as granite, but it had less warmth. "Sit," he said, his pale, slitted eyes watching me warily.

I eased into the chair opposite him, forcing myself to remain calm. Even though his teammates chose not to sit with him, if he and I were to fight they would have to come to his aid out of team loyalty.

Pruett downed another shot of whiskey and exhaled so hard that I could feel a slight spray. "What do you want to talk about?" he asked.

"I hear you got a little side business going. Charging players five bucks a game to keep their heads intact."

"Now where'd you hear something like that?" Pruett's slight smile indicted that he felt no insult at the accusation.

"It ain't exactly a secret."

He flinched slightly, and I found it satisfying to have given him at least a small reason for concern.

I went on, "I never heard of a protection racket in baseball before. How'd you come up with it?"

After a moment's thought, Pruett elected not to deny the

357

charge. He answered with pride, "I'm smart. That's how." Leaning forward, he went on, "About three years ago, when I was still with Brooklyn, a buddy of mine on the Braves offered me five bucks to throw him a couple of fat pitches so he could boost his batting average. I'm not one to turn down a few extra dollars, so I figured why not? Then I realized: Hey, why not charge players for staying safe? I don't got to give up no hits or runs that way. All I got to do is collect their money, and then they're *happy,* if I throw strikes—it's better for them if the ball is in the strike zone than in their ear." He smiled with satisfaction. "Besides, baseball owes it to me. I been playing a lot of years, and this is the only retirement fund I'm gonna have."

I was astonished at the perverse thinking process this man had. "What if the League finds out?"

"They won't." Pruett chuckled. "Not a ballplayer anywhere is gonna admit that he's so scared of getting beaned that he paid off a pitcher."

"The ones who don't go along with you might tell."

His expression hardened to the point where I thought his face might crack. "No, they won't. They understand if they do something like that, they'll be *wishing* for something as gentle as a fastball to the head. It's a lot easier to get to a guy outside the ballpark—and there's a lot more ways to hurt him."

"Can't be any worse than what you did to Archie Hines. You *killed* him."

Pruett slammed his hand on the table. "Hey, you can't blame me for that. Even if I wanted to kill the kid, you can't depend on a beanball for that. All I could be sure of is hitting him, not killing him."

"So you did want to hit him. Why? He turn down your offer?"

There apparently was some limit to Pruett's arrogance. He answered, "I ain't saying nothing about Hines." But after another sip of whiskey, his natural cockiness returned. "Just for the sake of argument," he said, "let's say the kid did turn me down. Then hitting him would have been strictly business. It wasn't nothing personal."

While I pondered my next question, Pruett turned it around. "Now let's talk about *you.*"

"What about me?"

"You haven't donated to my retirement fund yet." He smirked. "Five bucks a game."

"Like hell. I'm not giving you a penny."

"Don't have to yet. Next series we play—that's in about two weeks I think—you leave five bucks for me at the hotel desk." His teeth almost gleamed in a smile. "Or I drill ya."

I fought the urge to remove some of those teeth with my fist. "I'll think about it," I said facetiously, as I stood to leave. A few more minutes with Jake Pruett, and one of us was going to be badly hurt right in this room.

"Don't think too long. Tomorrow the price goes up to ten bucks." He slowly poured another shot of rye. "With Hines getting himself killed the way he did, I figure other players will want to be real sure it don't happen to them. And they ought to be willing to pay a little more for that insurance."

I was too astonished to summon up the strength to punch him. Almost numb, I pulled myself up from the table and walked unsteadily out the door.

It wasn't until I was back in my room that I was able to think clearly again. During the entire walk home, my head had been foggy. What Jake Pruett had told me wasn't what confused me—he was straightforward enough about what he was doing. What I couldn't fathom was his utter lack of shame or regret. He was actually proud of his extortion scheme.

What I needed to figure out now wasn't what Pruett was doing, but what I should do.

I went over to Archie Hines' bed, where his old glove still lay on the pillow. Sitting down, I grabbed the mitt and stared at the repairs to the stitching. To Archie, every five dollars was that much closer to buying his girl an engagement ring, and he wouldn't even buy himself a new glove. There was no way he would pay protection to Pruett. And he was dead because of it.

Floyd Geer, on the other hand, thought paying off Pruett was worth it to keep playing baseball. Archie had made his choice, Geer had made a different one. What, I wondered, were my choices?

One thing was sure: Jake Pruett would take advantage of more ballplayers—the younger ones, who could be more easily scared—now charging them ten dollars to avoid his beanballs. More would probably pay; others might refuse—and maybe end up like Archie.

If I went to the cops or the league, the best they *might* do is start an investigation. That could take weeks, or months, and if no other ballplayers came forward it would accomplish nothing. There wasn't time to try that route, I decided. Pruett would be pitching again in a few days.

I had just gotten a table and was racking up when Jake Pruett came into the pool hall. Simply by being here I was breaking two club rules—billiard parlors were off-limits and I was out after curfew—but I wanted to give Pruett my decision tonight.

The pitcher made his way toward me, slogging through thick sawdust soaked with tobacco juice and spilt beer. "Got your message." I had phoned the Hamilton Hotel, where a bellboy found Pruett still in the bar.

"Thanks for coming." I leaned over to break.

He looked around. "You couldn't have found a worse dump to meet?"

Probably not. The rickety clapboard structure near the Neches River differed from an outhouse only in its size and the presence of half a dozen pool tables and a small bar. Except for dim light bulbs over the four tables in use, and a kerosene lamp behind the bar, the room was in shadows. Men seated along the walls were more audible than visible, as they argued over bets and clinked their whiskey glasses. "This seemed like the best place for what we got to talk about. I don't especially want to be seen with you."

Pruett proved impossible to offend. He sniffed, "Well, I been in worse joints than this in Red Hook."

I carefully positioned the cue ball and took a few practice strokes.

Pruett asked with some derision, "You called me for a game

361

of pool?"

"No, I was just killing time. But I'll play a game if you want." I tried not to sound too eager.

"All right." He took off his hat and coat, and went to the rack for a cue. After rolling four of them on a table to check for straightness, he found one that he liked and chalked the tip. "Want to make it interesting?" he asked. "Say five bucks?"

"Nah, I'm lousy at this game."

"Two bucks then."

"Oh, what the hell. Why not?"

"Break," he said.

I did, but the balls didn't exactly scatter.

Pruett took his turn, pocketing two balls before missing a relatively easy shot. "Why did you want to meet?" he asked.

"To give you your answer." I pocketed the ball he'd missed, but got no more.

He then opted for a difficult bank shot although there were several easier possibilities. "Damn!" he said when he missed. "So, what's it gonna be? You gonna make your payment before next game?"

Pruett had left the cue ball where I could again make an easy shot. "Nope. I'm not paying you nothing—except two dollars if I lose this game."

"You sure about that? You know I might get a little wild if you don't."

"Like today? All you did was put me on base, and I didn't get hurt a bit."

Pruett winced as I missed another easy shot. "Damn, you're having a rough night." No rougher than any other time I'd attempted this game. Hitting a ball with the end of a stick felt odd to me, and I'd never developed any skill at billiards.

I leaned on my cue as he went over to take his shot. "Anyway, you go ahead and throw at me if you want. I'll watch out for myself."

"That's your choice." He paused to watch a couple of roughly dressed men begin a game at the table next to us. They each laid several bills on the rail before racking. Pruett turned back to me. "No hard feelings. Same as I said about Hines, it's just business."

We played on, Pruett trying valiantly to lose to me, and increasingly frustrated at my failure to capitalize. Finally, he lost the game by scratching. "Damn," he said, pulling two silver dollars from his pocket. "You'll give me a chance to win my money back, right?"

I took the coins. "Not tonight." I wasn't going to be hustled at pool any more than I was going to be extorted in baseball.

Pruett continued to press me for another game until I returned my cue to the rack. Then he looked around the room. There was a glint in his eyes when he said to me, "Maybe another time then. I think there might be some *real* players here."

I left the pool hall feeling confident that he would have even less success hustling them.

I had finished suiting up, and was about to leave for Magnolia Ball Park, when a breathless kid of about seventeen burst into my room. He had a canvas satchel in one hand and a small suitcase in the other. "You Rawlings?" he gasped.

"That's me."

He dropped the luggage and took off his boater, revealing a thick mop of straw-colored hair. "Erv Olson," he said, offering his hand. "Your new roommate."

I flinched. Here was Archie Hines' replacement. I knew somebody would have to come to take his spot on the roster, but I didn't like it.

Still waiting for me to shake hands, Olson said, "My train was late. Sorry to rush in like this."

I wanted to blurt out, "You can't replace Archie," but told myself to give the kid a chance. What had happened to Archie wasn't his fault. "Welcome to the club," I said, finally returning his grip. "Where you play? Shortstop?"

"Short, second, third," he answered. "I'll play anywhere they put me. I just wanna play ball." Olson reached into his bag and pulled out a folded Oilers uniform. "I went right to the park from the station. The manager gave me this, but said I'd have to come back here to change."

I sat down on my bed. "I'll wait for you. We should still make it in time for batting practice."

"Thanks!" Olson began peeling out of his cheap khaki suit. It reminded me of something Archie would wear.

As he started to don his new flannels, I said, "You should like it here. Got a decent ball club, and George Leidy's easy to play for. One thing you got to be careful about, though, is where you go in town. Stay away from the bars and joy houses, and don't *ever* go into the pool halls down by the river. If the toughs there think you're trying to hustle them, they'll break every bone in your hands."

"You don't have to tell me," Olson answered. "I heard what happened to that Houston pitcher a couple days ago. They say he'll never pitch again." According to what I'd heard, Jake Pruett would be lucky if he could ever hold a baseball again never mind throw one.

"I'm telling you anyway," I said firmly. "They warn everyone about the pool halls as soon as they get here. In fact, you'll probably hear it a hundred more times in your first week." Just as I had when I joined the team.

BIBLIOGRAPHY

Here is a list of recommended further reading in the world of baseball mysteries. It is fairly comprehensive without making claims to being complete. Some are entirely about baseball and some only touch it on the outside corner, but all are mystery, crime or suspense fiction.

Abrahams, Peter	*The Fan*	Warner	1995
Avallone, Michael	*Dead Game*	Holt	1984
Bagby, George	*The Twin Killing*	Doubleday	1947
Ball, John	*Johnny Get Your Gun*	Little Brown	1969
Benjamin, Paul	*Squeeze Play*	Avon	1982
Block, Lawrence	*The Burglar Who Traded Ted Williams*	Dutton	1994
Bouton, Jim and Eliot Asinof	*Strike Zone*	Viking	1994
Bowen, Michael	*Fielder's Choice*	St. Martin's	1991
Cronley, Jay	*Screwballs*	Doubleday	1980
Curtis, Richard	*Strike Zone*	Warner	1975
DeAndrea, William	*Five O'Clock Lightning*	St. Martin's	1982
DeMarco, Gordon	*Frisco Blues*	Pluto	1985
Engleman, Paul	*Dead In Center Field*	Ballantine	1983

Enger, L.L.	*Comeback*	Pocket	1990
Enger, L.L.	*Swing*	Pocket	1991
Enger, L.L.	*Strike*	Pocket	1992
Enger, L.L.	*Sacrifice*	Pocket	1993
Enger, L.L.	*The Sinners' League*	Otto Penzler Books	1994
Estleman, Loren	*King of the Corner*	Bantam	1992
Everson, David	*Suicide Squeeze*	St. Martin's	1991
Evers, Crabbe	*Murder In Wrigley Field*	Bantam	1991
Evers, Crabbe	*Murderer's Row*	Bantam	1991
Evers, Crabbe	*Bleeding Dodger Blue*	Bantam	1991
Evers, Crabbe	*Fear In Fenway*	Morrow	1993
Evers, Crabbe	*Tigers Burning*	Morrow	1994
Faust, Ron	*Fugitive Moon*	Doherty	1995
Fish, Robert with Henry Rothblatt	*A Handy Death*	Simon & Schuster	1973
Fitzsimmons, Cortland	*Death On The Diamond*	Stokes	1934
Geller, Michael	*Major League Murder*	St. Martin's	1988
Geller, Michael	*Three Strikes You're Dead*	St. Martin's	1992
Gordon, Alison	*The Dead Pull Hitter*	St. Martin's	1988
Gordon, Alison	*Safe at Home*	St. Martin's	1990
Gordon, Alison	*Night Game*	St. Martin's	1992
Granger, Bill	*Drover and the Designated Hitter*	Morrow	1994
Guthrie, A.B.	*Wild Pitch*	Houghton Mifflin	1973
Holton, Leonard	*The Devil to Pay*	Dodd, Mead	1974

Honig, Donald	*The Plot to Kill Jackie Robinson*	Dutton	1992
Honig, Donald	*Last Man Out*	Dutton	1993
Hoyt, Richard	*Japanese Game*	Forge	1995
Irvine, Robert	*Gone To Glory*	St. Martin's	1990
Klein, Dave	*Hit and Run*	Charter	1982
Lupica, Mike	*Limited Partner*	Villard	1990
Magnuson, James	*The Rundown*	Jove	1977
Maxes, Anna	*Dead to Rights*	St. Martin's	1994
McBain, Ed	*The Heckler*	Simon & Schuster	1960
Morgenstein, Gary	*Take Me Out to the Ballgame*	St. Martin's	1980
Newman, Christopher	*Dead End Game*	Putnam	1994
Nighbert, David F.	*Strikezone*	St. Martin's	1989
Nighbert, David F.	*Squeeze Play*	St. Martin's	1992
Nighbert, David F.	*Shutout*	St. Martin's	1995
Parker, Robert B.	*Mortal Stakes*	Houghton Mifflin	1975
Platt, Kin	*Screwball King Murder*	Random House	1978
Pomeranz, Gary	*Out at Home*	Houghton Mifflin	1985
Rosen, Richard	*Fadeaway*	Harper Row	1986
Rosen, Richard	*Saturday Night Dead*	Viking	1988
Rosen, Richard	*Strike Three You're Dead*	Walker	1984
Russell, Randy	*Caught Looking*	Doubleday	1992
Spencer, Ross H.	*The Stranger City Caper*	Avon	1980
Spencer, Ross H.	*Echoes of Zero*	St. Martin's	1981